'A page-turning, emotional rollercoaster I found difficult to put down'
Samantha Tonge

'Parts of this story will have touched most of our lives, and the sensitivity the author gives to it is wonderful. This is a real tear-jerker.'
The Sun

'... don't realise how quickly this story draws you in and then takes ... n an emotional roller coaster ride.' **Welsh Country Magazine**

'...atdownable. A real page-turner.'
Maria Felix Vas, BBC Radio Lancashire

'N ...ody writes about the tenderness and brutality of life like S.D. R ...rtson.' **Miranda Dickinson**

'A ... art-warming and thought-provoking story of grief, redemption an ...einvention.' **Imogen Clark**

'W ... great skill and humour, S.D. Robertson guides us through a m ...field of family misunderstandings and discontent. I'm not sure I've se ...such dynamics tackled better.' **Stewart Foster**

'A ...nderfully told tale of devastation, grief and ultimately hope, with a ...ative that grips from the start and doesn't let go until the final p...' **Kathryn Hughes**

'A ...der and beautifully told heart-tugging story.' **Caroline England**

'...'s really, really clever about this book is that you don't realise ...been drawn in until it's too late to stop. The story leaves you ...g down an emotional knife edge until you freefall. It's soft, subtle, ...ngaging, then devastating.' **Helen Fields**

'R... Emotional. Powerful. A must-read for anyone who loves to lose h...lves completely in a book.' **Claudia Carroll**

ABOUT THE AUTHOR

Former journalist S.D. Robertson quit his role as a local newspaper editor to pursue a lifelong ambition of becoming a novelist. *The Daughter's Choice* is his sixth novel, and he is a *USA Today* and #1 Kindle bestseller.

Stuart is a reluctant DIYer and unofficial tech support provider for his family. He lives in a village near Manchester with his wife and daughter. There's also his cat, who likes to distract him from writing – usually by breaking things.

Also by S.D. Robertson

Time to Say Goodbye
If Ever I Fall
Stand By Me
My Sister's Lies
How to Save a Life

The Daughter's Choice

S.D. ROBERTSON

avon.

HarperCollins*Publishers*
1 London Bridge Street
London SE1 9GF

www.harpercollins.co.uk

HarperCollins*Publishers*
1st Floor, Watermarque Building, Ringsend Road
Dublin 4, Ireland

A Paperback Original 2021

First published in Great Britain by HarperCollins*Publishers* 2021

A catalogue copy of this book is available from the British Library.

ISBN: 978-0-00-837479-2

This novel is entirely a work of fiction. The names, characters and incidents portrayed in it are the work of the author's imagination. Any resemblance to actual persons, living or dead, events or localities is entirely coincidental.

Typeset in Sabon Lt Std by
Palimpsest Book Production Ltd, Falkirk, Stirlingshire
Printed and Bound in the UK using 100% Renewable Electricity
at CPI Group (UK) Ltd

MIX
Paper from
responsible sources
FSC
www.fsc.org
FSC C007454

This book is produced from independently certified FSC™ paper to ensure responsible forest management.

For more information visit: www.harpercollins.co.uk/green

For Kirsten

PROLOGUE

She runs out of the hotel lounge, gasping for fresh air, head spinning.

In the corridor, she almost collides with a waiter carrying a full tray of cups and saucers, but he deftly swings to one side to avoid her.

'Is everything all right, madam?' he asks, face creased with concern.

But she ploughs on past like he doesn't exist, his voice fading into the distance.

She needs to get outside. Right now.

It's stifling in this place.

She'll suffocate if she doesn't get away from the pair of them and their lies.

She races onwards. Barges through door after door in the twisting, never-ending passageway. Feels the alternate frowns and looks of pity from guests and staff as she rips past them on a torrent of tears, her face screwed into a tight red knot of anguish.

How the hell has today ended up such a disaster?

Where did it all go so wrong?

She felt more or less on top of things when they arrived, just hours earlier.

Now that feels like a lifetime ago.

It wasn't supposed to be this way.

How could she could ever have predicted today's staggering events?

She's been blindsided – trapped in a living nightmare – and all she wants to do is escape.

PART ONE – A FRIENDLY ENCOUNTER

CHAPTER 1

EARLIER THAT DAY

She watches from the small sofa as the two young women enter the hotel reception on cue, arm in arm and giggling at some previously uttered private joke. Striding past her with barely a second glance, each pulling a small trolley case, they look so happy – like neither has a care in the world. She clenches her jaw in the knowledge that this will not remain the case. Then she turns the page of her newspaper to sustain the illusion that she's reading it.

Her deadpan expression hides a struggle to steady her breathing in the face of her racing heartbeat. Not long now, she thinks. Stay calm and play your role.

It's already proving harder than expected, though: the reality of the situation, as compared to the theory. Sharing the same physical space as *her* – seeing her in the flesh, with her own eyes, instantly distinguishing her from the friend – is far more powerful than she imagined.

She finds herself fighting an unforeseen urge to walk up to her right now and say something, although she knows that can't happen. Instead, she bites the inside of her cheek hard enough to draw blood. As the metallic taste spreads across her tongue, she tries not to be too obvious while watching the vibrant pair – both petite blondes, barely more than girls – approach the front desk.

'Hello there,' says the smiling, immaculately groomed receptionist. He looks even younger than they do, although his confidence and efficiency suggest otherwise. 'Welcome to Hornby Lodge Spa Hotel. My name's Clive. How can I help you today?'

'Hello, I'm Rose Hughes and this is Cara Wilson. There should be a twin room booked for tonight, under my name. I know we're a bit early to check in, but we're planning to have some lunch soon. Could we leave our bags somewhere, or—'

'No problem,' Clive replies with a polite nod. 'I can help you with that. If you could bear with me, I'll check the system and see where we're up to.' After a few swift taps on his computer keyboard, he confirms the reservation, which has already been paid in full, before adding: 'And you're in luck: the room is ready right now.'

'Oh, brilliant,' Rose replies.

'See,' Cara says to her friend in a low voice, making her jump with a gentle dig in the ribs. 'What did I tell you?'

Rose frowns playfully and whispers: 'Behave, will you?'

Clive asks the pair to fill in the same brief check-in form that she – still discreetly observing them from the sidelines – had to complete on her arrival yesterday.

Once that's done, he gives them all the necessary information about the spa facilities, treatment rooms and meal arrangements, before explaining how to get to their room. 'Would you like any help carrying your bags?' he asks next, to which they both reply no at the same time, setting them off giggling again.

'I hope you have a wonderful stay,' Clive adds, unfazed. 'Do let us know here at reception if there's anything we can do to make your visit more comfortable.'

'Thanks, we definitely will,' Cara says, nudging and winking at her friend as she does so, provoking yet more laughter as they walk off in search of their room.

Clive watches them for a few seconds, a puzzled look spreading across his face, before calling out: 'Excuse me! Sorry, but you're heading the wrong way. It's left, not right, to get to your room.'

A couple of giddy snorts and screeches later, they head off in the correct direction. Soon the reception area is quiet again, although this lasts for barely a minute before the phone rings and Clive is back in action, sounding as calm and courteous as ever.

She tunes out and, still holding her unread newspaper, closes her eyes in a bid to steady her nerves and reflect. The idea of being here when they arrived was purely to prepare herself for later, like dipping a toe or two in cold water ahead of jumping in. She definitely hadn't predicted feeling so much at this early stage, when all she had to do was observe, but at least she got through it without incident.

Will Rose or Cara recall seeing her here? She doubts

that very much. Not consciously, anyway. If luck is on her side, she may have made a small dent in their subconscious minds, which could prove handy in the very near future. Feeling like you recognise someone can be a powerful thing – a good icebreaker – which was why she used the paper as a prop rather than to conceal herself. Her face was on display the whole time they were in the reception area.

She hides in plain sight again a short while later in the restaurant, where she arrives for lunch a few minutes after them and requests a table in full view but not right next to theirs. It's no accident, although she does her best to make it look that way, when she knocks and smashes her full glass of red wine all over the table and the poor waiter's white shirt, instantly drawing the attention of all of her fellow diners.

'Oh my gosh!' she says in a voice loud enough to be heard over the gasps echoing around the room. 'I'm so, so sorry. I can't believe I just did that. I'm so darn clumsy.'

'Don't worry, madam,' the dazed but deferential waiter replies, making her feel bad for picking him as her target. 'It's fine, honestly. Please don't worry.'

Nonetheless, she stands up with a serviette to offer her help, but it's declined. As the clean-up takes place, she's ushered to a new table, on the other side of the dining room, away from Rose and Cara.

This no longer matters. If they didn't notice her before, they definitely have now.

CHAPTER 2

ROSE

She knows there's something wrong when Cara's expression changes after answering her mobile.

It rang while they were roaring with laughter at Cara's bad but hilarious impression of an English teacher they'd both been taught by at secondary school. Now she's deadly serious, which is unusual in itself.

Rose should know: they've been BFFs since they were tots. Rose's dad and Cara's parents were friends before the girls were born; the two families live within walking distance of each other's homes. Cara is the eldest of three children, but her brother and sister are four and six years younger than her, so for a while at least, she too was an only child like Rose. The friendship went from strength to strength as they grew up, surviving all the stages of their lives so far, from Rose starting school a year earlier than Cara, to them attending universities in totally different parts of the UK.

Rose never even considered asking anyone else to be her maid of honour. They might not always be able to see each other in person as often as they used to, thanks to the logistics of their early twenties day-to-day lives, but they still message each other all the time and phone or video chat at least once a week. When they are together, like now, they pick up right where they left off.

'Yes,' Cara says into the phone, perched on the edge of her bed in the swanky hotel room, to which they just returned after a lovely lunch in the restaurant. 'But can't you at least—'

She tucks a strand of her long, wavy blonde hair behind one ear while whoever she's talking to on the other end of the line continues speaking. Eventually, before hanging up, she adds: 'Fine, I understand. I will. See you soon.'

'Everything all right?' Rose asks, moving to sit next to her friend and squeezing her hand. They're both in their swimwear, ready to head down to the spa; Rose has covered her navy one-piece with the obligatory fluffy white bath-robe provided in the room, while Cara, thanks to the unexpected phone call, is still in just her floral bikini.

'Not really, no,' Cara replies. 'That was Dad. There's some kind of family emergency going on, apparently – although he wouldn't tell me what it was, which is a bit weird and, um, slightly worrying. He needs me to head home.'

'Straight away?'

'I'm afraid so. Sorry, I—'

'Don't be ridiculous. It doesn't matter. Family comes first. Let's just go.'

'No, you're not going anywhere, Rose. You need to stay and enjoy this. Dad was categoric about that. He emphasised that while it was important for me to come home, everyone was okay and there was nothing you'd be able to do to help.'

'What? That's crazy. How can I stay here and let you go? We're in my car, anyway. You'll need me to drive.'

'No, Dad's coming to pick me up.'

'But I'll be worrying about you. Besides, it wouldn't be the same on my own. Seriously, I'm coming too.'

Cara shakes her head and, placing both hands on Rose's shoulders, looks her square in the eye. 'Seriously, you're not. Listen to me, bride-to-be. This is an order from your maid of honour and oldest friend: you're staying, end of discussion. I'll speak to you later to let you know what's going on and, if I can, of course I'll come back. Your dad has already paid for all of this so you can relax ahead of the wedding, and it's not going to waste. You're going to enjoy your treatments, go on the tranquillity tour, as planned, and make the most of this gorgeous hotel, all right?'

Rose continues to resist for a while longer, but Cara's having none of it. She rebuffs all of her arguments and won't take no for an answer. In a matter of minutes, Cara's out of her bikini, dressed and packed, standing at the door of the hotel room, arms open, offering her friend a farewell hug.

'At least let me see you off outside,' Rose protests.

'In your dressing gown?'

'Oh right, yeah. Um, I can quickly throw on some clothes.'

'Don't be silly. We can say goodbye now and then I want you to forget about me, clear your mind and unwind. This time next week will be your big day! You deserve this chance to chill out and take a break from all the arrangements. Please make the most of it.'

As they embrace, Rose presses her cheek against Cara's and whispers: 'I love you so much. If you do need me for anything, let me know. I'll be there in a flash.'

'Thanks,' Cara replies. 'Love you too.' A slight waver in her voice betrays her true anxiety about whatever this family emergency might be, but when they pull apart, her mask is back in place and she's all calmness and serenity.

Once she's gone, Rose flops on to her bed and sulks for a bit. She's genuinely worried for Cara and her family, whom she thinks of like relatives of her own. However, she takes some comfort from knowing Cara's dad told her everyone was all right. She contemplates phoning her own father, Dave, to see if he knows anything about what's going on, but she talks herself out of it, bearing in mind everything Cara's just said, and knowing how disappointed he'd be to hear they weren't having the wonderful Saturday he'd planned for them.

He only sprang this trip on her and Cara a few days ago, having secretly booked it on their behalf, wanting to give them a last-minute treat ahead of the wedding. 'Dad, it sounds fantastic, but you shouldn't have,' she told him when, at breakfast earlier that week, he handed her an envelope containing the details.

'Why not?' he replied, standing behind her chair at the dining table and leaning around to plant a kiss on her forehead. 'You're my only daughter. I like to spoil you, especially knowing you won't be my little girl for very much longer. I thought it would be a nice way to spend your last weekend before whatever it is you've got planned for next Saturday. Remind me again what we're doing?'

'Very funny,' she said, rolling her eyes at his feeble dad joke. 'I'll always be your little girl, incidentally, just a bit bigger, older and wiser. Oh yeah, and with a husband, in a few days' time.'

She paused before adding: 'It still feels weird to say that, even though it's so close to being a reality. I've barely got used to calling Ryan my fiancé rather than my boyfriend. Having a husband – being a wife – sounds so grown-up. Anyway, thanks very much for this, Dad. It's really thoughtful of you. It'll be lovely to have something relaxing to keep me occupied and away from tinkering or worrying about things.'

Back in the present, Rose looks at her mobile and, seeing it's just gone two o'clock, gives herself an imaginary slap around the face and jumps to her feet.

'Come on, Rose. Pull yourself together,' she says to her pale, makeup-free reflection in the mirror, willing some energy and renewed enthusiasm into her sorry-for-themselves green eyes. She runs her hands through and shakes some life into her straight, shoulder-length fair hair. Without further ado, she grabs the keycard for the room, slides her feet into the complimentary white slippers and heads for the spa.

CHAPTER 3

Having checked in at the spa reception and explained about Cara no longer being able to attend, Rose is shown into the women's changing room by a friendly member of staff.

'Help yourself to a spare locker,' the motherly woman says, handing her a large, soft towel and a pair of flipflops. 'There's no key: you set a four-digit PIN of your choice. You'll find instructions on the inside of the locker door, but if you have any problems, please give us a shout.'

'Thank you,' Rose replies. 'And how exactly does the tranquillity tour work? I get that it's a series of different saunas, steam rooms, hot tubs and so on. But do I have to move around in a specific order, or—'

'It's up to you really. There are signs on the wall to guide you on the recommended route, but you don't have to follow it. And you can spend as much or as little time in each area as you like. There are no hard and fast rules. It's all about your relaxation, so please do whatever works for you.'

'Okay. And are there clocks in there so I can keep track of the time and not be late for my treatments?'

'Absolutely.' With a gentle smile and a hand on Rose's arm, she adds: 'What a shame your friend got called away, my dear. Don't worry about being on your own, though. There are several others flying solo today. It's quite normal. You'll find most people in there are very friendly. Sitting around in the warmth in a swimsuit tends to lower folks' inhibitions. And the bar's open too, if you fancy a little drink, which you can charge to your room if you don't have cash or a card handy. Anything else I can help you with?'

'No, that's great. Thanks again.'

A few minutes later, having had a quick shower on the way in, Rose finds herself standing before the glass door of the journey's first stage. Would adhering to the prescribed order of things make her terribly boring? There must be good logic behind the sequence, she thinks. Why stray just for the sake of being different? There's no one else currently inside the small room, described on the sign next to the door as 'gently warming and fragrant', so she steps inside and plonks herself down on the tiled seating that runs in a U-shape around the edge of the softly lit space. Soothing music is being played from a small speaker in the centre of the ceiling and there's a gentle floral aroma.

After a brief feeling of self-consciousness passes, Rose stops shuffling about and looking around, leans back and slowly exhales. Maybe doing this alone won't be so bad after all. If she could manage to clear her mind of everything that's been occupying it for the past several months

– primarily wedding, wedding, wedding – that would be really nice. And, trying to look at things positively, perhaps being here by herself will even make that a bit easier, since it would have been hard to avoid discussing the arrangements for next weekend with her maid of honour beside her.

Unfortunately, in trying to take a break from the wedding plans, Rose ends up doing the exact opposite. Ongoing niggles about flowers, music, table decorations, last-minute seating tweaks and various other anxieties bob to the surface of her mind, one after another, shattering her serenity. And then the glass door swings open, wafting in cooler air plus a hirsute man and a woman so orange from fake tan that she looks as though she might glow in the dark. The mid-thirties pair both nod politely at Rose, who returns the gesture, and proceed to sit down opposite her. They talk quietly to each other, continuing a discussion about whether or not their teenage neighbour would make a suitable babysitter for Calvin, who she assumes to be their young son.

Their presence puts Rose on edge. Despite being here first, she feels like an intruder, eavesdropping on a private debate. She wants to leave the room but fears coming across as rude by doing so too soon. She hangs on for a short while before finally surrendering to the urge and walking out, offering them a pursed smile on the way.

Following the corridor, en route to the next leg of the tranquillity tour, Rose arrives at what she assumes to be the hub of the spa complex: a small indoor swimming pool and lounging area. Another helpful sign informs her that the pool isn't a formal part of the journey but may be enjoyed at any point along the way. Since it's fairly busy with other guests, she decides to skip it for now and, having grabbed a quick drink from a water cooler, walks up to the door of stage two: a menthol steam room.

She notes that other people have brought their bathrobes and towels with them. Many are walking around wrapped up, hanging them on hooks outside the rooms or on the backs of chairs and loungers, as required. Rose left hers tucked away in her locker. She considers going back to the changing room to grab one or the other but decides against it. Why bother? She's perfectly warm and body confident enough in her swimsuit.

She tries to peer through the door to see how many people are already in there, but thanks to it being a steam room, there's no real way to tell. As she opens the door, a minty cloud wafts out and the heat hits her immediately. It's quite a step up from the previous room, although once she sits down, so her head's no longer in the hottest spot, Rose finds it more manageable and starts to acclimatise.

There are two other women already inside. They both smile at her through the fog and say hello.

'Hi,' she replies. 'Toasty in here, isn't it?'

'Certainly is,' one of them says, letting out a noisy puff of air. 'I reckon I've only got another minute or so in me before I'm all steamed out. I feel like a lobster. I probably look like one too.'

'No comment,' the other replies, making all three of them giggle.

Since the pair seem happy to chat, Rose asks: 'How

long are you supposed to stay in each room? I've not done this before. Is there a recommended time?'

'It really depends on how much you enjoy each stage,' lobster woman replies. 'If you start feeling too hot, it's best to get out. As I shall now demonstrate.' She jumps to her feet and exits the room, adding: 'See you later, ladies. Enjoy.'

'Bye,' Rose says, surprised that the other woman remains behind, having assumed they were here together. Apparently not.

The two of them are silent for what feels like ages. 'Have you done this before?' Rose says eventually, more due to feeling awkward than because she's desperate to know.

The woman, who looks to be somewhere in her early forties – a little younger than Rose's father – replies: 'It's my first time staying at this hotel, but I arrived yesterday and I did pop down here then. I didn't do the full tranquillity tour, as they call it. I just had a dip in the pool and a quick sauna. But today's a new day, right? I quite fancy working my way around the whole thing. It sounds like the best kind of challenge – a relaxing one.'

'Definitely,' Rose says. 'I'm planning to do the same. How long are you staying here?'

'Oh, only a few days. What about you?'

'I'm just here for the one night,' Rose says.

The woman nods, adding: 'Lovely, isn't it?'

'Absolutely. Really nice and luxurious.' Rose is tempted to explain why she's here and what happened to Cara, but it seems a bit much when they're just making small talk, so she reins herself in for now.

'The surrounding area is gorgeous too,' the woman adds. 'The countryside is breathtaking.'

This warms Rose's heart. She might be a guest here in the hotel today, but she's very much a local to these parts. Lancashire's Ribble Valley – a beautiful area of calm, green, undulating countryside dotted with picturesque villages and small towns – is her home. She's hugely proud of it and loves nothing more than to hear visitors wax lyrical about its allure. As part of the Forest of Bowland, much of the district is an officially designated Area of Outstanding Natural Beauty. If Rose had her way, all of it would be.

'It's stunning, right?' Rose says. 'I live nearby, so I'm used to it. I try never to take it for granted, though. There are few burdens that can't be lightened by a stroll here. That's what my dad always says – and I can't disagree.'

'What a nice way of putting things,' the woman replies. 'Anyway, I don't know about you, but I'm starting to get a bit too hot.'

Rose wipes some of the accumulated sweat from her forehead and blinks. 'Totally.'

They get out at the same time and, without specifically agreeing to do so, walk to the next stage of the tour together. It turns out to be a large outdoor hot tub with spectacular views over a gorgeous stretch of luscious meadows and pastures – a stream winding its way through them – and the impressive sight of the mighty Pendle Hill as a distant backdrop.

'Wow,' the woman says, surveying the scene while standing in her bathrobe before the bubbling, steaming water. 'It looks like a scene from *The Lord of the Rings*.

I know they actually filmed the movies in New Zealand, but blimey, this is impressive.'

'It's interesting you say that,' Rose answers. 'Tolkien was a regular visitor to this area in the 1940s, staying at Stonyhurst College, while he was writing the story. It's often said that Middle Earth was largely inspired by where Tolkien grew up, around Birmingham, but I think the evidence that he was inspired by the nature all around us speaks for itself.'

'You like to read?'

'Definitely. Books have been a big part of my life ever since my father started reading to me at bedtime. He's always been a bookworm and I guess it rubbed off on me. There was a brief period when I stopped, in my early teens. I'm not sure why. Maybe it was a minor form of rebellion. But I soon picked up the habit again. Don't get me wrong, I like films and TV shows too, but books are my favourite form of storytelling. I love how personal the experience is; how much of a role your own imagination plays in it.'

'That's refreshing to hear. It seems like everyone's always saying how people your age don't read books any longer; that they're too busy on social media, watching YouTube videos or taking selfies. Good to get a different viewpoint.' She holds out a hand. 'We haven't properly introduced ourselves. I'm Cassie Doyle.'

'And I'm Rose Hughes,' she says, accepting the handshake with an enthusiastic grin. 'It's very nice to meet you, Cassie.'

Considering it's an overcast but warm afternoon in late

July, Rose is surprised not to find the tub rammed with bodies. In fact, the only other people in there at the moment are the same pair that she encountered in the fragrant first stage – Mr Hairy and Mrs Orange. They must have skipped the steam room. At least she won't be alone with them this time.

Slipping off her flipflops while Cassie hangs up her robe, Rose climbs the three steps up to the hot tub and slides into the wonderfully warm, soothing water, muttering a brief 'hello' to her fellow bathers, then promptly avoiding eye contact. Instead, she looks in the direction of Cassie, whose slender form is now approaching in her red and white striped halterneck swimsuit. She looks great for her age, Rose thinks, hoping she'll manage to stay so trim into her forties.

Cassie's hairstyle is short – honey blonde, parted to the side with a sweeping fringe – very feminine and glamorous. As she steps into the water, nodding gracefully at the other couple and sitting down directly opposite Rose, she lets out a contented sigh. 'Oh, yes! This feels sublime. Having the fresh breeze on your face is such a nice contrast to the heat, don't you think? It's heavenly, especially looking out on such a lovely landscape. Given half the chance, I could probably stay here all day, easing my achy limbs. But don't let me do that, Rose. There could be something even better waiting around the corner, right?'

Rose chuckles. 'That's possible. This is really nice, though.'

CHAPTER 4

'A bit odd,' Cassie mouths to Rose, drawing a smile, after the other two have climbed out of the hot tub. She pulls a face but says no more while they remain within earshot, putting on their flipflops and robes.

Following the earlier discussion Rose had overheard the couple have about babysitting, this time they were busy talking, in loud voices, about the pros and cons of him getting a vasectomy.

Having first looked over her shoulder to double-check the coast is clear, Cassie adds: 'I can't believe they were discussing that so blatantly in front of us! You'd think they'd want to keep such matters to themselves, wouldn't you? And when he burped and they both started laughing. Honestly. How uncouth. What's your view, anyway?'

'Sorry?' Rose replies, unsure what she's being asked.

'Do you think he should get the snip or not? I reckon he should. I have a feeling we don't need any more of their offspring than absolutely necessary.' She giggles. 'It's okay, Rose. You don't have to answer. I'm being bitchy, aren't I? Sorry, I can't help myself sometimes. Ignore me.'

'You do have a point,' Rose adds with a wry grin. Recounting how she came across them earlier, she almost makes a joke about the pair's appearance. However, she bites her tongue, reminding herself that she's not with Cara now; she needs to be careful not to overstep the mark.

'What were they talking about then: sex toys?'

'Thankfully not. It was regarding whether some young neighbour of theirs would make a suitable babysitter for their son.'

'For Calvin, you mean?' Cassie asks, raising one eyebrow. 'Not that they mentioned him a lot or anything. Only every other sentence. Doesn't look like he's going to be getting any brothers or sisters, does it? Not if the procedure goes ahead. Anyway, enough about our over-sharing friends. Tell me something about yourself, Rose. What brings you here today?'

Before Rose answers this, she has to ask a question of her own; something that's been bugging her ever since she and Cassie started talking. 'I will tell you, of course,' she says. 'But first – and I'm sorry if this sounds weird – have we met before? You seem familiar and I can't put my finger on why.' She holds her hand up to her mouth as another possibility dawns on her. 'Oh, gosh, you're not famous, are you? Do I recognise you from the television or something? I'm so sorry if that's it. I—'

Cassie tips her head back and laughs. Toned arms out of the water, extended in both directions along the curved edge of the hot tub, she says: 'No, you can relax, Rose. I'm definitely not famous. Not by any stretch of the imagination. And I doubt you'd recognise me from us meeting previously, since I don't live nearby. I'm visiting the area.' She clears her throat before adding, with a sheepish look on her face: 'I have an inkling I might know what it is, though. You didn't by any chance have lunch in the restaurant here earlier, did you?'

'I did. You too?'

'Yes. Let's just say I was a bit clumsy with my wine glass.'

It only takes a couple of seconds for the penny to drop and, once it does, Rose has to bite her bottom lip to stifle a giggle.

'Yes, that was me,' Cassie says, bowing with a mock hand flourish. 'I can be a bit accident-prone. That poor waiter. He was probably calling me all kinds of names inside his head, but he remained very professional on the surface, I must say. I made a right spectacle of myself, didn't I?'

'Accidents happen,' Rose replies. 'It could just as easily have been me or someone else. Anyway, at least that answers my question and I know I'm not delusional. It's always so frustrating when you recognise a face but can't recall where from. So, you wanted to know why I'm here. Believe it or not, I'm actually getting married next weekend. My dad treated me to a last trip away as a single woman to take my mind off the wedding planning and help me chill out.'

'Oh, how wonderful,' Cassie replies. 'Congratulations!

And what a lovely gesture by your father. Is he here with you?'

'No, no. This isn't really his kind of thing. I came with my maid of honour. We were together at lunch and then, unfortunately, she got called away.'

Rose is surprised to find herself feeling emotional, even shedding a few tears. 'Sorry,' she says, fanning them away. 'I don't know why I'm reacting like this now. I thought I was fine about it, but—'

'You poor thing,' Cassie says, reaching across the bubbling water and squeezing her hand. 'Of course you're upset. It's totally understandable, with your best friend getting whisked away like that at the start of your special time together. And considering you're about to get married. Everyone knows how emotional and stressful that can be.'

She pauses briefly, looking upwards like she's considering something. Rose almost breaks the silence, but her new acquaintance continues, with a twinkle in her eye and an infectious, dimple-framed smile: 'It sounds to me, Rose, like you need a wing-woman. If you don't mind being accompanied by someone clumsy, mature, but chatty and young at heart, I'd be delighted to keep you company on this tranquillity tour. No pressure. It's entirely up to you if you'd rather go on alone, but the offer's there. What do you think?'

'That sounds like a lovely idea,' Rose replies, speaking slowly and steadily in a bid to hide the lump in her throat that this near stranger's kindness has elicited. 'Thank you.'

'Oh, it's my absolute pleasure.'

The door leading back to the indoor section of the spa

swings open and two men and two women emerge, heading for the hot tub.

'I think this might be our cue to move on,' Cassie says in a low voice.

Rose agrees and so, before the others get in, they both climb out. They continue following the outside signs to the next stop on the tour, walking around the corner along a paved path that leads to a lively terraced area. Seeing it for the first time, Rose is impressed.

There's a well-stocked, log-fronted bar next to a seating area with a mix of tables and chairs, alongside some hammocks and recliners. It's surprisingly quiet, with only a few places occupied by fellow guests. To one side of the terrace is a glass-fronted Himalayan salt sauna. Opposite that is a quirky, rustic barrel sauna: literally a large wooden barrel resting on its side, on a pair of legs to keep it elevated off the ground. This looks full. As for the salt sauna, which should technically be their next stop, there is definitely space for her and Cassie. However, unfortunately, that would mean joining and having to listen to that over-sharing couple again, who are currently on display through the glass, each sprawled across a separate bench, treating the place like they own it.

'Are you thinking what I'm thinking, Rose?' Cassie says, her eyes first darting towards the salt sauna and then to the bar. 'How about we have a brief pause in our journey and a drink – my treat? I don't know about you, but I could murder a G&T right now, even if it is early. I promise I'll do my utmost not to spill it – especially not on you.'

Rose giggles, enjoying her new companion's self-deprecating humour. She's very easy company. It occurs to her that not all twenty-somethings would be as comfortable making conversation with someone twice their age and unfamiliar. But having grown up as an only child, raised by a single father, it's second nature to Rose. She was happy chatting away to adults back when she was a toddler and, over the years, that hasn't changed. There are folk who think they can only get along well with those of their own generation, but that's nonsense, as far as she's concerned. People are people, just at different stages of their lives.

Rose is glad she's wired this way – and knows it's largely thanks to her dad. She often refers to Cara as her best friend, and yet the truth is she thinks of her father in the same breath. Is that weird? It might seem so to some people, but not to her. She even calls him Dave sometimes, mainly for a bit of cheeky fun and occasionally to be annoying, knowing it winds him up.

They've always had a special kind of father–daughter relationship. It no doubt stems from the two of them living alone together for so long and, perhaps, him being younger than the average parent of a child her age. But that sells her dad short. He's key to this, because of the way he brought her up . . . not only as a wonderfully supportive parent, but equally as a mentor, playmate and confidante. He has that rare ability to be both incredibly fun to spend time with, while also being the first person you'd turn to in a crisis.

Having taken Cassie up on her kind offer of a drink, Rose grabs a spare table with two seats and watches her approach the bar. Her dad told her as a child that you could learn a lot about a person by watching how they interacted with serving staff in hotels, restaurants and so on. The idea stuck in her mind and so, ever since, particularly when meeting new people, this is something that Rose likes to observe to help get a sense of their true character.

From what she recalls of seeing Cassie spill red wine all over that poor waiter at lunch, she was very apologetic, which bodes well. Confirming this, she watches her laugh and joke with the young bartender in a shirt and waistcoat who takes her order, thanking him sincerely when he offers to bring the drinks over to them and even instructing him to round up the bill to include a tip for himself.

'Thank you, that's very kind,' he says.

'Not at all,' she replies. 'You're grafting while we lounge around, spoiling ourselves. It's the least I can do.'

'The drinks will be over in a minute,' Cassie says as she sits down at the table, facing Rose. 'Are you warm enough in just your swimsuit, by the way? Sorry, I didn't think. Here's me wrapped up in my robe and—'

'No, no. I'm fine. I left my robe and towel in the locker. I can always go and grab them if I get cold, but I doubt I'll need to. The sun might not be out, but it's still warm. Anyway, I've told you what I'm doing here, Cassie. How about you? What brings you to Lancashire's lovely Ribble Valley?'

'I'm from the North West originally, as it happens. I grew up around Blackpool; Preston way for a bit. Later, I lived in Manchester for a little while.'

'Really?' Rose replies. 'I wouldn't have guessed from your accent.'

Cassie chuckles. 'I've not been back for ages. Where do I sound like I'm from?'

Rose pauses briefly to weigh up this question, before answering: 'Nowhere in particular. Not that I can put my finger on. You sound kind of neutral, if that makes sense. How would you say the word for the green stuff that grows in people's gardens and needs mowing?'

'Grass,' Cassie replies, pronouncing the word like Rose would, with a short vowel, as in the word *cat*.

'And the large container you, um, fill with water to soak and wash yourself in?'

Cassie laughs. 'This is starting to remind me of a TV quiz show. Bath?' She says this in the same way, also with a short vowel.

Rose nods her head in reply, smiling back at her. 'Sorry, was that weird? I'm just doing my best to gauge your accent. If I'm honest, I thought you were probably from somewhere down south to start with, but as we've just determined, you speak with northern vowels. There's a hint of something else too, which I can't put my finger on. I want to say New Zealand or maybe Irish, but, sorry, I'm stumped.'

The two G&Ts arrive, courtesy of the friendly bartender. 'Enjoy,' he says, placing the balloon glasses on the table. They're covered in condensation from all the ice inside and, aided by a swirl of grapefruit running through the middle of the glass, look utterly mouth-watering.

'Wonderful.' Cassie nods enthusiastically. 'Thank you so much, Greg. You're a star.'

'Wow,' Rose says to him. 'This looks fantastic. It's not going to blow my head off, is it?'

'Don't worry,' he replies. 'It's not as much as it looks. There's plenty of ice and tonic in there to keep you refreshed. Have a taste, though. If it is too strong for you, I can certainly change it. No problem at all.'

Rose leans forward and has a sip. 'Oh, no. That's lovely. Just perfect. Thank you. And thank you too, Cassie.'

'Cheers!' the women say to each other after Greg has returned to the bar.

'Tranquillity in a glass,' Cassie adds with a twinkle in her eye. 'Anyway, my accent. What you said actually makes a lot of sense, as I've lived all over the place – all around the world. I had a real passion for travelling when I was younger and I suppose my accent did its best to keep up. Nowadays I'm settled just outside of Dublin; before that, I did spend a little time in New Zealand – probably not long enough to have picked up an accent, though. Still, that was some impressive guesswork on your part. You have a good ear, Rose.'

'Thanks. Whereabouts outside Dublin is it that you live? I know the area a little, because Dad and I went on holiday there a few years back, when I was sixteen. We stayed in a couple of places; my favourite was a lovely seaside resort to the north-east of the city. Now what was it called? Mal something, I think. It had a castle.'

'Malahide?' Cassie replies, open-mouthed.

'Yes, that's it.'

'No way.'

'What, is that where you live?'

'Not in Malahide itself. It's very popular and property there's expensive. We're really nearby, though, just across the estuary in a place called Donabate. We're in and around Malahide all the time.'

'How funny. Maybe our paths have crossed before, then. Do you think your accent changes depending on where you live?'

'Sorry?' Cassie replies with a satellite delay, eyes suddenly distant. It's like her mind has darted elsewhere but then, with a quick shake of her head, her focus returns.

Rose repeats the question.

'Oh, right. I think it does a little, in my case. Not deliberately. It just happens. Perhaps I'm a natural born mimic.'

'Can you do impressions of people?'

Cassie shrugs. 'It's not something I've ever really tried. You don't have a strong accent either, Rose. I can tell you're northern, but that's about it.' She winks. 'You are from a posh part of Lancashire, though. Have you always lived here or—'

'Pretty much. Other than the three years when I was at university in Sheffield.'

'What did you study?'

'English and philosophy.'

Cassie raises an eyebrow. 'Wow. You must be very academic.'

Rose pulls a face. 'It was a great course. I had a brilliant time. But I have wondered since whether I should have done something more geared towards a particular job. My dad encouraged me to choose something I found "enjoyable and intellectually stimulating".' She makes air quotes with her fingers as she says these last four words. 'It was lovely of him to take that view. Very liberating. However, I must admit that I've found myself a bit lost, career-wise, since graduating last summer.

'I shouldn't say this, but I occasionally envy my friend Cara still having another year left of her degree. She's on a four-year history course in Edinburgh, which she started twelve months after I went to Sheffield. It's currently her summer holidays.'

Cassie nods, a frown etched into her forehead. 'So what are you doing at the moment?'

'Does being a wedding planner count when it's your own marriage?' She rolls her eyes. 'I did have a job in a call centre for a while, although I found it soul-destroying. It suits some people, but it wasn't for me. Especially when what was supposed to be a temp role started to slip into permanent territory. The instant career progression and management prospects were discussed, I knew it was time to leave. Next, who knows? I'm not thinking further than a week today.'

'Fair enough. I wouldn't worry, anyway. You have your whole life ahead of you, Rose. Once you've decided what it is that you'd like to do, I don't doubt you'll make it happen. I can tell that you'd come across well in an interview, based on our conversation so far.'

'I'm not sure that's true, but it's nice of you to say.' It dawns on Rose that she's been busy talking about herself again when, a minute ago, she was trying to find out something more about Cassie. How did that happen?

'You didn't say what it is that brings you here,' she

says, taking a sip from her icy drink and throwing an expectant look in her companion's direction.

'No,' Cassie replies after taking a slug of her own drink. 'It's a little complicated, to be honest. I have a suggestion, though. Since we're going to be spending a little time together as we make our way along this tranquillity tour, how about we share our stories?'

'Sorry, I'm not with you. Stories?'

'Our life stories. How we got to where we are now. As I said, mine's a bit complicated – I need to build up to it – but if you were to start . . .'

'Hmm, that sounds daunting. How do I know you'll hold up your side of the bargain? This could be a cunning plan to get me to do all the talking.'

Rose speaks with a half-smile, but she looks Cassie in the eye as she does so, hoping to drive her point home. She's not sure why, but she really does want to know more about this woman. It's probably because she's not been very forthcoming so far; the air of mystery has piqued Rose's interest. And yet there's something else. Nothing she can put her finger on. Just a faint gut feeling that Cassie's story is one she'll want to hear, as though it could prove somehow useful. Rose is a believer in fate and everything in life having a purpose. Maybe she was supposed to meet this woman here today. Perhaps she's meant to learn something from her that will prove beneficial in her own life, moving forward. Who knows?

'You have my word,' Cassie says. 'Brownie's honour! And please don't pull the age before beauty card on me.' She grabs Rose's hand, squeezing it as she gazes at her.

'I'd really love to hear your story, Rose. Go on. What do you say?'

Rose wrinkles her nose as she briefly considers the proposal. 'Fine, if I must. What would you like to know? Where shall I start?'

'At the beginning, of course. As far back as you can remember. Tell me everything you can.'

'I don't know about everything – there are only so many hours in the day – but I can certainly try to give you the highlights, if you really want to know.'

'Absolutely. Fire away, my dear. I'm all ears.'

PART TWO – ROSE'S STORY

CHAPTER 5

I don't remember the very beginning. Who does? From what I've heard, memories that adults claim to have from before the age of three tend to fall into one of two categories: received memories, passed on from others, often parents; and traumatic events that etch themselves with a permanent marker on young minds.

In terms of the latter, I do recall an injury I suffered when I was around two and a half. My dad was showering and I was waiting for him in his bedroom. On the wall opposite his bed was a small oil painting of a black horse in the middle of an otherwise empty field. It's still there now. Anyway, for some reason it caught my eye that day and I decided I wanted to touch it, to feel the texture under my fingers.

Discovering it was out of my reach, I climbed on to a nearby wooden chair covered in a pile of my dad's clothes. I stood up on it, reaching over to the painting, only for the chair to tip over, taking me with it. Suddenly my mind was flooded with pain and there was blood everywhere.

I'd smacked my chin at speed, while falling, on the sharp corner of a chest of drawers. My howling soon had my poor father out of the shower, dripping wet, eyes wide with panic. Next he was pressing a clump of tissues on the wound, trying to stem the bleeding, before instructing me – a terrified, sobbing mess – to do the same as he drove us to the nearby GP surgery. A temporary patch later, we continued to A&E, where they stitched me up with what Dad called my 'cat whiskers'. If you look closely, there's still a small white scar on my chin today. It looks a little like a bird or an aeroplane.

Some of this memory is probably received rather than actually remembered, as Dad and I have spoken about it many times over the years. That moment of injury, though – my first true experience of real pain – that part of the memory is all mine.

Despite the trauma, I think it's a fitting first recollection of my childhood, because it demonstrates something that was true throughout: Dad was always there for me. He still is today. I couldn't wish for a better father. And the fact he brought me up as a single parent, despite only being twenty-two when I was born . . . There aren't many fathers who can say that. I'm twenty-two now, for goodness' sake. I'd definitely like to have kids one day, maybe even soon. But would I be ready to go it alone right now? I'm not sure. It would be a challenge. I might technically be an adult, but I still feel much the same as when I was a teenager.

You're no doubt wondering what happened to my mother. Sadly, she died when I was only a few weeks old, after she had a brain haemorrhage. Consequently, I have no memory of her whatsoever, other than what my dad has told me over the years, which isn't a huge amount. That's not really his fault, though. He does his best, but he finds it hard to talk about her without getting upset. Nana – my father's mother – is not much help either, as I don't think she knew her very well, and my mother was an orphan, so there's no family on her side who could tell me more. My parents weren't together for long before they had me and it seems they spent much of that time alone, just the two of them, a pair of lovebirds.

Reading between the lines, it appears to have been a whirlwind romance cut short by tragedy. I was probably a mistake, although Dad's never said as much.

I've never even seen a photograph of my mum. There aren't any I'm aware of, as weird as that might sound. I remember yelling at Dad about it once during a teenage strop when, for whatever reason, I felt like the world was conspiring against me and nothing was fair.

'How can there be no photos of her?' I demanded, stomping my feet on the tiled kitchen floor. 'It's ridiculous. There must be some pictures of her somewhere. Are you hiding them from me? Why would you do that?'

In response, he looked at me with this awful pained expression: a fragility behind his eyes that I didn't recognise. It freaked me out to see him that way and instantly put a stop to my acting up.

When he eventually spoke, his voice rasped with an

unusual hesitancy. 'I mean, she – your mother, that is – wasn't a big fan of being photographed. I'm not sure why. She never really explained. It must sound strange to you: especially these days, when people take selfies every other minute on their phones. But it wasn't like that back then. And we had such precious little time together. There were a few snaps I did manage to take, but I made the mistake of keeping them all in one place – one envelope. Then there was this fire and, well, they were all destroyed.'

'A fire?' I asked, knowing nothing about this.

He let out an exasperated sigh. 'Yes! It was a very long time ago, Rose. Listen, I wish I did have photographs of her that I could share with you, I truly do. But I'm sorry, I don't. I wouldn't keep them from you if I did.'

'Okay,' I replied in a tiny voice. 'It's fine, honestly, Dad. I shouldn't have said what I did. I didn't mean to accuse you like that. Please forgive me.'

'Forgive you?' he said, eyes stretching wide, beaming spotlights on me. 'There's nothing to forgive. It's me who should be apologising.'

We hugged it out after that. Dad's always given the best cuddles: big, all-enveloping embraces that make you feel loved and safe like nothing else.

I felt so bad, I never asked him about this again. I did mention the fire to Nana once, a little while after-wards, curious about what had happened. She told me she hadn't been there at the time, but as far as she knew, it had been an accident – some kind of mix-up – while he'd been destroying old paperwork, burning it off in the garden. He'd always felt terrible about it, she said, which kind of explained the way he'd reacted to my earlier interrogation.

It's not the end of the world. I just have to imagine her in my head. I've been doing it for so long, it's second nature now. She was younger than me when she died – only twenty – which messes with my head if I reflect on it too much.

It's not strictly about me, but the way my parents met is certainly a key part of my life story, so I'm going to cover that here very briefly too. Not that I was around for it, obviously, but Dad's told me the tale on enough occasions for me to be able to recount the basics.

They met at a wedding, although not in a conventional fashion. It was a swanky do at some very grand hotel. The groom was an old schoolfriend of Dad's, a couple of years older than him. Only a handful of other guests were fellow former pupils, meaning Dad felt a bit isolated once the meal was over and the evening do was in full swing. He's always been more of a talker than a dancer, so while the few people he knew were all busy boogying, he found himself propping up the bar and chatting away to a pretty bartender.

It was love at first sight, the way he tells it; the meeting of two minds. They just clicked. In fact, they were so busy clicking that my mother, who'd picked up the job through a temp agency, ended up getting fired by her manager for doing no work. Not that either of them cared. It gave them the perfect excuse to run off together and spend some time alone.

Have you ever seen the movie *Before Sunrise*? It's that

super romantic one from the mid-1990s with Ethan Hawke and Julie Delpy as two young strangers who meet on a train journey and spend the rest of that day and night wandering the sumptuous city of Vienna together. They have these intense, exhilarating, nuanced conversations with each other – dialogue playing a huge role in the film – as a romantic attraction quickly blossoms between the two kindred spirits.

I like to imagine my parents having a similar connection when they first met: the kind of pure, potent chemistry that only happens when true soulmates come together. I even tell myself that's why Dad has never shown any interest in other women, as far as I'm aware. I'm probably over-romanticising things, but what's a girl supposed to do when she's never known her mother? Can you blame me for wearing rose-tinted glasses?

Anyhow, from what I gather, they were inseparable after that night. I came along less than a year later and, far too soon afterwards, my mother was taken from us.

Although she was an orphan, I do have family on my father's side. The only problem is that none of them live nearby. Not any more. And it's not a huge family by any stretch of the imagination.

There's my nana, Deborah, who helped us out a lot when I was little, but several years ago she moved to an expat community not far from Marbella in Spain. The official reason was because she couldn't handle the British winters any longer. 'They're so long and dreary,' she still tells anyone who'll listen whenever she makes a rare visit home. 'They make me depressed. Even when summer finally comes along, there's no guarantee of it being nice. Not in Lancashire. You usually get just enough decent days in May and June to give you hope, only for it to drizzle incessantly once the schools break up at the end of July. At least you know where you are with the weather in Spain. And people are nicer to one another when the sun's out. Honestly, it's like being on holiday all the time. I love it.'

In truth, I think she went there because she was lonely and needed a change to reinvigorate herself and give her life purpose. Her husband Stephen – my grandad – died years ago, when I was six. I do remember him, although he was never around much, like she was at that point, so I don't feel as if I knew him very well. He was always busy with work, but she worshipped him. That's still clear today from the way she talks about him. Dad says she'll never marry again, although we suspect she has had one or two boyfriends since moving to Spain. She's never fully come out and admitted it, though, like she feels to do so would be a betrayal of my grandad. Maybe that's another part of the reason she moved so far away, so she could do such things out of sight of her family and old friends.

I usually speak to her at least once a week. Despite the physical distance between us, we still have a strong bond, as she's the closest thing I've ever had to a mother. Video calls make keeping in touch so easy. It's not the same as her living nearby, but it's better than nothing.

I actually spoke to her yesterday evening. I told her about coming on the tranquillity tour, but she struggled to understand the concept. 'What do you mean?' she said. 'How's it a tour. Where do you go?'

I explained: 'There are various different saunas, steam rooms and so on. You go into them one after another.'

'So they're in different places, are they? How do you travel between them? On a bus?'

'They're all on one site, Nana. You just walk out of one and head on to the next.'

She screwed up her face, clearly still not grasping the concept. 'Will you be naked?'

'What? No, of course not. I'll be in my swimsuit.'

'Good. Make sure it's not too revealing. You never know who might be watching. There are perverts everywhere these days, you know. I was only reading the other day—'

'Nana, chill out! It's a country spa hotel I'm going to, not some seedy inner-city sauna. Dad booked it for me and Cara, remember? Do you really think he'd send us somewhere dodgy?'

'Listen, Rose, all it takes is one person with a camera phone and, next thing you know, there might photos or videos of you on a sex website.'

If I hadn't been visible to her, I would have banged my head on the table in front of me. Instead, I smiled patiently and promised to be careful. 'Anyway, are you looking forward to the wedding, Nana?' I asked. 'I can't wait for you to fly in next Thursday. I'm dying to show you my dress, for a start.'

'My favourite granddaughter's wedding? Of course I'm looking forward to it. And I can't wait to see you in your dress. Goodness knows how I'm going to stop myself from sobbing throughout the ceremony. My little Rose – all grown-up. How's the weather forecast looking, by the way?'

'Oh, I'm not wasting time looking at the weather, Nana,' I said. 'I'd rather focus on the things I can control. I'm sure it'll be fine. Probably not as warm as you're used to in Spain, but I'd rather not be covered in a sheen of sweat in all the photos, anyway.'

'I'll have a word with Him Upstairs and ask him to sort it for you,' Nana replied. To be honest, I wondered if this was a little dig at me for having a civil ceremony, rather than a church wedding, which I know my grandmother would prefer. Nana didn't elaborate, though, so I gave her the benefit of the doubt.

'By the way, Rose, before I forget, do you know when Bridget and family are arriving? I forgot to ask her when we last spoke.'

'Friday, I think. Sorry, I'm not entirely sure. Dad will know, but he's not around to ask.'

Bridget, my dad's elder sister, makes up the rest of my core family. Well, her and her husband Joseph plus their two sons, Patrick, seventeen, and Harry, fifteen. There are a few other more distant relatives – second cousins and so on – but none that we see regularly.

It's not like we see Bridget and family that often either, to be honest. They live up in Scotland, in a small village north of Dundee; it's a fair trek for us to travel up or them down to see one another. That said, I've always enjoyed spending time with my younger cousins. They're good fun to be around, if a little exhausting. Whenever we meet up, which tends to be once or twice a year, they usually end up involving me in some kind of game, typically requiring lots of running around and shouting. They're definitely not the type to spend hours on end sitting behind a computer screen or tablet, playing video games, like a lot of boys their age. I suppose you'd call them outdoorsy, athletically built and ruddy-cheeked, with Scottish accents occasionally so strong that I have to ask them to repeat themselves.

When I was younger, there were moments when I used to wish I had brothers or sisters, just like I used to yearn for a mother. It was only normal in the circumstances – I see that now – although at the time it often led to feelings of guilt, like I was letting Dad down in some way by thinking such things. Like I wasn't appreciating him enough and taking everything I did have for granted.

Anyway, sometimes when I met up with Patrick and Harry, I used to pretend to myself that they really were my brothers. I even remember saying so out loud to them on a few instances, making it part of a game. Thankfully, they always played along without saying it was weird.

We went on a short summer holiday with them to Northumbria when I was around twelve, for instance. I recall playing on the beach one day with a bunch of other children we'd got talking to.

'Let's trick the others and say we're sister and brother,' I whispered to Patrick, throwing in a conspiratorial wink for good measure, before doing the same to Harry. Both boys grinned and nodded in reply, happy to oblige. And so I referred to them as my brothers at every available opportunity after that; it felt particularly good to hear them reciprocate.

I really missed them after that trip. I felt so glum driving home alone with Dad once the break was over, even though he did his utmost to cheer me up by doing silly impressions and singing along to songs on the radio in an exaggerated falsetto.

'Cheer up, Dimples,' he said eventually. 'Returning home isn't that awful, is it? Holidays are fun, I know, but if they went on forever, they'd just be normal life. And there would be no holidays to look forward to, would there? Plus you'll get to see Cara and your other friends again.'

'I'm fine,' I replied with a grunt. 'I'm tired, that's all. How much longer do we have to drive? Are we nearly there yet?'

'Seriously, Rose?' Dad replied, shaking his head. 'We only left forty-five minutes ago. You do remember the journey up here, right?'

I turned away from him to look out of the window at my side, not yet ready to stop wallowing.

He started snorting and talking in this silly pig voice he used to use when he'd read me 'The Three Little Pigs' as a bedtime story.

'Little Rose, little Rose, don't be glum,' he said, reaching over with one hand to gently tickle my neck.

'Don't!' I said, jerking away from him but already finding myself struggling not to smile. By the time he'd grunted and squealed his way through a suggestion to stop for a burger and a milkshake when we were halfway home, my bad mood was broken.

Dad's always been good at doing the right thing to cheer me up when I'm down. He knows me better than anyone else in the world – and yes, that includes my fiancé.

CHAPTER 6

The next really clear memory I have after the bloody chin incident is probably my first day at primary school.

I'd been looking forward to it for ages. Don't get me wrong, I loved spending time at home or out and about with Dad and Nana. Plus Cara and I were already great pals by that point. But I wanted to spread my wings and start my journey towards adulthood. Obviously I wasn't thinking in quite such defined terms, as I was only four years old, but I was itching to move on to the next stage of my little life. I was super keen to learn as well as to meet new people.

I've always been studious and gregarious. Some students work hard because they feel like it's the right thing to do, keeping one eye on their future. However, my key driver has always been knowledge. I've had a thirst for it for as long as I can remember. I enjoy learning for the sake of it. Nerdy, right? And yes, I've achieved good grades as a result, but that's never been the be-all and end-all for me.

Maybe this goes some way to explaining my current lack of a job. If I'd focused on a career endgame from the beginning, things might be different.

As for the gregarious thing, I'm pretty sure that's a reaction to my home situation: a response to the way I was nurtured. I don't mean this as a criticism of my father. I owe him everything. However, he's not always the most sociable of people. He's fine with me and other family members and friends – put him in the right situation and he can be quite the live wire – but generally he's not a fan of situations where he has to mingle with lots of people, particularly when it's a group he hasn't met before.

Dad's comfortable in his own company and happy to leave home as little as possible. It helps that home is a roomy Victorian house: a secluded former vicarage with large gardens and a private drive, off a winding country road, surrounded by open fields.

It's even called The Old Vicarage. It's lovely. I couldn't have wished for a nicer home to grow up in – I wouldn't have agreed to have my wedding reception in a marquee there, otherwise. And yet I do think that growing up in such a place, with my father being the person he is, shaped me into someone far more convivial than him.

'Ready?' Dad asked on my first day of school, having taken twenty-odd photos of me in my itchy, stiff new uniform outside the house. It was a gloriously warm, sunny morning that felt more like July or August than early September.

'Yes, yes, yes!' I ran over to the car and banged my palms on the window, impatient for him to unlock the door.

'No need to smash your way in there, Dimples! I do have keys.'

'You can't call me that at school, Daddy,' I said a few minutes later, as he drove the short journey to my new school.

'Sorry, I'm not with you. Call you what?'

'Dimples,' I replied, referring to the pet name he'd called me for as long as I could remember.

'Oh, right. Why? Don't you like it any more? I just love those cute little dimples of yours when you smile, that's all.'

'It's fine at home,' I said. 'But my teacher might think it's my real name – and it's not.'

'I see.' He nodded and flashed me a serious look. 'No problem, Rose. I'll be sure to use your actual name while we're at school. Okay?'

'Okay.'

Oakfield Lane Primary School, where I spent a large chunk of my time for the next seven years, was located about three miles from our house in a charming little village in the middle of nowhere with one general store, two pubs, a playground, a church and a chip shop. Today it remains much the same.

It's the kind of village where everyone knows everyone else and people definitely don't mind their own business. Not that I was aware of this back then. However, when we were waiting in line outside the reception classroom, I did notice that most of the other children and their parents already seemed to know one another. They were busy making conversation while Dad said nothing to anyone other than me. Meanwhile, I was already excitedly eyeing up my future classmates, wondering who to make friends with first.

On the first day there were plenty of other dads there, as well as all the mums, though their numbers soon thinned out as the weeks passed and the novelty of their child being a new starter wore off.

I felt like people were staring at us. With hindsight, there were several potential reasons for this. Firstly, living a few miles outside the village, we were outsiders. Secondly, it was just me and Dad. That might not seem especially unusual nowadays, but it was less common at that time, particularly in a small rural community. Thirdly, Dad was something of a celebrity in his heyday. He wasn't always such a recluse. At the tender age of nineteen he published a novel, *A Child's Scream*, about the abduction of a young boy from a quiet village. Rather than focusing on the crime, it deals with how the kidnapping affects a group of friends who, while having a barbecue, ignored the lad's cry for help, assuming it to be the sound of kids playing. The book was a huge international bestseller and Dad was the darling of the literary world for a while. His face was plastered across newspapers and magazines, here and abroad; he did various book tours and even made some TV appearances.

A few years later, when the novel was turned into a blockbuster movie, things had changed somewhat for my father. I'd been born, for a start, and my mother had died. Plus he'd been struck by a chronic case of writer's block, so he was nowhere near producing the brilliant second novel that was more or less expected of him.

His initial experience of being in the limelight, which he'd naively accepted without question as a young author, grateful to be published, had been draining and intrusive.

For all these reasons, plus the fact he wasn't mad about the film, he withdrew from the spotlight, refusing to give further interviews or do any publicity at all.

Of course, at the time of my first day at school, I didn't know any of this about my father. I was vaguely aware of the fact he'd written a book, but only from things my nana and other people had said. Dad himself had yet to discuss it with me and I'd never brought it up with him because I simply wasn't interested. What four-year-old genuinely cares how their parents earn a crust? And it wasn't like I'd ever seen him do any writing. As far as I was concerned, his main job was looking after me. I assumed most children's parents had probably written a book and it was nothing remarkable.

So why did I think the other parents were staring at us? A small part of me suspected it might be something to do with my mum not being around, as by that age I'd already picked up on this not being the normal state of affairs. But as getting to know the other kids was such a big deal to me, I also thought they were weighing me up, wondering whether I'd make a good friend or not. So I stood tall and beamed my biggest smile, catching the eye of everyone I could, regardless of age.

We must have made a strange pair, the two of us: me desperate to connect with new people, and Dad only interested in his daughter. He was probably counting down the seconds until he could get into the car and head home, hopefully without being recognised.

If he did feel that way, though, he didn't let on to me when the doors opened and it was time to say goodbye and head inside. Instead, the picture of calm, he took my hand and knelt down in front of me so we were eye to eye. 'Rose,' he said, winking as my actual name left his lips rather than my nickname. 'This is a special moment. Look at you. You're such a grown-up girl now; I couldn't be prouder of you. I hope you have a wonderful day.'

He kissed me on the forehead before adding: 'Off you go. I'll be right here waiting for you at home time.'

And so he was, joined by Nana. I ran out into the playground and leapt into his arms, not because I'd missed him or had a bad day. To the contrary, I'd loved every minute; I was high on life and couldn't wait to tell the pair of them all about it.

'Well?' Nana said as I bounced from Dad's embrace to hers. 'How was it?'

'Super, fantastic, amazing! I made lots of new friends. Do you want to know their names?'

'Absolutely,' she replied.

Breathlessly, I reeled off as many names as I could remember.

'Wow,' Dad replied. 'That's a lot.'

'That's not even everyone,' I said. 'And guess what!'

'What?'

'You're meant to guess.'

'You met a friendly badger on the school field?'

'Daddy! Don't be silly.'

'What? That was my guess.'

'Well, it's wrong.'

'You'll have to tell me, Rose.'

'Fine.' I lowered my voice. 'One boy weed himself during story time.'

'Oh dear,' Dad replied. 'Never mind. These things happen. I hope you were nice to him about it.'

'I didn't laugh,' I said. 'Some of the others did and the teacher was cross. She says we have to be kind koalas, like in this book she readed to us. Koalas are so cute. Could I get one for Christmas, Daddy? I promise I'll feed it every day.'

He flashed a look at Nana before turning back to me with a patient smile. 'Christmas is a while off yet, darling. Plus, I don't think real-life koalas make good pets. I know they appear soft and friendly, but they're actually wild animals with very sharp claws. It's also a bit cold for them here in Britain. The only place they can live safely is somewhere like a zoo. We could always go and see some, though, if you like.'

'At a zoo?'

'Yes, I'm sure there must be one with some koalas nearby.'

I turned to my grandmother. 'Have you ever stroked a koala?'

Nana shook her head. 'No, love. I did ride on a camel once, though.'

'A camel?' This sounded ridiculous to my little girl's mind. 'Are you telling fibs, Nana?'

'No, really, in Morocco. It wasn't very comfortable.

Come on, I'll tell you all about it in the car on the way home.'

'Yes, yes, yes!' Waving to some of my new friends on the way out of the school gates, I called: 'Bye, bye. See you tomorrow!'

Primary school was a happy time for me. I wasn't always quite as enthusiastic as on that first day, but I really enjoyed it. I never dreaded returning after the holidays, even during the final years, when there was quite a lot of real work and tests to do. Such was my enthusiasm, in fact, that I ended up being head girl, which was a huge honour for me at the time.

It meant I got to represent Oakfield Lane at various external events and, when things were going on at the school – sports days, concerts and the like – it was my job to help the teachers and greet visitors, etc. I was in my element and, when the time to move on to secondary school came along, I was genuinely sad to leave.

It probably didn't help that I went to a different secondary school from the majority of my classmates. Most of them went to the nearest comprehensive. However, I'd fallen for the ivy-clad, scholarly charms of Riverside Grammar School. Having attended an open day with Dad and being really impressed, I took the entrance exam and passed. So that was where I headed to start the next major chapter in my life.

Ironically, considering my enthusiasm to make new friends at Oakfield Lane, the only person from primary school that I'm still in touch with today is Cara. And she doesn't really count, seeing as we were already friends before attending. Plus she followed me to Riverside. The lack of continued contact with others, however, is no reflection on my classmates. With the odd exception, they were lovely. If I bumped into one of them tomorrow, assuming we recognised each other, I'd relish the opportunity to catch up. We just went down different paths in life. It happens.

As for my secondary school friends, several of us are still in good contact via social media. We also have occasional in-person reunions that usually involve getting a bit tiddly in a pub and recounting amusing shared anecdotes from the old days. There will be quite a few of them at the wedding. Ryan, my fiancé, went to Riverside too, you see. That's where we met. And shared friends are, in my experience, easier to manage as a couple than separate ones. You know where you are with them. There's less room for misunderstandings.

Female friends from secondary school also made up the majority of those on my hen do, which was in Manchester just over a month ago. I had told Cara I didn't want one, having convinced myself they were corny and unnecessary. However, she went ahead and organised it regardless. She did manage to rope in a few of my uni friends, bless her, and I enjoyed it in the end, despite them making me wear L plates and a tutu.

'Kelly sends her apologies,' Cara told me in the minibus on the way there.

'Sorry?'

'Ryan's mum: your almost mother-in-law? I invited her, but she already had some do on that she couldn't get out of. She said she'd have loved to come otherwise and wished you a wonderful time.'

'Ah, that's nice of her.'

'Probably as well she's not coming,' Cara said with a cheeky wink and a giggle. 'She might have cramped your style.'

I rolled my eyes. 'Whatever happens, no karaoke.'

'Don't worry, Rose,' she told me, arm wrapped around my shoulders. 'I think I know you by now. You're going to love what I've got planned. Trust me.'

Cut to a few hours and countless cocktails later.

The pair of us were having the time of our lives belting out Taylor Swift's 'Shake It Off' in a large private karaoke room, surrounded by our friends.

'Best idea ever!' I slurred into her ear as we embraced afterwards. 'I love you so much.'

'I love you too,' Cara replied. 'And I'm so glad you're having fun. It really is an honour to be . . .' She paused to hiccup and giggle. 'You know, your maid of honour. Do you think that's why they call it that?'

'It could be.' I winked. 'Although the *maid* bit suggests you ought to be cleaning up after me. That might come true if I keep on drinking cocktails at this rate and end up spewing my guts everywhere.'

'Anything for my BFF,' Cara replied, unfazed. Tugging my arm, pulling me in really close, she locked eyes with me before adding: 'We've known each other basically our whole lives and I've always looked up to you, admired you so much. I love you like a sister. More than I love my actual sister, or brother, for that matter. But that's our secret.'

'Totally. I feel the same, sis.'

'This feels like the end of an era,' she said, tears appearing out of nowhere. 'Do you think you being married will change things between us?'

'No, of course not, Cara. Why would it?'

'I don't know,' she said, half-laughing, half-sobbing. 'Getting married sounds so grown-up. I'm still a student; I feel like a child most of the time. I worry you're leaving me behind.'

'Never.'

'Sorry. I can't believe I'm doing this to you on your hen do. I'm drunk. Ignore me.'

'No need to apologise. If anyone should be sorry, it's me, for making it harder than necessary for you to organise things. Well done for ignoring my wishes, especially with it being Ryan's stag do this weekend. I'd have been miserable sitting at home wondering what he was up to in Brighton.'

'That's what friends are for, right? Have you spoken to him today?'

I shook my head. 'No, I told you earlier: we agreed to leave each other to our own devices.'

'Oh, yeah. See, I told you I was pissed.'

I leaned forward to wipe away the remains of Cara's tears from her cheeks. 'Are you all right now?' She nodded in reply. 'Good. Come on, then. Let's get back to the others.'

CHAPTER 7

I'd better tell you some more about Ryan, seeing as I'll be marrying him in a week's time. His surname is Thorne, believe it or not. You couldn't make it up, could you? I've already specified that there's no way I'm taking it as my own once we're husband and wife.

I'll be sticking to Hughes, my maiden name, rather than having to put up with people making jokes about what I'm called for the rest of my life.

It still shocks me how many people are surprised when I say I'm not going to take Ryan's surname.

'Really? Can you do that?' I've been asked more times than I can remember. 'How does it work?'

'You just don't change it,' I usually reply. 'Simple. It's not a legal requirement. Husbands and wives can have different surnames.'

Why is this still considered unconventional in a modern, supposedly progressive society?

'Okay,' Ryan said with a shrug when I first told him.

'It's only a name. Whatever you're most comfortable with. You do definitely want to marry me, though, right? This isn't some kind of weird hint that—'

'No, absolutely not,' I replied, giving him a reassuring kiss. 'I'm simply not prepared to put up with all the jokes and comments that Rose Thorne would inevitably have to face for the rest of her life. Come on, you know what I'm saying. You remember how it was at school.'

He chuckled. 'Fair enough.'

'You could always become a Hughes if you'd really like us to share a surname.'

'What?' he said, a perplexed look knotted into his face. 'You're kidding, aren't you? How bizarre would that be? My parents would never forgive me, I reckon. Surely it's not even possible.'

'Of course it is,' I replied. 'Also, you can change your name by deed poll to whatever you like. We could create a whole new shared surname if we wanted to. How about Hughorne?'

'Now I know you're winding me up.' He poked me playfully on the end of my nose. 'Why would either of us want to be called something so ridiculous?'

'You've got me,' I said, holding my hands up.

I definitely wouldn't want to be called Hughorne. That sounds almost as ridiculous as Rose Thorne. I was half serious about him taking my name, though. If he hadn't been so against it, I might even have attempted to cajole him into doing so. However, I figured it was better to quit while I was ahead.

I suspect Ryan hasn't said anything to his mum and

dad yet about me not taking his name; they'll probably have something to say on the matter, to him at least. They're pretty conventional, so I don't doubt it will come as a surprise. But on the other hand, I know they like me, viewing me as a good influence on their son. I'm sure they'll manage to get their heads around it. They'll have to.

As for what happens when we have children, ideally, I'd like them to be called Hughes; another discussion for down the line. Perhaps we could reach a compromise via middle names or going double-barrelled. Mind you, Ryan wasn't particularly keen on the latter idea when I suggested it as another option for the two of us.

'Hughes-Thorne?' he said, wincing with distaste. 'No, it's too much of a mouthful. Plus it sounds pretentious.'

'What about Thorne-Hughes?'

'Yeah, that's *so* different, Rose. No, thanks.'

He might soften with time. At least we're agreed on having babies. We're young to be so sure, but we've always seen eye to eye on wanting a family one day, probably due to us both being only children. The debate is how many kids would be the perfect number. He thinks two or three; for me, it's three or four. Hopefully, we'll settle on three. That would be wonderful. Fingers and toes crossed that we don't have any issues conceiving. All the more reason to start young!

When people ask a couple how they met, there's usually an anecdote. The best we've got is that I initially didn't remember meeting Ryan for the very first time. We weren't in the same form at school, so we didn't have any lessons together at the start. That only happened later when options were chosen, sets formed and so on; even then, we only ever had a few shared classes.

It was in one of these – year nine, set two maths – that I first noticed Ryan. I honestly had no prior recollection of him. The boys generally were little more than an annoyance to me before that. Most of them blended into one with their farting, football talk and pathetic attempts to be funny. But when he and I were instructed to sit next to each other each lesson by our waspish maths teacher, who was fastidious about keeping friends apart to avoid 'chitter-chatter', I remember not minding.

I was just starting to view certain members of the opposite sex through fresh eyes and he looked really nice: tall, athletic build, chiselled jawline, big brown eyes and short, stylishly ruffled hair. He wasn't quite as perfect as that might sound. We were teenagers, so both of us had our share of zits; he had this pathetic, downy part-moustache and his teeth – later fixed with braces – were all kinds of wonky. But I didn't notice any of the negative stuff at the time. I was more interested in how he smelled. Not in a weird way. He just didn't stink of sweat or cheap deodorant, like most of the lads did. On that first occasion, at the beginning of term, he was wearing some kind of subtle but alluring aftershave – an aquatic, musky smell. It was probably something he'd nicked from his dad. I don't remember him smelling quite so amazing again, so maybe I've over-romanticised it; it certainly helped him make an impression.

I decided on the spot that I wanted to get to know him

better, but it took me a few weeks to build up the courage to strike up a conversation that wasn't to do with maths.

A month or so later, following lots of hair twirling, giggling, and little 'accidental' touches on my part, he got the message and asked if I wanted to hang out after school sometime. I agreed, obviously, and so we ended up back at his house, which was a twenty-minute walk from school. To my surprise, his mum was there. Kelly and I were briefly introduced as the kettle boiled and Ryan made all three of us a cup of tea. Then, having grabbed us some crisps and a bag of Maltesers, he led me upstairs to his bedroom.

Does that sound seedy? It wasn't. Far from it. We were only thirteen! He still had posters of *Transformers* and football players on his wall. We just had a good laugh together, giggling about teachers, classmates and so on. We didn't even kiss. I kind of hoped we might. There were a couple of moments when I thought it was about to happen, but there was no way I was going to instigate it. I wasn't confident enough, having never properly kissed a boy before, other than the odd playground peck at primary school.

It took another week for him to make the move, pouncing on me, so to speak, in an empty classroom one lunchtime, when no one else was around. And yes, it was worth the wait. I was walking around in a daze for hours afterwards, drunk on lust and already yearning for my next fix.

Back in his bedroom, though, on our first date of sorts, when locking lips with Ryan was still a fantasy, I teased him about meeting his mother so soon. 'Does your mum vet everyone who comes around?' I said with a wink, sitting across from him on his bed. 'Especially the girls.'

Ryan blushed. 'Of course not.'

'Joke!' I said, not yet knowing his limits. 'She seems lovely.'

'She's okay,' he replied, 'when she's not getting on my back about doing homework and stuff. She loves threatening to take away my Xbox if she thinks I'm not working hard enough. And she's forever telling me to read a book, which just isn't my thing. I read magazines sometimes, but that's not good enough for her. She loves novels – always has her head in one. They feel like school work to me. I don't get the appeal.'

'Hmm,' I replied, assuming this meant he didn't already know about my father being a fairly famous author. Mind you, Dad's star had waned considerably in the years since my first day at primary school, when he was still getting recognised. Withdrawing from the public eye and not publishing anything else for so long had seen to that, although it was quite possible that Kelly might be aware of him, being a keen reader. 'I'm with your mum, Ryan,' I told him. 'I enjoy reading. I think there are books out there to suit everyone. It could be you've just not picked up the right ones so far.'

He screwed up his nose. 'If you say so. You're in set one for English, aren't you?'

'Yes, but what's that got to do with anything?' I was in set one for all subjects apart from maths – our shared set two class. I wasn't sure if Ryan was aware of this, although I knew he was mainly in sets three and four. I had no issue with that being the case. Why would I? And yet, in light of his question, I feared that me being a 'swot' might put him off me. Hence the defensive reply.

'I'm in the bottom set,' he said. 'It's one of my worst subjects.'

'And? Let's keep things in context here. You're a Riverside Grammar pupil. You passed the entrance exam just like I did. Don't try and make out you're some kind of dummy. I sit next to you in maths, remember? You're usually the one helping me.'

'Yeah, but that's maths.' He grinned. 'It's probably my best subject.'

And my worst, I thought. Opposites attract?

'Anyway,' I added. 'Let's change the subject. How come we never ran into each other before this year at school?'

Not the best choice of moving-on question, as it turned out.

'I knew it!' he said in a loud voice, jumping to his feet and shaking his arms in the air.

I didn't know what was going on. 'Sorry? I'm not with you.'

An energised Ryan did a strange kind of jig around the bed. 'I've been wondering this the whole time since we got put next to each other in maths, but I wasn't a hundred per cent sure, so I kept shtum. I knew it!'

'You knew what? Ryan, please explain, because I'm totally lost.'

'That you didn't remember me. We met before, Rose.

Right back at the start of year seven. I knew you'd forgotten.'

'Um.' I was lost for words as I racked my brains for some hint of what he was talking about; nothing came. 'Is this a wind-up?' I said eventually, clutching at straws.

He shook his head slowly. 'Still nothing? Wow. Good to know I made such a lasting impression. At least it explains why you blanked me in the corridor when I smiled at you all those times afterwards.'

'I did?'

The awkwardness I was feeling must have shown in my face, as Ryan took his foot off the pedal. 'Okay, it wasn't that many times. Only a couple really. I stopped after that. It, er, was only a brief encounter when there were so many new things and people to get to know. I feel a bit stupid now, to be honest, for making something out of nothing. It's just, what you said – what you did – really stuck in my mind. You were kind to me. I—'

'Please put me out of my misery, Ryan.'

'It's embarrassing. I wish I'd not said anything.'

I threw him my best no-nonsense glare.

'Fine,' he said. 'So, yeah, it was right at the start of our first term at school. The second or third week, probably, when we were all still very green. Getting used to being small fish in a big pond again.'

'And?'

He let out a long sigh. 'These two older lads I knew from primary school, who didn't like me much, decided to play a prank on me. One of them held me down while the other pulled my shoes and socks off. Then they—'

'Threw them up on the roof,' I said, finishing his sentence with a barely concealed gasp. 'Oh my God, I do remember. That was you? I'd never have guessed. You looked so different. The boy I remember helping was so—'

'Short and fat?' Ryan said. 'Wimpy?'

'No, that's not how I'd put it, but you've definitely grown up a lot. That was really you?'

'It was.'

'And I ignored you in the corridor afterwards? That wasn't deliberate, I promise.'

Ryan, sitting down on the bed again now, squirmed, his hands kneading the quilt. 'Yeah, that was a bit of a misrepresentation. It was quite a bit later. Year eight, probably. I'd already shot up a bit by then and shed some of my puppy fat. I can't believe I brought this up. I should have kept quiet.'

'No,' I told him. 'I feel awful for not having made the connection.'

So I did remember meeting Ryan after all. I just hadn't twigged that it was him. The stubby eleven-year-old boy I'd seen fighting back tears that day was far removed from the teenage hunk he'd sprouted into. The incident stood out in my memory but not the fine details. As Ryan had already pointed out, there was so much going on in those early days of settling into secondary school, new faces merged into one big blur; the ones that got remembered tended to belong to regular classmates, not kids from other forms.

'What did I do that day that made you remember me?' I asked. 'I wasn't the only one around. There were several of us.'

'Yeah, but most were laughing and pointing, amused by my predicament. You came over to introduce yourself. You asked me my name and if I was all right; if there was anything you could do to help. "Ignore them," you whispered into my ear. "They're just idiots who'll be laughing at someone else tomorrow." I remember those words clearly.'

I nodded, chewing on my lip, feeling awkward that I couldn't recall anything so specific about the episode. 'What happened in the end?'

'A teacher came along and cleared everyone away. He got one of the caretakers to come out with a ladder to retrieve my shoes and socks from the roof.'

'Did the boys who did it get in trouble?'

'No,' he replied. 'I never said who it was. I pretended not to know them. I'd have been labelled a grass, otherwise, which was the last thing I needed. Anyway, now you know.'

I was glad to have made this discovery. I was mad keen on him anyway, but what I'd learned made me like him even more. It gave him extra depth – a vulnerability I hadn't seen before. Despite his earlier words about Kelly nagging him, I could also tell that Ryan had a close relationship with his mum. It was the easy way they'd spoken to each other when we got in from school; the fact he'd automatically made her a brew without her even asking for one. He hadn't flinched when she'd greeted him with a hug and kiss in front of me.

He was definitely boyfriend material, so when he formally asked me out – a couple of days after our lovely classroom smooch – I was delighted. 'About time,' I was tempted to reply.

I didn't say anything of the sort, obviously. Instead, I pretended to think about it, somehow managing to keep a straight face, before nodding and uttering a calm, simple 'okay'.

I didn't want to look too keen at such an early stage. I knew, based on the experience of friends, how quickly boys could lose interest in the absence of a chase.

CHAPTER 8

'Clearly that wasn't a problem,' Cassie says.

'Sorry?' Rose takes a second to return from the pull of her memories. She blinks away the sweat running down her face, thanks to the heat of her present surroundings: the rustic barrel sauna. She and her new friend have this latest stop on the tranquillity tour to themselves for the moment. And boy, is it warm! The G&T they each drank before coming inside may have made it feel even more so.

'Well, if you're getting married now, Ryan obviously didn't lose interest.'

'Oh, I see what you mean,' Rose says. 'No, I suppose not.'

'Have you been together the whole time since then, Rose?'

'Um, not the whole time, no.' She fans her face with both hands, wondering if it's as red as she fears. Cassie doesn't look especially flushed, which only makes her feel more paranoid. Maybe it's not as hot as Rose thinks.

Perhaps it's more down to the fact she's a bit of a light-weight when it comes to alcohol. She still can't believe how much she managed to drink on her hen do. It was as if she'd been granted temporary boozing superpowers for the night.

Cassie is looking at her expectantly from the wooden bench opposite, clearly wanting to know more about the not entirely smooth course of her and Ryan's relationship. 'We split up briefly a couple of times at school. You know how it goes when you're young. Stupid arguments about nothing. But we never managed long without getting drawn back to each other.' She pauses before saying anything else, weighing up how much she wants to reveal to Cassie, whose own background remains a mystery. 'We also parted ways for a while when I was at university, but that didn't take either. When you're meant to be together, you're meant to be together, right? Love's a powerful thing.'

'It is,' Cassie says.

'I'm guessing it was love that led to you settling in Ireland. Am I right?'

Cassie raises an eyebrow and squeezes her lips into a tight smile. 'You might be right, you might not. I will tell you, I promise, but not yet. That was our deal, remember.'

'Oh, come on. Why else would you move there from New Zealand?'

'I never said I went straight from one to the other. Maybe I did, maybe I didn't. And even if I did, it could have been for work. Or perhaps I simply fancied a change of scenery.'

'Don't get me wrong,' Rose says, 'the Emerald Isle is

absolutely lovely, but New Zealand looks so spectacular! I bet it's an amazing place to live. Fine, I'll admit that work is another possibility for the move. It's such a long way, though. I'm convinced it was down to love. If you want to persuade me otherwise, you'll have to actually tell me something. As for why you're here in the Ribble Valley, I'll admit that has me stumped for now, but it has to be linked to the past, one way or another. It can't be a coincidence that you grew up in Lancashire, even if it was elsewhere in the county. A family matter, perhaps, or something to do with an old friend?'

Cassie doesn't respond straight away. She stares at Rose with a calm, impenetrable expression on her face. Finally, she says: 'All in good time. But let's stick to our agreement and continue with your story first. I'm really enjoying hearing all about you and your life. I'd love to hear some more.'

'What else do you want to know?'

'That's up to you. It's your story, Rose. There is one thing I'd like to you to tell me, though, if that's okay: your mother's name. I didn't want to interrupt you when you were full flow, but I'm fairly sure you didn't mention it.'

'Oh, right. Didn't I? Sorry. I guess that's because I usually just think of her as my mum. Although it's hard to think of her at all, considering I have no actual memories of her and so little to go on from my dad. Anyway, she was called Catherine, for what it's worth. I'd tell you more, but—'

'No, no. I quite understand. I just like to know a name. It's easier to picture people in your mind that way, don't you think?'

'I suppose you're right. I do have a picture of her in my mind, purely imaginary, and I suppose she looks like a Catherine. But in truth, I tend to imagine her as looking rather like me now, partly because she died so young. Is that weird?'

'No, I think it's perfectly understandable.'

'Anyway,' Rose adds, shifting gear to conceal how self-conscious she suddenly feels. 'Would you like to hear some more about me and Ryan or should I return to family stuff? There's so much I could cover from the past. It's hard to know where to focus.'

Cassie nods, throwing a pensive look at the small sauna's curved wooden ceiling, apparently weighing up the two options, before replying. 'Fair enough. Let's go with the latter. I'm particularly intrigued by your father, I must admit. It sounds like there's a really strong bond between the two of you.'

'There is,' Rose replies. 'He's my only parent: the one constant I've always had in my life. The fact I'm now the age he was when I was born helps me to appreciate the sacrifices he must have made in his life to focus every-thing on me. Not that he's ever said that; nor would he. But, of course, it goes through my head that maybe I'm to blame for the abrupt end to his literary career. If I hadn't come along – if he hadn't had to bring me up alone – would he have written loads more books by now? Had he written a novel a year, or even every two years, as many authors do, he'd have a huge body of work today. And he was good. Really talented. I've read his book and I'm not surprised it garnered so much praise and attention. It made me really proud. Imagine what else he might have gone on to write.'

'You can't think like that. It's pure speculation. He may have only written the one book whatever happened, for all you know. What did he end up doing instead?'

'Initially, he focused almost entirely on me. He was in a fortunate enough position to be able to do that on the back of the major success of *A Child's Scream*, especially with it also becoming a movie.'

'Right.' Cassie nods.

Rose has always tended to explain her father's wealth this way. It is partly true – and people are always willing to believe that authors are loaded, even though it's rarely the case these days, from what she's heard. However, it's most certainly not the whole truth, especially now, so many years after the success of his one novel. No, there's family money at play too.

Stephen, Rose's grandad, was a man of means. He once set up and ran a large frozen foods business, which he sold for a huge sum, investing that money wisely and building up a healthy portfolio of stocks, shares and property. When he died, his family were all well taken care of, more than making up for Dave's dwindling literary earnings.

This is not something Rose's father has ever spoken much about. She's thankful for the money, though, knowing it allowed her to grow up in comfort and with her father around all the time, rather than out at work.

'He was a stay-at-home dad until I started at primary school. Then he converted an outhouse in our garden into a workshop and started his own business.'

'Really?' Cassie asks. 'Doing what? Something related to his writing?'

'No, totally different. Still creative, but in another way: he builds furniture.'

'Wow. That is quite different. What kind of things? How did he get into that?'

'He can make most things, but he specialises in chairs and tables of all kinds, shapes and sizes. He creates them from scratch, either bespoke, to a particular customer's specifications, or from his own imagination. They're really nice. Unique. Totally different from the usual kind of thing you find in shops. He started out by making me some items for my bedroom when I was little: a reading chair and two bedside tables. He did it for fun, but ended up finding it really enjoyable. He then made a couple of things for family and friends, who were really impressed, and it escalated from there.'

Rose doesn't know the financial ins and outs of her dad's business, but she suspects he doesn't make a huge profit. He's still a one-man band with no apparent desire to expand beyond his workshop. And he definitely doesn't charge enough, especially to people he knows, to cover the considerable time each of his wonderful creations takes him to make. The way she looks at it, though, if it keeps him busy and makes him happy, that's what counts. How fortunate not to have to be money-driven. He's generous too. She knows he has monthly direct debits set up to a variety of charities.

Last year, he supported a fundraising auction for the church Nana used to attend, donating two spare creations:

a lovely rustic oak coffee table and the cutest child's stool with a sheep carved into the top. And that was despite him not being a churchgoer. He did it because he knew how much it would mean to his mum. Not that he told her about it. Deborah only found out from Rose, who knew her dad wouldn't have said anything.

When she was younger, on occasional evenings and weekends when he was busy with a particular project, she sometimes used to do her homework alongside him in his workshop. They'd beaver away independently, soft classical music or jazz playing in the background. Always instrumental, as Dave said lyrics were bad for concentration.

She tells Cassie most of this, skipping the part about her hunch that he makes little profit from his furniture building. That's none of her business. Not that any of it is her business, come to think of it.

Why is she telling so much to a stranger?

Reflecting on this suddenly makes Rose suspicious.

Hang on. What if Cassie is a journalist trying to dig up dirt on her father, the reclusive literary figure? Oh my God! How has she not thought of this until now, after running her mouth about all sorts? And today of all times: a week before the wedding. What if a terrible exposé comes out in the papers next weekend, breaking her dad's heart and ruining everything?

Rose's heart is pounding. Her breathing is laboured and shallow; she feels woozy.

And then, somehow, she's on to thinking about Cara, feeling awful that she's not been in her thoughts while she's been chatting to Cassie; wondering how she's dealing with her family emergency, whatever it might be. She should have left with her best friend, no matter what. Cara would never have abandoned her in such circumstances.

'Everything all right, Rose?' Cassie asks, a shadow of concern falling over her face. 'You look like something's wrong. Are you too hot? We can move on if you like.'

'Good idea,' Rose says, jumping to her feet and storming out of the small sauna at speed. She doesn't look back until she's outside, resting on a wooden bench, appreciating the much cooler air as she greedily sucks it into her lungs.

Cassie follows her. She wipes perspiration from her furrowed brow as she approaches. 'Can I get you some water, Rose? You look parched.'

'Yes, please.'

Cassie wraps her bathrobe around her slender figure and disappears in the direction of the bar, returning a short time later with two large plastic cups of iced water. 'Here you go,' she says, sitting down next to her. 'You can have both, if you like. I feel better than you look.'

'Thanks,' Rose replies, taking the cup Cassie's extended arm holds out to her. She has a swig before adding: 'One's fine. Please, you have the other.'

The intensity of her moment of panic has passed. Her head is clear again. Outside the heat and enclosed space of the barrel sauna, she's no longer gripped by the suspicion of Cassie being a wolf in sheep's clothing. She seems too nice, for a start, concerned about Rose being dehydrated. Plus, it's not as though Cassie approached her. They bumped into each other by chance. And Rose was the one who started their conversation. She was being paranoid. It was surely a result of the alcohol followed by the intense warmth. It caused her to have a funny turn, that's all, fuelling silly suspicions based on nothing.

Why on earth would a journalist appear out of nowhere now, wanting to dig up dirt on her dad so many years after he stopped being well known? And even if there was a good reason, such as if he was about to bring out a new book, it would be utterly unethical for any journalist to approach his daughter in this way without first properly announcing themselves and their intentions. What newspaper or magazine editor would sign off on such practices in modern, privacy-sensitive times? Perhaps if it was to unearth a terrorist or a dangerous undercover spy – something in the public interest – but not to find out what a former literary darling has been up to since eschewing publicity to enjoy a quiet life in the countryside.

As for her feelings of guilt over her maid of honour, they haven't gone away, although they have at least eased. Cara did *insist* on her staying.

Finishing her lovely, refreshing drink, Rose realises Cassie is staring at her expectantly, like she's awaiting an answer. 'Sorry?' she says. 'Did you, um . . .'

'I asked if you were all right now, that's all.'

'Right. Sorry. I was away with the fairies for a minute. I'm okay now, I think. Thanks for the water.'

'You're welcome. What happened in there?' She nods back towards the barrel sauna, which a group of three laughing woman are now entering. 'Did the heat get to you?'

Rose exhales. 'Think so.'

'How about something less intense next?'

'That sounds like a good idea. Any suggestions?'

'I'm glad you asked.' Cassie takes a quick sip of her water and tilts the cup in Rose's direction like she's making a toast. 'When I was getting these drinks, I asked Greg, the bartender who served us earlier, if there was anything a bit cooler that might be a good next stop on our tranquillity tour.'

Rose holds her head in her hands. 'How embarrassing. I must be the only person in the world who has a meltdown on a spa day. It's supposed to be relaxing!'

She immediately regrets using the word *meltdown* and hopes Cassie doesn't read too much into that. It's too late, though; she can already tell the cat is out of the bag from the older woman's sudden jagged frown.

'Is that what happened?' Cassie says. 'I thought you overheated. What was actually going on? Was it the wedding? Did something about that make you panic?'

'I, er, don't really want to get into it, if that's okay. It's passed now. Where did, er, Greg, recommend we go next?'

'If we continue along this path, it leads to another entrance inside. There we can apparently find a chillout room with gentle, ambient sounds and heated, tiled spa loungers.'

'A tiled lounger? How does that work? Doesn't sound very comfortable to me.'

'They're very relaxing. I've used them before in Ireland, assuming these are much the same. They're hard, but rather than being flat, they're ergonomically shaped to be a nice, natural fit with your body. In combination with the heat, they're very comfortable. I've fallen asleep on them in the past.'

'I'll take your word for it.'

'If you don't like them, we can move on again.'

'Fair enough.'

As they're making their way along the path, Rose has a sudden urge to blurt out her earlier fear about Cassie being a journalist. She resists initially, but once they're in the chillout room, where the tiled loungers are indeed very comfortable, the thought returns and won't go away.

They don't chat a lot to start with, as there are a couple of others in the room with them – a mother and daughter, by the looks of things – who say very little, seemingly enjoying the peace and quiet. The other women get up and leave after five or ten minutes, though, which Rose takes as a green light to restart her conversation with Cassie. She's keen to keep talking – not so much to finish telling her story, but rather so they can get on to that of her mysterious companion. The longer she knows nothing about her, the more she's intrigued. Why is that? Why does she even care? Who knew she was so nosy? It's human nature, she tells herself, that's all. People naturally want what they don't or can't have.

But that's not quite it. There's something enigmatic about Cassie, like there's more to her than meets the eye. Rose senses a depth of soul in the shadow of the image she presents to the world.

Rose doesn't doubt for an instant that she has something to learn – to gain – from hearing Cassie's story. But first, before she continues her own narrative, she has to get that lingering doubt, that fear, off her chest.

'This is going to sound weird,' Rose says. 'Can I ask you a question?'

'You just did,' Cassie replies with a warm-hearted wink. 'No, I'm joking. Ask away.'

'You won't be offended, will you?'

'Impossible to say for sure, but I do have quite thick skin.'

'I was wondering . . .' Rose hesitates again, looking up at the white painted ceiling while taking a deep breath. Redirecting her gaze at Cassie, she comes out with it. 'You're not a journalist, are you?'

The bewildered look that flashes up on Cassie's face in response is answer enough. Cassie would have to be one heck of an actor to fake that. She struggles to find the right words to respond, humming and hawing, apparently fighting to comprehend where on earth this question has come from. Eventually, she lets out a puff of air, shakes her head and, eyebrows raised, simply says: 'No, I'm definitely not a journalist.'

'Good,' Rose says. 'I didn't think so, but I had to check.'

'I see.' Cassie's green eyes, glowing an almost emerald colour, wander around the room, like they're looking for clues, answers. When they land back on Rose, they narrow, scrutinising her face. 'Would you like to talk about this some more or—'

'No, I believe you. You're not offended, are you?'

'Not offended. A little taken aback, but I guess I can

just about see where it came from. You must have inherited your father's sense of imagination.'

Now it's Rose's turn to be taken aback. 'Sorry? What do you mean? How can you—'

'Whoa,' Cassie says, levering herself upright on the lounger, palms held aloft in a surrender gesture. 'I'm only referring to the fact he wrote a novel. Don't take it the wrong way. It was meant as a joke. You said he was very creative with his furniture building too. I loved what you were telling me earlier about how the two of you would work alongside each other in his converted outhouse. It sounded wonderful – really special. Wouldn't you say that some of his creativity has rubbed off on you? You certainly know how to tell a story.'

'Do you think?' Rose replies as Cassie eases herself back down.

'Absolutely.' Cassie throws her a wink. 'So, you know, feel free to carry on.'

CHAPTER 9

I have fond memories of the times Dad and I spent together in his workshop, each busy with our own tasks. There would be long periods when not a word was uttered. It was nice to be so at ease with each other that we could do so without any awkwardness. I remember feeling incredibly comfortable there, like I was wrapped in a snuggly blanket; happy and safe.

When I look back on the countless occasions we spent together there, I mainly remember two times of year: the depths of winter and the peak of summer. I either picture it as really cold – frost lining the windowpanes and various electric heaters glowing or blowing to keep us from freezing – or boiling hot, with an open door and windows working alongside rattling fans to keep us cool.

I had my own desk in one corner of the room. It wasn't right in the corner; there was just enough space for me to sit behind it, my back to the wall, allowing me to watch whatever Dad was up to on the other side. I also had a desk in my bedroom, like most children of school age, but if Dad was busy in the workshop, I preferred to be there with him.

In my younger years, this was probably a lot to do with being scared of not having my father within sight or sound. He'd set up an intercom linking the workshop with several rooms around the house, but that wasn't enough for a single child with a vivid imagination. The fact we lived in a sleepy rural spot with next to no crime was lost on me. My main fears were witches, goblins, ghosts or the bogeyman coming to get me.

When I was at my desk in Dad's workshop, he'd warn me on the rare occasion he had to do something noisy; I had a bright orange pair of ear defenders on hand. He never painted or varnished in my presence, for fear of me inhaling noxious fumes.

On many of the occasions we were in there together, he was busy planning his creations, making drawings and calculations. At other moments, he was chiselling, sanding, shaping and putting things together by hand. That's what I really used to love watching him do. It was wonderful to see how much care he took over every little detail of a project, like he was infusing a piece of his heart and soul into it with every movement.

'What are you looking at, Dimples?' he'd say to me with feigned affront if he caught me watching him. 'I thought you had homework to do? You're not spying on me, are you? Rose Bond, I should call you: licensed to stare. Except you're not. What you most definitely are licensed to do is fetch your starving dad a banana, giving him a hug along the way. So, what are you waiting for? Get a wiggle on. And pick something from the fruit bowl for yourself. Growing girls need fuel.'

'Can't I have a biscuit instead?'

'Not unless it comes with a fruit chaser.'

'What's a chaser?'

'It's a dad who hunts down his daughter when she doesn't eat enough healthy stuff.'

'That doesn't make sense.'

'Really? Oh dear. I think you might be losing your marbles due to lack of fruit. Best grab two pieces for yourself, if not three.'

This was a typical kind of nonsense conversation Dad would have with me when he was feeling playful. There was the odd occasion when it would wind me up, particularly during my teenage years, but even then, more often than not, it would make me smile. Now, as a young adult myself, I know how important it is to be able to look at life in a light-hearted way whenever possible, especially when times are tough or things aren't going to plan. In my experience, most people tend to be better at one or the other: being light-hearted or serious. Dad's always been good at juggling both and, most importantly, knowing the right hat to wear – clown or counsellor – at the right moment.

Being a single father to an only child, a daughter no less, must require a lot of juggling. It's not something I truly appreciated as a kid. It was only really when I went to university that I gained some perspective on our situation, realising how close we were compared to other people and their parents.

I remember a conversation we had in the car on the way home when he came to pick me up at the end of my first term. 'How did you manage alone when I was a baby and you were just a young guy in his early twenties?' I asked him. 'Wasn't that hard?'

'What's brought this question on?' Dad asked, keeping his eyes on the road.

'I don't know. I was thinking about it the other day, that's all. I'm only a few years younger than you were then.'

'You're not pregnant, are you?' he asked. I think he was joking, having drummed the importance of safe sex into me from my early teens, although his face didn't give anything away, so he may have been serious.

'Dad!' I replied. 'Of course I'm not pregnant. Having a baby wouldn't exactly be conducive to my studies, would it? I'm trying to compliment you. I think it's impressive what you did. Nappies, feeding, teething, all that. Not many young blokes would be able to handle that alone. I can't picture any of the guys I know at uni being able to manage in those circumstances.'

'I was twenty-two when you were born, Rose, not a teenager. A few years count for a lot at that age.'

'True, but it can't have been easy. Plus you had the trauma of Mum's death to contend with.'

'Hmm,' he replied.

'Don't play down what you did, Dad. It was amazing.'

'I did what any father would do in the circumstances, love. I brought up my child to the best of my ability. Was it always easy? No, especially not at the start. I definitely couldn't have managed without the help of your nana. It felt like she was around at the house or I was on the phone to her all the time to begin with. I was certainly no super dad. I often didn't have a clue what I was doing. I went from one panic to another, but eventually I started to get the hang of it, thank goodness, and the phone calls to Nana became less frequent.'

'For what it's worth, Dad, I don't remember any of that. From my perspective, you always knew exactly what you were doing. Sure, there were times, growing up, when I wished I had a mum. As a child, you want what others have – what seems to be normal – but it was only an occasional thing. A stab of envy, for instance, when Cara and her mum went to the hairdresser together or painted each other's nails. The fact that the feeling was so infrequent, well, that was down to you, Dad. The crux of my rambling is that you're an awesome parent and I really do appreciate you.'

Dad's sea-blue eyes glistened as he slowly nodded, reaching over and squeezing my hand. 'You couldn't be more welcome, Dimples,' he said with a catch in his voice. 'I've missed you at home.'

'Me too,' I replied. 'There's nowhere I'd rather spend Christmas.'

'Oh gosh, yes, it is Christmas soon, isn't it?' Dad said, slipping into a typical wind-up. 'I'd better start thinking about a tree and presents before it's too late.'

He spoiled me with gifts that festive period, as he does every year and, of course, the tree and decorations were already up when we arrived home.

Dad and I have always had traditions that we follow at specific times of the year. At Christmas, for instance, we always watch certain seasonal movies in a specific order, honed over the years. It's *Elf* first, followed by *Jingle All the Way*, then *Home Alone*, *Arthur Christmas*, and finally, preferably on 25 December, *National Lampoon's Christmas Vacation*. We've seen all of these films so often, we usually spend most of the time while they're on the TV eating, drinking and chatting. On Boxing Day, we have lasagne for lunch followed by a game of Scrabble. Similarly, weather permitting, we always try to climb nearby Pendle Hill at some point over the Easter weekend. And we have a two-part chocolate egg hunt around the house on Easter Sunday morning, first with Dad hiding and me seeking; then the other way around.

As for Halloween, we hosted a fancy-dress party at the house just about every year that I can remember up until I went to university. I really missed it that first term I was away, despite attending a Halloween disco with a group of my new friends. It was fun but not the same. Does that sound weird, that an eighteen-year-old would rather be at home with her dad, apple bobbing and 'mummifying' people by wrapping them in toilet roll, than out with her uni pals? The following year, when I was out of halls, living in a rented house with four close friends, I suggested we host a party and incorporated many of the traditions I missed. That worked out much better.

Dad also likes to make a special effort to mark my birthday. As a girl, school day or not, it always began with breakfast and presents in bed, nice and early, so as not to waste any of the day. And I could expect a series of surprises right up until bedtime, which, as a one-off, if I had the energy, was allowed to be as late as midnight. These surprises could be anything, from extra presents in strange places – such as a ring in a box baked into my birthday cake one year – to unexpected visitors.

On one memorable occasion, Nana jumped out of my bedroom wardrobe as I was drinking a glass of milk from the breakfast tray Dad had carried upstairs for me. It was my first birthday since she'd moved to Spain and I wasn't expecting to see her at all, never mind have her burst out of my closet. Consequently, I spat the drink all over my quilt as I nearly leapt out of my skin. Then I started sobbing, which definitely wasn't the desired result. The pair of them looked horrified, obviously fearing the cunning plan they'd cooked up between them had proved a disaster. I was fine a few minutes later, though. The shock of it all had thrown me.

For my first birthday away from home, during my fresher year in Sheffield, Dad phoned me at seven o'clock in the morning.

'Congratulations, Dimples!' he said, having started the call by singing 'Happy Birthday' down the line. 'Nineteen years old. Wow. My little girl is all grown-up. I didn't wake you, did I?'

'No,' I lied. 'I was just getting up.'

'Good, good. What have you got planned for today? Something exciting with your friends, I assume.'

'Oh, right. Yeah, we'll probably go out for a few drinks this evening,' I said, hoping he couldn't hear the disappointment in my voice. I hadn't actually made any plans. Naively, I'd assumed he'd come to see me, having never spent a birthday apart from him before in my life.

'Did you get my present?' he asked.

'No. Should I have?'

'It didn't arrive yesterday? But they told me . . . Damn, seriously?'

'Don't worry, I'm sure it'll be somewhere safe. I can ask—'

'Could they have left it in the corridor, outside the door of your room?'

'That's not how the post works here.'

'Do your old dad a favour and check anyway, would you?'

'What, now? Seriously?'

'Go on, please. It'll only take you a second and you'll be putting my mind at ease.'

This was an odd request, but since I wasn't yet fully awake, I didn't give it too much thought. 'Fine,' I said, 'but I'm telling you it's a waste of time. Hang on.'

I put the phone down and threw on a dressing gown, catching a glimpse of myself looking far from my best in the mirror. Shaking my head at the pointlessness of Dad's request, I walked over to the door of my room and opened it. I expected to see nothing other than perhaps an early-bird student; to my surprise, there was a parcel around the size of a loaf of bread, wrapped in bright red paper. It had my name on the front in handwriting I recognised as my father's, but there was no address or stamp, which struck me as odd.

Intrigued, I picked it up and went back inside, sitting down on my narrow single bed and picking up the phone again. 'Dad?' I said. 'There was a parcel. You were right, although I don't understand it, because—'

'Ah, fantastic,' Dad replied, cutting in. 'Have you opened it yet?'

'Give me a chance.'

'Oh, hang on,' he said. 'Can you bear with me? I have to do something. You go ahead and open it, Rose, and I'll call you back in a minute.'

He hung up.

Rubbing my still-sleepy eyes, I turned the parcel over in my hands, imagining Dad sitting at the kitchen table at the house, taping it together. The thought made me homesick and a little teary. 'Come on, Rose. Pull yourself together,' I said out loud, blinking repeatedly and wiping the corners of my eyes with one finger. 'It's your birthday, for goodness' sake. Smile.'

I focused my attention on opening the parcel, only to find another layer of wrapping – pink tissue paper this time. 'Oh, Dad,' I said, looking at the phone and willing him to ring it again. 'Ever the joker, aren't you?'

He'd really gone to town. Every layer of wrapping I ripped open revealed another of a different colour. It was only when I finally reached the nineteenth layer, which was a shiny gold colour, that I realised this would be the last one, to mark my age. The size of the parcel had shrunk considerably by now; it was about as big as a large matchbox.

I didn't actually expect it to be a matchbox, though.

When that was what I found, I was confused and, dare I say, disappointed. Wait, I thought, wondering again why Dad hadn't phoned me back yet: there must be something exciting inside.

In fact, all the matchbox contained was a small piece of plain white paper, folded in half. I removed it, opened it up and found a short message written in black biro. It read: *Knock knock. There's somebody at the door.*

'What?' I stared at the note, confused, until my mind started to whirr, calculating possibilities. I jumped to my feet, scattering wrapping paper all over the floor, and ran to the door. Opening it, I was serenaded with another rendition of 'Happy Birthday' by Dad – yes, he was there in person, smiling ear to ear – accompanied, bizarrely, by one of the security staff, also singing and playing an acoustic guitar.

CHAPTER 10

Dad's never shied away from grand gestures. It's kind of his thing, especially when it comes to me. I think there's little, if anything, he enjoys more than making his only daughter feel special. Subconsciously, it's probably a case of him over-compensating for the fact I've no mother or siblings, although I'd never say that to him.

It's a very different side to his character from the reclusive one. He's really good with people when he wants or needs to be. However, he turns this charisma on and off like a tap, depending on the situation.

Not everyone would have been able to persuade that security guard to let them into my accommodation block unannounced to surprise me on my birthday. Dad went one step further, managing to convince the guy to join in on the fun, like they were best pals. Up until that moment, I hadn't thought of that particular chap as being very friendly. And yet from my birthday onwards, we always had a smile for each other.

I've seen Dad in recorded TV interviews from when his book was released. He comes across well, like a friendly, easy-going, gregarious type. That's also how he is with me and other people with whom he's comfortable spending time. And yet it's rarely the persona he portrays publicly. Introduce him without warning to someone new and you'll often struggle to get two words out of him. Even at my school parents' evenings or when he took me to look around universities, he made all the right noises, but that was it. There was little or no small talk with other mums and dads. There were even times when he was downright rude, asking people to stop dawdling and move out of his way in a narrow corridor, for instance, or ignoring what he considered to be a ridiculous question. He was out of his comfort zone, I guess. Perhaps such occasions were painful because they reminded him of what our family might have looked like if my mum hadn't died.

I think the main reason Dad withdrew from the public eye originally was probably grief. He and my mother might not have been together for long, but I'm sure he adored her. It's the way his eyes glaze over when he finds the strength to talk about her. Had she lived, I have a feeling he'd have kept on writing, with her as his muse. The way he talks about her, it sounds so powerful what they found in each other: that click, spark, chemistry, whatever you want to call it. I'm probably guilty of over-romanticising things again. But, in my head at least, they were soulmates, and losing her when he did – the way he did – shot down his creativity.

I've read that the human brain is capable of adapting

itself following a traumatic injury. Patients can sometimes recover lost functions, at least to a degree, through the formation of new connections and pathways, as the brain reorganises to try to compensate for damage. This reminds me of what Dad achieved by getting into his furniture building. He's an imaginative, artistic type – always has been, according to Nana – but he lost his original outlet for that when he stopped wanting or being able to write. Instead, he discovered an alternative way of expressing himself creatively and thus found new purpose in life. Dave the furniture maker is undoubtedly a very different person to Dave the successful young author. He's older and wiser, bearing the scars of the journey that changed him. And yet the creative essence at his core probably remains much the same as it was at the start.

Dad has never, to my knowledge, had a romantic relationship with anyone since my mother. It's not because he's ugly or anything. The physical nature of his work keeps him in good shape. He has a full head of dark brown hair, which he keeps short and relatively tidy. He definitely doesn't shave every day, so he often has stubble, but I suppose that gives him a ruggedly handsome look. It's hard to consider your father in that way, but I know other women find him attractive, in spite of his tendency to clam up or even be ill-mannered in social situations he finds awkward.

One of my English teachers at school used to virtually swoon whenever she met him, although it's possible a lot of that was down to his novel, which I know she adored.

He's had several admirers over the years, from mothers

of my schoolfriends – some divorced, some bored – to women he's made furniture for. And they're only the ones I know about. I recall one customer in particular who wouldn't leave him alone: Madge. A wealthy, glamorous widow with a vivid mane of burgundy hair and too much time on her hands, she was maybe five or six years older than Dad. She originally commissioned him, based on a personal recommendation, to make her a fancy garden bench. But after meeting him in person, she wouldn't leave him alone. There was a period of six months or so when he seemed to be constantly making things for Madge, and she was forever coming around or phoning up.

'You know she has a thing for you, Dad,' I remember telling him at the dinner table one evening. I must have been sixteen or seventeen.

'I think she's just lonely,' he replied. 'She's nice enough. A little demanding of my time and attention, perhaps.'

'That's because she's hot for you.'

'Rose!'

'What? She is. Anyone can see that. And you can't say she's not attractive. She has one heck of a good figure for her age. You're not bad-looking either, you know, for an old man.'

'Old? Don't be so cheeky. I'm younger than a lot of your friends' parents.'

'Yeah, yeah,' I said with a cheeky grin. 'Anyway, the question is: what will you do when Madge asks you out on a date or throws herself at you? Because that is what's going to happen, Dad.'

He was having none of it until, a few days later, she

made her move. He came to me with his tail between his legs.

'You were right,' he said. 'What do I do now?'

'Would you like to go on a date with her? It would probably do you good to get out there again after all these years. And in case you're wondering, I'd be fine with it.'

He pulled a face. 'No, thanks. Madge isn't my type. She's very full-on. She, um . . . This is embarrassing—'

'Don't you dare stop now. What did she do?'

'Promise you won't tell anyone? I mean it.'

'Who would I tell, Dad?'

'Well now, let me see. How about Nana, Cara, Ryan, perhaps?'

'Fine, I won't tell them, or anyone else. So?'

'She turned up unannounced at my workshop this lunchtime, while you were still at school.'

'And?' I rotated my hands in front of me, gesturing for him to continue with his story and get to the point.

'She was wearing this small summer dress. One minute we were chatting about an idea she'd had for a coffee table to give her sister as a birthday present and the next . . . she slipped the straps off and the dress was on the floor.'

'No! Seriously? Wow, she's not backward in coming forward! What did she have on underneath?'

Dad had gone bright red by this point and was covering his face with one hand. 'Um, she was just in her sandals.'

Now this might sound like a strange conversation for a father to be having with his teenage daughter, but remember that he and I have always been incredibly close. I'd confided in him about so many embarrassing, personal things, it didn't feel weird or uncomfortable at all to hear this. Plus, had anything actually happened between him and Madge, or if he was remotely interested in her, he would never have shared such details with me. But this was a very different situation; my jaw was on the floor at what I was hearing.

'She was starkers?'

'Basically.'

'So what did you do?'

'Stepped away and asked her politely to put her dress on again. I was really taken aback.'

'You should listen to me next time. I did warn you.'

'I know, Dimples. I probably wouldn't be telling you this otherwise. Anyway, what do I do?'

'What happened next? How did you leave it? I assume she put the dress back on eventually. Was she upset? Offended?'

'She didn't seem to be. She brazenly stood there, in her birthday suit, and said: "I'll put it back on if you agree to take me out to dinner – now you know what's on offer." She's certainly confident, I'll give her that.'

I chuckled. 'Let me guess, Dad: you agreed to go on the date?'

'I had to do something to get her dressed again.'

We chatted the situation over and eventually decided the best thing for him to do was to take her out somewhere busy, so as to avoid any more potential nakedness; to have a nice meal and let her down gently. Apparently, she didn't get the message, though, and tried to pounce on him when he drove her home in the car afterwards.

'I had to give her a reality check,' he told me over a cuppa when he got back.

'Oh, no. You didn't let Rude Dave out of the cage, did you?' I asked, already wincing.

Dad bared his teeth and growled. 'Sometimes I have to set him free.'

'What did you say?'

'Don't worry, I'm exaggerating. It was nothing too awful. I was quite blunt, though. I told her: "Madge, you're a lovely person and I enjoyed our meal together, but I don't find you attractive. You're not my type. Please don't pursue this, because you'll only embarrass yourself. Invest your time elsewhere. I'm sure there are plenty of men out there who'd jump at the chance to be with you – but I'm not one of them. Sorry." That was it, pretty much.'

It definitely could have been worse, although I did feel a tad sorry for Madge. Not that I could ever have imagined her and Dad as a couple, but rejection is never nice. She got the message. Her frequent furniture orders stopped and I don't ever recall seeing her at the house again.

As for what *is* Dad's type, who knows? I'd like to see him find someone, especially now I'm about to get married. I worry about him being by himself in that big house. I mean, it's nothing new. He's lived there alone, on and off, since I went to uni. But then, at least, I was always coming home for the holidays. And after uni, I moved back on a more permanent basis. I still nominally live there now, although I spend a lot of time at Ryan's place. He has a flat in Clitheroe, which is only a short drive away. The plan is that I'll move in there full-time after the wedding and we'll look for somewhere bigger together.

I love where I grew up and I'm sure I'll still visit the house regularly, but it'll have to be different once I'm married. For that reason, I've been spending more rather than less time alone there with Dad recently. I've told Ryan this is to make it feel more special when we shift to being permanently together after tying the knot – and that is partly true. If I'm totally honest, though, it's more about enjoying 'the old days' for a little longer while I still can; being a daughter rather than a wife.

I'm looking forward to the wedding, of course. I've thought about little else for months now. And yet a part of me is also afraid, because once it's over, I know reality will start to kick in. And that means serious things like finding a job and a house, which I've been putting off to focus on this one big event for ages now. House hunting should be fun, in theory, but it likely won't happen until I've got my career on track. And I don't want to get stuck in Ryan's flat for too long. Clitheroe is great. It's a lively market town, which even has a castle, like Malahide does. But where he lives is little more than a bachelor pad. I'll always think of it as his rather than ours. There's only the one bedroom and a small lounge/kitchen that doesn't even have room for a dining table, so meals have to be eaten on laps.

I could ask for Dad's help to get set up somewhere else, but he's already done so much in terms of our wedding. I want the two of us to try to get to the next stage of our lives by ourselves. That's important to me.

We have a honeymoon planned first, thank goodness: two luxurious weeks on the luscious island of St Lucia in the Caribbean. That's Nana's wedding present to us, which is so lovely of her. It should be absolute bliss. We're due to jet off a few days after the ceremony and I can't wait. At that point, I'll do my utmost to close my mind off to future concerns, and focus on enjoying myself in the lap of luxury with my new husband.

CHAPTER 11

Ryan doesn't stay over at The Old Vicarage very often. He and my dad don't really get along. Fingers crossed that will change one day. It's not a great state of affairs, but it's something I've had to learn to accept.

It wasn't always this way. They've known each other a long time already, considering Ryan and I first got together when we were only thirteen. Initially there was a little tension between them: typical father–boyfriend issues, I suppose. That soon eased, though, and for several years they got on fine. But the tension returned, for reasons I'll explain soon, and things never improved beyond where they are now, which is kind of a stand-off; an enforced peace treaty, brokered by me, which both parties warily observe. Most of the time.

That must sound awful, considering our imminent nuptials; not least the fact that Dad will be hosting the reception in a marquee in the grounds of The Old Vicarage, following a civil ceremony at a pretty village hall a short drive away. However it's really not as bad as all that. They're polite to each other, when they have to be, but any conversation they have will be superficial – most likely about sport, TV or movies. The sad truth is that neither is genuinely bothered about the other, apart from their interactions with me, who they both care about. Hopefully one day that will spread to children/grandchildren, which might be the best chance we have of a thaw in relations. A shared love of little ones could have a bonding effect, I reckon. I know Dad would be brilliant with grandkids, based on how he was with me. I also think Ryan would make a fabulous father. I wouldn't be marrying him otherwise.

So what went wrong between Dad and Ryan? Well, as I already indicated, they didn't get off to a great start when they first met.

To begin with, I didn't tell Dad that I had a boyfriend. I'm not entirely sure why, considering I told him most other things. I suppose I feared he wouldn't like the idea of his little girl growing up in that way, or that he wouldn't approve of Ryan. I kept our relationship secret for about a month and then, out of the blue, Dad asked me over breakfast one morning: 'So who's this Ryan chap?'

'Sorry, what?' I asked, confused, having never mentioned him to Dad. I'd not told Nana or anyone else that might have let it slip either. Cara knew, but there was no way she'd have told him behind my back. So where on earth had he got the name from? I worried that I might have called it out in my sleep. Since I usually left my bedroom door ajar at night, that was an embarrassing possibility. I prayed for it not to be the case.

'Ryan?' Dad repeated.

'What exactly are you asking me, Dad?' I said, feeling the heat of my cheeks flushing. 'What do you want to know?'

'I wondered who Ryan was, that's all. No need to get worked up about it. You don't have to tell me if you don't want to.'

Dad started talking about the weather; I couldn't stop thinking about where he might have got Ryan's name from. It niggled away at me until I finally broke. 'Fine. I'll tell you who Ryan is, but only if you tell me first where you heard of him.'

Dad nodded towards my school bag. It was hanging over the back of an unoccupied chair next to him at the kitchen table, unzipped so the contents were on display from where he was sitting but out of my view.

'What?' I snapped to my feet and reached over to grab the bag. As soon as it was in my hands and I could see inside, the answer was obvious – and mortifying. My blue rough work book was sitting there on top of all my other stuff, covered in doodles, some scribbled on by me; others by my friends and classmates. It was hard to miss the one Cara had added, in bright red felt-tip pen, when we'd been hanging out at her house after school the day before: Ryan's name inside a heart, slap bang in the middle of the front cover. I'd forgotten she'd done it. I hadn't been impressed at the time and, having told her not to do so again, I'd intended to cover it over with a sticker. Frustratingly, it had slipped my mind.

I looked up from the offending exercise book and saw

Dad digging into his bowl of muesli, avoiding my eye. Sighing, I said: 'He's my boyfriend. I've got a boyfriend. I probably should have told you before, but . . . I don't know . . . it never felt like the right time.'

'Okay,' Dad said, nodding once and continuing to focus on eating his breakfast.

'What does that mean? Are you mad at me?'

He placed his spoon in his bowl and finally looked up. 'Mad at you? For what? No, of course not. It's not unusual to have a boyfriend at your age, Rose. And I don't expect you to tell me everything.' He paused for a few seconds before adding: 'That said, I hope you don't feel embarrassed or awkward to mention such things to me. I was a teenager too once, believe it or not.'

'I was going to tell you,' I said.

'Good. If you'd like to invite this Ryan over for tea after school one day, he'd be very welcome. No rush. Whenever you're ready.'

It took me a few weeks, but eventually I did invite Ryan over. Dad didn't say much to him initially, other than introducing himself. He spent most of the afternoon crafting his latest creation in the workshop, leaving us to our own devices in the house. There was some snogging in my room, but not too much, as I found it weird having an actual boyfriend in my home for the first time. Plus I appreciated the fact that Dad trusted me enough not to watch over us, so I didn't want to take advantage.

We mainly talked, about all sorts, in the kind of leisurely way that's not possible when you're constantly surrounded by other pupils and teachers at school. I'd briefly mentioned to Ryan before about my mum dying when I was a baby and he brought it up that afternoon.

'So it's just you and your dad?' he said.

'I have other family too.' I listed Nana and so on. 'But yeah, it's just the two of us living here.'

'It's a big house,' he added, eyes gazing up at the high ceiling above my bed. 'Your room is twice the size of mine.'

'I guess so. Yours is lovely. Just different.'

'Does it ever bother you, not having a mum?'

'I do have one, Ryan. I wouldn't be here otherwise. She's just not alive any more.'

'Sorry, um, I meant do you wish that she was still . . . alive?'

'Yes, definitely. I don't remember her, though, being so young when she passed away. I'm not sure if that makes it harder or easier. I've only ever known life with one parent. Dad's great. I can't complain. How did you find him?'

Ryan looked a bit taken aback by this question. 'Yeah, he seems nice. What do you reckon he makes of me? I feel like we haven't, um—'

'You'll get to chat more when we have tea. He's left you alone here with me, which means he must think you're reasonably trustworthy.'

It was more awkward than I'd hoped when the three of us sat down together to eat. Dad had made lasagne, which is one of what he likes to call his 'signature dishes', served with salad and garlic bread.

'This is delicious, Mr Hughes,' Ryan told him. 'Really, really nice.' It was decent of him to say so, and such a comment would usually have put him straight into Dad's good books. It might even have led to a 'call me Dave', which hadn't happened so far. Unfortunately, Ryan said these flattering words without first having swallowed the food in his mouth – and people talking with their mouths full has always been one of Dad's pet hates. He's drummed it into me not to do this for as long as I can remember; as soon as I spotted Ryan doing so, I looked over at Dad to see if he'd noticed. To my dismay, he most certainly had and was already frowning.

I cleared my throat to get Dad's attention and, when he looked at me, I shook my head ever so subtly, in the hope that he'd get the message not to say anything, while Ryan would be oblivious.

Amazingly, it seemed to work. Dad replied: 'Thank you, Ryan. It's one of my specialities.'

'My dad can't cook at all,' Ryan said, thankfully in between mouthfuls this time. 'My mum's always moaning at him that he should learn, but I think he deliberately messes it up whenever she makes him have a go.'

'What about you?' Dad asked. He'd been teaching me the basics of cooking for years, being a firm believer in key life skills being passed on to children from a young age.

'Me?' Ryan replied, wide-eyed. 'Oh, er, I've never really tried, apart from the little bit we had to do at school. I made a pizza then and it tasted like cardboard. I think I probably take after my father when it comes to cooking.'

I didn't even need to look at Dad to know that he was frowning again. It was evident enough from the tone of his voice. 'That's a rather defeatist attitude, don't you think, Ryan? Cooking is a skill that needs to be learned. Please don't tell me that you think of it as women's work.'

Ryan seemed to almost choke on his food at this point, throwing a 'help me' look in my direction before adding: 'No, no. Not at all. I wouldn't—'

'It's okay, Ryan,' I said, shooting daggers at my father while kicking his foot under the table. 'He's only messing with you. Aren't you, Dad?'

'Um, sure,' Dad said. 'But I do think it's important that everyone learns the basics of cooking as early as possible. It's not hard. Anyone can do it with a little focus and dedication.' Staring intently at me, he added: 'Wouldn't you agree, Rose?'

'I guess so.'

Dad redirected his gaze at Ryan. 'Rose is downplaying her knowledge and experience. She's already very accomplished in the kitchen.'

'Really?' Ryan looked first at Dad and then me. 'You never said. What can you make?'

I shrugged. 'Bits and bobs. I'm hardly the budding chef Dad suggests.'

'Nonsense. She made us a delicious shepherd's pie the other week. And her cheesecake is to die for.'

'Wow, I love both of those,' Ryan said, having stuffed his mouth with more lasagne only a few seconds earlier. My heart sank.

'Ryan, please!' Dad said before I could stop him.

'Sorry?' Ryan replied, his mouth still not clear of food. 'What do—'

'Please stop talking with your mouth full,' Dad said. I hoped he would leave it at that, but – to my dismay – he continued. 'It's a pet hate of mine. I can't bear it when people do that. I find it disgusting.'

'Oh. Right. Sorry, I didn't realise I was doing it. I'll, er, try not to, um, do it again. Sorry.' Ryan's face turned an increasingly deep red colour as he spoke; I felt so mortified, I wished I could shrink myself to the size of an ant and scuttle away from this awkward scene.

Instead, I was stuck there, piggy in the middle, no idea what to do. Part of me was tempted to rip into Dad, but I had a feeling that if I did this, he'd hate Ryan forevermore, thinking of him as the boy who turned me against him. Equally, if I defended Ryan's actions, this would probably only result in Dad further emphasising his point, thus dragging out the cringy situation. I did the only other thing I could think of and changed the subject. 'Did I tell you, Dad, that Ryan and I are in the same maths class? That's actually how we got to know each other, because the teacher sat us together.'

'Isn't that a bit distracting?' Dad asked.

'No, not at all. Ryan's really good at maths. Much better than me. He's been a big help.'

Dad nodded. 'Good to hear. It's important to stay focused.'

I almost kicked him under the table again, but I managed to resist. He was doing my head in, not being himself at all. I'd never seen him behave this way towards any female friends I'd brought home; it was weird to see him so stern and protective.

After we'd finished the main course, Ryan politely asked if he could be excused to go to the toilet. As soon as he was out of earshot, I asked Dad in hushed but angry tones what on earth he was playing at. 'Why are you being like this? No wonder he's escaped to the loo. He probably needs to splash cold water over his face to cool down, thanks to you. I thought you were going to be nice to him? I can't believe you picked him up on his table manners. Couldn't you have let it slide for once?'

'I did let it slide once. Then he spoke with his mouth full for a second time. Sorry, but he needs to be told. It's for his own good. Maybe that's considered normal behaviour in his house, but it's definitely not acceptable in polite company. In fact, as far as I'm concerned, it's unacceptable in any circumstances.'

'Most people aren't as obsessed about it as you, Dad. Put yourself in Ryan's shoes. He must be so humiliated. Is this why you asked me to invite him over: so you could make him look stupid and not want to come back? Well, congratulations. You've succeeded. Thanks a bunch.'

We heard the toilet flush, signalling Ryan's imminent return, so we curtailed our private chat. When he got back to the table, Dad didn't explicitly apologise to him, but there was a notable change in his manner. For instance, when he was divvying up dessert – apple pie – he said to Ryan: 'This is unlikely to be quite as delicious as Rose's cheesecake. It's shop-bought, I must confess, but the local bakery I got it from is good. I'll give you a nice big piece and I hope you enjoy it.'

'Thank you, Mr Hughes,' he said in a quiet voice. It

broke a piece of my heart to hear the difference, the reduction in confidence and enthusiasm, from how he'd spoken to Dad before. It reminded me, although I never told Ryan this, of a nervy dog being fed by an owner who'd previously hurt it.

'Please,' Dad said, finally. 'There's no need for such formalities. Call me Dave.'

'Right,' Ryan said, a perplexed but relieved look in his eyes. 'Thanks. I'll try to remember.'

He ate his pie slowly and carefully, clearly aware of potential scrutiny, and didn't utter another word while his mouth was full, thank goodness. Meanwhile, Dad played nice, restricting further chat to light-hearted small talk and even giving Ryan a few encouraging nods and smiles.

Later that evening, he drove Ryan home. I went along too, both of us sitting on the back seat. Although Dad asked questions about school and his family on the way, it was all very amicable. When we arrived, Dad complimented the appearance of his house before reaching across to offer him a handshake. 'It's been very nice to meet you, Ryan. I do hope you'll come to visit again. You'll be most welcome.'

'Thank you, Mr, um . . . sorry, Dave, I mean. Thank you very much for having me and for the ride home.'

'No problem.'

Ryan stepped out of the car, having squeezed my hand to say goodbye rather than kissing me, which felt like a good decision. He started to close the door, only to open it again and lower his head to address Dad. 'Sorry, I forgot. Mum made me promise that I'd give her a chance to pop out and meet you. Would that be okay?'

'Sure.'

Kelly appeared and Dad got out of the car to shake her hand and say hello. She seemed nervous, her voice jerky and a bit giggly, although when after a few minutes she brought up Dad's novel, it made sense. 'I apologise. You must get this all the time, but I have to tell you I'm a big fan of your writing. *A Child's Scream*: what a powerful book!'

'That's nice of you,' Dad said with a gracious smile. 'I'm glad you enjoyed it.'

As the two of us drove home afterwards, Dad having also briefly met Ryan's father, Jeremy, he told me: 'His parents seem very nice. And despite what you may think, I like Ryan too. Sorry about being a bit hard on him initially. I don't know why I did that. It won't happen again.'

True to his word, it didn't. Not for a long while, anyway. Not until Ryan brought it on himself.

CHAPTER 12

CASSIE

'That sounds ominous.'

'Relationships aren't always easy,' Rose replies.

Cassie nods, shifting herself into an upright position on her tiled lounger and swinging her feet to the side, so she's facing Rose. 'It feels like we've been in here for ages. Do you think we should move on?'

'Sure,' Rose says. Cassie thinks she spots a look of relief flash across the younger woman's face, like the next bit of the story is something she'd rather not talk about. Cassie knows why. It wouldn't be too hard to guess, even if she wasn't already privy to key information about Rose's backstory before they started talking.

Rose looks up at the clock on the wall of the chillout room, still echoing with gentle, ambient sounds, and does a double take. 'Wow. We have been in here a while, haven't we? I lost track of time. They're so comfy, these loungers.

I'm surprised no one else has come in here after us.' Sliding off her lounger and up on to her feet in one smooth motion, she adds: 'We definitely need to get on with our tour. It'll be time for my treatments before I know it. Where to next? Any suggestions?'

Also standing up and having a good stretch, resisting the temptation to yawn, Cassie shakes her head. 'Not really. Whatever you fancy, Rose. Or if you're not sure, we can always follow the signs and see where they take us.'

'Let's do that,' she replies, 'but first I need another drink.'

'Good plan.'

'There's a water dispenser in the corridor, I think.'

Cassie nods, not letting on that she thought Rose was talking about alcohol until she qualified her statement. She'll certainly need some more booze inside her before she starts to tell her story. But water will do for now.

They end up in a steam room with moody green lighting and a menthol aroma. It's not dissimilar from the one in which she and Rose first encountered each other, earlier in the tour. However, the temperature here is higher and the steam seems thicker.

The smell takes Cassie back to her younger days, when she used to enjoy smoking menthol cigarettes. Apart from the fact they tasted better to her – much smoother than harsh regular cigarettes – they also looked better, more elegant, thanks to having a white rather than a brown filter. Or so she thought at the time. Nowadays, like most people, she finds all cigarettes disgusting, full stop. She hasn't had one for years. But still she finds herself inhaling and exhaling, secretly imagining she's puffing on a ciggie.

Rose's story is temporarily on hold, due to the fact there's an undesirably chatty man in there with them: a skinny bald chap in his early sixties with a silly, thin-lined white goatee beard, groomed to within an inch of its life. It reminds Cassie of when she lived in Amsterdam for a while in her twenties. She worked in a bar in the heart of the city, close to Rembrandtplein, where one of her Dutch colleagues told her the local nickname for such a beard was *pratende kut*, or talking vagina, to apply the politest translation. She struggled to take anyone with a goatee seriously after hearing that; thinking about it now makes her giggle.

'What's so funny?' Rose whispers.

'Nothing.' Cassie bites the inside of her cheek in a bid to stop laughing; it doesn't work. She lets out a loud, involuntary snort, which sounds so ridiculous, it makes her laugh more.

'A joke is best shared,' the man says from across the room. Cassie does her utmost not to look at his face, for fear of picturing a talking vagina again, and says: 'There's no joke to repeat, I'm afraid. I think the heat went to my head for a minute.'

'That can happen,' he says. 'Maybe you should try the ice bucket around the corner. I've seen other people using it, although I've not had a go myself. It's not actually ice in there, just very cold water. You stand underneath and pull a chain – if you dare.'

'Right.' Cassie says no more for fear of encouraging him. In the short time they've spent in his company, he's already launched into diatribes against the government, the police and, bizarrely, Wellington boots. It's clear he loves the sound of his own voice and she can't bear much more. Not to mention he has something of a wandering eye that is particularly focused on Rose, which is all kinds of wrong and creepy, considering he's old enough to be her grandfather.

Turning to face Rose at an angle where her expression is out of his view, she says: 'I'm going to head to the ladies. Are you coming?' What she doesn't say but conveys with facial expressions, is: 'Let's get out of here and as far away from this weirdo as possible.'

'Yes, I need to go too,' Rose replies, thankfully.

'Do you really need the loo?' Rose asks her as they wander away from the steam room.

'A little,' Cassie says. 'You?'

'Same. That's not really why we left, though, is it?'

Cassie rolls her eyes. 'I figured the last thing either of us needed was to get stuck with that annoying bloke for any longer. He could barely take his eyes off you.'

'Ew, seriously?'

'You didn't notice?'

'No, I guess I assumed, because he's so old, he wouldn't, um—'

'Never assume that, Rose. Not when it comes to men. They're not all like your father, you know – far from it.'

Oops. Cassie fears she may have said too much. She stops talking, waiting to see how Rose reacts. Fortunately, she doesn't appear to have noticed the slip. She seems to have taken the comment to refer to fathers and daughters in general – or perhaps to be based on what Rose has already said about her dad. Phew, a lucky escape.

'What a horrible thought,' Rose says of being ogled. She pulls a face like she's just eaten something unpleasant.

'I know.' Cassie winces.

'How are you enjoying my story?' Rose asks. 'I'm not boring you, I hope. I wish I'd led a more remarkable life, but it is what it is. Sorry, I know that's a vacuous expression. Cara and I tend to say it to each other ironically, because of how often it's said on reality TV. I don't want you to think of me that way – like I'm brainless.'

'I could never think that about you,' Cassie says automatically, quickly adding: 'You're obviously a very intelligent young woman. That's already crystal clear from the short time we've been acquainted.'

As a diversionary tactic, Cassie asks Rose what treatments she has lined up for later. However, she already knows the answer: a hot-stone back massage followed by a marine mineral purifying facial. Cassie is nothing if not thorough. She's done her homework.

'What about you?' Rose asks.

'Just a facial for me.' She winks and lowers her voice. 'The age protecting kind. But don't tell.'

Rose laughs. 'Doesn't look like you need it to me. You look great.'

'That's kind of you. But you're never too young to start looking after nature's gifts. It's easier to preserve than repair.'

'I'll bear that in mind.'

When the pair return to the main pool area, thankfully

there's no sign of their annoying male acquaintance. The pool is the emptiest Cassie has seen it so far; there's a free spot with a raised underwater shelf next to some massage jets, so she suggests they give it a try.

'It should be easy for us to keep on talking there without interruptions and, if that guy or anyone else unsavoury appears, we'll be able to see them coming without getting boxed in.'

'Good idea,' Rose replies with a broad smile.

Cassie feels a stab of pain every time she sees her like this – radiating happiness. It's exactly what you'd expect of a bride-to-be a week before her wedding. And yet soon she'll have to burst that bubble.

Once Cassie's told her own story, everything will change for Rose.

Cassie finds herself thinking of Hans Christian Andersen's 'The Little Mermaid'. She read this fairy tale as a girl and it had a profound effect on her. One aspect of the story that leapt off the page then, and which she recalls now, was how when the little mermaid got her wish of having legs, it was agony for her, like walking on knives. Spending time with Rose now, enjoying her company while knowing what's to come and how things will change, Cassie has a sense of that pain.

Not that she has any right to feel sorry for herself or expect the sympathy of others. Her pain is incidental and irrelevant. The one to be pitied is Rose. Her entire world is about to come crashing down around her, through no fault of her own, and she doesn't have a clue.

'So where was I?' Rose says after they've settled into

their latest spot on the tranquillity tour, Cassie continuing to mask her inner turmoil behind a friendly smile.

Rose's face darkens as she adds: 'Oh, yes. The reason for Ryan and my father falling out.'

CHAPTER 13

ROSE

My father and Ryan got along fine for a good number of years – right through our time at secondary school, really. It took Ryan a little while to believe this, following his first encounter with Rude Dave, but he got there eventually.

There were a few hiccups along the way, such as when Dad learned we'd started sleeping together and told me he wanted to 'throttle that lad'. This wasn't until we were both in sixth form. Ryan would have been happy to do it earlier, of course: he was a lustful teenage boy. But he was great about respecting my desire to wait until I was seventeen. I'm not sure exactly why I picked that age as the turning point, but it felt right.

It also felt right to tell my father after the event. I wanted to be adult about it. I was hoping that, given time to wrap his head around the idea, Dad might allow Ryan to stay over in my bedroom once in a while. Plus I was considering going on the pill and I knew this would be easier with Dad's knowledge.

'Do you want to throttle me too?' was my response to Dad's overreaction.

'Of course not.'

'Well, I was a willing party in what happened and Ryan was the perfect gentleman. Would you rather I hadn't told you about it and we'd carried on in secret? I thought we'd agreed to be honest with each about such things.'

'Yes, well, wanting to throttle Ryan is my honest reaction to this news,' Dad said. 'It's a really big step at your age. I still think you're both too young and that you'll regret not waiting. Where did you even . . . do it?'

'I'm sure you don't want to know the gory details, Dad, and it's too late for regrets. Ryan and I love each other. We've been together forever and it felt like the right time.'

'I wish you'd discussed it with me first.'

'I'm glad I didn't, based on how well this chat is going.'

Dad stared into the distance. 'Please tell me you were safe. You used a condom, right?'

'Of course. You've warned me often enough about that, Dad. I'd have to be stupid for that particular message not to have sunk in by now.'

Dad was still for ages, blinking repeatedly, before he replied: 'That's something, I suppose. You haven't told your nana, have you? I doubt she'd approve. She doesn't believe in sex before marriage, never mind while you're still at school. It goes against her religious beliefs.'

'I'm not sure your mother is quite the prude you think

she is, Dad. I hoped you'd be cool with this. You're reminding me now of what you were like that first time Ryan came over to the house, when you told him off for talking with his mouth full.'

'That was a good life lesson I gave him.' He wagged his finger. 'He's never done it since, at least in front of me, so he learned something valuable.'

'Seriously, Dad?'

He did get used to the idea eventually, although he flat refused to let Ryan stay the night in my bedroom until we'd finished secondary school. He said he had no issue with me going on the pill, on the proviso I promised to continue using condoms as well. 'You can't be too careful, and it's not only pregnancy you need protection against, Rose. You need to think about STIs too.'

'You make it sound like I'm sleeping around, Dad. Ryan and I are committed to each other. We were both virgins before this.'

'You can't be too careful,' he repeated. 'Even with the best of intentions, things can change quickly at your age. I need to know you're not taking any risks at all.'

'You don't trust Ryan, do you? That's what this is about.'

'I didn't say that, Rose. The simple fact is that the pair of you are only seventeen. Everyone's prone to making mistakes at that age. It's part of growing up. I want you to be safe. Is that so awful? It's not like I'm banning you from seeing your boyfriend. Quite the opposite.'

'Fine.' I let it drop and accepted his terms. We'll show him how dedicated we are to each other, I thought; we'll prove his assumptions wrong.

And we did for a while. Ryan and I stayed together right through sixth form without any major issues. We loved each other and spent most of our free time together. That final long summer, after A levels and before university, when Dad and Ryan's parents finally let us stay over together at each other's houses, we were more or less inseparable. We even went on holiday to Gran Canaria together. Well, us and a group of ten schoolfriends. There was the odd minor argument, of course, but nothing significant. Secretly, I'd already started to think that one day we might get married. I knew we were young, with so much still ahead of us. But I was happy. We were happy. I didn't want or need anyone else; I was certain Ryan felt the same.

We didn't even have to worry about what might happen next, because we'd got that covered. We were heading over the border to Yorkshire together: me to study English and philosophy at the University of Sheffield, and Ryan to study economics at Sheffield Hallam University.

That was the plan. We'd both been offered conditional places, which our teachers expected us to achieve, so naively it felt like a done deal.

Unfortunately, that didn't factor-in Ryan making major blunders in two of his A-level subjects, which saw him crash spectacularly out of the race for uni places.

I still remember his face on results day like it was yesterday. We'd gone into school together but got separated in the rush. I was absolutely over the moon to get all As. It was what I'd been predicted, but I'd convinced myself it wouldn't happen.

I'll be honest, on seeing my results, a tiny part of me wondered if I ought to have applied to Oxbridge after all, as some of my teachers had suggested. I hadn't done so, despite or maybe partly because of Dad being an Oxford English graduate himself. The official line had always been that I wanted to stay in the north, where there were plenty of excellent universities, but of course the truth was more about Ryan than I cared to acknowledge. That and the fact I genuinely didn't believe I was good enough.

'Just because you went to Oxford, doesn't mean I have to, Dad,' I remember shouting at him during one particular hissy fit. 'Next you'll be telling me to write a bestselling novel before I graduate. But I'm not you, Dad, and I don't want to be. I need to tread my own path in life.'

My anger was rooted in the fact that Dad had, rightly, queried whether my decision was being influenced by my relationship with Ryan. There was no way I was going to admit that to him. I barely even admitted it to myself.

Anyway, there I was on results day, feeling totally chuffed at what I'd achieved, while entertaining the notion that I could perhaps have held my own at Oxford or Cambridge. Then I saw Ryan's dazed, devastated face coming towards me from further down the corridor and everything else was forgotten. My self-centred what-ifs vanished. I knew before I spoke a word to him that Ryan's dreams had been shattered. He looked punch-drunk, his usually sparkling eyes unfocused, clouded over; shock and ruin were etched into every pore of his sheet-white skin.

So, yeah, there weren't many celebrations that day. Ryan and his parents urged me to go out and enjoy myself with our friends in the pub, but I didn't. I couldn't. I went back to his house and stayed at his side, comforting him as best I could. Trying desperately to help him formulate a new plan and understand that, however bad he felt, his adult life absolutely wasn't over before it had begun.

I wish I could travel back in time to that moment, when Ryan was so incredibly low, and tell him that it all turns out fine in the end. He's a qualified electrician these days, having completed an apprenticeship with flying colours, gaining all the key certifications he needed to set up his own fledgling business. Now he's in the process of building it up and things are going swimmingly. He's never short of work or money coming in, which is more than can be said for me with my degree.

It took him a little while to work out what he wanted to do after the disappointment of his A-level results. He had to look at things from outside the box that had been presented to us by our very traditional-minded school. But eventually he discovered the path that was right for him, away from academia. Seeing how happy he is now with his job, I know that studying economics at Sheffield would have been a bad fit for him. If only Ryan had been able to see that back then, as well as to know that we'd eventually be getting married. Things would likely have gone smoother for him – and for me.

Instead, as I went off to Sheffield and he stayed at home, it didn't take long until problems arose. We'd had loads of conversations about how we would make our relationship work in spite of the distance between us. We both knew it would be hard and that most school relationships didn't survive university. However, we convinced ourselves that, by going into it with our eyes open, we could be the exception to the rule.

We agreed to chat regularly – every day where possible – and to take it in turns visiting each other at weekends several times per term. We had a plan, which we intended to stick to, and that included a pledge to be completely faithful. But since we were keeping our eyes open, we recognised there could be minor slip-ups along the way; we promised total honesty with the aim of nipping any such problems in the bud.

Dad didn't get involved, saying it was none of his business, which was probably the wisest move. Nana, on the other hand, had plenty to say from Spain whenever I spoke to her around that time.

'Don't get me wrong,' I recall her telling me in one video call, 'Ryan's a lovely boy, but do you really think this is the best idea?'

I fought to keep calm. 'Of course I do, Nana. We love each other and we want to stay together.'

'You do *now*,' she said. 'But you're both so young. Think of all the other people you've yet to meet in life. How can you be so sure he's your perfect partner with so many other possibilities out there? Going off to university will give you a great opportunity to explore new people and situations; to discover who you really are, on your own, away from the ties of the past. Maybe even to reinvent yourself, if that's what you want. Why go into that experience with one arm tied behind your back? If Ryan is perfect for you, you could always get together again later, after university.'

Considering Nana never went to university, I suspect she based most of this advice on her experiences since moving abroad, which she'd clearly found liberating after years of being married to a workaholic, who cast a long shadow even after his death. I've said before that she worshipped my grandad, but I don't think she always found it easy sharing him with his business interests. He remained occupied right to the end, by all accounts, refocusing on his investments after selling his frozen foods firm, but never really slowing down. She dealt with this by managing his personal life and running their busy social calendar like a well-oiled machine. After his death, I think she felt incredibly lost. Helping me and Dad filled the gap for a while, but as I got older and increasingly self-sufficient, she needed more – a life all of her own – and she found that in Spain.

Not that I thought any of this qualified her to advise me on my relationship with Ryan as I headed off to uni at eighteen. But the last thing I wanted to do was fall out with the one really close family member I had other than Dad, especially when she was already so far away. I let her say her piece and then ignored it.

One particular snippet of guidance she offered did come back to haunt me, though. 'If you agree to stay together when you go off to university, he'll be the one who'll struggle with it, mark my words.'

'Why do you say that, Nana? I thought you liked Ryan.'

'I do, but he's a boy, Rose. Okay, a man now, I suppose,

technically, but that doesn't change my point. Men might be physically stronger than women, much of the time, but mentally – particularly when it comes to love and lust – it's often a very different story. I think he'll struggle being the one left at home while you're off doing new things. He'll imagine all sorts: fear and jealousy will run wild in his mind. And that's when he'll end up doing something stupid, breaking your heart in the process.'

'I appreciate your concern, Nana,' I said. 'Respectfully, though, I think you're wrong. Ryan's not like that. You'll see.'

Unfortunately, I was the one who was wrong.

CHAPTER 14

It must be pretty clear by now that Ryan cheated on me. I still find it tough to say that about the man I'm due to marry, but it's part of our past I can't deny. Forgiven but not forgotten. And yes, you've probably guessed that this is also the reason things turned sour between Ryan and my dad.

In my father's case, what Ryan did is neither forgiven nor forgotten. It's merely acknowledged and, for my sake, tolerated.

So what exactly happened and when?

It was right at the end of my first term in Sheffield, during the start of Christmas party season at the beginning of December. I didn't find out about it until New Year's Eve, though, which made that a particularly memorable occasion for all the wrong reasons.

So much for Ryan's pledge to be totally honest about any slip-ups. Mind you, it was more than a little mistake. It was a drunken one-night stand with a thirty-something stranger he met on a pub crawl in Preston. There, I've said it. Never gets any easier to repeat.

It took me a long time to get over; to accept his apologies. Initially, having ended the relationship, I didn't think I ever would. I hated Ryan for what he'd done and how utterly betrayed, devastated and humiliated it left me feeling. I couldn't even look at him. For ages, I refused to see him in person or communicate with him in any way whatsoever.

I cried myself to sleep night after night at the start. For a good while after that, I was numb, protecting myself from further hurt by shutting down any other such feelings.

I became a bit of an ice queen at uni with boys I was attracted to. I had flings with some of them, mainly to help me move on, but I kept these brief and free of emotion. However, it did, undeniably, feel good to be desired by others. And such boosts to my self-esteem were welcome after the sucker punch Ryan had dealt me.

As for why he did what he did, it was almost exactly what Nana had predicted. The night when he cheated was only a few days after he'd come to visit me in Sheffield for the weekend. He'd been quiet when we'd gone out together with a large group of my friends on the Saturday. Then on the Sunday morning, hungover, we'd rowed. He'd accused me of flirting with some of the boys we'd been out with, making him 'look like a mug'.

I firmly disputed this, plus his ridiculous claim that everyone was judging him for being 'a country bumpkin, too thick to go to uni'. This annoyed me, because I'd seen

130

how much effort they'd made to include him, while he'd been surly and monosyllabic. He'd also drunk twice as much alcohol as anyone else, tried to pick a fight with the boyfriend of one of my closest pals, and been sick in the corridor outside my room, leaving me to clean up after him.

He left on bad terms, although when we spoke by phone a couple of days later, I thought we managed to iron things out. Apparently not. He went off and did what he did, then hid it from me right over the festive period.

I had a feeling something was wrong even before we saw each other in person again. I never suspected the terrible truth, though, or anything close to it. I genuinely didn't think he had it in him to inflict such pain on me. But after him being weird throughout the holidays, avoiding being alone with me and making one excuse after another not to have sex, my suspicions were through the roof.

We were attending a party at the house of an old school friend on New Year's Eve and at 11.30 p.m., I dragged him into the back garden and confronted him. Finally, he broke down and told me everything. He was crying and shaking and begging and pleading; I just had to get away from him.

'Please, Rose. It was a mistake. A dreadful one, I know, but it didn't mean anything. I was hammered. The whole thing's a blur. It was—'

'Didn't mean anything?' I spat, raging. 'You're disgusting. What did I ever see in you? We're done. Once and for all.'

'No, don't say that! I'll never do it again, I promise. I

love you so much, Rose. Please forgive me. At least hear me out.' He tried to grab my hand, but I shoved him away as hard as I could and, before he could react further, stormed alone into the busy kitchen, slamming the door behind me and turning the key in the lock to keep him outside.

'Rose, is everything all right?' I heard a female voice call over the loud music. But I couldn't deal with anyone, so I continued into the empty hallway, quietly let myself out of the front door and slipped off into the darkness. I walked for a bit, not allowing my brain to think about anything at all, and it wasn't until the cold air started to bite that I even realised I'd left without my coat. I pulled my mobile out of my handbag and looked at the time: 11.48 p.m. Almost midnight. Fantastic. What was I supposed to do now?

There was only one thing for it: I rang Dad, who was meant to be over at Cara's parents' house for a dinner party.

'Rose,' he said down the line. 'Is everything all right?'

'Where are you?' I asked, surprised not to hear any background noise from his end.

'Oh, I'm at home. I couldn't face going in the end. Don't judge me. I thought I'd have a quiet one by myself instead. Where are you? It doesn't sound like there's much of a party going on.'

I burst into tears and it took Dad a couple of minutes to get any sense out of me. As soon as he did, he jumped in the car to fetch me, insisting that I walk to a nearby pub and wait inside for him, rather than staying out in the cold. Having promised to do this, I entered the bright lights of the packed bar area on the stroke of midnight.

I distinctly remember standing there, like a spare part, as everyone around me erupted into an elated cry of 'Happy New Year!', kissing and hugging each other, shouting, cheering and clapping.

Soon someone started singing 'Auld Lang Syne' and most people joined in, slurring and fudging their way through the song as I continued to stand there, alone and silent, wishing the sticky wooden floor would swallow me up.

I looked at my phone, which was on mute; I saw there were now several missed calls from Ryan as well as a couple from Cara, who'd also been at the party. I texted her back to say I was safe and not to worry. As for Ryan, I ignored that bloody bastard, which was the only way I could think of him at that moment.

'Cheer up, love,' a boozy man's voice said close to my ear as he passed by carrying a round of drinks. 'It might never happen.'

It already has, I thought, ignoring him and his stupid comment.

I considered going to the bar myself, mainly to kill time and give me something to do. However, it was jam-packed and there was nothing I wanted, anyway, other than for Dad to arrive to rescue me.

Eventually, feeling awkward and terribly alone, I decided to hide out in the ladies for a while, only to get there and find a long, slow-moving queue to enter. I joined it briefly before giving up. Instead, I continued along the corridor, turning the corner on the hunt for a quiet spot to hide, only to come across a separate accessible toilet that appeared unoccupied.

When I opened the door, seeing no harm in using it for a minute or two to spend a penny, I came across a woman kneeling on the floor, head in the toilet bowl, vomiting. She had short grey hair and was wearing a sparkly black dress.

'Sorry,' I said. 'I didn't know anyone was in here.' She didn't acknowledge me, too busy emptying her stomach. The smell made me gag, so I closed the door again and took a step back.

I did consider walking away, but with nothing better to do, I decided to remain there to stop anyone else barging in on the puking woman, as well as to make sure she emerged in one piece and didn't need any assistance.

To my surprise, when she did exit the toilet, staggering, wet-faced and generally looking the worse for wear, I recognised her. It was one of my old teachers from secondary school, Miss Murdoch, who must have been in her mid-fifties by that point. She'd taught me history for the two years leading up to GCSEs and I'd always thought of her as strait-laced and boring. I turned my head in a bid to avoid her eye. However, she remained standing right in front of me, a puzzled look on her face.

'Hello,' I said when it became apparent that she wasn't moving on.

She hiccupped. 'I know you, don't I?'

'Yes, Miss Murdoch,' I said, flashing her a swift smile. 'You used to teach me at Riverside.'

Her eyes widened. 'Shh!' she said, hiccupping again before holding up her forefinger, trying to place it in front of her lips but missing and hitting her nose instead. 'Oops, I'm a bit squiffy.' She giggled. 'I should know your name, but . . . I can't stop – *hic* – yes that. So annoying.'

'It's Rose. Rose Hughes.'

'Yes!' she said, far louder than necessary, waving her finger in my face so I took a step back. 'Rose, that's it. Rose and . . . don't tell me . . . Ryan, right? I remember you two lovebirds – *hic* – always holding hands when you thought no one was watching. Are you still together? Is Ryan here too?'

This caught me off guard. A swell of emotion rose up in my chest and my eyes flooded with tears. I wanted to say something in reply, but it was like my throat and mouth had seized up.

Miss Murdoch looked horrified. 'I – *hic* – sorry, I didn't mean to, um, upset you. Are you all right?'

She leaned in close enough so I got a whiff of vomit, forcing me to step back again. I nodded that I was okay but still couldn't get any words out.

Thankfully, at that moment, my father came around the corner at a pace. 'Oh, Rose, there you are,' he said. 'Thank goodness. Why aren't you answering your phone? I've been looking all over the pub for you. I was on the verge of barging into the ladies.'

I ran into his arms, squeezed my eyes shut and hugged the only man in the world I knew I could trust.

He stroked my hair. 'I'm here now. I've got you.'

I'm not exactly sure what happened to Miss Murdoch

after that. I wasn't paying attention, although she probably slinked off back into the bar.

I remember Dad did ask me who she was in the car on the way home. He may even have said she looked familiar, but I was too worn out to explain, so I pretended she was a drunk passer-by.

'Do you want to talk about what happened?' Dad asked while making us both a hot chocolate in the kitchen at home.

'Not tonight,' I replied. 'I don't have the energy. Tomorrow?'

'Whenever you're ready, Dimples. You're okay, though?'

'I will be, but it might take a while.' I felt my eyes well up yet again as I added: 'Ryan broke my heart into little pieces tonight.'

Dad handed me my hot chocolate, ruffling my hair as he did so. 'I'm really sorry to hear that, Rose.'

He reserved passing judgement until I eventually found the strength to tell him the full story the next day, as much as it pained and shamed me to repeat Ryan's misdeed. Meanwhile, he was just there for me.

'Thanks, Dad,' I told him. 'For everything. I'd have been lost without you tonight.'

'That's what dads are for. Me not going to that dinner party was meant to be. It didn't feel right. Now we know why. I was needed elsewhere.' He shook his head. 'Plus I think they were trying to set me up with this single friend of theirs. I've met her once before and she's definitely not my type. She's nice-looking enough, but so timid and jittery. I remember feeling on edge just talking to her for a couple of minutes, like I'd had five double espressos.'

'Oh, Dad,' I said, taking a sweet sip from my steaming mug. 'You shouldn't be so closed off to new possibilities.'

'I take your point, but trust me on this one, love. Her name is Drusilla and she's a taxidermist.'

'What? As in someone who stuffs dead animals? Gross.'

Dad winked. 'I may have made that bit up, but she's definitely not for me.'

'I'm surprised Cara didn't mention her,' I said. 'Mind you, she was busy familiarising herself with her new boyfriend's lips most of the night.'

'Was she now?' Dad raised an eyebrow. 'She did find time to call me to ask if I knew where you were. She was worried, but I told her it was under control. You should give her a call tomorrow, Rose.'

'I will. But I've turned my phone off for now, in case you-know-who calls. If he rings the home phone or turns up here, will you get rid of him? I really don't want to see him.'

'Consider it done.'

CHAPTER 15

Ryan came round to the house on New Year's Day. He drove his mum's white Vauxhall Corsa on to the drive at around three o'clock that afternoon. I happened to be looking out of the window at the time. I ran to my bedroom, shouting: 'Dad, he's here! You can't let him in.'

'Don't worry,' Dad said in a steady voice. 'I've got this.'

He knew the full story by that point. His eyes had burned with fury as I'd told him exactly what Ryan had done. I wondered if he might take a swing at him on the doorstep, something I both did and didn't want to happen.

Too curious to stay in my room, I crept out on to the landing, near the banister at the top of the stairs, where I could hear but not see what was happening at the front door.

I heard the sound of the door opening, immediately followed by my dad's voice. 'What do you want, Ryan?'

'Is Rose here? Please could I speak to her?'

'No, just go. You're not welcome here any longer. She

doesn't want to see or hear from you and neither do I. You've got a real cheek coming here after what you did, do you know that?'

'I want to apologise; to explain. I also have her coat. She left it at the party last night.'

'Fine, I'll take that. But don't expect a thank you. Let me explain this to you, Ryan. If you come here again, you'll leave with a black eye or worse. Are we clear? And don't bother calling her either, because she won't answer. You've burned your bridges. Live with it. Now sling your hook.'

If Ryan had anything else to say, he didn't get a chance, as the door was slammed shut.

I crept back into my bedroom, where I'd already closed the curtains, and lay on my bed feeling utterly miserable.

Dad appeared at the door a short while later. 'He's gone.'

'Are you sure?'

'Yes, I watched him drive away. Hopefully he won't be back any time soon. I told him not to call you either, but you may be best to block his number. He brought your coat back, by the way.'

'I know. I was listening from the landing.'

'Oh, I see. Fair enough.' He cleared his throat and shuffled his feet, still hovering in the doorway.

'I thought you handled it perfectly, Dad,' I said, sensing he needed to hear this. 'I know it must have felt a bit weird. Thank you.'

I didn't see Ryan again for ages after that, not even to exchange the bits and bobs of each other's stuff we had.

There was nothing I wanted back badly enough to go through the pain of facing him. At uni, I immersed myself in my studies as well as partying more than before. I tried not to think about Ryan, although it was harder when I was home again for a long period over the summer holidays between first and second year, especially as we'd talked about going away together then.

I saw a lot of Cara, who'd recently finished her A levels and was looking forward to starting at the University of Edinburgh that autumn. The two of us booked a last-minute trip to Mallorca for a week in August, which was amazing fun. We both made the most of being single, partying until the early hours every night and flirting left, right and centre without ever letting things get too out of hand.

A couple of days after we got back, when I was still sun-kissed and nicely chilled, I finally bumped into Ryan for the first time while out catching up with some other old schoolfriends in a pub garden.

'Hello, stranger,' he said, approaching me as I was waiting to get served at the outside bar. 'I've missed you. You look amazing, like you've just stepped off the beach or something.'

He looked good too, in dark jeans and a fitted white T-shirt that showed off his muscled physique. However, I'd seen more than enough good-looking guys in tight clothes during my week abroad to be impressed – and there was no way I was complimenting him back.

I realised I no longer felt angry at him. Apparently, I'd moved on at last. 'Hello, Ryan,' I said. 'How are you?'

We didn't chat for long – five minutes probably – before going our separate ways, but it was enough to clear the air. When we next ran into each other, some months later, while I was back for Christmas, I was able to greet him with a peck on the cheek. Even though it brought back memories of the disastrous previous New Year's Eve, I was strong and confident enough not to be fazed. I almost enjoyed our conversation that time, particularly when we spoke about our schooldays. I'd be lying if I said it didn't hurt when he told me he was going out with a pretty girl I vaguely remembered from Cara's year at school and 'things were going well'. I took it in my stride, though, telling him in turn that I'd been seeing a few people at uni but nothing serious. I walked away feeling like a line had been drawn under our relationship once and for all.

Of course, it hadn't. I wouldn't be getting married to him next week, otherwise, would I? But it wasn't until the summer holidays after that – at the end of my second year at uni – that it occurred to me I might still have feelings for Ryan.

I must mention Dad at this point. Having already explained that he's never really forgiven Ryan for what he did to me, I don't want to make him sound unreasonable. Quite the opposite. He didn't take the opportunity to bad-mouth Ryan to me after we split up. He largely kept his feelings to himself.

Dad was a huge comfort to me in the cold early January days after I finished with cheating Ryan. Cara came over to see me several times, and yet she was distracted by that new boyfriend with whom she'd spent New Year's Eve sucking face. In the absence of my BFF, there was Dad. Mainly he listened to me as I spilled my heart out and cried enough tears to fill a swimming pool. He hugged and comforted me, bringing me my favourite food and constant cups of tea; we watched countless classic feelgood films like *Big*, *Matilda*, *The Sound of Music*, *The Princess Bride*, *Mamma Mia!* and *Ferris Bueller's Day Off*. Luckily, Dad's always enjoyed these kinds of movies as much as I have. He was the one who got me into them in the first place, coming up with the idea of Sunday Evening Film Club when I was ten or eleven years old, complete with microwave popcorn and a rotating variety of other tasty snacks, such as hotdogs and nachos. He kept it going right through my teenage years until I moved to Sheffield.

I took it for granted a bit towards the end, skipping some Sundays to see Ryan and so on. But boy did I miss it when I got to university. So much so that I started a boozy student version with a couple of my new friends, which we dubbed the Cheesy Film and Wine Club.

No, Dad's a total softie at heart, whose literary credentials go out of the window when there's a Hollywood ending to enjoy. As a child, I thought most men liked watching such films, because Dad, who could reel off his top ten romcoms without having to think about it, was my prime point of reference. But as I grew older and more worldly-wise, I realised this wasn't typical. Dad's always been far more in touch with his emotional side than a lot of men, including Ryan – but not in an effete way. He comes across as a tough, manly man most of the time. It's a rare combination that I love and cherish; secretly, I like

142

to think it's partly down to me, in that he brought me up and lived alone with me for all those years. It feels nice to believe that some of me rubbed off on him. Although, let's be honest, he must have been pretty darn special to begin with. Not every man could handle raising a baby girl single-handedly from his early twenties – never mind do such a great job of it.

I have no doubt he would make someone a brilliant boyfriend or husband. He could help them plait or curl their hair one minute and fix a leaking radiator or lay some laminate flooring the next. He's a man of many varied talents, my father. I'd love for him to find a woman to appreciate what a wonderful guy he is and for him to share his life with. I don't like the idea of him rattling around that big house by himself without me. Maybe I'll try again to get him online dating after the wedding. Or I could even fill out an application form for him to go on a TV show like *First Dates*. They'd lap him up with his past. Fat chance he'd agree to it.

Anyway, back to the other man in my life, Ryan, and how, against the odds, he eventually managed to win me back.

Having not seen him for months, I bumped into him in a supermarket, of all places, in the August before I started my third and final year in Sheffield. I'd been at home less than usual that summer, having spent a chunk of it on a trip to Spain with Dad to visit Nana. I'd also visited the family homes of some of my best uni friends, including a guy called Simon from my course, who was the closest I'd had to an actual boyfriend since Ryan, although we were 'keeping things casual' and 'avoiding labels'. I can't believe how pretentious that sounds now, although, I'm embarrassed to admit, it was all my doing. Poor Simon was head over heels in love with me, while I was still working through my commitment issues.

Ryan and I were both alone when we bumped into each other looking at pizzas late one afternoon in the chilled foods aisle. We got chatting and, neither of us having plans, we didn't stop. We finished our shopping alongside each other, kept chatting in the car park and agreed we might as well enjoy our pizzas together. So I went back to Ryan's parents' house, where he was still living at the time. We had the place to ourselves, since his mum and dad were on holiday in France. It was weird as hell to be back there with the boy who'd broken my heart, but it also felt nice.

Having spent so long apart, we talked nonstop. Over our pizzas and a glass of white wine, followed by ice cream and coffee, we caught up on each other's lives while also reliving some of the highlights of when we were together.

I didn't totally lower my guard, playing up my relationship with Simon, for instance, by calling him my boyfriend and pretending I was really into him. This was important not only for my pride, so Ryan knew I'd moved on, but also for the practical purpose of making it clear there was nothing but friendship on the cards. A little voice in the back of my head warned me that Ryan might have other ideas. I possibly even wanted him to, so I could have the satisfaction of shutting him down and saying no. But it didn't happen, even though he was single at that point.

It wasn't like that. We just had a nice time together as old friends.

We were both in a good place: me enjoying the holidays and enthusiastic to resume my studies; Ryan well on track to becoming a fully-fledged electrician, already looking forward to getting his own place and setting up his own business.

Later he offered to give me back some of the things he still had of mine from when we were together.

'What is there? It's been so long; I can hardly remember.'

'Um, a few T-shirts, a hoodie, a toothbrush and some toiletries.'

'Wow, that's very precise. How do you—'

'I have them in a box in my room. I dug it out when I popped upstairs earlier. I wasn't sure if, er—'

'I'll take them. Thanks for keeping them for me. I wish I could say the same about what you left in my bedroom, but . . .' I winced as I continued. 'I'm afraid I threw it all in the bin in a fit of rage.'

Ryan took this in good humour. 'Fair enough. I deserved that.'

I didn't join him when he disappeared upstairs to get the box. It didn't feel appropriate, so I waited in the lounge, privately reminiscing about the enjoyable evenings I'd spent there with him and his parents. To my surprise, there was still a framed photo on the mantelpiece of the four of us, taken when we went to a fancy steak restaurant in Manchester to celebrate Ryan's eighteenth birthday. He and I both looked so young and happy: me surprising him with a kiss on the cheek as the photo was snapped by the waiter. It was looking at that simple picture, I think, on the back of our impromptu meal together, that I first felt the timid reawakening of feelings I'd long considered dead and buried.

I turned my back on the picture as I heard him coming down the stairs. Shaking my head to clear it, as if from a daydream, I swatted those feelings away. They terrified me.

'Ah, there you are,' he said, handing over the box. 'Everything all right? You look a bit—'

'I'm fine.'

'Hang on. That reminds me. Back in a sec.' He ran up the stairs and returned almost immediately with two paperback books: J.D. Salinger's *The Catcher in the Rye* and *Life of Pi* by Yann Martel.

'These are yours too, right?' he said. 'I think you wanted me to try reading them.'

'And did you?' I asked. 'They were meant as gifts, not loans.'

'Oh, right. That's awkward. Sorry, Rose.' He shrugged. 'You know I'm not much of a reader. If you'd rather someone else had them – this Simon, perhaps – that's absolutely fine.'

'No. They're yours. Keep hold of them. If you gave reading for pleasure a chance, I still think you'd enjoy them. Besides, Simon has plenty of other things to read.'

Ryan smirked. 'Unlike me, you mean?'

'Am I wrong?'

'Fine, but don't hold your breath.' He winked. 'There's a lot of good stuff on the telly these days. It's hard enough to keep up with that.'

We didn't specifically discuss our breakup until I was leaving, picking up the bits of shopping I'd kept cool in his fridge. He touched my shoulder from behind, making me jump, fearful he had got the wrong idea after all. Then he came out with this apology I hadn't been expecting. 'Rose,' he said. 'I know we've not discussed what happened – what I did to you. I've wanted to all evening, but . . . I didn't want to spoil things or upset you. I can't not say anything, though, especially after such a nice catch-up.'

I felt short of breath and panicky. Tears were waiting in the wings, but I really didn't want to get upset in front of him. I put the last bit of shopping in my bag, shut the fridge and said: 'Sorry, Ryan, but I really need to go now. The past is the past. Let's leave it alone.'

'Fine, I'll stop. Whatever you want, Rose. I owe you that and a lot more on top.'

'You don't owe me anything,' I snapped without thinking. 'We're not anything to each other any longer.'

His face fell. 'Not even friends? After tonight, I thought—'

'I didn't mean that,' I said, my head all over the place, awash with opposing thoughts and feelings.

'I'm glad. I miss you so much, Rose. Every day.' He held up his hands defensively as he added: 'I don't expect anything from you. I understand it's all my fault and that you've moved on. But it's been so great to see you properly again. And, I know I said I wouldn't, but I have to tell you this while I can: I'm truly sorry for what I did to you, Rose. It was the worst mistake of my life. You're a wonderful person and Simon is a lucky man to have you. I hope he realises that.'

It took all of my inner strength not to cry as he said this. But I managed somehow. I couldn't stay, though, or answer him properly. All I said, in a tiny, barely steady voice, was: 'I have to go now. Goodbye.'

And that was it. I left and didn't see him again until Christmas.

CHAPTER 16

'There you are,' Cassie says from across the changing room. 'How were your treatments?'

'Wonderful,' Rose replies. 'So relaxing. I had the hot-stone massage first, which was super chilled, and then the facial; I actually fell asleep during that. Can you believe it? The therapist had to wake me up when the time came to remove the minerals. I was mortified.'

'Oh, you shouldn't be. I'm sure it happens a lot. They'll be used to it.'

Cassie is busy towel-drying her short hair, having already had a shower; Rose still needs to go for one.

'How was your massage?' Rose asks. 'Deep tissue, wasn't it?'

'That's right. It was great. I feel quite limber after that and all the spa facilities we used beforehand.' She chuckles. 'I didn't get any opportunity to nod off like you did, though. It was rather intense.'

'Really?' Rose wrinkles her nose. 'I had a massage in

Spain once, when I was out there visiting my nana, and that was really, um, vigorous. Quite uncomfortable at times. I did feel rejuvenated the next day, so I guess it was worth it.' She runs her hands gently down her cheeks and chin.

'Is your skin really soft now?' Cassie asks.

Rose giggles. 'Like a baby's bottom.'

'I thought so. You're literally glowing, you beautiful thing. Oh, to be young again!'

'Stop it,' Rose says. 'I can only hope I look as amazing as you do when I'm older.'

Cassie grins. 'Flattery will get you everywhere in life, my dear, even if it's not true. Anyway, I'm itching to hear the rest of your story – how you and Ryan got back to where you are now. It was cruel to leave me hanging like you did. Are we still on for meeting in forty-five minutes?'

'Absolutely,' Rose replies. 'I'm not letting you go now when I'm finally so close to passing on the baton and hearing your story.'

'So I'll see you at the bar where we had the G&T earlier, after you've showered and so on?'

'Yes.'

'What drink should I order for you?'

'No, it's my round next.'

'Nonsense. You've done all the talking so far and that's thirsty work. Another G&T?'

'Go on, you've twisted my arm. Thank you.'

'Not a problem. Oh and one more thing: what are your dinner plans this evening?'

'I don't really have any,' Rose says. 'Did you have something in mind?'

'Well, since we're both here alone and I still have a story to tell, I thought perhaps it might be nice for us to dine in the restaurant together. Only if you want to. No pressure. If you'd rather have room service, or—'

'No, that sounds nice. Let's do it. Now I think about it, Cara and I did have a table booked for eight o'clock, which I haven't altered. We could use that, if the time suits.'

'Perfect.'

'Are you planning to dress up for dinner? What's the etiquette? You ate here last night, right?'

'They're pretty chilled about that, as most of the guests are in and out of the spa. Some were a little dressed up yesterday, others definitely weren't. Whatever you fancy, really. I'll be keeping things casual.'

'Suits me.'

'Great. They're lovely monsoon showers here, by the way. Enjoy!'

Rose wonders what Cassie meant by a monsoon shower as she walks through to the cubicles. Once she gets in, it's obvious. There's a dinnerplate-sized showerhead fixed to the ceiling as well as jets from the wall on either side. It's the perfect end to her tranquillity tour, which leaves her feeling thoroughly clean and refreshed.

How lucky that she met Cassie here today, she thinks, walking back to her locker wrapped in a large towel, damp feet squelching in her flipflops. It wouldn't have been half as much fun on her own. It's so strange how comfortable she feels in the company of someone she didn't even know a few hours earlier. Will they somehow remain friends after today, keeping in touch online perhaps? More likely they'll go their separate ways, never to see each other again. That's a weird thought, considering everything she's already told this woman.

She's looking forward to hearing Cassie's story now, having almost reached the end of her own. Despite the older woman's apparent interest in what she's recounted, part of Rose still fears her own life will feel dull and insignificant in comparison. People who've travelled a lot, as Cassie clearly has, usually have plenty to tell. And Rose is dying to know what it is from her past that's brought her back to Lancashire.

First, though, she'd like to speak to Cara. After agreeing to have dinner with Cassie, it occurred to Rose that there was a small chance her maid of honour might return. She wants to touch base with her to check this, as well as making sure she's okay.

If Cara was to come back now, it would make things a little tricky, but they'd find a way for it to work. The three of them could always eat together.

Conscious of the time and her drinks appointment with Cassie, she hurries up to her room, where she tries to call her best friend but gets no answer.

She messages her instead: *How's it going? Hope not too bad. Thinking of you and missing you. Any chance you'll be back for dinner?* X

Meanwhile, she dries and brushes her hair before picking out a skirt and top to wear, going for a smart-casual look. She's just finished applying eyeliner when her mobile pings with a response from Cara: *Can't make it back. So sorry! Bit complicated, but no need to worry. Forget about me. Let your hair down. Chat tomorrow? Love you. X*

Rose replies to say that's fine and reaches for her lip gloss. As she's applying it, she wonders again about Cara's mysterious family emergency. It's good she says not to worry, and yet it's unlike her not to answer a phone call, even just to say a couple of quick words. What if something really bad *has* happened and Cara's covering it up for her sake, so as not to spoil her break?

'Stop overthinking things,' she tells her reflection in the mirror, resisting the urge to make another call. 'You've been over this before, after she first left. Drop it now. Tomorrow will come around soon enough.'

Time to go. She slides a thin shrug over her top. Taking a deep breath, she pops her mobile on silent, sticks it in her handbag and, throwing that over one shoulder, heads down to meet Cassie at the bar.

'So, come on,' Cassie says once they've each had a few sips from their large, delicious G&Ts, made this time with strips of cucumber folded through the middle of their glasses and garnished with lemon wedges. 'I'm absolutely dying to know how Ryan won you back and got you to agree to marry him.'

Rose smiles, admiring how effortlessly elegant her companion looks now she's dressed for dinner, wearing light blue linen trousers, a cream short-sleeved blouse and a turquoise crew-neck cardigan. 'It was very romantic.'

Cassie runs a hand through her short, neatly groomed

hair. She's fresh-faced with only a light hint of makeup to emphasise her natural gifts. 'I should hope so.'

Rose wonders for a moment whether Cassie might be the kind of woman her dad would go for. She must be around his age and she's undeniably attractive. A chic, sophisticated woman.

'Do you read much?' Rose finds herself asking.

'I do enjoy a good novel,' Cassie replies, 'although it's not always easy to find as much reading time as I'd like to these days. Sometimes I turn to poetry instead. I've been enjoying Yeats recently. It's a good fit, I suppose, living in Ireland as I do now, although I liked his work before that.'

'I know a little Yeats from university. I remember enjoying "Byzantium", I think it was called. Is that right?'

'Absolutely. Did Ryan do something inspired by literature to win your heart? That would sound out of character from how you've described him so far, but—'

'No, not at all. I'm not sure why I asked you that. My mind flew off at a tangent. No, Ryan will never be a literary type. He probably still hasn't read those two books I left at his house. It was incredibly sweet what he arranged, though, and jaw-droppingly memorable. It was the kind of grand gesture I wouldn't usually expect from him. Something truly special.'

'Are you going to tell me what it was?' Cassie says with a wink. 'I'm on tenterhooks.'

'Sorry, I'll get on with the story . . .'

CHAPTER 17

During my teenage years, I went through a period of listening to old music. Not really old, but things my dad used to enjoy when he was younger, probably with the volume turned up far too loud, knowing what he's like. He wasn't cool enough to have a vinyl collection, but he did buy loads of CDs, which he still to this day keeps in pride of place on a huge rack in the lounge.

Not that he listens to any of them. He uses a streaming service, like most other people. I think he likes how the CDs look, reminding him of the old days.

He's the same with books. Although he reads a lot of ebooks nowadays, he has stacks of paperbacks and hardbacks slotted into various shelves and bookcases all over the house. And thank goodness for that, as I've taken great pleasure in reading many pieces from our home library and I intend to do so for a long time to come.

Anyhow, when I went through my phase of listening to Dad's old CDs, it was on an ancient portable player of his with a built-in speaker, which I commandeered for my room. I particularly enjoyed listening to whole albums. I'd pick one and play it in its entirety, again and again, until it became like an old friend. It made a nice change from singles and playlists.

Listening to these albums, which varied from R.E.M. and Radiohead to Björk and Daft Punk, was something I shared with Ryan whenever he came to visit. Our tastes weren't always exactly the same, but the one album we both grew to love, to the point where it pretty much became 'our album', was *The Miseducation of Lauryn Hill* from 1998.

I adore the whole album. However, my favourite song of all – my favourite Lauryn Hill song, full stop, which I've sung along to so often I know every beat – wasn't originally on the official track listing. It appeared as the first of two hidden songs at the end of the record.

Why am I telling you this? It's important: a teaser of what's to come.

First, let's return to how Ryan and I got back together. By the time the Christmas holidays came around in my third year at uni, he was back on my mind a great deal. We hadn't met up again since our impromptu reunion at his parents' place in August. Nor had we even spoken on the phone. However, we had messaged loads. It started really gradually, here and there. I can't even remember who sent the first one. But by December we were messaging back and forth numerous times a day – and getting along famously. I was busy as hell with my final year uni work and going out a lot less than I had previously. I'd used this as an excuse to end things with Simon in October and, since then, no one else in Sheffield had piqued my interest romantically.

Ryan wasn't seeing anyone either, busy with his own work.

It probably seems odd that we didn't move on to phone or video calls, but neither of us suggested it. Why? Who knows? It was working as it was; I suspect we were both afraid of making a wrong move and shattering that.

We'd message each other last thing at night, first thing in the morning and countless times in between. Whenever something out of the ordinary happened to either of us, we'd immediately message the other with details.

I didn't tell anyone we were doing this – not my house-mates or Cara, and definitely not Dad. This was probably because I knew they'd all advise me against it. And I didn't want to stop.

My housemates knew I was messaging someone a lot, but I pretended it was Cara; they guessed that wasn't true, as I found out later, but Ryan wasn't a suspect, since I hadn't mentioned him in ages, nor told them about our summer meet-up. They thought I was seeing one of my tutors, believe it or not.

Anyway, as the Christmas holidays grew ever closer, Ryan and I tentatively started to discuss meeting up when I got home. It was him who brought it up first, although it had been on my mind for a while before then.

Ryan: *It's nearly Xmas! Excited to come home?*
Me: *Obvs. It's one of my favourite times of the year.*
     You know that.

Ryan: Are we finally gonna catch up in person after all our chatting?

Me: Sure. Everyone's meeting in the pub on Xmas Eve, right?

Ryan: Yeah, true.

I could tell he was angling for something more personal: a one-to-one meeting, like a quiet drink together or dinner.

Part of me wanted a more intimate reunion too, but, equally, the idea terrified me. How could it not feel like a date? While it was only messaging going on between the two of us, it was manageable, containable. I knew that would change once we saw each other in person. Keeping it within a group setting, where no one else knew we were back in regular contact, felt like a wise safety precaution.

The irony was that I'd never felt closer to Ryan than since we'd started sharing so much with each other via these messages. I'd be lying if I said I hadn't fantasised about us falling into each other's arms again. This image and various more graphic ones had been regular fixtures in my mind, waking and sleeping, for some time by that stage. But although our chats had included some flirting, particularly on occasions when I'd had some wine, I'd never gone so far as to admit my feelings. I was too scared. He'd hurt me so much once before. How could I be sure he wouldn't do so again?

Ryan hadn't specifically said that he wanted me back. However, I knew that boy like the back of my hand, having spent the best part of my teenage years as his girlfriend. I found it obvious from the fact he was messaging as often as he was, and from the things he did say, that he still had strong feelings for me. He'd say, for instance, that he couldn't open up to anyone else about his hopes and fears like he could to me. He'd regularly reminisce about stuff we did together as a couple when we were younger. And he'd often mention – particularly after a few beers – how much he missed me and how he regretted what he'd done to ruin our relationship. Thankfully, he no longer gave off jealous vibes about me being at university, doing things with other people.

He didn't have much to worry about there, anyway, considering how hard I was studying. Although there was an incident with a lad called Bill, who I knew from halls in first year and bumped into on a rare night out when I was feeling a bit frisky. You can use your imagination about what happened. It was a one-time thing and a bit disappointing, if I'm honest. I think I did it partly because of the growing feelings I had for Ryan, because they scared me and I wanted to try to turn them off. It had the opposite effect, if anything, reminding me of what I was missing. I didn't mention the episode to Ryan.

Did he have similar secret dalliances? Possibly, although not to my knowledge. It's not something we ever discussed; if he did, like me, it was no business of mine at that point, because we weren't together. We were simply friends who messaged each other a lot.

So, despite very much looking forward to seeing Ryan, I avoided making any formal plans to meet up other than at the Christmas Eve do. I only got home a couple of days before that and wanted to enjoy some quality time with

Dad; I thought I'd play things by ear and see what happened. Meanwhile, Ryan and I were still messaging loads, to the point where Dad asked me why I was glued to my phone, and I had to pretend I was hooked on a puzzle game. There was no way I was telling him the truth.

When Christmas Eve came around and Dad was driving me and Cara to the pub where we were all meeting up, I was a bundle of nerves.

'Are you all right?' Cara asked me after he dropped us off outside. 'You seem on edge.'

'I'm fine. I've had a bit too much coffee, I think. I'm a little hooked on the stuff these days.'

'Me too. Is that all?'

'Yep.'

She looked unconvinced as she squeezed my hand. 'You know where I am if you need anything. I've missed you!'

'I've missed you too. Now let's get inside and have a drink.'

I don't know what I was expecting to happen when I eventually saw Ryan, but as it turned out, my heart pretty much exploded in my chest. The minute I walked into the busy pub, I was looking for him, my eyes scouring every corner until I finally spotted him waiting to get served at the bar. I waved. His big brown eyes zoomed in on me. He threw me a wink and a cheeky grin that made me want to run over there and jump on him.

'What do you want to drink?' Cara asked, squeezing my arm.

'Vodka and tonic, please.'

Nodding, smiling and greeting familiar faces all around,

I had to steady my breathing, I was so worked up inside. As I made pleasantries, my thoughts were elsewhere. I knew what I wanted – what I desperately desired and was now within my grasp – but there was a silent alarm flashing in the corner of my mind's eye.

Did I really want to do this?

There would be no going back if I went down that road. I knew I wouldn't be able to stop myself.

Next thing I knew, he was back from the bar and barely more than a metre away from me, greeting others, laughing and joking, gradually getting closer. Was that his aftershave I could smell? I could hardly function as I waited for him to approach me. Then, finally, his lightly stubbled cheeks were pressed ever so briefly against mine as we said hello with two kisses and a momentary hug, just like everyone else. There was a look, though, that passed between us that said so much more.

I knew at that precise moment I was going to give in to my feelings before the night was over.

As Cara returned with our drinks, whispering a question about whether Ryan's presence made me feel uncomfortable, I smiled and shook my head.

It must have been about half an hour later, when I was at the bar, that I felt a presence behind me and knew it was him before I even turned around. 'Would you step outside to meet me for a quick chat in a few minutes?' he whispered into my ear; the intimate sensation of his warm breath on my skin sent shivers down my spine.

I nodded, helpless, incapable of resisting now he was next to me.

We slipped outside separately, meeting in a shadowy spot around the corner, away from prying eyes. I found myself standing toe to toe with the boy who two years earlier had crushed me, staring into his eyes and willing him to kiss me.

'Hi,' he said.

'Hello,' I whispered, a kaleidoscope of butterflies bursting out of my stomach.

'It's really, really good to see you, Rose. You look . . . amazing.'

'You too,' I replied, gasping at the sudden, unexpected feeling of his hand gently running up my back.

'Sorry!' he said, stepping back, like he'd done something wrong.

'No, don't be.' I reached forward, grabbed the lapel of his leather jacket and pulled him into the most passionate, intense kiss I've ever experienced. Each tiny movement seemed to convey a dozen thoughts and emotions. I didn't want it to end, but when it did, I was speechless.

'Wow,' was all Ryan managed to utter as he held me tightly in his arms, my head resting on his chest, feeling his every breath as we both took a moment to recover.

'I've dreamed about this happening for so long, Rose. I didn't know if it ever would. I wasn't sure if you could—'

'Shh,' I said gently, not wanting to have that conversation yet.

'What next?' he added after a brief pause. 'When we go back inside the pub, I mean.'

'Let's keep this between us for now,' I said. The truth

was that I wanted to rip his clothes off on the spot, but I knew I couldn't allow myself to do that. If Ryan and I were going to work again, we'd have to take things slowly, at least to start with, as long as I could hold out. It wouldn't be easy, but if I gave him everything in one go, there was a danger he'd take it for granted and mess up again.

'Okay,' he said. 'One request, though. Well, two actually. Please could I have another kiss first, and would you agree to meet me again while you're home? Preferably as soon as possible.'

I giggled. 'Yeah, go on then.'

CHAPTER 18

We got engaged early the following July, soon after I'd finished my finals and moved back home.

As our relationship had progressed and solidified past that Christmas Eve kiss, we'd gradually come clean to all of our friends and family. Many had been shocked, not least my father, although he had managed to keep his cool.

'Right,' he replied when I first told him over breakfast one morning early that January, when I felt sure enough to say something. Frowning, he fell silent for what felt like ages, finally adding, 'This is a surprise, I must admit, but it does at least explain a few things I've been wondering since you got back from university for the holidays.' He paused. 'It's your life, Rose. You're an adult and more than capable of making your own decisions. I really hope he doesn't hurt you again, though. I'll be civil to him, for your sake, but I can't promise anything more.'

Not exactly a ringing endorsement of my decision, but

better than I'd feared. Cara's response, on the other hand, had been more animated. 'I knew it! I spotted a spark between you two on Christmas Eve. Why the hell didn't you tell me?'

'I thought you might not approve.'

'Why? What's it got to do with me who you get with? I'm a disaster zone when it comes to relationships and I'd be the last one to dole out advice. Yes, he was an idiot in the past, but if you've forgiven him, who am I to stand in the way? Life's too short to hold a grudge. Whatever makes you happy, Rose.'

Ryan's parents were over the moon to hear we were together again.

'It's so nice to have you back,' Kelly said, taking me to one side after inviting me over for a Sunday roast to celebrate. 'Jeremy and I have both missed you so much. We've always considered you part of the family, so it was an awful wrench when the two of you split up. I was so angry with Ryan for . . . well, let's not go into all of that. The important thing is you're back together. He loves you and we love you too.'

My uni housemates were less forgiving, remembering how hard it had been on me when Ryan cheated; not really knowing him very well and never having seen us at our finest as a couple. They came around to him, though, after a few visits when he was on his best behaviour.

He was very supportive when I went through my finals and he kept the green-eyed monster at bay this time. It probably helped having an end in sight for my studies and thus for the long-distance aspect of our relationship.

'What are your plans after you graduate?' I remember him tentatively asking during a surprise Valentine's Day visit when he turned up on the doorstep with a huge bunch of roses and took me for a slap-up meal at a swish French restaurant.

'I'll be returning home to the Ribble Valley. What do you think?'

Perhaps not the best decision career-wise, as it turned out, but the pair of us are still young. Once we're married, who says we can't move somewhere with better job prospects? If we were a bit closer to Manchester, that would open up a lot of opportunities. Once the wedding is out of the way, I plan to test the waters.

That's where he proposed to me, as it happens, on a gloriously sunny Monday in Manchester's Piccadilly Gardens. He'd lured me there with the promise of a day's shopping, only to drag me out of a shoe shop with a sudden urgency I didn't understand, supposedly to grab an ice cream. I almost had a go at him for it, but thank goodness I bit my tongue because, as he was leading me by the hand across the open space at the heart of the city, he suddenly stopped, with no ice cream stand in sight, and threw me this weird grin.

'What's going on?' I said as I heard the unmistakable opening bars of my favourite Lauryn Hill song: her amazing cover of Frankie Valli classic 'Can't Take My Eyes off You'. The music was pumping from the boombox of a man sitting on a bench in front of us.

Before I had a chance to say anything else, the man started to sway in time to the music. Mouth agape, I turned back to Ryan only to notice other people on benches also moving in sync with the song.

'Oh my God. No way,' I said under my breath, frozen to the spot, as the lyrics began and at least twenty, possibly even thirty people – men and women of various looks and ages – stepped out of the background to come together as a flash mob, forming a circle around me and Ryan. They were clicking their fingers, dancing in sync with one another and miming along to the song, like they were in a music video.

It's hard to describe exactly what it felt like to be at the heart of that wonderfully choreographed moment: to have so much positive energy focused on me and for it to be such a bolt from the blue. It was magical, dream-like. I was grinning ear to ear and crying all at once. I couldn't even bring myself to look at Ryan, knowing he'd organised this for me, for fear of breaking down in front of all those people.

He was squeezing my hand tightly and then he was moving in front of me and getting down on one knee, pulling out a ring box and holding it up before me. I could only just hear what he said over the spectacle unfolding all around us.

'Rose, I'm madly in love with you,' he told me. 'Let's spend the rest of our lives together.' He paused for breath before adding in a shaky voice: 'Will you marry me?'

'Of course I will,' I wailed, barely able to see any more, due to all the tears in my eyes. There was clapping and cheering and Ryan was hugging me; as the music drew to a close, we were locked in the most passionate kiss, despite all the people watching us. And when it ended and I pulled away, opening my eyes, everything had returned to normal. We were two people among a crowd of strangers again, everyone going about their own business. It was as if I'd imagined the whole episode.

'What?' I said, my jaw still dragging along the floor. 'Where have they all gone?'

'Where have who gone?' Ryan said, deadpan. 'What are you talking about?'

'Are you frigging kidding me?' I replied, drying my sodden cheeks with the palms of my hands. 'What are you trying to do: convince me I'm going loopy?'

This made Ryan laugh. 'Don't worry, you're not. It was real, I promise. That's part of what they do: disappear the same way they appeared, blending back into the crowd. It's all part of the flash mob experience. Anyway, we have witnesses to prove it really happened.' He waved at someone behind me and, when I turned around to see who, my eyes landed on a teary Cara. She was walking towards me with her arms outstretched for a hug, followed by an equally emotional Kelly and then Jeremy, whose eyes also looked watery.

'You three were in on this?' I said after we'd greeted each other and got the initial shock and excitement out of the way.

'Yep, sorry,' Cara said as Ryan's parents nodded and shrugged. 'It was hard not to say anything, but Ryan swore me to secrecy – and the last thing I wanted to do was ruin the surprise.'

'Did you all come in together?'

Cara nodded. 'Kelly and Jeremy were good enough to give me a lift. We've been so excited, haven't we?'

'You're not kidding,' Jeremy said, rolling his eyes. 'Honestly, these two in the car. I could have done with some earplugs for all the squealing.'

'Your face was a picture, Rose,' Kelly added. 'Oh, I'm so glad you said yes. It's wonderful that you're going to be an official member of the family soon. When do you think the wedding will be?'

'Hold your horses, Mum,' Ryan added. 'Give us a chance to talk everything through first.'

'Sorry.' She fanned herself with her hand. 'I'm just so thrilled. What a shame that your dad wasn't able to make it today, Rose. He was invited, of course, but he was busy with some work stuff. Not to worry, though, Jeremy recorded the whole thing on his camera phone, didn't you, love? You didn't mess it up, did you?'

Jeremy shook his head wearily. 'No, I already told you, Kelly. It's fine. I'm perfectly capable of making a video recording; thanks for the vote of confidence.'

Kelly planted a kiss on her husband's cheek, ruffling his hair, and adding with a wink to everyone else: 'Well done, you. I'm sure you've done a great job of it. Now take your grumpy hat off and enjoy the moment. You've got the pleasure of buying everyone lunch next.'

'Actually, I don't,' Jeremy said. 'I didn't tell you this yet, Kelly, but I had a phone call from Dave earlier. He apologised again for not being here, insisting that he would pick up the bill for all of us to have lunch in Manchester today.'

Kelly beamed at this news. 'Oh, that's nice of him. What

a gentleman your dad is, Rose. You must say a big thank-you to him for us all when you get home.'

'Sure,' I replied. 'Will do.'

I wondered why on earth he hadn't come. I struggled to believe he was genuinely that busy with anything that he couldn't find time to watch this. What was the point in being his own boss if he couldn't use this flexibility when required? I worried that he hadn't wanted to see it, having still not come to terms with the two of us being back together.

I planned to have a serious chat with my father after I got home that evening. But ahead of that, I refused to let Dad's absence ruin an otherwise amazing day. Lunch, including bubbly, was at a lovely tapas restaurant. Then Ryan and I bid farewell to the others and went ring shopping, since the one he'd presented to me in the moment was a piece of costume jewellery he'd borrowed from his mum.

'Is that okay?' he'd asked me after explaining this. 'You wouldn't rather I'd picked one in advance, would you? I could have done that, but I thought you'd prefer to choose something yourself. You have much better taste than me and you'll be the one wearing it for the rest of your life, right?'

'It's perfect like this,' I said, kissing my fiancé and future husband. 'The whole day has been amazing. I couldn't dream of a more special way to get engaged. Thank you for everything. I mean that from the bottom of my heart. I don't know how you arranged it all, but hats off. I'll be telling this anecdote for years to come.'

'I was getting worried when you didn't want to leave that

shoe shop,' he said, chuckling. 'I thought I might have to throw you over my shoulder and carry you out of there. And when the ice cream ruse miraculously worked, you still looked kind of mad at me. You're welcome, anyway. A special day for a special person. You deserve the best, Rose.'

Ryan wanted to spend more than he could afford on a ring, but I wasn't having that. The flash mob must have cost him enough already.

'I don't need a showy ring,' I told him before we entered the first jewellery store. 'In fact, scratch that, I don't *want* that kind of ring. I'm not into having a huge diamond or anything really bling. A thin band with a very small stone in it will be perfect. And I want traditional gold – not platinum or palladium or whatever's fashionable.'

'Seriously?' Ryan looked perplexed. 'I mean, it's really nice of you to say that, but I want to do this properly. I don't want people thinking I'm a skinflint.'

'Who cares what people think? This ring is for me and you, no one else. And I'm not saying this to be nice or to save you a few bob – it's what I want. I've no intention of wearing something I don't like or feel comfortable in simply because it's what society expects.'

'What about your dad?'

'What about him?'

'Well, he's not exactly my biggest fan, Rose. If he thinks I've got you a bargain basement engagement ring, how's that going to help?'

'Don't be ridiculous,' I said, although a part of me secretly wondered if he might be right.

Ryan held up his palms in surrender. 'Whatever makes

you happy. But don't hold back if you see something you love that's expensive. I've come prepared.'

I didn't ask what he meant by this, but already knowing the rough ins and outs of his finances, I suspected he'd had a word with his mum or dad and arranged the terms of a loan.

Anyway, after touring the shops, I eventually found this lovely simple gold ring with a subtle diamond, which made me very happy. We ordered one in the perfect size, including an engraving of our two names on the inside.

Later, following a saucy stop-off down a quiet country lane, which held fond memories from when we were together the first time, Ryan dropped me off at home. We agreed that he should come inside so we could make the formal announcement to Dad together.

'I'm a bit nervous,' Ryan admitted before we got out of the car.

'Why? There's no need to be. He already knows, anyway.'

'Yeah, the thing is, I'm wondering if I messed up.'

'Are you serious?' I placed my hand on his cheek. 'I told you already: today was perfect.'

'Do you think I ought to have asked for his approval first, though? I mean, I invited him to the proposal and that, but maybe the reason he said no was because I hadn't formally requested his permission.'

'Are you joking? This is the twenty-first century, Ryan! Were you expecting a dowry? Also, I'm not a possession passing from one man to another, you know.'

He scowled. 'Of course you're not. I don't mean it that

way. It's just . . . people still do it, don't they? Because it's nice. A nod to tradition.'

I let out a puff of air. 'It wouldn't even have occurred to me, if you hadn't mentioned it.'

'It did go through my mind right at the start, when I decided I was going to ask you, but if I'm totally honest, I was worried he might say no.'

I took both of Ryan's hands in mine and looked deep into his eyes. 'It's not for him to say yes or no. It's my decision and I said an emphatic yes. I want to marry you, Ryan, so stop worrying and come inside.'

To be fair to Dad, he made an effort to be magnanimous. He smiled and hugged me, congratulating us and shaking Ryan's hand. He even offered to open a bottle of bubbly, but we declined. 'That's nice of you, Dad, but Ryan has to work tomorrow and I'm shattered.'

'See, that wasn't so bad.' I kissed my fiancé farewell at the front door.

'No, I guess not.' Relief was written all over Ryan's face. 'Goodnight, darling. I love you.'

'I love you too. Loads and loads. Thank you again for such a special day.'

Having waved him off, I took a deep breath and went to probe Dad about his actual feelings regarding our engagement.

CHAPTER 19

'So, Dave, I'm fascinated to know why you were so incredibly busy today that you couldn't find time to watch your only daughter get engaged.' I deliberately used his first name to emphasise my irritation.

Dad let out a low groan and reached for the whisky glass sitting on a coffee table at the side of his chair in the lounge. The fact he was already drinking this when we got home – certainly not something he did on a regular basis – spoke volumes. As did the silence that filled the room while he took a swig, seemingly choosing his eventual words carefully.

I waited, eyeballing him from where I was perched on the sofa opposite, forcing myself not to say anything else until he'd replied.

'We're doing this now, are we?' he said eventually.

'Yes, absolutely. You should have been there. It really hurt me that you weren't.'

He rubbed his temples with one hand. 'That, um,

definitely wasn't my intention, Rose. I'd never do anything to deliberately hurt you. I didn't think there was a lot I could add to the situation. If anything, I thought there was a danger I might put a downer on things.'

At least he wasn't trying to pretend to me that he really had been too busy to come.

'Why would my father being there have put a downer on things?' I asked.

'I think you know why.'

Pressing my fingers into the spongy material of the sofa cushion, I took a couple of steady breaths before replying. 'Why can't you move on from what happened back then? It was two and a half years ago. If I can leave the past in the past, why can't you? Ryan makes me happy. Honestly, the effort he went to today. I felt so special. If you had been there to witness it, perhaps you'd find it easier to see what I see in him; how much he's grown and changed since . . . what you keep focusing on.'

'I'm sorry I wasn't there for you, Rose,' Dad said after a lengthy pause. 'I ought to have been. I should have put my reservations aside.'

'You have reservations about us getting married?'

'You're still so young. It seems needlessly soon. Why tie yourself down now when you have your whole life ahead of you; so many possibilities?'

'Maybe that's exactly what I want, Dad. Did you stop to consider that I might like to build a family of my own: a nice big one with lots of children. I've never had that. Now it's within my grasp.'

There was a deep sadness in his eyes when he next

spoke. 'I know you've found it hard sometimes, especially when you were younger, being an only child and having just one parent. It wasn't something I planned. The reality of life, as I see it, is that you can only control what goes on to a certain degree. There's always a bigger picture unfolding around you, which is largely out of your hands and never afraid to surprise you. Some of what happens is caused by other people and their decisions. Some isn't: it's fate or chance, depending on your viewpoint. You have to respond as best you can. Try to make it work for you.'

He paused to take a sip of his whisky. 'Thanks for not laughing at that. I'm no philosopher, Rose. I know you could put it better and out-debate me, if you chose to. What I'm trying to say, in a roundabout kind of way, is that I'm sorry I didn't give you the big family you'd have liked. I did the best I could with the hand I was dealt. When you were a baby, I used to imagine meeting another woman who could be the glue to fix our family unit. However, as time passed and the right person didn't come along, I came to realise that we didn't need fixing, because we had each other. If the perfect woman had shown up, I'd have been open to that. But why try to force the issue for the sake of it?'

I was tempted to give Dad a hug at this point, although I held off, having not yet forgiven him for skipping Ryan's proposal. I think what he wanted to say, but avoided specifying for fear of further offending me, was that I didn't need to get married to Ryan this young in order to have a big family. He'd have preferred me to put

176

my career first, for the time being, probably in the hope that I'd grow apart from Ryan and meet someone else.

'Listen, Dad,' I said. 'You've nothing to apologise for when it comes to my upbringing. You managed amazingly in tough circumstances; I'll always appreciate that, more than you know. And I wouldn't have expected, or wanted, you to settle for a woman you didn't really love for the sake of giving me a mother figure. That's ridiculous. But we're miles off the real issue here. Ryan is my fiancé now, whether you like it or not. One way or another, you need to come to terms with that. We're getting married and, to be clear, I'd like that to happen sooner rather than later.'

Dad nodded slowly, looking past me into the distance. 'I'll do my best, love. I was polite to him tonight, wasn't I?'

'I guess. You'd better be nice about the ring when I get it. It's very simple, with a tiny diamond, but only because that's what I want. Ryan was all for getting me something far grander, but I was having none of that.'

'I'm sure it's lovely, Rose,' Dad said. 'My reservations about Ryan have never been related to his means. The only thing I care about is that he loves and cherishes my only daughter.'

'So you're not mad at him for not asking you in advance for my hand?'

Dad scratched his head. 'What? Is that even a thing these days? When or who you get married to is your decision, not mine. Was he really considering doing that? Thank goodness he didn't. It would have been excruciating.'

We spoke for a while longer and did eventually end up having a hug. I'm glad we had that conversation. It was needed to clear the air and, afterwards, things did improve between Ryan and Dad, gradually reaching the plateaued point where they remain now: the peace treaty, as I referred to it earlier. Saying that, the improvement was mainly on Dad's side. If anything, Ryan has slipped a little the other way since we got engaged. I think he's accepted that he'll never be Dad's favourite person, whatever he does, which has hardened his attitude, leading him to make less effort than he once did.

Anyway, they're pleasant enough to each other when we're all together and, for that, I'm thankful. It has been tough at times, though, and I'm not sure my dad will ever entirely stop thinking badly of Ryan. Even since we've been engaged, Dad's tried several times to warn me off him. Eventually, I had to say that I wouldn't stand for it any longer. I told him in no uncertain terms to keep such thoughts to himself. I've made the decision to forgive Ryan and move past what happened, so Dad needs to as well.

Will the very act of us all going through the wedding ceremony and reception improve matters? Here's hoping. It does already seem to have brought Dad closer to Kelly and Jeremy. It's all been extremely amicable between them so far, in terms of making arrangements for the big day; if Ryan's parents are aware of any residual tension between him and Dad, they certainly haven't let on to me.

Kelly, in particular, is bursting with excitement about next week. I got her involved, together with Cara, in helping me to find my perfect wedding dress. The three of us visited several bridal shops together, eventually finding exactly what I was looking for in the lovely village of Whalley. It was great having her along for the ride – someone who's actually been a bride – and we definitely bonded through the experience.

No one has a clue what the dress looks like, other than the three of us and the staff at the shop. On Kelly's recommendation, we made a pact not to discuss it with anyone else before the big day. 'My mother told me it was bad luck to do so,' she said. 'I'm not sure why. Maybe it's to reduce the chance of the groom finding anything out about it. I think it's fun, anyway. If you can manage to keep it from your father, his reaction when he first sees you wearing the dress on the day, before giving you away, will be priceless. You'll both be in tears, I reckon.'

'Perhaps I'd better show him before I get my makeup done, so as not to ruin it. But otherwise, good idea. What do you think, Cara? Will you be able to keep it secret?'

Cara gave me a playful poke in the ribs. 'Oy, what are you suggesting, Rose? Are you calling me a gossip? Of course I can keep it under my hat. So long as you don't stitch me up with an embarrassing maid of honour outfit.'

'Deal.' Winking at my soon-to-be mother-in-law, I added: 'But remember that means you not saying anything to Jeremy either, Kelly. And especially not to Ryan.'

She mimed locking her lips and throwing away the key. 'You have my word.'

For fun, we all did a pinkie promise – and that was that. As agreed, I've not shown it to Dad. I wound him up initially, saying it was short and very revealing. But fearing this might lead him to try to sneak a look ahead of the big day, I told him not to worry. 'It's very elegant,'

I said. 'But that's all you need to know. It'll be a nice surprise.'

It should go without saying that Dad and Ryan haven't been suit shopping together. I wouldn't have dared to suggest that to either of them, for fear of upsetting the delicate balance in relations ahead of the main event.

PART THREE – CASSIE'S STORY

CHAPTER 20

ROSE

Rose and Cassie walk along the passageway towards the restaurant where they'll be having dinner together.

'Do you think they'll put me in a highchair?' Cassie asks.

'Sorry?' Rose replies. 'I'm not with you. Like a bar stool, you mean? I doubt it.'

Cassie chuckles, brushing Rose's forearm with her fingers. 'I mean like the kind of seat they put babies in, because of how clumsy I was last time I was here, spilling wine all over that poor waiter. Gosh, I hope he doesn't serve us tonight. I'd be mortified – and he'd probably be terrified to come near me again.'

Rose feels a bit merry already, having finished telling Cassie her story at the outside bar. She plans to slow down at the dinner table and drink plenty of water. Cassie's clearly a lot more used to drinking than she is, as she doesn't seem remotely affected, despite being a drink ahead of her. Maybe she's good at hiding it.

At least Rose has done most of her talking; now she mainly needs to sit back and listen to Cassie tell her story. She did try to get her to start it while they were still in the bar, but the older woman resisted.

'Relax,' she said. 'Let's have a short breather, rather than me racing straight in.' Apparently picking up on Rose's frustration, she added: 'Come on, you've waited this long. I'm sure you can manage a few more minutes. I'll begin when we're seated for dinner, I promise. And thank you for telling me your story, Rose. I feel like I know you an awful lot better as a result. Not hard, I suppose, considering we met as strangers only a few hours ago. It seems so much longer, though, don't you think? Probably because of everything we've discussed.'

She was tempted to disagree, on the grounds that she still barely knew anything about Cassie. However, not wanting to be churlish, Rose nodded and smiled. Had she revealed too much about herself? It felt like she'd been talking forever. And yet it wasn't like she'd actually recounted her *entire* life story. It was an abridged version at best – little more than a precis in parts. And yet she had covered most of the key moments. The substantial stuff.

'I suppose I can wait a little longer,' Rose said with a diplomatic smile, sipping on her G&T. 'If I absolutely must. You certainly know how to whet my appetite, Cassie, I'll give you that. The longer you make me wait, the greater expectations I have of a truly scintillating story.'

As they approach the entrance to the restaurant, Rose worries that Cassie might make another excuse to delay finally opening up about herself. If so, she'll call her on it this time, knowing she has no means of escape, short of leaving the table and causing a scene, which she doubts Cassie will want to do on the back of her lunchtime misadventure.

As it happens, there's no need. Once they've been led to the table and had their initial drinks order taken, Cassie begins.

'Right,' she says. 'Here we are. No more excuses. Time for me to pay my dues and return one story with another.' She takes a deep breath. 'Ready?'

'Definitely.'

'Good. I'll start at the beginning, but I'm not going to dwell on that part. It's not pertinent compared to the stuff that follows and, honestly, it's hard for me to talk about. Please bear with me on this, Rose. My reasoning will make more sense once you've heard more of what I have to tell you. And it's not that I'm deliberately glossing over the difficult bits. There are plenty of those that I will be recounting in detail, believe me. We only have so much time, so I'm going to focus my storytelling on what has most relevance to, er, the bigger picture.'

Rose shrugs, wondering what on earth she's about to hear; she feels a mixture of excitement and, inexplicably, trepidation. 'Whatever you think's best,' she says in a quiet voice, nodding and raising her eyebrows.

'So, I was an only child and my parents were both junkies,' Cassie says, which is absolutely not what Rose was expecting to hear. 'Heroin mainly, but whatever they could get their hands on, truth be told.'

Rose gasps without meaning to. Drug addicts have never really existed in her sheltered existence. She's read about them in books. Watched them in films and TV shows. At uni, she knew a few people who dabbled occasionally in so-called recreational drugs – but she steered clear. The idea of Cassie being brought up by heroin users sounds absolutely terrifying to her ears.

'I don't remember a huge amount about my dad,' Cassie says. 'He died when I was nine and wasn't around much beforehand. He drowned in the sea in Blackpool, where we were living at the time. Who knows exactly what happened? His veins were brimming with smack, by all accounts, so it was written up as an accident. Mum always suspected foul play, as he owed money to a lot of people, apparently. She was quite paranoid, though. I don't know. Honestly, I don't really care either. He was a nasty piece of work. That's probably why I don't recall much about him: he wasn't worth the effort.

'He didn't live with us; he used to turn up from time to time, usually looking for cash. He'd be all nice to start with, but it was an act, to try to get what he wanted. If he didn't – and often even if he did – he'd turn on Mum, shouting at her . . . or worse. I saw him hit her a number of times. He never did that to me, which was something, I suppose. But he probably would have eventually, if he hadn't been killed.

'As for Mum, I do have some fond memories of her, mainly from when I was little. She didn't do drugs then.

Not that I know of. If she did, she hid it well, or I'd never have been allowed to stay with her. We didn't have much. The various houses and flats we lived in together were grotty. But I remember her playing hide-and-seek and various make-believe games with me: goblins and fairies; charades; pretending to run our own little café. The kind of thing that required little more than a good imagination. She'd take me to build sandcastles on the beach, eat ice cream and pink candyfloss. Occasionally, especially when there were cheap showings on, we went to the cinema. Mum loved her movies almost as much as her discount vouchers and special offers, so it was the perfect combination.

'She was fun originally. It was only after Dad died that things started to change. I'm not sure why that made such a difference. I suppose she must have loved him, although he didn't deserve it. Anyway, whatever the reason, she ended up falling in with some of his old crowd and getting into the drugs herself. It started small, but before long she went full downward spiral. Social services came knocking and I started a long tour of temporary homes, mainly in foster care.

'I grew used to only seeing Mum occasionally, as part of supervised visits, which she didn't always show up for. And when she did, she always looked gaunt, listless and on edge – a shadow of her old self. Her once sparkling eyes were permanently glazed over and she was forever making promises I knew she wouldn't keep. Then, a few weeks after my fifteenth birthday – which she'd forgotten about – my social worker turned up unannounced to

187

break the news to me that she'd died. It was an overdose, no surprise. And so there I was . . . an orphan.'

'Oh no, how awful,' Rose says. She's about to reiterate the fact that her late mother was an orphan too when a waiter appears at the side of the table to take their order. Flustered, Rose looks to Cassie. 'Have you decided yet? I haven't even had a proper look at the menu.'

'Could you give us a few minutes, please?' Cassie says. Her voice sounds far calmer and steadier than Rose feels in light of what she's just been told. Beaming at the waiter – a short-haired woman around Rose's age – she adds, with a wrinkle of her nose. 'Sorry. We've been too busy gossiping.'

The waiter nods and returns the smile. 'Not a problem. Can I get you any bread or olives in the meantime?'

Cassie looks at me across the table, eyebrows raised.

'Not for me, thanks,' I say.

'No, we're fine for now,' Cassie adds. 'Thank you.'

Once the woman is out of earshot, Cassie says: 'Thank goodness it's not the guy from lunch. I've had a good look around, but I haven't seen him. Hopefully he's not working tonight.' She raises her palms. 'Not that he was in the wrong. It was all me. But it'll save a few blushes if he's not around.'

Rose can't believe Cassie is talking so casually about such insignificant things, while her own mind continues to reel from the shock of what she's heard. Mind you, Cassie's had her whole life to get her head around these heartbreaking facts. She lived through them, poor thing. You wouldn't guess it to look at her now. Until a moment ago, Rose assumed, naively perhaps, that Cassie came from a similar background to herself. How could she have been so wrong?

She's already looking at the older woman in a new light, wondering what kinds of hell she must have experienced as a child. How did she end up so normal? She seems incredibly balanced, well mannered and comfortable in her own skin. What strength of character she must have!

And to think Rose spent so long talking about her own largely shielded life: her supposed problems, which already seem utterly insignificant. How mortifying. And how gracious of Cassie to allow her the space to do so. It no longer feels appropriate to bring up her mother being an orphan, particularly since she's already mentioned it to Cassie. Rather than coming across as empathetic, it could end up sounding as if she wants to turn the spotlight back on herself.

'I don't know what to say,' she mutters, barely able to look her dinner companion in the eye. 'That all sounds so dreadful. I had no idea. I feel—'

'You don't need to say anything, Rose,' Cassie says in a near whisper. 'It's my turn to do the talking. How could you know any of this? It's fine. I'm not looking for sympathy. It was a long time ago – a world away from my life today. It often feels like a half-remembered dream or something that happened to another person. I arguably am a different person now, for all manner of reasons, although moving on from my childhood was a gradual process. It wasn't something I did easily or quickly. But as I say, this isn't the part of my story that I want to focus on.'

'Right.'

'And first, before I continue, we both need to make our meal choices. Agreed?'

'Yes, absolutely.' Rose blinks as she picks up the menu and tries to focus on the choices available. 'Are we having starters?'

'Yes, let's. I like the sound of the minty pea soup on the specials.'

When the waiter returns, Rose orders a halloumi salad to start, followed by seafood risotto. For her main course, Cassie opts for grilled seabass. And they agree to share a bottle of rosé with the meal.

'I nearly went for the risotto,' Cassie says once they're alone again. 'It was a toss-up between the two, but I thought it would be boring if we both ordered the same, so I went for the fish. Anyhow, I'd better continue with my story. After Mum died, it was just me.'

'Didn't you have any other family?' Rose asks. 'Wasn't there a grandparent, an aunt or uncle, someone?'

'Nobody that cared or wanted anything to do with me,' Cassie replies.

'That's awful. I can't begin to imagine.'

Her mother would have been able to, though, Rose reflects. It does seem a little odd that Cassie hasn't acknow- ledged this. Hasn't made the link. Or didn't pipe up to say that she was also an orphan when Rose mentioned it earlier. Unless . . . what if there's a reason for that?

It occurs to Rose that Cassie might have actually known her mother. What if she was a childhood friend of hers back in the day or, God forbid, an enemy even? Maybe the two of them shared a foster home for a while. It's a heck of a leap to make, with little justification, and yet once the thought has entered Rose's mind, she struggles to contain it. Cassie *is* around the right age to have been in care at a similar time. And clearly something specific has brought her back to Lancashire. Could that be to track down Rose or her father? The logistics of this wild theory are dizzying. Rose reminds herself it's irrational – probably more to do with her own hang-ups about growing up without a mother than anything else – but it's too late to stem the tide.

'Is everything all right, Rose? You look like you've seen a ghost.'

Cassie's words jolt her back into the moment.

'Sorry, yes, I'm fine.' Blurting out the first excuse she can think of, Rose adds: 'I just felt a bit weird for a second there. I guess I need to eat soon. I'll be okay, though, honestly.'

'Should we order some bread?'

'No, no. Really. The starters will be here before long. Please continue.'

'Okay, if you're sure.' Cassie clasps her hands together and squints across the table at Rose. 'I won't pretend it was a good time for me. Those final years before I became an adult were hard. There was the odd happy moment, but it was tough. I thought I was used to being alone after years of not living with Mum, but knowing she was gone for good, that was far harder. I suppose, before that, a tiny part of me hoped she might miraculously change one day, holding on to the old happy memories from when I was little. After she died, there was no hope. Then and

191

only then, I knew true loneliness. I hated her so much for leaving me behind. For not caring enough or finding the strength to survive her addiction for my sake. That particular wound took a long, long time to heal.

'My focus from that point forward was reaching adulthood. I longed for the day when I could finally become my own person – out of the care system and free from the shackles of my miserable past. I bided my time, keeping my head down at school; avoiding trouble wherever possible. And I started to dream of travelling: making my way around the world, free as a bird. I bought a battered old atlas from a second-hand bookshop and studied it from cover to cover, over and over again, planning in my head where I'd like to go. I borrowed guidebooks and travelogues from the library. Fantasising about the amazing places I'd visit one day kept me sane.'

'And you made that happen, didn't you? The travelling, I mean.' Rose recalls Cassie saying she'd lived 'all around the world'.

'Absolutely. I'm settled now and very happy. But it took me years to reach that position. Everything was temporary before that – how I liked it. I was a drifter. I stayed in a place for as long as I was enjoying it, or while I felt welcome, and then I moved on. Sometimes that meant being somewhere for a few days or weeks, maybe a month or two; other times, I stayed longer, still knowing in the back of my head that one day I'd move on. It was liberating. No ties, no real consequences. Plus I got to see all kinds of amazing places and to meet people I otherwise never would have met.'

Despite doing her utmost to focus on Cassie's words, Rose can't quite manage to put her fresh concerns to bed. Pull yourself together, she thinks, fearing another query about her wellbeing. She presses her fingers into her knees under the table and tries to sit still, to look calm, while attempting to shove these intrusive thoughts to the back of her mind. She needs to concentrate on what Cassie's finally telling her about herself, rather than wasting her time on self-absorbed flights of fantasy.

She reminds herself of her previous fear about Cassie being a journalist, which now seems ridiculous. Surely this is more of the same: the result of an overactive imagination, having no basis in fact.

And yet a nagging doubt remains.

'You must have some stories,' Rose says, trying to look suitably engaged.

'Oh, I do – and nowhere near enough time to tell them all to you today, I'm afraid. But there's plenty I will tell you. Hopefully, by the end of our chat, you'll feel like you know the essence of me. That's how your story made me feel about you.'

Rose smiles and nods as a waiter appears with their wine bottle. 'Would you like to try it first, madam?' he asks, automatically looking at Cassie rather than Rose, which grates. She almost says something to him but bites her tongue, realising he probably assumes they're mother and daughter and that Cassie is paying. It's not like she'd mind if he did the same when Dad was taking her out for a meal. Still, he shouldn't make assumptions. It's unprofessional.

'Just pour it, thank you,' Cassie says to him with a smile. 'I'm sure it will be fine.'

'Why do they still ask that?' Cassie says once he's gone. 'It's totally unnecessary with a screwtop bottle. Old habits really do die hard, don't they?'

Rose scratches the side of her neck. 'I guess. Did you go travelling as soon as you turned eighteen?'

'No, not straight away. I needed to find work and save up a bit of money first.'

'Was university an option?' Rose says – and then worries how this question might be perceived. 'Sorry, I don't mean in terms of whether you were clever enough. It's obvious to me that you're very intelligent. I mean, um—'

'Relax, Rose. I know what you're asking. I did okay at school, despite everything. Against the odds I got decent GCSEs and A levels, but no, university was never on my radar. Some of my teachers tried to talk me into it, but the financial practicalities concerned me. It wasn't something I really wanted either. My focus was on working hard for a couple of years, doing whatever jobs I could find, and saving up enough to get me started on my travels. Things didn't quite go to plan, though.'

'How do you mean?'

Cassie takes a deep breath before she continues. 'I met someone. Someone special.'

Rose's ears prick up at this. Could Cassie be about to reveal that she knew her mother?

Mind racing again, Rose can't stop herself trying to fill in the blanks, chasing yet more speculative theories. She feels bewitched by the idea of potentially being able to forge some kind of new connection with her late mother, whom she knows so little about.

She revises her earlier guess about how and when the two orphans could have come across each other. Perhaps they didn't meet as children but as young adults, some time before Rose's parents got together. It might have been totally unrelated to living in care, only for them to discover how much they had in common and develop a powerful bond.

That must be what she means by 'someone special', right? A really close friend. Or could it have been something more than that between them?

Could they have once been . . . lovers?

CHAPTER 21

CASSIE

Meeting someone I really liked at that stage wasn't part of the masterplan. However, life has a habit of doing that, I've found over the years, particularly when you try to plan things in too much detail. Almost like it's urging you not to bother.

This was something I learned to accept once I did manage to get away on my travels. I became less of a forward-thinker and more impulsive: living for the moment and dealing with issues one at a time. Travelling is much more relaxing that way. Most things are, actually.

Anyhow, I fell head over heels in love. It happened when I least expected it . . . at work. We totally clicked, and things between us got serious really quickly. The travel bug was too ingrained in me by that stage to put off my plans for long, but they did take a back seat for a while. I even asked this special person to consider joining me.

I'll come back to this relationship in a bit. As you may have guessed, it's a key part of the reason I've returned to Lancashire. It makes most sense to tie these matters up together at the end of my story.

For the time being, all I'll say is that things got far more complicated and confusing than I expected; I had some really tough decisions to make. I did what felt right at the time, based on who I was at that point and everything I'd been through leading up to it.

Would the woman I am today do the same? I don't think so, to be honest. But that's a moot point. You could also argue that I wouldn't be who I am now if I hadn't made the decisions I did, no matter how hard.

I was barely an adult, with none of the family support structure that most people have. I'd been putting myself first for a long time, because I'd grown to realise that if I didn't, no one else would. That was my default state before falling in love so unexpectedly. It shouldn't come as too much of a surprise that I returned to it when things got tricky.

Anyway, we'll deal with that soon enough.

What you need to know for now is that I headed off on my long-awaited travels a little later than intended and with a heavy heart.

I started in Europe, mainly because of the proximity, the ease of being able to work in so many different countries at that time, and the lower initial cost of getting there, as opposed to making a long-haul trip.

Greece was my first stop. I went island hopping in the Aegean, staying in budget accommodation, picking up casual work here and there to keep my funds topped up, but mainly enjoying the weather, the gorgeous beaches, the azure sea, so many stunning views, the water sports and, of course, the food. I largely avoided the nightlife side of things. I only made the odd casual acquaintance outside of any work I took on. Considering how I'd left things in the UK, I wasn't in the right headspace to go partying or make loads of new friends. I read a lot. I thought a lot. I took up yoga, which I still enjoy to this day and have always found hugely beneficial to body and mind. Crucially, I tried to get to know myself better, making my first tentative steps on the long journey towards accepting my challenging early years; working to forgive others, as well as myself, for past mistakes, in a quest to find inner peace.

Was it hard travelling alone? Yes and no. There were difficult moments, not least because I was a young woman, which inevitably attracted some unwanted male attention. However, my years in the care system had taught me how to stand on my own two feet and to look after myself. I was street savvy and knew the kind of risks to avoid. I didn't take grief or inappropriate comments off anyone. Mainly, I enjoyed the new-found freedom of being able to do whatever I wanted, when I wanted.

If I liked a spot on a certain island, I stayed for a while, maybe even looking for a job. If not, I moved on. Took a ferry and started again. This was exactly why I chose island hopping to kick off my travels. I thought of it like a microcosm of the world at large, with nice manageable distances between destinations. I travelled all over, from the bigger, well-known islands like Crete and Rhodes, to the various islands of the Cyclades, including tiny places like Kimolos and Antiparos. They were each wonderful in their own unique way. Some were commercialised, others pure and pristine, like magical gateways into a serene bygone era before the onslaught of mass tourism.

It was a great place to find my feet as a traveller. My next stop, decided on a whim at the end of summer, was the very different setting of Berlin, where I spent a bitterly cold few months working in a series of bars and restaurants, doing my best to get by on the very basic German I remembered from studying it for a year at school. The fact is you can get by almost anywhere with English as your first language, but the locals embrace you much more readily if you at least make an effort to speak in the native tongue. Luckily, I've always been good at picking up the basics of other languages. It's been a major help over the years, particularly since people in other countries are so used to meeting Brits who can't or won't speak anything other than English. It helped me to stand out from the crowd and definitely led to more work opportunities than I might have expected to find otherwise.

The temperatures may have been cold, but the German locals were lovely and so welcoming. I don't think I've ever spent time in a capital city that's felt safer or more relaxing. It's not the most beautiful or elegant place, but it more than makes up for that with its vibrant culture and hip, artistic vibe. Thanks to the kinds of jobs I was doing, I did dabble in the nightlife there and even made some friends. But by the following spring, I was ready to move on again. First I took the train to Paris, another of the great European cities I'd always wanted to visit, where I loved absolutely everything apart from how much it all cost. And then, a month or two later, thanks to a chance encounter with another young British woman in a busy Parisian café, I found myself on a long train journey down to the South of France.

Angela, having overheard me speaking French to the waiter in Paris, had struck up a conversation, as we were both alone on small separate tables that were pushed so close together, we were basically sitting on top of each other.

'British, right?' she said in a warm Brummie accent, after catching my eye.

'Is my pronunciation that bad?' I replied. 'I must be getting rusty.'

French had been one of my strongest subjects at school.

She flashed me an infectious smile. 'Not at all. You speak French very well, but there aren't many foreign language speakers who can truly hide their natural accent. I know I can't.'

We hit it off and talked for hours, first there in the café and then in a succession of bars. It turned out Angela, who was a few years older than me – stunning looking, with mesmerising deep-brown eyes and long braided hair – had recently landed a job running a team of holiday reps over a couple of campsites near Fréjus on the French Riviera, in between Cannes and Saint-Tropez. She said they were in the process of hiring staff and someone around my age, fluent in French and English, would be a perfect candidate.

'I'll be honest,' she said. 'It doesn't pay well, but there's free accommodation and plenty of time off to enjoy the gorgeous surroundings. You get to sample lots of the excursions on offer – visits to Cannes and Monaco, diving trips, etc. – to help you flog them to the holidaymakers, plus a decent staff discount at the campsite bar and shop.

'Part of the job involves entertaining, holding drinks receptions and so on; we encourage reps to let their hair down and have fun, within reason. There's also a fantastic social scene, as the reps from the various firms all know each other and tend to go out together most nights. It's very much a work hard, play hard kind of thing.'

'What's the catch?' I asked. 'Other than the low pay, it sounds too good to be true. Is the free accommodation a tent or something?'

She threw her head back and laughed. 'It actually is a tent, but not like you're thinking. It's a roomy one you can walk around in, with a kitchen and a proper bed. It's the same kind that a lot of our guests stay in, although we do offer static caravans too.'

'Not for the reps, though?'

She winked. 'Not unless you're in a management role, like me. A mobile home is one of the perks.'

'Any other catches?'

'There's cleaning to do once a week. Saturday is change-over day, so that's usually busy, tidying one lot's mess up before the next arrives. That's probably the worst part of the job, especially in the full heat of summer, but you get used to it. Most of the holidaymakers we get are families, not wild singles. There's not usually too much mess.'

I nodded.

'So, what do you think. Interested? I'd need to run the usual checks, get references and so on, to keep head office happy, but I wouldn't need to interview you any more than I already have.'

'What?' I replied with exaggerated indignation. 'You never told me this was a job interview. I'd have worn something smarter if I knew that and I'd have stuck to sparkling water.' I paused for a long moment as those entrancing eyes of hers scrutinised me. With a grin, I caved. 'Fine, I'm interested.'

It was a great decision. I had one of the best summers of my life that year. Other than the aforementioned cleaning, which was a weekly drag, it rarely felt like work. I met some fantastic people; did loads of sunbathing, swimming and sightseeing. I socialised a lot with the other reps and, sometimes, the guests. I had a few flings. It was hard not to when permanently surrounded by people letting their hair down on holiday.

The one thing I occasionally found hard was seeing all the happy families who came to stay with us. It's not that I begrudged them their happiness. But every now and again, certain kids – particularly the shy, quiet only children who sometimes came along – would remind me of myself growing up. And seeing loving parents doting on them, pride in their offspring written all over their smiling faces, would, for various reasons, make my heart ache. I don't remember being taken on holiday anywhere as a kid, not even in the UK. I suppose that's one of the key things that drove me to travel far and wide once I was an adult. It's human nature to want what you've never had, right? The grass is always greener and so on.

I'd never wanted a family of my own. It was something I'd decided after my mum died and I found myself as an orphan. Is that a strange reaction? Would it have been more normal for me to try to fill the void by settling down at the earliest opportunity and trying for children? Maybe, maybe not. I think everyone has the right to deal with traumatic events in their own way. That was how I responded to my difficult childhood. A part of me was afraid that I'd turn out to be a no-good parent. I feared it was written in my DNA to fail as a mother. Plus the last thing I wanted to do was drag another child into the miserable world I had to grow up in. It felt like a responsible decision.

Focusing on myself, as I'll freely admit I did, probably sounds egotistical. But I didn't see it that way. It was all I'd known for a long time. It was my shield.

CHAPTER 22

I made friendships on my travels before becoming a holiday rep, but not deep or lasting ones. I didn't open myself up enough for that to happen. This changed during my time on the Côte d'Azur in France.

I bonded with a lot of the other reps, several of whom were British, like me, while others came from countries including Germany, the Netherlands and Belgium. It was hard not to bond when we spent most of our days and nights together. We were like one big family, which was a new experience for me. Still, I knew we'd eventually all go our different ways; I kept my cards close to my chest when it came to talking about the past, our families and so on. I stayed silent or made an excuse to leave when the others discussed things like making phone calls home to chat to their parents or siblings. I bit my tongue if I ever heard them grumbling about their upbringings, which always sounded far nicer than anything I'd experienced.

One night, about halfway through the season, I ended

up alone with Angela at a small bar a mile or so from the campsite at about three or four in the morning. I say alone – there were other people in there, mainly French locals – but we were the only two reps. Everyone else who'd been out with us had disappeared by that point, off to bed to sleep or fornicate, after a typical boozy night. It had started hours earlier with drinking games around a sangria-filled cool box. Somehow, Angela and I still had a couple of nightcaps left in us.

The stout, middle-aged bartender, who we knew fairly well by that point, having been in there many times previously, was called Hector. He was one of those guys who wears a grumpy face for show but has a heart of gold. We nicknamed him Tache, due to his bushy salt and pepper moustache. I only ever called him this to his face when I was tipsy, so most nights. Since *tâche* is a French word meaning *task*, and he spoke barely a word of English, I'd decided on this occasion, while ordering us two Manhattan cocktails, to try to explain why we called him that. He nodded and smiled politely at my drunken French, but whether I made any sense or not is another matter.

As he moved to the other side of the bar to serve someone else, I looked at Angela, on a bar stool next to me sipping her drink. 'Do you think he got any of that?'

'Who knows? It was fun to watch, that's for sure.'

She wasn't always around, Angela. Sometimes she spent a few days at the other campsite she covered, mainly if there were problems or staffing issues. But ours was her primary base, where her official mobile home was located, and where she spent most of her time. She wasn't a standoffish boss, not in the least. She came out with us most nights and I felt like I'd already got to know her well.

'Thanks for the drink, Cassie.'

'You're welcome. You've bought me plenty. Do you know what? You might be the best boss I've ever had.' I pressed one finger to my lips. 'But don't tell anyone I said so.'

'Glad you took me up on the offer I made in Paris, then?' she asked, a twinkle in her eye.

'Absolutely.'

'You looked a bit lost. Like you needed someone to give you a break. Is that fair?'

'Possibly,' I said, a little taken aback by the comment.

'You don't talk much about your personal life back home, do you? Which is fine. Totally your prerogative. But if you did ever want to chat about anything like that, in confidence, I'd be happy to listen.'

'There isn't really a back home,' I said, the alcohol and my affection for Angela making me unusually loose-lipped. 'There's where I grew up, in Lancashire, mainly around the Fylde coast. Blackpool, among other places. I moved around.'

I paused, trying to remember whether any of the paperwork I'd filled out, when I formally applied for this job, had contained details of my growing up in the care system and so on. Stuff it. Whatever. I'm just going to tell her, I thought. I found I wanted to offload it, not least because Angela was someone I'd grown to trust.

'I spent much of my childhood in care. My parents are both dead.' I found my voice wavering as I said this last bit. Tears pricked my eyes.

Next thing I knew, Angela was pulling me into a warm,

soothing hug and I pretty much told her the lot – up to when I left secondary school, anyway. I skipped over the next bit about meeting someone and . . . yeah, the, er, tricky stuff I'll come on to later. It was still too fresh a wound to talk about with anyone. I barely even allowed myself to think about it. Not because I didn't want to. The thoughts jostled to enter my mind numerous times every day. However, I did my utmost to push them aside. Mainly because I didn't dare to dwell on them, fearing what they might do to me and my mental state.

'You poor thing,' she said afterwards, squeezing my hand with such genuine affection, I almost started sobbing. 'I can't imagine what it must have been like, having to grow up through such pain and trauma. It's remarkable what a wonderful, intelligent, talented person you are, in spite of everything. You should be proud of yourself, Cassie. I know I'm proud to work with you and to call you my friend.'

Angela and I had always got on well before that point, but we became very close afterwards. She tucked me further under her wing than I was already. We're still friends to this day. I'm sad to say it's been a good while since we've seen each other in person, but that's purely down to the logistics of us settling in different countries.

Angela played a key role in that stage of my life. She really helped me to find my feet as a person: to know who I was, how to make the best of myself, and how to be happy in my own skin. And to think it was all down to that one chance encounter in Paris. Was it chance, though? That's something I've often wondered over the years. I used to call her my guardian Angela. She always brushed this off, but the more I think about it – especially now I'm older and more sentimental – it's a rather accurate description of our relationship at the time.

We continued to work together after the season ended in Fréjus. I was starting to wonder what to do with myself next, as things were winding down at the campsite, when she announced that she would be spending the winter working a ski season in the French resort of Alpe d'Huez. She invited me to join her.

'Um. Wow,' I said, pulling up a seat at the plastic white table outside her mobile home. 'This is unexpected. I don't know anything about skiing or ski seasons. The one time I've ever skied was when a girl from my form at secondary school had a birthday party at a dry ski slope. I made an idiot of myself, falling over left, right and centre. I wasn't a natural.'

'Everyone falls over a lot at the start,' she said. 'I didn't feel like a natural when I first went, but I soon got the hang of it. I think you'd be great with a little practice – and there would be plenty of time for that. Besides, being a good skier isn't a requirement. Some reps are required to accompany guests while out on the slopes, but that's not the role I have in mind for you.

'You'd be hosting, organising, advising, assisting and so on. You'd still have to get your hands dirty, like here, with things like cleaning and snow-clearing. There would be airport coach pickups to deal with too, but nothing you couldn't handle. It's cold there, obviously. But you're a hardy northerner, right? What do you say?'

I agreed. I'd have been crazy not to, considering I had

nothing else lined up to do next, other than pick another place to head to and take my chances.

There was a break between the two jobs, during which Angela headed home to the UK to spend some time with her parents in Solihull. She'd invited me to join her, which was a lovely gesture. However, not wanting to impose, I chose instead to continue on my solo travels, embarking on a budget whistle-stop tour of Italy, taking in Milan, Venice, Bologna, Florence, Rome and Naples. Finally, I caught the cheapest flight I could find to Geneva, then the train to Grenoble, where I was met by a far more wrapped-up version of Angela than I was used to seeing, who drove us to our new workplace and got me settled in.

For the second time, Angela's job offer proved a good one. I had a great winter. I met another fantastic crew of fellow reps. I also enjoyed the après ski very much, had a couple of pleasant but forgettable 'holiday romances' with tourists from other travel companies, and I learned to ski almost passably. If I'm honest, though, as much as I enjoyed the experience, I didn't really catch the winter sports bug. It was the one and only time I worked a ski season. I think it's hard to adore the experience if you're not mad keen on the actual throwing yourself down a slope side of things. And I wasn't. It scared me. With the odd nerve-racking exception, I rarely trusted my newly learned skills enough to attempt more than green and blue runs.

Plus, I couldn't help but notice that quite a few of the people who went skiing were from fairly wealthy backgrounds. Not all, but a significant proportion. It's an expensive hobby. This made me uncomfortable at times, due to my own background being so different. It's not that anyone ever specifically said something to me to suggest I didn't belong. My role as a rep and pre-existing friendship with Angela allowed me to hide my lack of skiing and social credentials in plain sight for the most part. It was more something I felt from time to time, like when money was being splashed about on excessive, showy drinks orders in bars and so on. Or when talk turned to posh boarding schools that folk had attended or fancy university courses and high-flying jobs. Usually I'd fall quiet or make an excuse to leave at such moments.

It was the casual sense of entitlement I found hardest when I encountered it, especially among young wealthy tourists, in their late teens and early twenties. They often appeared to think nothing of how lucky they were in life, taking their luxurious lot for granted.

It wasn't only the youngsters. I experienced two unrelated incidents when older men – both married and on holiday with their 'lucky' spouses – mistakenly assumed I'd be interested in having a quickie with them when their wives were looking the other way. Clearly not used to hearing the word *no*, each seemed genuinely surprised when I sent them packing with the threat of telling their families if they tried it on again.

I remember recounting the second of these incidents, which took place near the end of the season, to Angela. The first had happened near the start of my season in Alpe d'Huez and I hadn't even mentioned it to her. I'd been a bit drunk, making my memory of what he'd said sketchy.

Plus I'd slapped him hard around the face, which I'd worried could land me in trouble.

Anyway, when I told her about the second incident, over a hot chocolate the morning after it happened, she got serious.

'Would you like me to write it up? He should not be making indecent proposals like that to you, Cassie. That's sexual harassment. Bloody pervert.'

'I know. He had the cheek to say I'd been leading him on. Called me a prick-tease.'

'Seriously? That's so out of order. And how gross that he even thought he had a chance. He must be twice your age! What is it about these old rich guys? They think their money can buy them anything they want.'

'I know. All I did was smile at him, like I do to all the guests.'

I told Angela to drop the matter, seeing as he hadn't actually put his hands on me and he'd left me alone afterwards.

That sounds so weak and pathetic in the context of modern times, I realise. Looking back, I should have made an official complaint. However, things were different in those days. Men used to get away with all sorts of unwanted behaviour towards women, because it wasn't taken half as seriously as it is now. I can only hope that neither of those men who harassed me went on to do anything more serious to anyone else. That's the point. In letting them get away with it, I enabled them to continue acting like pigs going forward, potentially with women less able to stand up for themselves than I was.

'Are you sure?' Angela asked, looking me in the eye. 'Because, trust me, I'd be very happy to—'

'I'm sure. It's fine. Nothing I couldn't handle.'

'Would you like me to have a stern word with him at least? Or maybe with his wife?'

'Tempting, but no, thanks. I'd rather put it behind me.'

'Okay. I'm just sorry you had to go through that. If you change your mind, you know where I am.'

Angela was a great friend as well as a brilliant boss. So when she told me she would be returning to the South of France again that summer, in the same role as the previous year, a part of me was tempted to join her.

'I was thinking you could be my deputy,' she said, 'running the show when I'm not around. There would be a decent pay bump, and it would be a good stepping stone for you towards becoming a manager. I think you'd be great.'

'I'm flattered, but it's time for me to do something different – see somewhere else. The traveller in me is getting itchy feet.'

Angela's face fell for an instant before she regained her composure. 'That's a shame. Please tell me it's nothing to do with—'

'Absolutely not. I promise. I wouldn't let that idiot man affect my life like that. This is about my needs and desires, full stop.'

'I'm disappointed, but I respect your decision, Cassie. Where are you planning to go instead?'

'Amsterdam.'

CHAPTER 23

The Netherlands was a country I'd always fancied visiting. Originally, when I was a teenager clinging on to my battered old atlas and dreaming of a foreign future, this was largely due to it being nice and close to the UK. Cheap and quick to get to, in other words.

However, I think it was also inspired by a group of Dutch kids that came to visit my school once, touring our country as part of an award-winning youth orchestra. They performed for everyone at school and were put up for the night by selected pupils' families.

I'm not entirely sure why their brief visit stuck in my mind. None of them stayed with me, for obvious reasons, and I barely even spoke to any of them, despite being around the same age. It struck me how healthy and happy they all looked in their jeans and colourful T-shirts. Every single one of them, as I remember it, looked confident, content in their own skin. They all spoke fluent English and sounded amazing when they played together. I remember hearing one of them – this tall, handsome, fresh-faced boy with dark blond hair in curtains – remark about how pupils didn't have to wear a uniform in their country.

'I can't believe you all have to dress in a jacket and tie,' he said with an almost American-sounding twang. 'Isn't it hot and uncomfortable?'

I'd never considered the possibility of not having to wear a school uniform before that and, although I'm sure it's also the case in lots of other countries, at the time I imagined it was unique to the Netherlands. Combined with everything I saw of those chilled-out, talented young-sters, it led to me idealising the country as a wonderfully calm and civilised place.

Amazingly, that wasn't far off the mark, as I eventually found out when I headed there after Alpe d'Huez. With Angela's encouragement, I'd contacted one of our fellow reps from Fréjus from the previous summer – a Dutch woman in her early twenties called Bianca. She'd worked for a different travel company, a small Dutch operator, but I'd got to know her well, nonetheless, since we all socialised together. It hadn't occurred to me to contact her before heading to Amsterdam, not knowing where she lived in the country, or indeed if she had even gone back there. However, Angela revealed that she'd been in recent contact with Bianca, having approached her to return to the South of France and work for her this year. Consequently, she knew that Bianca was settled in the capital city and working as a duty-free sales assistant at Schiphol, the Netherlands' huge main airport.

'She also turned down my job offer,' Angela had said

to me with an exaggerated sad face. 'I must be losing my touch. It's enough to make a person paranoid.' Winking, she added: 'My loss is Amsterdam's gain, twice.'

I took my time travelling up to the Netherlands, stopping off in the French cities of Lyon and Strasbourg, then Luxembourg, followed by Brussels, Bruges and Antwerp in Belgium. Lastly, determined to see more than just Amsterdam while in the Netherlands, I took advantage of the short distances and fast rail connections between towns and cities there, dropping in on Eindhoven, Arnhem, Utrecht and The Hague before arriving at my destination.

Bianca was waiting for me amid the hustle and bustle of busy Amsterdam Central Station with rosy cheeks, long legs and a huge smile. 'Your hair! It makes you look so different,' I said after we'd greeted each other with the three cheek kisses I knew were customary in Holland.

Last time we'd been together her hair had been long with blonde streaks from the sun. Now it was light brown and in a short pixie cut. 'It really suits you,' I added. 'You look lovely.' I'm not sure I'd have recognised her if she hadn't waved at me and called my name to get my attention. Other than the hair, she was also much paler than I remembered, her rep's tan long since faded away.

'Thanks so much for letting me come to stay with you,' I said. 'It won't be for long, I promise. I am hoping to hang around for a bit, if I can find a job, but I don't expect you to put me up for more than a day or two.'

'Don't be silly,' she said in the same near-perfect English that nearly every Dutch person I'd encountered so far seemed to speak. 'Stay as long as you like. I have plenty of space; I'll be glad of the company.'

'That's very generous of you,' I said, taken aback and assuming she was exaggerating and being polite. Mind you, that wasn't typical of the Bianca I knew from the Côte d'Azur. She was very much the kind of person who spoke their mind, saying things as they were rather than standing on ceremony. 'How far away do you live?'

'Oh, it's close. Five minutes by bike, maybe less. Would you like to get a coffee here, or shall we go straight back?'

I opted for the latter, since I was feeling tired and had all my belongings with me.

'Is that all you've got?' Bianca asked, pointing at my backpack.

'Um, yeah, that's it.' Travelling light had become second nature to me by that point. I found it liberating rather than restricting. I'd accumulated a few odds and ends during my period in the Alps, as I had before that in Fréjus, but before leaving, I'd ditched everything unnecessary to my onward journey.

'I should be able to carry you with me on the bike,' she said.

'Right. So you actually came here by bicycle?'

'Of course.' She flashed me a puzzled look, like she could barely understand the question.

When I saw the countless bikes shoved into row upon row of racks a short stroll from the station, her comment made more sense. I'd seen a similar state of affairs outside other Dutch railway stations on my journey here – but not to this extent. I don't think I'd ever seen so many bicycles gathered in one place before.

'How do you even know which is yours?' I asked Bianca as she strode off ahead of me.

'Oh, it's easy once you get the hang of it,' she replied without looking back.

'I'll take your word for that.'

'Careful!' she warned me a minute later after I was nearly mowed down by another bell-ringing cyclist while Bianca was busy unlocking her bike.

'Hop on,' she said once perched on the traditional, high-seated and rather decrepit-looking two-wheeler.

I stared blankly at her. 'Sorry, where?'

'On the back,' she said, twisting around and nodding at a small rectangular metal bag rack fixed over the rear wheel.

'Really? Are you sure it'll hold the weight of me and my bag? I could always walk alongside you instead, if you don't go too fast.'

'No, come on, Cassie. Don't be a wuss. We do this all the time here. You'll be fine.'

'If you say so.' Still hesitant, I started to straddle the rack, one leg on either side, until the sound of Bianca's laughter made me stop.

'Not like this?'

'No, silly. You should sit sideways on it, like the posh ladies used to do on horses. It won't be comfortable otherwise. And you might be better holding your backpack on your lap rather than wearing it.'

'You're the boss.' I took her instruction and, next thing,

we were off at a surprisingly fast pace, giving me quite the bumpy, white-knuckle ride among various other cyclists and pedestrians. At least we were separated from the cars, trams and so on for the most part, thanks to a series of cycle lanes. It definitely wasn't very comfortable; I closed my eyes and gritted my teeth for much of the journey, which felt longer than five minutes, but according to my watch was actually just under.

'Here we are,' Bianca said, drawing to a halt outside a terraced row of tall, skinny, brown and white canal-side properties. They couldn't have looked more typically Dutch if they tried. There were a few people around, but they mainly looked like residents rather than tourists. It wasn't busy at all compared to some of the streets we'd passed through. It was clearly an affluent spot.

'What a gorgeous neighbourhood,' I said, mouth agape. 'It looks like a scene from a postcard.'

'Nice, eh?' she replied. 'Wait until you see inside. It's my aunt's home. I'm looking after it while she's working in Singapore. I'd never be able to afford to live here, otherwise. This is the main reason I turned Angela down when she asked me to return to the South of France. I've never had the opportunity to live in central Amsterdam before – especially not somewhere like this.'

She walked up to a big, solid wooden door and opened it to reveal a long hallway with a steep flight of stairs at the end. After wheeling her bicycle into the narrow space and leaving it there, she led the way up to the duplex apartment, which was on the top two floors of the building.

The stairs were even steeper than I thought, not far

removed from a ladder, with twists and turns on the way to keep things interesting. Bianca, having first grabbed my bag to save me the effort, bless her, shot up with practised ease.

'Wow, that's quite a flight of stairs,' I said on catching her up. 'How on earth do you get large things in here, like washing machines, beds and stuff?'

'Ah, now that's interesting,' she replied. 'I'm not sure if you noticed, but there's a big hook at the top of many of the buildings here. That's for, um . . . what's the word? Pulling up with a rope?'

'Winching?' I offered.

'Yes, that sounds right. Winching things up on the outside and in through the windows, which are nice and big, so also plenty of daylight. A lot of the buildings lean forward a little. Did you notice?'

'No, I wasn't really looking at that on the way here.'

'Anyway, this leaning is often mistaken by tourists for, er, how do you call it: movement in the ground?'

'Subsidence?'

'Yes. That definitely can be a problem here in the Netherlands, but it's not the reason for this leaning, which is deliberate. This is so that when things are pulled up on the outside, they don't swing into the building and damage the bricks and such.'

It didn't take me long to fall in love with Amsterdam. The process began as Bianca showed me around the gorgeous apartment, which was surprisingly spacious and airy, with amazing views over the canal and beyond from the living area and master bedroom. The first floor contained a large open-plan lounge and high-spec kitchen. It was all wooden floors, clean white walls and what I'd probably describe as cosy minimalism – functional without being clinical. A couple of large modernist-style paintings adorned the walls and there was a big, well-filled bookcase next to the sofa, but little in terms of clutter. I adored the place, including the simple but very comfortable guest bedroom that Bianca told me was all mine.

'Make yourself at home,' she said. 'And seriously, stay as long as you want. It's wonderful to see you, Cassie. Now, how about some good Dutch coffee and a tasty treat while we catch up?'

'That sounds lovely.'

'Have you ever heard of *tompouce*?'

As a Netherlands newbie, I hadn't. But it was something I had a lot more of while I was there: an iconic, delicious Dutch take on the vanilla slice, with sweet yellow pastry cream sandwiched by two layers of puff pastry, topped with pink icing.

I stayed with Bianca for the whole time I was in Amsterdam – nearly a year as it turned out. It was longer than I'd intended, but it was so nice, I couldn't help myself. It was rent-free too, amazingly. Bianca refused to charge me anything, since she wasn't being charged by her aunt. All I had to contribute was my share of the supermarket shopping and utility bills.

It was news of her aunt's imminent return from Singapore that was the eventual catalyst for my departure. I knew nowhere else would be able to live up to that amazing apartment, where the two of us had made such wonderful memories. Plus Bianca had found a serious boyfriend by that point and, although she mentioned the possibility of us looking for somewhere else to live together in Amsterdam, I could tell her heart wasn't in the suggestion. Sure enough, soon after I left, she moved in with Jeroen and they got married a couple of years later. They have two daughters. We're still in touch. I stayed with them on a trip to Amsterdam about a year ago.

Funnily enough, they met through me. For most of the time I was there, I worked at a bar close to Rembrandtplein, which is right in the buzzing heart of Amsterdam.

It's one of the city's major squares, named after the famous Dutch painter, and always a lively hub of activity, particularly at night, thanks to the many nearby shops, bars, clubs and restaurants.

I was waiting tables, inside the bar and on the large terrace outside. It was a lot of fun, for the most part, other than the regular late nights and sore lower limbs I experienced from being on my feet for hours on end.

Originally, Bianca had tried to get me a job working alongside her at the airport. But that hadn't worked out due to the fact I didn't speak Dutch. Luckily, this wasn't a problem at the bar, since a large proportion of the customers were foreign tourists and the owner, Frits, loved Brits. Plus I'd done bar work previously in the UK. And my skill for picking up languages paid off again, as I soon managed to learn enough Dutch to have a basic conversation.

I went out with a Dutch law student called Joost for a few months. He lived near the bar and often drank there.

Jeroen was a friend of his, who I introduced to Bianca. And while Joost and I fizzled out, their relationship went from strength to strength.

It's funny. When I left the Netherlands, I told myself that perhaps it would be a good place to return to one day when I was ready to settle down. I felt really at home there. The Dutch are generally so practical, friendly and relaxed. They combine good sense with good humour. Also, you don't see the same kind of class divide or social snobbery that you do here and in so many other countries. It's refreshing.

Maybe I'll end up retiring to a houseboat there one day. Who knows?

CHAPTER 24

'Do a lot of people live on houseboats in the Netherlands?' Rose asks after Cassie pauses her monologue, draining the remnants of her wine prior to pouring them both some more.

'What's a lot?' Cassie replies. 'It's not *that* common. Most people live in apartments and houses, but you definitely do see houseboats, particularly in the towns and cities with canals running through them, like Amsterdam, Haarlem and Utrecht.

'They're probably not very practical in reality, but there's something romantic about living on one, I've always thought. Not that you have to be in the Netherlands to do so. People live on barges in the UK too, of course. But I've never seen as many in one place as when I was in Amsterdam.

'I have such fond memories of living there; the hundreds of colourful houseboats, of various shapes and sizes, were a key part of the backdrop. Ever since, I can't see any kind of canal boat without having flashbacks to that time.'

Biting her lip, Rose replies: 'I've never been to Amsterdam.

Ryan often suggests we should go on a trip there, but I always say no, on the grounds that it's probably full of stoners and sex tourists. After everything you've said, I feel a bit stupid.'

'Plenty of potheads do go there for the coffee shops,' Cassie says. 'Especially from the UK. As for the famous red-light district, it's self-contained and you can easily avoid it. Amsterdam has an enormous amount to offer in terms of culture, food and drink, shopping, you name it. The rest of the country is wonderful too – and less touristy.'

'So I should go?'

'Definitely.'

'I can't believe all the places you've been to, Cassie. I'm guessing there are plenty more to come. What a fascinating life you've led.'

Cassie smiles, but her heart's not in it. She wants to be flattered by these comments, but she knows they're meaningless, soon to be usurped by very different feelings and words.

Once Rose knows the full story.

Her true identity.

What she did.

'The mains are taking a while,' she says, fanning herself with her hand. 'Sorry, but I must nip to the toilet. Back in a minute.'

She walks across the room to the ladies, which she's glad to find empty. The main reason she's come here isn't to use the loo, although she does that anyway. It's to take a minute to clear her head. She's getting anxious. Scratch that. She's been fearful the whole time – before she and

Rose even had their first conversation. But now she's way past the point of no return. All those years to prepare for this moment, which part of her always suspected would one day come to pass, and still she doesn't feel ready. She's so nervous she could throw up.

How she's managed to keep talking about the past over the dinner table without faltering, she doesn't know. Now she's paused for breath, too many thoughts have crept in. There's a tightness in her chest and throat; breathing feels like an effort.

Cassie exits the cubicle and crosses to the sink on unsteady legs. She grabs the edge of the porcelain basin, holding herself up, and stares into the large mirror attached to the tiled wall. 'You can do this,' she says. 'You have to.'

The door swings open and a smartly dressed elderly woman enters the room, covering her mouth with the palm of one wrinkled hand as she clears her throat. 'Hello,' she says in a soft polite voice, smiling at Cassie's reflection in the mirror.

'Hi,' Cassie replies, forcing a smile.

The woman nods her head and walks into the cubicle Cassie just vacated . . . without having pulled the chain, it dawns on her. Oops. How uncouth.

There's a tutting sound followed by a flush. Cassie scowls at the mirror, slaps her cheeks and splashes some water over her face. Taking a deep breath, she attempts to clear her mind, willing herself back into whatever zone it was she occupied previously.

*　*　*

225

'Ah, the food's arrived,' she says, seeing two full plates billowing steam into the shaded lamp above the table as she returns. 'Excellent.' Taking her seat and smoothing the napkin back on to her lap with rhythmic strokes, she adds: 'It's not been here long, has it? I quite like returning to find my meal waiting, but it's less fun if you're the one left at the table watching it go cold.'

'It's barely been here a minute,' Rose says, as though she's not bothered, although Cassie thinks she spots a flicker of annoyance cross her face. 'Did you want any condiments? I can call the waiter back if—'

'No, no. It looks perfect as it is.' Cassie leans forward over her plate. 'Mmm. Smells great. I love seabass. And your risotto looks delicious. Please dig in; ignore my chatter. I've done enough delaying already.'

'So where did you head next after Amsterdam?'

Cassie winks. 'Keen to get back to my story, are you?'

'You did make me wait all day for it.'

'Touché. Have a guess.'

'Seriously?'

'Why not? Just for fun.'

'You'll have to give me a clue first.'

'It wasn't in Europe. This time I travelled further afield. Working in the bar left me better off than expected, thanks to decent tips from tipsy tourists and seeing as how I didn't have to pay any rent. I was finally able to afford a long-haul trip, so I seized the opportunity. Go on, guess. Where do you think I went?'

'America?' Rose offers.

'North or South?'

226

'North – the United States?'

'Nope.'

'South?'

'Sorry. Wrong again.'

'Oh, that's not fair. You tricked me. Fine, New Zealand? I know you definitely went there at some point.'

'I did indeed, but not then. Would you like me to tell you?'

'Yes, please.'

Again, Cassie thinks she spots a flash of irritation in her companion's gaze. Is Rose starting to realise that all is not quite as it seems? Hmm, best tread carefully. It's not time yet for the big revelations. She needs to finish her story first.

'You weren't far off, as it happens: I went to Australia. It wasn't hard to get a visa that allowed me to work over there, you see. That's what swung it over other places, like the US. I didn't have enough money to travel without picking up jobs along the way. Plus I'd always wanted to go there. Who wouldn't? It's an amazing country.

'Things didn't get off to a great start, though, when I made a stopover in Kuala Lumpur en route. I had my backpack slashed open by pickpockets while fighting my way through the crazy busy noisy streets to reach my hostel.'

'No! What did they take?'

'Cash, a camera, some clothes. Not my passport or airline ticket, thankfully. I was lucky not to lose everything. A kindly young American couple came to my aid. They helped me gather what was left, although it still wasn't easy, scrabbling around in such a hectic spot – people everywhere, street traders hawking their wares, vehicle horns honking. They accompanied me to the hostel and even pointed me in the right direction of where to buy a new bag. I was in bits. If those two hadn't shown up when they did, I don't know how I'd have managed.'

'Anyway,' Cassie continues, in between bites of food, 'having my stuff nicked like that taught me the importance of being vigilant at all times, particularly as a lone female traveller. I eventually arrived at my planned starting destination of Cairns, at the top of Australia's east coast, after entering the country in Darwin and taking an internal connecting flight. I wanted to work my way down to Sydney and Melbourne via the likes of Noosa, Brisbane and Byron Bay. It was a popular route with backpackers, according to the *Lonely Planet* guide I'd been studying nonstop ever since deciding to head Down Under. Thank goodness they didn't steal that in Kuala Lumpur, with all my pencilled notes inside. There was no Internet in your pocket, like today.'

'I can't imagine doing that kind of travelling without a smartphone,' Rose says.

Cassie shrugs. 'It's what your generation has grown up with. I'm sure it makes things much easier. How's the risotto?'

'Lovely thanks. And your fish?'

'To die for, melt-in-the-mouth delicious. Would you like to try some?'

Rose shakes her head. 'I'm fine, thanks.' She doesn't reciprocate the offer.

Cassie returns to her story.

CHAPTER 25

I was in Australia for the best part of four years. That definitely wasn't the plan, but it's what happened. I did the backpacker thing for most of the first year, sometimes travelling alone, sometimes with other people I'd met in youth hostels along the way. I picked up all kinds of temporary jobs in all kinds of places, from door-to-door sales in Townsville to washing freshly picked courgettes, or zucchinis as they call them in Australia, at a remote farm near Mackay.

The farm job only lasted for one morning. I was reliant on a lift there with two other travellers; the driver got sacked after four hours of backbreaking work out in the fields, picking the zucchinis for me and my colleagues to wash. He was too slow, apparently. It meant all three of us had to leave or there'd have been no way out of there at the end of the day.

I did various other jobs too: telesales, bar work, waiting on tables, pot washing. I even cleaned trains for a fortnight in Sydney, which involved a lot of waiting around playing cards in between frantic bouts of hoovering, bin-emptying, mopping and wiping whenever a train pulled into the depot.

I loved the freedom of flitting from one place, one job, to another without repercussions.

In Brisbane, I landed a sales job in a second-hand car lot, despite not knowing a thing about motor vehicles and, at the time, not having a driving licence. With hindsight, it was no skin off their nose to employ me, seeing as it was purely commission-based work. 'You'll be right, darling,' the slimy sales manager told me when, naively, I mentioned my cluelessness. 'Most of our customers are blokes. Just bat your eyelashes and flash some leg.'

That should have been enough to warn me off. Instead, more fool me, I put up with being ogled, even wolf-whistled at, by colleagues and customers alike for a couple of hours without making a single sale. I eventually had enough when I overheard two of the sales guys betting, while on a cigarette break, or 'smoko' as they called it, to see who could 'root' me first. That's Aussie slang for having sex. I turned on my heel and walked out of the door without a word to anyone. I didn't look back. Oh, yeah, and I'm embarrassed to admit this, but as a goodbye gift, I ran my room key along the side of a Ford Falcon I'd failed twice to sell. That felt great in the moment, although afterwards I started to worry about the car damage catching up with me. Easily solved: I hopped on a coach the next afternoon and moved on. No consequences.

In Sydney, after the train-cleaning shifts dried up, I

landed on my feet with a cushy office job, selling adverts over the phone for a popular city-based food and drink magazine. Next thing I knew, after offering my services up when one of the writers unexpectedly quit, I was working in editorial. Initially I was a junior, doing the more menial tasks, but I became a full-on food and drink critic, paid to go wining and dining across Sydney's many bars and restaurants.

How on earth did I manage this with no journalistic or culinary training? Good question. I'm not entirely sure. I was in the right place at the right time and my editor took a liking to me. 'You have a flair for this,' I remember her telling me after I first reviewed a restaurant, covering for a critic who was away on holiday. 'I like your writing style. It's different. Raw. Edgy. We need more of this kind of thing to stay relevant and attract younger readers. Good work.'

It was thanks to this job that I was able to remain in the country long beyond my initial twelve-month visa, since my employer agreed to sponsor me to stay. I went from being a traveller living out of a backpack and hostel dorm rooms, to a professional with a better salary than I'd ever earned before and a cosy apartment in the trendy inner-city suburb of Surry Hills.

There was plenty of socialising, not least because of all the establishments I had to visit for work. I settled very quickly into that lifestyle. I had a circle of friends. A place to rest my head at night that felt like home. And Sydney was such a wonderful place to live, especially in summer. I'm yet to discover another destination that manages to merge modern, big city life so effortlessly with such an amazing selection of glorious beaches, perfect for swimming, surfing or simply basking in the heat. As someone who grew up without holidays, I felt like I was living one every day. Work didn't feel like work and, for most of my time in Sydney, I was incredibly, unbelievably happy.

I'd been in Australia for approaching three and a half years when things started to go wrong. My lovely editor left and was replaced by a guy called Mark, who'd previously worked in newspapers. I liked him initially. He was charming and, I'll admit it, handsome. In fact, I liked him rather too much and, against my better judgement, let him pursue me romantically. After weeks of flirting, and plenty of wooing on his part, we eventually entered into a relationship. It was nice while it lasted. Then he cheated on me with an eighteen-year-old intern and I could barely look him in the eye, never mind work for him, so I quit. No sooner had I done so than the old urge to travel reawakened in me. Barely two weeks later, I was back on a coach with just a backpack of belongings to my name again, having given away the larger things I'd accumulated to friends and neighbours.

I'd managed to save up quite a bit of cash during my time in Sydney, so I spent several weeks seeing more of Australia's amazing attractions: Melbourne and the Great Ocean Road; Adelaide and its wonderful wineries; the opal mining outback town of Coober Pedy; Alice Springs, Uluru and Kata Tjuta in the Red Centre; Kakadu National Park and Darwin.

I flew to Bali for some lovely relaxation, then on to

Singapore, from which I travelled up to Peninsular Malaysia, skipping Kuala Lumpur after my bad experience there last time. Instead, I headed up to the Cameron Highlands on a rickety bus.

It got me there in one piece, thankfully, despite having to navigate some rough, narrow and very windy roads, particularly towards the end of the journey. It was worth the effort, though. The highlands were magnificent and, thanks to the high altitude, the air there was significantly cooler than I'd grown used to, which was a lovely refreshing surprise. I stayed in a former military Nissen hut – essentially a half-cylinder of corrugated metal with a door and windows – which was roomy, protected from the sun, and very comfortable. It was part of a sprawling guest house near Tanah Rata, full of other international travellers. While staying there, I enjoyed treats such as an oriental-style fondue, called a steam boat, in which you cook various meats, vegetables and seafood in a broth. I also went on a tour of a local tea plantation and factory.

It was on to lively Penang Island next, connected to the mainland's west coast by the impressive Penang Bridge, nearly eight and a half miles long, over which I was delivered by another typically battered-looking bus. A day or two later, just about reacclimatised to the intense heat, I crossed the width of the peninsula in another couple of lovely buses, one of which broke down along the way. Eventually, I reached Kota Bharu, right at the top of the country's east coast, near the Thai border.

I'd booked ahead at a local inn, but due to my late arrival, thanks to the bus breaking down, they'd assumed

I wasn't coming and sold my room to someone else. Not to worry, the young owner told me with a smile: they still had space for me. This was actually the laundry room, into which a bed, fan and light were quickly carried and installed, making for what turned out to be a surprisingly good night's sleep. However, that may partly have been down to the nip of locally produced, very potent rum I had before bed, having bought a small bottle while visiting a nearby street market for food that night.

I only picked it up because of the name, Orangutan, and the striking image of the ape on its label. Saying that, it was probably in the back of my mind that the Perhentian Islands, where I was heading next, were officially 'dry', meaning no alcohol could be bought there, so taking a little of my own made sense.

The following morning, I shared a taxi with some German travellers to the coast, from which we took a ferry to the idyllic Perhentian Kecil. Having found simple, beach hut-style accommodation, I spent a few days lounging on sunbeds and hammocks, swimming in the crystal clear, warm water, chatting to other travellers, and eating barbecued fish fresh from the sea. Paradise! Oh, and I needn't have worried about buying that strange rum, as despite the island being officially alcohol-free, there was in fact beer available to buy, courtesy of a mysterious man with a cool box, who appeared on the edge of the beach after dark.

Next I crossed into Thailand, spending time on the islands of Koh Phangan, famous for its wild full moon beach parties, which I thankfully avoided, and Koh Samui.

They were a lot more touristy than my last island stop, but gorgeous nonetheless. Afterwards, I took the night train up to Bangkok, where I sweated and scratched my head for a few days, in between seeing the sights, wondering how anywhere so humid could be so hectic, and generally feeling paranoid about the possibility of getting scammed or pickpocketed in such a busy place. It made Kuala Lumpur look relatively tame in comparison.

I hadn't yet made my mind up about where to head next. I had various ideas and, thanks partly to the bargain cost of living in Southeast Asia, plenty of money left to keep on going.

Then an email picked up in a busy Internet café made the decision for me. It was from Angela, my old friend and boss, sent a few days earlier. Despite not seeing each other for years, we'd stayed in touch. It had been a few months since I'd heard from her, though, so I hadn't yet told her about leaving Australia. Last I heard, she was working a 'boring desk job' in the head office of a travel firm in London.

'Exciting news' was the subject of her email, which revealed that she'd met someone while working in London: a woman called Melissa, from New Zealand, who'd swept her off her feet. They were madly in love, she said, and – get this – they'd decided to move to Christchurch together to make a go of it. Angela had jacked in her job and, at the time of writing, was due to fly out to New Zealand the next evening.

I still remember her exact words: 'I know it's all very quick, Cassie, but when you know, you know.'

Thinking I was still in Australia, she ended her message by pointing out that you could fly between Christchurch and Sydney in three and a bit hours. She said it would be wonderful if we could use this opportunity to meet up again after so long.

Believe it or not, New Zealand was one of the places I'd been considering heading next. I'd heard so many great things about the country during my time in Australia, despite the Aussies loving to poke fun at the Kiwis and vice versa.

The only thing that had been putting me off was the fact it would mean flying back the way I'd come from, which wasn't logical. And yet, it would be amazing to see Angela again and meet her girlfriend.

So I took the email as a sign. I made a snap decision to shelve my plans to see more of Southeast Asia and to get myself on the cheapest New Zealand-bound flight I could find.

CHAPTER 26

So began the next chapter of my life. A crucially important one, as it happens, which ultimately led me to who and where I am now – settled in Ireland.

Where I am literally right now, here in this excellent hotel restaurant, enjoying your very lovely company, is more complicated, as I've indicated. We'll be getting to that soon, trust me.

Anyway, I flew into Wellington rather than Christchurch, partly so I could travel alone for a bit and see the North Island, but also to give Angela a chance to get settled.

After enjoying the capital city for a few days, immersing myself in the culture and culinary scene, I signed up for some tours, taking in sights such as the enormous Lake Taupo, Waikato River and the thunderous, mesmerising Huka Falls. Among other things, I also enjoyed two nights in Auckland and several days visiting vineyards and super sandy beaches.

I had a fabulous time.

When I finally came to take the ferry across the Cook Strait to Picton on the South Island, knowing I'd soon be reunited with my old friend Angela, I was in a cracking mood.

'Looks like New Zealand definitely agrees with someone,' a voice from nearby said. I was standing there on the boat's open top deck, around a third of the way into the three-hour-plus crossing, soaking in the morning sunshine and marvelling at the magical, rugged coastlines, uninhabited as far as the eye could see since leaving Wellington behind.

'Incredible views, right?' the same male voice added with an Irish lilt. 'Truly breathtaking.'

I'd assumed up until then that he'd been talking to someone else. But since no one appeared to be answering him, it dawned on me that I ought to turn around to check. I did and, sure enough, there was a shortish chap with windswept dark, curly hair and these intense blue eyes looking straight at me. He was standing about a metre back, a wonky grin leaning across his stubbly chin. 'Oh, hello there,' he said. 'Wow, even more beauty! I'm not sure my eyes can handle it. I should probably walk away now. You must get tired of chancers like me approaching you. Sorry, I can't contain myself sometimes. Ed the eejit, my pals back home like to call me. You can probably see why. At least they don't use my full name.'

Seeing as I was in a good mood and had a couple more hours to kill on the ferry, I decided to humour him, since he seemed harmless and jovial. 'What's wrong with your full name?' I asked.

'Ah, she talks! And a lovely English voice too. It must be my lucky day. Yes, my full name. It's not Edward or Edmund or Edwin, all of which would be preferable. Can you guess what it is . . . without laughing?'

I allowed the hint of a smile to form at the edge of my pursed lips. 'You'll have to tell me.'

'Don't make me say it in public,' he said. 'Please, no! Oh, okay. If I must. It's Edgar. There I've spoken it out loud. What can I say to explain? It's not very Irish, unlike my surname, which is Doyle. It's not a tribute to an old relative or friend either. Character-building, that's what it is. And proof that my parents have a wicked sense of humour. Anyway, enough about me. What's your name?'

And so I met Ed, my future husband; the yin to my yang; the man I'm still madly in love with today, who tamed my restless spirit.

When he asked if I'd like to join him for coffee and cake, I agreed.

'What brings you to New Zealand?' he asked when we were sitting opposite each other on a small circular table in the sun-soaked onboard café. 'Business, pleasure, bit of both?'

'Pleasure; potentially business. Depends if I decide to stay here for a while and find work.'

'That sounds very fluid and liberating. I like it. Where are you headed next, if you don't mind me asking?'

'Christchurch. I'll be catching up with an old friend who's recently moved there from the UK.'

'Taking the train once we reach Picton?'

'That's right.'

He grinned. 'Me too.'

'What about you, Ed? What brings you here?'

He took a slow sip from his coffee before replying: 'Pretty much a midlife crisis.'

'Aren't you a bit young for that?'

'I suppose that depends how long I live. I'm currently thirty-six, so if I popped my clogs in my early seventies, now would be about right.'

I enjoyed the black humour of this statement, delivered with tongue firmly in cheek. I was also a little surprised to discover he was eight years older than me, as he looked younger. If anything, that only made him more appealing, though. I liked the fact he had some life experience.

'I'm technically on a sabbatical,' he said. 'I'm a university lecturer in Dublin. Psychology, ironically, considering it was my poor mental state that led to me running off to the other side of the world to find myself. Yes, I know what you're thinking: a living, breathing cliché. And it gets better. My meltdown, for want of a better word, followed the breakdown of my marriage.'

Ed paused for a moment and looked me square in the eye. It was really intense, moving somehow, like he was opening up a window into his soul. I wasn't used to men being like this with me, so honest and upfront, and it punctured my defences, made me let him in. It didn't feel like he was looking for sympathy, not in the least, particularly as he kept everything light-hearted as he spoke. It was more like he didn't have the energy any longer to play games or wear a mask – and this was refreshing.

Lowering his eyelids, so he was squinting at me, he

added: 'I can imagine what you're thinking. Thanks to countless books and films, people imagine us lecturers to be regularly fornicating with our students, feeding on their vibrancy like academic vampires. Well, not this lecturer. I was very happily married, with four amazing children – two sets of twins – until my soon-to-be ex-wife told me she was no longer in love with me. "How do you know?" I asked her. "Let's see a counsellor who might be able to get us back on track." It turned out she was in love with someone else, a moneyed muscleman she'd met at the gym. They'd been sleeping together behind my back for months. Cue the sabbatical request and subsequent long-haul flight. I'm not bitter, though.' He winked. 'If none of that had happened, I wouldn't be sitting here enjoying these amazing views with you. Any questions?'

I scratched my head. 'Two sets of twins?'

Stretching his eyes wide open, so they were almost bulging out at me, he nodded slowly. 'Unusual but not impossible, as we discovered. I have identical twin sons, Rory and Niall, who are six, and non-identical twin daughters, Niamh and Shauna, who are three.'

'That sounds like a handful. Your wife's having to manage on her own now?'

'Oh, no. What do you take me for? I'd never have left her in the lurch, midlife crisis or not. Maria has an au pair to help out, don't you worry. Plus she's moved in with lover boy in his swanky beachfront mansion. I was barely getting to see them before I left, which was one of reasons I ran off. I miss them terribly. Is it weird to say that, considering I chose to put so much distance between us?'

241

'No, I don't think so. Sometimes you have to do what's right for you. How long are you here for?'

'I'm not sure, to be honest. I've already spent nearly a month on the North Island and there's loads I want to see on the South Island. My onward flight is in four weeks, but it's transferable, so I guess I'll see where I'm up to. My sabbatical is for a year, as things stand, but I'm not sure I'll be able to stay away from the nippers for that long. They might not even remember me, otherwise.'

'Where are you going after New Zealand?'

'Tasmania and then Perth in Western Australia.'

This answer surprised me. 'Really? I recently spent quite a long time in Oz; I didn't make it to either of those places, although I'd have loved to.'

I gave him a potted history of my Australian travels.

Nodding, Ed explained: 'I went backpacking there with Maria when we were both in our early twenties. Sounds like we travelled a similar path to you, minus the long stay in Sydney. Perth and Tasmania were the two places I really regretted missing. I've always fancied going up the remote west coast in a campervan. I think it would be heavenly to have all that open space, all those wild, empty beaches, to yourself. It would be like travelling back in time.'

I could almost see the untamed sea he was imagining, reflected in those striking blue eyes of his – and I had this feeling in my stomach. It was a sensation I'd only ever experienced anything like once before, with one other person. A meeting of hearts and minds is the closest I could probably get to describing it. It was something

I hadn't ever expected to feel again, and I knew exactly what it meant: I was falling in love with this man already, despite the fact we'd only just met.

Not that I had any intention of letting him know. But the really interesting thing, for me, was that the last time I'd experienced such an amazing sensation, the timing had been off. I hadn't been ready for it. I'd been too young and restless.

On this occasion, I didn't feel that way. The main thing I wanted, sitting in that café on the ferry with this exciting new person, was to keep talking to him. The mere act of doing so was giving me a head rush. I wanted to know more about this man, whose words had made me feel a broad spectrum of emotions – from joy to sorrow – in the space of a few sentences.

I also wanted to do the unthinkable, something I rarely did with close friends, never mind new acquaintances. I wanted to tell Ed about myself – not everything, not yet – but I was ready to open the door.

We really hit it off. We talked nonstop for the rest of the ferry journey. Then we boarded the Coastal Pacific train together, enjoying yet more splendid panoramic views. By the time the train pulled into Christchurch that evening, it felt like we'd known each other for ages.

I was dying to kiss Ed by that point – to hold him close and not let go. I just wasn't confident enough to make a move. I had a hunch he liked me, not least because he kept paying me compliments. But at the same time, paradoxically, he was hard to read. I kept wondering if he was simply a flirty guy who often made such comments to people. It was so unusual for me to like someone as much as I already liked him, I felt vulnerable.

I recall taking myself off to the loo several times during that long journey and looking at my giggly, glowing reflection in the mirror. 'Calm down,' I kept telling myself. 'Don't get over-excited. He's a man on the rebound, in the throes of a self-confessed midlife crisis. Remember what happened to you in Sydney.'

Honestly, that last warning to myself was a hollow one, though. What had happened with my ex-boss, Mark, while unpleasant and the trigger for me to move on, was entirely different. I'd never felt anything even approaching love for him. I'd fancied him, he'd been nice to me until he wasn't, and the sex had been enjoyable but not mind-blowing. The main reason I'd left wasn't heartbreak. It was because I'd felt humiliated. Besides, I'd already stayed there too long.

As the train drew closer and closer to Christchurch, I couldn't stop thinking about what would happen when we got there. I knew Angela would be waiting for me. She'd insisted on putting me up, despite me saying it wasn't necessary. I knew that once the train pulled into the city, Ed and I would have to go our separate ways. He knew this too, from our marathon conversation, but so far neither of us had addressed the elephant in the railway carriage.

Finally, minutes before the journey came to an end, Ed reached over and took my hand in his, giving me that intense, hypnotic gaze again. 'I've really enjoyed taking this journey with you today, Cassie,' he said. 'I don't know how to say this without sounding cheesy, but I feel like we've made a real connection. I know you'll be busy catching up with your friend, but do you think you might be able to spare a few hours one evening to let me take you out to dinner? I'd love to talk with you some more. Get to know you even better. What do you think?'

'I'd love to,' I said, resisting the urge to tell him I thought he was never going to ask. 'Let's swap email addresses. I also have a phone number for where I'm staying. I'll dig it out.'

There was a cheeky kiss right before we disembarked the train. It gave me butterflies in my stomach, left me dreaming of more, and cemented the strong feelings I already had towards Ed.

Then it was goodbye to him, at least for the time being, and hello to Angela.

CHAPTER 27

The pair of us started screaming when we saw each other. It's not the kind of thing I usually do, drawing attention to myself in public like that. But when Angela shrieked, running towards me on the platform, arms outstretched and tears rolling down her cheeks, I couldn't help but do the same. People were staring and rolling their eyes, but I couldn't have cared less. It was wonderful to see her again.

'Oh, Cassie!' Angela said after we'd almost hugged and kissed each other to death. 'I can't believe it's been so long. Now here we are, on the other side of the world, together again at last. You look amazing, by the way.' She reached forward and gently squeezed my cheek between finger and thumb, like a doting aunt. 'Oh, I've missed that face. I can't wait to catch up. How was the journey? What—'

She stopped mid-sentence, something further down the platform catching her eye.

I turned to see what she was looking at, only to find my eyes landing on Ed, who grinned and started waving.

'Who's that?' Angela asked. 'He seemed to be staring at us and now . . . Hang on. Do you know him?'

'I do. I'll tell you all about it later, I—'

Before I could stop her, Angela was marching over to Ed and introducing herself.

'Sorry,' I mouthed to him from behind. We'd already said our goodbyes, having agreed it would be easier that way, so this was unexpected.

'How do you two know each other?' Angela asked him. 'Cassie wouldn't say.'

'We met on the ferry,' he said with a friendly smile, followed by a subtle wink in my direction. 'And we sat together on the train. Cassie's great company, isn't she? I really enjoyed our time together.'

'Did you now?' Angela said, turning to flash me a private look of approval. 'Where are you staying? Maybe I could give you a lift or, I don't know, you could always come with us and have some food. My girlfriend is cooking, but I'm sure she'd be able to accommodate another mouth. She always makes way too much.'

'That's very kind of you,' he replied. 'But my hotel is only a short walk from here and you two need to catch up. Another time, perhaps? Cassie and I have each other's contact details, so—'

'You do, do you? Good. It's an open offer. You're welcome whenever. We've only recently moved here – I'm barely more than a visitor myself, still finding my feet – and any friend of Cassie's is a friend of mine.'

247

Once we were out of Ed's sight, I prodded Angela in the side, making her jump.

'Hey, what was that for?' she asked.

'You know what. I can't believe you ran after him like that. Here's me trying to play it cool and you—'

'Wow,' she said. 'You're into him, aren't you? I'm right, I know it. You're turning bright red. Wait, did you two get it on already?'

'No, it wasn't like that. We got on really well, that's all. Although he does want to take me out on a date. And there was a little kiss when we said goodbye the first time. You know, before you made me go back up to him and I ended up doing that awkward wave thing.'

Angela squealed before pulling me into a big hug. 'I don't think I've ever seen you so smitten before, Cassie. How exciting! He did seem very nice, I must say. Handsome too. And the Irish accent is sexy, right? I've always thought so. Oh, we'll definitely have to get him over sooner rather than later.' She stood back and gave me a sudden serious look. 'How long is he in Christchurch for? He's not just passing through, is he?'

'Chill,' I told her. 'You're the one so madly in love you dropped everything to move here. Tell me all about that. And I want the lowdown on Melissa before I meet her. You haven't even said how the two of you got to know each other yet. Come on, spill.'

That did the trick. She spent the rest of the journey back to her and Melissa's new home catching me up on her life, with a particular emphasis on their whirlwind romance over the past several months. They'd met in a

London restaurant after both being stood up by different dates. They'd compared notes before opting to eat together as a happy alternative.

'We were inseparable after that,' Angela said. 'I knew she was the one for me. We clicked in a way I've never experienced before. It's always felt effortless between us. I'm sure you two are going to love each other.'

Her words made me think of Ed. Bizarrely, I felt like I was missing him already. I pushed the notion to one side, but a mental image of him stubbornly remained in the corner of my mind, like an itch begging to be scratched.

When the phone at the house rang the next morning, as I was in the bathroom after breakfast, I hoped it was Ed. A minute passed, during which I waited, ears pricked, hoping for my name to be called. It wasn't, so I returned to brushing my teeth with renewed vigour. Finally, there was a knock on the door, followed by Angela's voice. 'Oh, lovebird. There's a gentleman caller for you on the phone.'

I spat my mouthful of toothpaste into the sink and flung open the door. 'Who answered?' I asked.

'Me.'

'Have you been talking to him all this time?'

She smirked. 'What can I say, Cassie? He's a chatty chap. I invited him here for dinner this evening, but he has other ideas. Sounds like he's desperate to get you on your own.'

'I don't want to ditch you. I've only just arrived. I'll tell him no.'

'You will not. He's already agreed to have afternoon tea with us beforehand. Come on, he's waiting.'

Ed took me to an amazing steak house in the heart of the city that evening, but only after first pretending we were going for a Thai meal. This was a joke, based on the fact I'd told him about my recent spell in Thailand and how I needed a break from that cuisine. I loved how this showed he'd been paying attention, particularly as I'd only mentioned it once.

The ability to really listen is a much-underrated quality in a potential partner. In my experience, men are good at pretending to lend an ear, in a bid to ingratiate themselves with you, while their minds are elsewhere. Serial daters are the worst: the ones who ask questions, rather than yakking about themselves, purely for selfish reasons. It's all a ruse to get you in the sack before moving on to the next target.

'Ed's fantastic,' Angela had whispered to me before we left on our date, having spent a couple of hours in his company. 'Definitely a keeper.'

This was great to hear, although it made me feel bad about my own feelings towards Melissa. I'd expected to love her, so I was shocked to find that I didn't immediately take to her.

'She seems a little cold and abrasive,' I told Ed in confidence, chatting over a post-dessert coffee. 'What did you think when you met her? Maybe it's me. Perhaps she sees me as some kind of threat. Could that be it? Wow, you must think I'm a right cow.'

'I don't think anything of the sort. You're not obliged

to like her because your friend does. She has to earn that. I do have a theory why she might have been a bit cold with you, if you'd like to hear it.'

'Sure.'

'I think it's to do with how incredibly gorgeous you are,' he said with a wink and his trademark wonky grin. 'Having someone as hot as you come to stay could easily make a person feel threatened, I reckon. It's a lot to live up to.'

'Behave yourself.' I tried to keep a straight face. 'Does that kind of corny line work for you in Ireland?'

'Ouch. It might have done twenty years ago. I'm out of practice.'

'I'd never have guessed,' I said, with a wink of my own. 'So what did you make of Melissa?'

'Hard to say. She didn't speak to me much – unlike Angela, who's lovely. They're definitely very different characters. But that can work in relationships. Opposites attract. My parents, for instance: they're nothing like each other. My father's quiet and loves sport; Mam's an extrovert who'd go to the theatre over watching a match any day of the week. What about your folks?'

I'd avoided mentioning the fact I was an orphan to Ed so far, despite our extensive conversations en route to Christchurch, as I didn't want his first impression of me to be coloured by pity. I suspect he'd noticed my evasiveness then and this was the reason he asked me such a direct question about my parents now. I could have avoided it again. I knew all the tricks. Instead, I told him.

'My parents are both dead. It's just been me for a long

time – even before my mum died. They were both junkies. I spent a lot of my childhood in care.'

This was a test. I looked Ed in the eye as I spoke and held his gaze as he responded.

'I'm so very sorry to hear that,' he said in a calm, steady voice, his eyes not straying from mine for a second. 'I can't imagine what that must have been like for you, other than bloody awful. You must be one heck of a strong person not to have been broken by that. To have grown into the amazing woman you are today.'

He paused before adding: 'I didn't think I could like you any more than I already did, Cassie, but now here I am, admiring the hell out of you.'

We saw each other daily after that. Soon, Ed had delayed his onward flight and was staying with me at Angela and Melissa's place while he and I made plans to travel around the South Island together.

It made sense for him to move in rather than wasting money on a hotel, particularly once we started spending our nights together. Angela suggested it and, after a little persuasion, Ed agreed, on the proviso that they at least accepted a contribution towards rent. Angela and Melissa lived in a smart three-bedroom town house in the Merivale area, just north of the city centre. It was owned by an old family friend of Melissa's, who'd apparently given them a great deal.

I'd warmed to Melissa considerably by that point, putting her early standoffishness down to the fact she was an introvert compared to Angela. She took her time to open up. I'd also grown to realise she had a very dry sense of humour, so much of what I'd initially considered abrasive hadn't been meant that way. I'd misinterpreted it.

I'd originally hoped that she and Angela might come travelling, but their primary focus was on finding long-term jobs and establishing their new life together. I accepted this and embraced my new travel partner instead, which wasn't hard considering how well things were going between us.

My long-term plan at that point, beyond touring the South Island's best bits, was non-existent. But as every day passed, with Ed and I spending increasing amounts of time together, I found myself liking him more and more.

'You two are so good together,' Angela said to me one night when the two of us were alone in the lounge, putting the world to rights over a bottle of vodka.

'I agree. It feels so natural and yet, if I think too hard about things, it's totally weird. We're so comfortable together, but we've only just met. And get this: it's not all about me any more. I often find myself pondering things in the plural – as a we. Where the hell did that come from? I barely knew I had it in me.' Lowering my voice to a whisper, I added: 'Don't tell anyone else I said this, especially not Ed, but I can't imagine my future without him in it. How nuts is that? Am I losing it?'

Angela threw her head back and laughed, the sound loud enough for me to get up and close the lounge door, worried about the possibility of waking Melissa or Ed, who'd both turned in for the night.

'Chill out,' she said. 'No one's listening.'

'They will be if you have anything to do with it, what

with your belly laughs. I suppose that means you do think I'm losing it.'

'No, don't be silly. A year ago, okay, I might have thought you were getting a bit ahead of yourself. But how could I think that now after everything I've experienced with Melissa? I left a decent job and all my family and friends behind to fly the best part of twelve thousand miles to a country I've never visited before. Why? Because I was following my heart. I don't regret it for one second, and neither should you. Go with it. Enjoy yourself. When you know, you know. Does that make sense to you now?'

'I suppose it does. Oh, it's so good to be here with you. Once again, you've led me to where I need to be at just the right moment. My guardian Angela strikes again.'

'I prefer to think of myself as your fabulous fairy godmother,' Angela replied with a cackle that sparked both of us into a giggling fit.

A few days later, Ed and I hit the road in a rental campervan, which seemed like the perfect way to tour the island together. Angela and Melissa waved us off, expecting to see us again after our road trip, when we'd pledged to return to Christchurch for another visit.

We spent the next three weeks in stunning surroundings: beautiful beaches, staggering national parks and so many lovely small towns. The air was so fresh and every time I breathed in I felt so alive. It was heaven, perfect. We may as well have been on honeymoon. I can't think of a time when I've been happier. I was madly, hopelessly in love. I hadn't told Ed yet, although I doubted I could hold it in for much longer. And I had a feeling he felt the same.

Then everything changed.

I knew it had the moment I spotted Ed walking out of the small Internet café where he'd gone to check his email. He was ashen-faced as he approached the campervan, where I was waiting. As he got inside, both of his hands were shaking.

'Whatever's the matter, Ed?' I said after he silently sat down beside me. 'What on earth's happened?'

'There was . . . an email,' he said.

'Right.' I realised this wasn't the moment to make a sarcastic comment. 'Who was it from? What did it say?'

'It was from Maria's email account,' he said slowly and quietly.

'Your wife Maria?'

He nodded. 'But it wasn't her who'd written the message. It was from her boyfriend, Ronan. He was writing to let me know what had happened. To her. There was an accident. She was, um . . . She was killed.'

CHAPTER 28

I gasped. 'No! You can't be serious. And the children?'

'They're fine, thank goodness,' Ed said. 'They weren't with her. Maria was hit by a car while she was out jogging alone. Ronan said she died at the scene.'

'That's awful.' I squeezed his hand in mine and kissed him hard on the cheek. 'I'm so sorry. When did it happen?'

'A couple of days ago, I think. His email was from yesterday. He asked me to come back straight away. I need to be there for my children. I don't know what . . . How . . . I can't wrap my head around any of it. I can't believe she's really gone. What do I—'

He started to hyperventilate.

'It's okay,' I told him. 'You're in shock. You need to calm down, yeah? I'm here for you. I'll help you. We'll get through this together. Breathe nice and slowly, in time with me. Can you do that?'

He nodded almost imperceptibly, but it was enough to know he could still hear me.

It took a while, but I eventually brought him back from the edge. Still shocked, naturally, but in control with some level of composure.

That's how I ended up going to Ireland with him. It was totally unexpected, but it never even occurred to me to do anything else. I felt he needed me at his side to get through the inevitably tough road ahead; I wanted to be there for him.

And yes, I went into it with my eyes open. I knew exactly what that meant – an end to my travelling, for one thing, and with it my independence. I realised there were four young children, who'd lost their mother, waiting for Ed to come home. But I didn't hesitate, even when he gave me an out.

'Are you absolutely sure you want to do this?' he asked me the evening before our flight, when we were back at Angela and Melissa's house in Christchurch for one final night. 'I want you to come, don't get me wrong. I absolutely want that. But I need you to know that I don't expect it. We have something amazing together, but it's still early days. I'm not the same prospect I was when you first met me. My life in Ireland is going to be very different with four children fully reliant on me. What I'm saying is, you don't owe me this. I'd totally understand if you wanted to walk away, even though I'd miss you terribly.'

'And you couldn't think to say this before I booked my flight?' I asked with a straight face, sitting next to him on the bed. 'Do you know if it's refundable?'

He looked worried for a split second before I grinned at him and stuck my tongue out. 'Got you! You're so gullible sometimes. I'm coming with you. I'm in, whatever that entails. I couldn't stay behind even if I wanted to. I'm totally in love with you.'

'Thank God for that,' he said, exhaling noisily. 'The truth is I don't think I could do this without you. I love you so much, Cassie. I feel bad saying this in the circumstances, but I have to, because it's the truth: I never felt anything approaching what I do for you with Maria, despite all the time we were together. It sounds soppy, but I think meeting you was the whole reason I came to New Zealand, like I was guided here, because it was meant to be. *We* were meant to be. Do you know what I'm saying?'

There were tears in my eyes as I replied. 'I do.'

That all happened around fourteen years ago. Ed and I got married a couple of years later, once things had settled down. Our first dance at the wedding reception – and this is a really bizarre coincidence – was to a song you know rather well, 'Can't Take My Eyes off You'. In our case, it was Andy Williams's version. However, true story, I was actually arguing for the Lauryn Hill cover you love. Ed's just not quite as hip as I am.

We're still very happy today. When I say we, by the way, I'm talking about all six of us. Rory and Niall are now twenty years old, while Niamh and Shauna are seventeen. They all know I'm not their birth mother. We've always been very open about that, especially with the girls, whose memories of her are sketchy because they were so young when she died.

Ronan disappeared from their lives more or less as soon

258

as Ed and I returned, certainly once the funeral had taken place. Showing his true colours, he made it quite clear that the four children had no biological ties to him and, with their mother gone, they were not his responsibility.

Luckily, they were all too young at the time to take this to heart, just as they were able to adapt fairly quickly to the new status quo, living with me and Ed. Which isn't to say they escaped the trauma of losing their mother in such a shocking way unscathed. How could they have? There were an awful lot of tears and tantrums, especially at the start, and I'd be lying if I said I found it remotely easy to transition into being a mother figure. I've formally adopted the four children, but it took a good while for us all to get to the stage we're at today.

Now, I love my family setup. I wouldn't change it for the world. It's my life; our house is my home. I still enjoy travelling, but I'm happy to do it in the form of taking holidays. Funnily enough, our last two summer vacations were to places you mentioned visiting as well: Gran Canaria and Mallorca.

Did I ever question the choice to give up my freedom: to reverse my earlier decision not to have a family so dramatically, by returning to Ireland with Ed and taking on his? Absolutely, lots of times, particularly in the first few years. But my love for him, and his for me, always managed to see us through any tight spots. He's an amazing father and husband, with such incredible patience and good humour. He's virtually unflappable.

Whenever I was finding it hard – flirting with thoughts of quitting and running away – I used to remind myself of my own troubled childhood. Knowing it could have been so different, had just one of my parents made better choices, motivated me to stand firm and do the right thing. That and the burden I'd carried with me for so long: from the time I've yet to speak of, right before I first left the UK to go travelling, when I'd made questionable choices of my own. Choices I was ashamed of, which had never stopped haunting me, despite my best efforts to bury them and pretend they weren't real. Guilt can be a powerful motivator, believe me.

But before we get to that, as we must, allow me to tie up a few loose ends.

Angela and Melissa are still together. They continue to live in New Zealand, but on the North Island now, not far from Wellington. Thankfully, they'd already left Christchurch well before it was hit by major earthquakes in September 2010 and February 2011. It made me so sad to see the devastation wrought on the city where I'd shared so many firsts with my great love. I imagine it's changed almost beyond recognition now. Ed and I will always have a special place in our hearts for Christchurch, and New Zealand in general. One day we hope to return to see for ourselves how it's changed and been rebuilt, but goodness knows when that will be.

Angela and Melissa have a young daughter now, Amelia, who's five, I think. Maybe six. I'd love to meet her in person one day. I still consider Angela a dear friend. I always will. Sometimes I wish we kept in more regular contact than we do, but it's hard living so far away from each other. Life moves on.

She and Melissa did come to visit us once in Ireland, following a trip to see Angela's family in Solihull, but that was nearly a decade ago now. How time flies. Last I heard, the two of them were in the process of setting up their own company, offering bespoke tours of lesser-known and off-the-beaten-track spots, aimed at the more intrepid traveller. I'm sure it's succeeding. Angela's not the kind of person to fail at anything she puts her mind to.

As for us, Ed is still at the university, where he's a well-respected professor. After spending a lot of time at home with the children – something the younger me never thought I'd hear myself say – I'm now working in education too. I'm putting my skill for languages to good use, teaching English to non-native speakers in Dublin. I've not been doing it for long, but I find it incredibly enjoyable and rewarding.

Anyway, that pretty much brings us up to now. All that's left really is the bit I've been dreading. The reason why I'm here today, back in Lancashire after so many years. You've probably already guessed that it's linked to this burden I mentioned. The one I've been carrying for most of my adult life.

Do you recall I spoke of someone special who I met at the wrong moment, when I was finally on the cusp of escaping my miserable youth and following my dreams? I skipped over it, promising to return to the subject later on. Now here we are.

Probably a good moment to top up our wine glasses.

Max was lovely, he really was, and I fell for him, head over heels.

I was nineteen when we met. He was older – a twenty-one-year-old graduate. I'd had a couple of boyfriends before, but nothing serious. Then he came along and blew my mind. Gave me my first experience of falling in love, and led me to re-evaluate almost everything about myself and my life.

He was from a well-to-do background with loving parents. He was fiercely intelligent, funny, kind, successful. And there was me: the orphan child of junkie parents, working low pay, low skill jobs, trying to scrape together enough cash to be able to run off and travel the world on a shoestring budget.

But something clicked between us. There was this instant chemistry, which made us crazily passionate for each other. And yet that was only part of it. Yes, I couldn't keep my hands off him, but I couldn't stop chatting to him either. The long, deep conversations we had, about all sorts – life, death and everything in between – used to electrify me. It's not that we agreed about everything. There was plenty we used to debate in those heady early days of our relationship, but it was always in an enjoyable, stimulating way.

The connection we had wasn't dissimilar from how Ed and I were when we first met. I'm very fortunate to have had that twice. Some people never experience it.

So why didn't we stay together? Timing, mainly. As much as I was in love with Max – and trust me, I really was in love – I equally wasn't ready to settle down. I had to get the travelling out of my system; escape the country in which I'd felt trapped and helpless for so long. I think

I needed to be selfish for a while in order to discover a part of me that was capable of settling down and wanting to become a wife, a mother. To learn to trust myself not to repeat the mistakes of my parents.

I was still licking the wounds of my upbringing then, desperately searching for my place in the world. By the time I met Ed, I'd become a woman. I had a firm grip on where my life was heading and was comfortable in my own skin.

And yet things could still have turned out so differently. Max and I did discuss the possibility of him coming travelling with me. He had a lot going on in his life. And yet, I think there was a good chance he'd have put it all on hold to join me if things hadn't taken the unexpected turn they did.

I fell pregnant. It was a huge shock.

Okay, we'd been having regular sex, but we'd been very careful . . . or so we'd thought. Having a baby couldn't have been further from what I wanted. Still in the early stages of recovery from my traumatic childhood, at that point I don't think there was a maternal bone in my body.

Regardless, I was pregnant and what I did about that pregnancy – how I dealt with it – is a secret I kept to myself for so long, even Ed didn't know until recently. He was the first person I ever told since leaving the UK, bound for Greece and beyond, all those years ago. I almost let it slip to Angela once, during a vulnerable moment, but I couldn't bring myself to do so in the end.

My actions back then have long been a source of shame for me, although I did what felt right at the time.

Was it the correct decision?

This is something I've wrestled with again and again over the years. My opinion still wavers, but my most consistent view is that morally it was wrong, while practically it was – and I say this with a heavy heart – probably correct. Still, that doesn't mean I wouldn't change it if I could travel back in time and inhabit the body of my younger self as the person I am today.

I'm jumping ahead. Look at me already ruminating on the rights and wrongs of what I did before even telling you what that was. Sorry. The simple truth is that I don't want to say it, because I know it'll change your view of me once and for all, despite everything you've heard up until now.

I'm still going to tell you, though.

I have to.

We're beyond the point of no return.

CHAPTER 29

The friendly young waiter appears out of nowhere at the side of the table. That's how it seems to Cassie, at least, because her mind is on far more important things and she's terrified of what's going to happen next.

Still, she's glad of the distraction, the momentary delay of the inevitable.

'How were your desserts?' the waiter asks.

'Very nice, thank you,' Rose says from across the table.

Cassie can tell there's something going on in Rose's head, but what that might be is anyone's guess. She's been very quiet for the last part of the story after initially looking anxious and then somewhat confused – maybe even disappointed, strangely – when Cassie started talking about her relationship with Max. Does Rose have any clue what she's on the cusp of being told?

'Yes, mine was very nice too,' Cassie adds, forcing her lips into a smile, hoping the way they quiver as she does so isn't visible.

'Tea or coffee for anyone?'

'Coffee, please,' they reply in sync, looking at each other across the table and both pulling a face.

'Jinx,' Rose says, although it sounds half-hearted to Cassie's ears. She responds with another painted-on smile. Her throat is like sandpaper, every swallow an effort.

'Perfect,' the waiter replies, hands clasped together. 'Would you like that here in the restaurant or would you prefer it in the lounge?'

After a quick consultation, they opt for the lounge. This suits Cassie, as the move from one spot to another allows for a natural pause in her storytelling.

'I'll take this opportunity to nip to the loo,' Rose says after the waiter has gone. 'Shall I meet you in the lounge?'

'Sure.'

'I'll see you in a few minutes. I'd like to pop back to my room and use the bathroom there, but I won't be long.'

'Take your time. I'm not going anywhere.'

When Rose has left the dining room, Cassie slowly exhales, glad of a few moments to herself, and yet thrown by Rose disappearing to her room.

What will she be doing there: calling someone? Looking Cassie up online?

She remains at the table, fighting to clear her mind and calm herself down.

'Relax,' she whispers under her breath. 'Keep your cool.'

Rose doesn't know anything, she tells herself repeatedly. There's no way. She can't do. She might believe she's on to something – a theory – but she'll have got the wrong end of the stick, surely.

She'd never have been able to keep her cool if she'd actually worked it out.

And how on earth could she have guessed the truth, anyway?

She thinks her mother is dead.

Only she's not.

She's right here.

How many times, waking and sleeping, has Cassie imagined herself breaking the bombshell news; finally revealing the shocking secret that's been kept from Rose for more than two decades?

I am your mother.

That short statement is all it will take.

But boy, do those four simple words carry some weight.

The thought of uttering them – as she must in a matter of minutes – fills Cassie with absolute dread.

From Rose's perspective, these words are impossible.

But the truth is the truth, however unlikely, however painful.

CHAPTER 30

Planning today's events beforehand, Cassie had intended to drop breadcrumbs while telling Rose her story, possibly even before then. But it was harder to do than she'd expected. How exactly do you hint to someone that you're the parent they've never known and believe to be dead?

If Rose has grown suspicious of her, which seems increasingly likely, goodness only knows what kind of conspiracy theories she has running around inside her head.

They can't be any worse than the truth, which is why the prospect of revealing it terrifies Cassie.

Perhaps she should have had the guts to refer to the boy she fell in love with at nineteen as Dave, rather than using her old nickname for him, but that would have risked giving the game away before she was ready.

She really did often used to call him Max. It had started as a joke when they were first together, based on the fact that he never did things by halves, giving

268

his all whatever he faced and often making grand gestures. That and his tendency to listen to music far too loud.

'It's because you always do things to the max,' she'd explained to him with a wink. 'Like becoming an author, for instance. You couldn't just be averagely successful. You had to write a global bestseller while you were still a teenager.'

He'd grinned, nodding approvingly. 'Well, why not? Go big or go home, I reckon.'

And so the pet name had stuck: their private joke.

As for her, she'd still been using her given name of Catherine when they were together. This changed when she left on her travels. She made a conscious decision to reinvent herself as Cassie: a name she'd heard in a movie not long before departing to Greece and taken a liking to. It came with the big advantage of being close enough to Catherine to pass as a diminutive, so that when she had to provide official details for matters such as applying for jobs or visas, it could easily be explained. And yet it was different enough to offer the fresh start she needed, helping her to shed the skin of her miserable childhood and move on from the shame of what she's about to confess to Rose.

She opens her handbag and takes out her mobile, which she put on silent earlier and hasn't looked at for some time.

There's a message from the number that, as a precaution, she's saved in her contacts as Max. Outside of her conversation with Rose, she doesn't actually call Dave that any more, though. A pet name is informal and affectionate; using it now would feel like an insult.

Telling Rose her story has been a fine balancing act from the start, not least concealing Dave's identity. It won't get any easier as she gets to the final part – the missing piece.

She could make it more obvious, by referring to her ex as a successful author who sometimes got recognised, for instance. Or she could refer back to how they met, which she's been deliberately vague about so far. Rose is familiar with that story: how her mother was working a bar job at a wedding and got fired for flirting with her father, so they ran off into the night together.

It is sorely tempting to reveal more, to better prepare Rose for what's coming. But Cassie knows it's not a good idea, even at this stage. Best to err on the side of caution. She needs to be able to get to the end of what she has to say before Rose cuts in. Despite spending so much time with her today, she's clueless how Rose will react when the penny drops.

After looking up to check that Rose hasn't returned for any reason, Cassie swipes to open the message on her mobile. It reads: *How's progress? Everything going to plan so far?*

She places the phone face down on the tablecloth and, closing her eyes, cups her chin in her hands, a cool palm resting on either cheek.

'Sorry to interrupt,' she hears after a few seconds, the waiter's voice slicing into her moment of calm. 'Is everything okay? You did say you wanted your coffee in the lounge, didn't you?'

Cassie slides open her eyes. 'That's right. I'll be heading there in a minute.'

'Oh, no rush,' the young woman says, cheeks turning pink. 'I wondered if I'd got it wrong, that's all. Sorry.'

'It's fine. No problem.'

Alone again, she picks up her phone and replies: *Yes. Nearly there now. Be ready.*

Shoving the device back into her bag, she stands up and heads for the lounge. She strides through the restaurant with her head held high, like she's confident and content. This is purely to try to make herself feel that way, although it doesn't work. Her insides are squirming. Part of her wants to head for the hotel entrance and run away. But that's not happening. She's done more than her share of running. It's time to face the music.

She and Rose arrive at almost the same moment.

'There you are,' Rose says. 'Where shall we sit?'

'How about over there?' Cassie points to the quietest spot she can see, in the far corner of the carpeted room, where no one else is currently sitting.

'Oh, okay,' Rose says. 'Right.' A hesitancy in her voice suggests it wouldn't be her first choice. However, she doesn't say anything further and follows Cassie to the table.

'The coffee should be here soon,' Cassie says after they both sit down in comfy armchairs. 'I'll, um, wait until it does before I continue, if that's all right. Less chance of us getting interrupted that way.'

'Yes, that makes sense, I suppose,' Rose replies.

An ominous silence fills the void, during which they

271

both stare at the door, as if willing a member of staff to walk through it with their drinks.

Cassie almost makes small talk about next week's wedding, but she bites her tongue, reminding herself of what's to come, and accepts the awkwardness instead.

'I'm going to check my phone, if you don't mind,' Rose says eventually. 'Make sure I've not got any missed messages or calls from anyone.'

'Of course. Go ahead.' Cassie plays along, knowing full well that Rose must have already done this while nipping to her room – and probably also when Cassie went to the toilet during the meal. She's spent more than enough time around Rory, Niall, Niamh, Shauna and their friends to know the crucial importance of a mobile to someone of the next generation.

While she watches Rose's eyes track whatever is displayed on the glowing screen, Cassie's stomach is doing somersaults; her palms are clammy and the corner of her right eye has started twitching, hopefully not in a visible way.

She's willing the twitching to stop – like she has any such control over it – when a waiter she hasn't encountered before, a stooped man in his early sixties, appears at the door and walks towards them with a tray containing two stainless steel cafetières plus milk jugs, cups and saucers, a bowl of sugar cubes and a small plate of plain biscuits.

Coffee poured and phone tucked away again, Cassie says: 'So, where was I? Ah yes, my unexpected pregnancy.'

CHAPTER 31

Falling in love ahead of my long-awaited travels was one thing. Falling pregnant was quite another.

Max and I hadn't been seeing each other for long when it happened. Less than two months. We'd been full-on, though. We'd spent most of that time together, mainly in the small bedsit I was renting in Withington, south Manchester.

I'd temporarily relocated there, rather than Blackpool or Preston, since there was more work in Manchester and it paid a little better. Plus it felt like a step in the right direction, away from my past. I was registered with various temp agencies in the city centre. I took whatever I could get, focused on the goal of getting away – leaving the UK – as soon as possible.

I worked less after meeting Max, if I'm honest, because I loved spending time with him. I couldn't believe someone so exciting was interested in me. It was electric between us. When we weren't, um, you know, we'd chat into the wee hours, never running out of things to say to each other.

I'd been embarrassed to take him to my bedsit initially, thinking he might go off me when he saw how small and simple it was, but he didn't care about that. Money wasn't an issue for him, as in he had plenty, but it also wasn't something he was particularly interested in. He said that far too many wealthy people he knew were obnoxious idiots. He was so down to earth. It was remarkable, really, considering his background and everything he'd already achieved himself.

He also knew better than to splash the cash around me after I'd made it clear to him that I wasn't interested in his money and I wouldn't accept his financial help in any way.

'You don't need to go out to work today,' he'd made the mistake of telling me once in the early days. 'Let me help with the bills or whatever.'

Our first argument had followed, during which I'd put him straight. I had zero interest in being his 'kept woman' and I warned that if he ever suggested such a thing again, we would be finished for good. Now that I was finally independent and free of the care system, the very last thing I wanted was to have to depend on anyone other than myself.

I let him take me out for the odd nice dinner and so on, as I couldn't see the harm in that, but I also made sure he knew not to shower me with gifts I'd have no use for when I went travelling.

Once the ground rules for the relationship were clear, we reached a happy equilibrium.

Yes, the travelling thing was hanging over us to some extent, but I still had a little way to go before I was ready financially. I was also warming to the idea of him coming with me and, had things not taken the unexpected turn they did, he may have done so.

But then, unusually for me, my period was late. Before I knew it, I was doing my fifth home pregnancy test, which came back with the same positive result as the previous four. Having not said anything to Max thus far, I gingerly broke the news, expecting him to be as scared and dumbstruck as I was, possibly even angry. I don't know why, I really don't, but I felt like I'd done something wrong and it was my responsibility more than his to sort it out. That was pure naivety, I guess. It feels ridiculous to even repeat such a thing now. But I was only nineteen at the time and had little experience of relationships beyond the one I was in.

His reaction was surprising. He was definitely taken aback, but there was never a hint of any anger or frustration directed towards me. In fact, half an hour later, he was beaming – almost bouncing off the walls in excitement.

'I think it's great news,' he said, kissing and hugging me. 'Yes, it's totally unexpected, but so what? Some of the best things in life happen this way. We have something special together, don't you think? I know it's only been about five minutes and, yes, we're young. But perhaps it's meant to be. What do you reckon?'

'Um, I reckon I'm supposed to be going travelling in a few months and having a baby is not something I've ever wanted. You know all about my childhood, everything I've

275

been through. How could I risk bringing a kid of my own into a world where stuff like that happens?'

'It's a totally different situation,' he replied, eyes wide and arms outstretched. 'You're not your parents and neither am I. We'd never let such a thing happen to a child of ours, would we?'

'How can you be so sure?' I asked him. 'Neither of us knows enough about the other to be able to say that for certain. I hope to hell I'm not like my mother or father, but what if I am? What if I end up getting hooked on drugs at some point? What if you do? What if we're not half as compatible as we think we are right now, still in the honeymoon period of our relationship? We could hate each other in a couple of months. Who can say? And this might sound selfish to you, but I've been looking forward to spreading my wings and finally going travelling for longer than you know. It means so much to me.'

'There would be time for that later,' he said. 'We could do it together – as a family.'

I shook my head. 'Yeah, right. Like that would ever happen with a baby or a toddler. Then they'd have to go to school. Come on, get real. Keeping this baby would mean giving up on my dream, full stop. You know it would.'

'So what are you saying: that you want to get an abortion?' He asked this in a quiet voice. There was a look in his eyes I'd not witnessed before – not from him – but I instantly recognised it as hurt. He appeared so vulnerable, whereas up until that moment I'd only ever thought of him as strong and resilient.

'I don't know,' was my answer – the honest truth. I was

sure I didn't want to be a mother. But could I actually bring myself to terminate the pregnancy? I kept contemplating whether doing so would make me better or worse than my late mum.

I'd learned about abortion at school, along with the arguments for and against. I remember standing up in class, when we had a staged debate, arguing the case for a woman's right to choose. But theory and practice are two very different things. And sitting there in my tiny Manchester flat, me on one side of the bed and him on the other, I felt far from certain about anything.

If I didn't want to keep the baby but I also didn't want to abort it, what other options were available to me? Adoption was the only one that sprang to mind. That didn't sit too comfortably with me either. The idea of giving away my child reminded me of my mother and how she effectively handed me over to social services. You could argue the move was against her will. But it's not like she made any great effort – at least not from my perspective – to try to get off the drugs and win me back. I know addiction is an illness and quitting a drug like heroin is far from simple. But try telling that to a young girl who desperately misses her mum.

'I feel really confused,' I confessed to Max. 'I don't know what the best way forward is, but I do know that I don't want to be a mother. Not now, not ever. I made that decision some time ago. It's far from a knee-jerk reaction to the test result.'

'I see,' he replied. Until that day we hadn't ever discussed our respective preferences about wanting children or not, despite confiding in each other about so much else. We were too new, too young, I suppose, for something so seemingly distant to come up. It hadn't felt relevant.

In my experience up until that point, most boys struggled to commit to anything more than a casual, no-strings-attached relationship, never mind having kids. Max was only a couple of years older than me, so I was struggling to comprehend his reaction to the pregnancy.

'I'm guessing having children is something you *do* want,' I said.

He frowned and chewed on his lip before answering. 'I haven't given it much thought until today. I suppose I kind of expected it might happen at some point in the future, when I was older and more settled. But it's happened now . . . and I don't hate the idea.'

He broke off, as though taking time to formulate his thoughts, before continuing: 'The timing of this ought to feel all wrong, but it doesn't, not to me, and I think a lot of that comes down to how I feel about you. Even though we haven't known each other for very long, I've never clicked with anyone else in quite the same way. Apart from the obvious attraction, I love being around you. I reckon you really get me and I get you too. To the point where I can comprehend why you feel like you do about being pregnant.

'Please don't think I'm trying to put pressure on you, one way or another, because I'm not. I wouldn't, I promise. I'm telling you how I feel, that's all. If you're not sure what to do, which *is* totally understandable, why not weigh up your options for a bit? There's no need to make a decision immediately.'

CHAPTER 32

I did consider the matter for a while. I gave it a great deal of thought and we continued to chew it over between us. It's not like I had anyone else to talk about it with, other than colleagues who barely knew me. Of my former foster parents, there were one or two who'd have probably been prepared to listen and give me advice, had I contacted them, but I had no interest in doing so. I was desperate to move on with my life, not to look backwards.

The big problem was that, as much as I knew having the baby wasn't right for me, I was massively struggling with the idea of having an abortion. I think this was related to me being an orphan. I kept having these awful, haunting nightmares featuring dead or dying babies. Sometimes they'd have my face. On other occasions, they'd have the face of my mother or father. I woke up screaming a couple of times and Max had to calm me down. He'd beg to know what had so upset me, but I could never bring myself to tell him. The thought of those bad dreams still sends shivers down my spine.

I eventually made the heart-wrenching decision to see the pregnancy through in order to give the baby up for adoption, delaying my travels in the meantime. I'd looked into how adoption worked and, despite my initial misgivings, it sounded like there would be plenty of people – particularly childless couples desperate for a family – queuing up to take a newborn into a loving home. I still wasn't exactly comfortable with it, but handled correctly, organised well in advance, it felt like the best available course of action.

Before I decided this, Max had quietly, calmly continued to try to convince me, without being pushy, that keeping the baby and bringing it up together was the best option. He'd even offered to marry me, bless his traditional heart, as if having a child out of wedlock was my big concern.

He'd caught me by surprise one evening after treating us to a takeaway curry. Having cleared away the plates, he got down on one knee in the bedsit.

'I've been thinking a lot over the last few days,' he said. 'And I hope I might have the answer. We're great together. I've never felt like I do for you about anyone else. I think of you constantly when we're not with each other and I count down the moments until we are. Looking at you makes me smile. When you smile at me, my heart skips a beat. Just being with you, talking to you, holding your hand, fills me with warmth and happiness. If that's not love, I don't know what is. I really believe we could make this work. Marry me. Let me take care of you and the little one. I know it's not what you planned, but I can offer you both a good life; I promise you won't regret it.'

It was so sweet, I started to cry. All those years of feeling alone and worthless, I'd never dreamed someone so wonderful would ever want to be with me, never mind ask me to be his wife. The tears kept coming. Goodness knows what he thought they meant. But eventually, I calmed down and found the words to reply to him.

'You're lovely,' I said, trying not to snivel. 'And I'm incredibly touched that you proposed. Part of me wishes I could say yes, but I can't. I'm sorry. If I kept this baby, I would regret it. I wish that wasn't true, but I know it is. There are things I still need to do with my life and, as self-centred as that sounds, I owe it to my miserable younger self – the one who dreamed of visiting far-flung destinations – to see them through. If I did what you ask of me, Max, I'd end up resenting you, our child and myself. Thank you, from the bottom of my heart, for asking me to be your wife; for being the sweet, kind, patient person you are. But I have to say no. I really am sorry.'

He took it on the chin, like he hadn't really expected me to agree. Thank goodness he hadn't presented me with a ring.

Anyway, when I later told him I'd made the decision to see the pregnancy through, but I wanted the baby to be adopted, his first response was to smile, nod and let out a gentle sigh of relief.

True to his word, at no point had he ever put pressure on me not to have an abortion or tried to make me feel guilty about considering it. He was too kind and sensitive for that. He didn't need to, anyway. I was already haunted by that hurt, vulnerable look I'd seen in his eyes when we'd first discussed the possibility.

Did that play a role in my decision? It was certainly a factor.

It was a week or so later that Max came back with another option, which I hadn't seen coming and threw me all over again. He'd been home for a few days with his family for his father's birthday. He had invited me, but I'd declined, blaming this on having to work, although in truth I couldn't face it. I hadn't yet met any of them, and the idea of doing so all in one go – in unfamiliar territory, while pregnant with Max's child – was far from appealing.

I could tell there was something on his mind as soon as he returned. He was restless, but I didn't ask why. I waited until he was ready. He was staying with me in the bedsit near enough full-time by this point. He'd been sofa surfing with friends before we met, in between staying at his parents' house in Lancashire, having previously been away at university.

His family probably didn't know I existed until he went back for his dad's birthday. I know he told them about me then, because of what he said on his return, once he finally stopped fidgeting and got to the point.

'I have something I want to talk to you about.' He took my hand and gently pulled me towards him. 'I need to say this before I chicken out.'

'That sounds heavy.'

'Yes.' He rubbed his eyes with the thumb and forefinger of one hand. 'It's to do with our baby.'

I'm not sure I'd ever heard him use the words *our baby* before. They sounded strange coming from his mouth. Made me feel weird.

'Right,' I said, gingerly, anxious about what was about to come next. 'Go on.'

He took a deep breath, cleared his throat and gave me this ultra-sincere look.

'I wonder if you might consider a slight amendment to the plan, whereby you still see the pregnancy through, but instead of giving up the child to some random family at the end, you, um . . . let me do it.'

'Sorry, I'm not with you,' I said. 'You mean you want to choose who adopts the baby? I'm not sure that's how the process works. I—'

'No, I didn't word that very well. Sorry. I'm a bit nervous, in case you haven't noticed. What I'm trying to say is that, rather than someone else adopting our baby . . . I'd like to raise it. By myself, I mean. You could still go off and do your thing. I wouldn't expect anything from you, financially or practically. We'd do it officially, ticking all the necessary boxes, so there wouldn't be any legal confusion or issues down the line. From your perspective, it would be much the same as having the child adopted, only you'd be passing parental responsibility to me – the biological father – rather than strangers.'

'Wow,' was all I could manage by way of an initial response. I really hadn't seen that coming.

He took my silence as an opportunity to make his case.

'I know this must be a shock,' he said. 'Not what you expected to hear. But it's not a spur of the moment suggestion. It's a possibility that first occurred to me a while ago, which I've been mulling over for some time. I've thought about little else for these past few days while I've been away. And, I hope you don't mind, but it's something I've also discussed with my family. I wanted to be sure it was feasible before I suggested it. I realise raising a baby as a single father wouldn't be easy. My whole life would change. But I want this. I'd get my own place near to my parents; Mum, in particular, would be on hand to help, point me in the right direction and so on, at least to begin with.'

'What about your career?' This was the first question I asked him, for some reason.

He wrinkled his nose. 'I'd put it on hold. I want this more than my career. I'm desperate to be a father to my child. I don't want someone else bringing them up. I want to do it, more than anything. Please let me prove to you how serious I am. How I've properly considered this. I'll jump through any hoops you need me to. Whatever it takes to get your blessing. We could prepare for it together.'

'Only for me to leave you in the lurch immediately after the birth,' I said, walking over to the sink to get a much-needed glass of water.

'No, you wouldn't be leaving me in the lurch. You'd be passing on the baton, as agreed. That's what we'd both be signing up for. There would be no hard feelings, no judgement, and no further responsibility for you.'

'What if something happened to you?'

'Then there's my mum and also my sister. But nothing

will happen. I'm young and healthy. I'd give our child a good life, I promise. The best. You wouldn't need to worry about any of that. After the birth, you'd be free to do whatever you wanted. There would be no ill will, honestly.'

I worried he was doing this in the hope I'd have a change of heart at the last minute and stay, but he shook his head and smiled when I raised this concern. 'If that did happen, I'd embrace it, of course. I'd never close the door to that possibility. But equally, I'm not trying to trick you. My suggestion is genuine. Anyway, listen, I'm not looking for an answer right away. Give it some thought, yeah?'

And I did. A lot.

The whole situation was bizarre, when you analyse it. There was me, growing bigger by the day, pregnant with his child, the pair of us enjoying each other's company, happy together. And yet, at the same time, I was counting down the days to being free again, so I could go off travelling, while weighing up this huge decision about our unborn child's future.

Before I gave Max an answer, I decided I ought to meet his parents, seeing as they'd potentially be playing a key role in raising my child.

Neutral ground felt most appropriate, so Max arranged for us to have dinner together in Manchester city centre. It was all a bit strange, especially at the start of the meal, when the conversation was stilted, but things improved as everyone relaxed. All in all, it was pleasant enough, considering.

The pregnancy was never specifically mentioned;

afterwards, Max revealed to me that he'd asked his mum and dad not to do so on this occasion.

'That wasn't necessary,' I told him.

'I didn't want anything to make you feel uncomfortable,' he said.

In the circumstances, the fact they'd shown up at all, giving me the time of day, was enough to inform my decision. They clearly doted on Max, who'd turned out just fine in their care, and they would no doubt love their grandchild every bit as much.

So I eventually concluded that entrusting our child's upbringing to Max and his family was the right thing to do.

When the minimum term passed on my bedsit, Max proposed that we move 'somewhere a little more comfortable' for the remainder of the pregnancy. He found a two-bedroom apartment nearby, still in Withington, which was nice without being too much. I agreed, on the proviso I still paid my own way. A compromise was reached and so we moved. I kept working until Max convinced me that being on my feet all the time, in bars and so on, wasn't good for the baby. So I spent my last couple of months taking it easy at the apartment and planning my travels.

Meanwhile, Max was busy finding a home in Lancashire, close to his parents, where he and the baby could live. We still got along really well together, but somewhere down the line – I couldn't put my finger on when exactly it happened – we transitioned from lovers to close friends and flatmates. It probably started with me having trouble sleeping at night, thanks to the bump, and him moving into the spare room to give me more space. But the overall shift was a lot more gradual than that. In hindsight, I think it was a natural, subconscious progression to prepare us both for what we knew was coming.

When the birth finally happened, ten days after the due date, it was an excruciatingly painful experience. Max was at my side the whole time. He stayed calm when I didn't. He held my hand even as I shouted and screamed blue murder at him. And when I first handed him our newborn child, the love I saw beaming from his eyes was so powerful, I wept.

Did I have second thoughts when I cast eyes on and held our beautiful baby girl to my bosom for the first time? Of course. I'm only human. Witnessing her entry into the world was a miracle I'll never forget.

But you already know that this part of my story ends with me leaving the country alone.

I stayed nearby for several weeks: long enough to take care of the legal practicalities, granting Max full parental responsibility and so on, while also ensuring everything was okay with the baby health-wise. But I distanced myself from her, letting Max take charge. I was afraid of forming a bond, knowing it would only make leaving more difficult. The two of them moved in with Max's parents until their own house was ready, while I remained at the apartment, finalising my travel plans.

It was hard staying away. I was up and down, all over the place emotionally. It was like my mind was fighting a war against my body and my hormones.

I shed a lot of tears, feeling empty and alone, laden with guilt; loathing myself for what I'd done to my own flesh and blood. I missed Max too, having spent so much time with him ahead of the birth. But despite all of this, somehow, I remained convinced that sticking to the plan was the best way forward for everyone concerned. I knew that taking myself entirely out of the picture as soon as possible would make it easier for all of us to adapt to our new lives.

So, as you know, I began my long-awaited travels in Greece.

A clean break. That was the deal.

It sounds so cruel and heartless when I say it now, but it genuinely felt like the right thing to do at the time, to avoid any more confusion or upset.

When I left the UK all those years ago, with no intention of returning, it was with the assumption I'd never hear from or see Max or my daughter again.

CHAPTER 33

'And have you?'

'Sorry?' Cassie blinks several times in a bid to refocus, so lost in her memories that she doesn't immediately register the question.

'Have you ever seen or heard from them again?' Rose says.

Cassie meets her intense gaze and finds herself speechless. She studies Rose's facial expression – trying to gauge her take on things – but it's no good. She can't read her, although she assumes Rose hasn't yet twigged the truth. Otherwise, how could she be so composed?

Cassie reminds herself that, as far as Rose is concerned, her mother is dead. Why would she link this story to her own, especially when Cassie has been so careful not to mention any specifics that might have let the cat out of the bag ahead of time?

Still, something is going on. Did Rose sound curt just now, when she repeated her question, or was that in

Cassie's imagination? Perhaps it's just a general sense of disapproval over what she's confessed. Giving up a child is the kind of thing people struggle to accept.

Even more so when they're personally involved.

Now the moment of revelation is all but upon them, the reality of presenting Rose with the terrible truth feels tougher than ever.

Stop, she tells herself. No more excuses, no more delays. Get on with it.

'Not until very recently,' she says, finally answering Rose's question. 'I'll explain in a minute. This may sound unbelievable, but I've thought about the two of them every single day since I left. They were constantly on my mind at the start of my travels, usually accompanied by feelings of guilt and self-loathing. And while those thoughts did eventually fade, they never went away.

'I often wondered over the years what they were both up to and how all of our lives might have turned out differently had I stayed. I considered making contact myself.'

'Why didn't you?' Rose asks, her eyes narrowing and lips tight. 'Especially once you moved to Ireland.'

Cassie grimaces, running a hand through her short hair. 'Because of something stupid I did. Something that made matters . . . complicated.'

'What do you mean?' Rose asks. 'And what's your daughter's name? You haven't said.'

Cassie's heart is thumping like a double-bass drum in her chest. She excuses herself for a minute, claiming to need the loo. 'Sorry,' she says, pulling a face. 'Needs must. I'll be back in a jiffy.'

She avoids eye contact at this stage, but it's not hard to sense that Rose is getting very frustrated now. 'I can't . . .' she starts to say, before breaking off, shaking her head and exhaling noisily.

As soon as Cassie is out of Rose's sight, she uses her mobile to send a short text message to 'Max': *Ten minutes.*

She darts to the ladies, splashes cold water on to her face, has a lingering stare at her reflection in the mirror, then heads back to the lounge.

'Right,' she says as she sits down opposite Rose again. 'Apologies.'

Rose looks up from whatever she's been viewing on her phone; without speaking, she switches off the screen and places it face down on the coffee table. Finally, she meets Cassie's eye and gives the slightest of nods.

Dammit, she's already fuming, Cassie thinks.

Smiling, mainly to hide how terrified she feels, Cassie says: 'This is hard to explain. After Max mooted the idea of him bringing up the baby as a single parent, I had a few concerns. One in particular kept niggling at me.'

She pauses in a bid to steady her breathing and calm herself down, although it makes little difference. She's sweaty and nauseous but soldiers on.

'This might sound ironic, hypocritical even, but I was really bothered at the idea of my daughter growing up feeling abandoned, having been through something similar myself. I was worried she's be scarred by that, spending her whole life wondering why her mother left; questioning whether it was something to do with her not being good enough. I recognise these feelings from

291

personal experience. I know how easily they can erode your sense of self-worth.

'After giving the matter much thought, I came up with a solution of sorts. I pressured Max to agree to it if he wanted me to support his suggestion. He was taken aback – as was his family – because it was controversial, to say the least. But after explaining my reasoning, I eventually persuaded him. I made him swear on our unborn baby's life that he'd stick to the story in my absence. That's how strongly I felt about it.'

Cassie signals a passing waiter and requests a jug of iced water.

'Would you like anything else, Rose?'

'No,' she replies in a tiny voice. Once the waiter's gone, she adds, in barely more than a whisper: 'What exactly was the story you got him to agree to, Cassie?'

Rose looks pale and anxious. She appears to be teetering on the edge of making the connection, while still holding herself back, probably not yet daring to believe the impossible whisper in her ear, the thud in her gut.

Cassie's mind flashes back to that moment in the hospital, more than twenty-two years ago, when she first held her newborn daughter.

The midwife gently passed her the baby for skin-to-skin contact, having previously explained the importance of this to help calm her and regulate her heartrate, temperature and breathing, easing her into life outside the womb.

'Would you like to do it instead, Max?' she'd offered when the two of them were alone earlier. They'd agreed not to say anything about their unusual situation to the birthing staff, deciding it was none of their business.

'No, no,' he'd replied, regarding the skin contact. 'I think it's best you do it, unless you really don't want to. It'll be most natural that way.'

At his request, they hadn't found out the sex of their baby in advance. He wanted it to be a surprise, and so it was.

'Are you happy to have a little girl?' she asked him as the tiny, hot little body wriggled against her chest, no longer crying like when she'd first emerged.

He smiled from where he was standing next to them, lightly stroking his daughter's bare arm and hand, effortlessly slipping into the role of proud father. 'I couldn't be happier.'

'Decided on a name?' she whispered, having promised to let him make the choice.

'Rose,' he replied without hesitation. 'It was already a front-runner, but now I see her, I know it's right. Just look at those rosy cheeks of hers. She's adorable.'

'Perfect.' She felt a strong urge to kiss Rose, who was absolutely adorable, on the top of her tiny head, where she had this cute little tuft of downy, dark hair. She resisted, aware of his eyes on her, not wanting to give the wrong idea and risk confusing matters.

'Don't worry, Dad,' the midwife said, returning into the room after nipping out. 'It'll be your turn soon. She looks like she might be a daddy's girl, this one.'

The two parents shared a private smile.

A few minutes later, the proud new father left to phone his own parents to tell them the good news. When the midwife also disappeared again, Catherine found herself alone with baby Rose for the first time.

Dazed and exhausted after everything she'd been through, her initial reaction was one of panic, afraid that she might do something wrong and accidentally hurt Rose. She'd never held a real baby before in her life – not a proper newborn like this – and with no intention of keeping the child, she'd barely done any research on the subject, meaning she felt utterly clueless. What if she started crying or wanted feeding? What would she do then?

Calm down, she thought, reminding herself that the midwife was still nearby. If she needed help, she could call out.

She kissed Rose's head without thinking this time, realising straight away that it was true what they said about babies' heads smelling amazing. She kissed her again, inhaling deeply, and found herself whispering to her daughter.

'Hi there, little one. Do you know who I am? I'm your mummy and I love you very much, even though I've only just met you. I'm so sorry I can't stay with you. It's . . . really complicated. You'll be fine, though. Your daddy isn't going anywhere and he's going to look after you, I promise. He's a special man – the best – and I know for a fact that he'll never let you down like I would if I stuck around. I'm not going to talk to you like this again, because . . . I can't make this harder than it is already. Know that I love you now and always, Rose. That's the truth, no matter how it looks. I wish you a wonderful childhood and a long, happy life, free from the scars of my own.'

It was only when she kissed her daughter's head again that she realised she'd been crying – a mother's tears. They'd run down her cheeks to her lips, moistening that wispy patch of hair.

The midwife reappeared. 'Everything good?'

'Yes, fine.' She sniffed and smiled.

'Don't worry, it's normal to get emotional at this stage, now that all the hard work to get her out is done. You did brilliantly today, love. You were a real star. And that little beauty you're holding is your reward.'

Snapping back into the present, her daughter now all grown up and staring at her inquisitively, desperate for the truth, Cassie feels something inside of her break.

'I'm so sorry,' she says, her voice catching as she feels the prick of fresh tears forming in the corners of her eyes. 'Rose, that was the name of my baby. It was you. I made your father agree to tell you I died.'

PART FOUR – THE TRUTH

CHAPTER 34

DAVE

He glances over at the time on the dashboard of the car and compares it to his phone, which is a minute ahead. He considers changing the car clock, knowing his mobile gets the information from the Internet, but he resists. The last thing he needs right now is a distraction from the job at hand.

'Stay focused!' he snaps, scolding himself.

He looks at his phone again: two minutes since he received Catherine's text message. Cassie's message, he means. He really needs to get the hang of calling her that. She says she hasn't gone by her full name for years. Plus she makes a point of only calling him Dave now, rather than Max, like she often used to in the old days. To his surprise, he felt sad about this when he noticed, but it makes sense, considering everything. Two decades – more than that – is a long period not to see someone.

They've both changed a great deal, physically and mentally. She's very different from the headstrong, fiery young woman he fell in love with, haunted by the wounds of her difficult childhood.

Not that they've had much of a chance to get re-acquainted in person: a quick face-to-face in an airport café before they travelled separately back to the Ribble Valley. He hadn't dared to give her a lift or meet her locally, for fear of some nosy parker spotting them and word getting back to Rose. Unlikely, perhaps, but he wasn't prepared to risk it. He'd already invested far too much time and energy into making today happen.

He's been on tenterhooks about this for weeks. He's firmly convinced it's the right thing to do. And yet he's terrified how Rose will react. What child wants to learn that their father has been lying to them their whole life about something so major?

Rose has been the centre of Dave's world ever since she was born. He'll never forget watching her arrive, seeing her beautiful face before even her own mother.

They say women become mums while pregnant, but for first-time dads the whole parenthood thing doesn't kick in until after the birth. That was true for him, even though he'd committed to being a single father long beforehand. He prepared for it as best as he could, but much of that effort was focused on things like finding the right house for them to live in, rather than studying the practicalities of raising a baby girl.

When the reality of being a dad did set in, it was with one heck of a jolt. He'd never felt so protective of anyone or anything as when he carried his fragile bundle of joy out of the hospital into the busy, noisy outdoors.

He wondered how on earth he would cope alone. He had no idea what he was doing. It took every ounce of strength he had not to get down on his knees and beg Catherine – Cassie now, he reminds himself again – not to leave.

Most of what he needed to know about being a father he learned 'on the job'. He'd probably never have made it through those early days of constant crying, feeding and nappy changes without the counsel and assistance of his own mother, Deborah. She was amazing, keeping him sane and regularly rising to the occasion when he couldn't or didn't know how, for much of Rose's early years.

Dave wishes she was here now, to help him through what's about to happen, but she's not due to fly in from Spain until next Thursday – a couple of days ahead of the wedding. He's not even told her what he's up to yet. He considered discussing it with her and possibly would have if she lived locally, but he was afraid that she might mention something to tip Rose off. The two key women in his life have an undeniably strong bond, despite the distance between them. They speak to each other more frequently than he himself talks to his mother.

He vividly recalls Deborah's opposition to the original idea of telling Rose, and the world at large, that her mother was dead. He wasn't keen on the idea either. Who would be? But Cassie – finally, he's getting the hang of using that name – was adamant.

He remembers the conversation he had with his mother

301

and late father, in the kitchen of the old family house, like it was yesterday.

'I'm sorry, what?' Deborah said to him, a look of utter disbelief emblazoned on her face. 'Are you out of your mind?' She turned to her husband, whose attention was divided between them and some financial reports piled in front of him on the table. 'Did you hear that, Stephen? Can you believe what our son said?'

'Pardon?' he replied with a satellite delay, shaking his head as if to clear it when he finally looked up and focused on the room around him. 'Sorry, they've made a right hash of this document. I'm . . . never mind. What's going on? Is there a problem?'

'I'll say there is,' she replied, so used to him being distracted by paperwork that she didn't bat an eyelid. 'David said that Catherine wants us to pretend she's dead once she's swanned off into the sunset. She wants the child to grow up believing that. Honestly, I'm lost for words.'

'That does sound very odd,' Stephen replied, rubbing his eyes before scrutinising his son. 'Why does she want us to do that?'

He made her case to his parents, emphasising once again her difficult childhood and explaining how she didn't want their child to grow up feeling abandoned.

'Not abandoning them in the first place would surely be a more normal approach,' Deborah said.

He cleared his throat before answering. 'Come on, Mum. Let's not go down that road. You've been great with Catherine so far. She really likes you. Don't spoil that now.'

302

'So you're fine with it, are you, David?' she asked. 'You're happy to lie to your child?'

He felt himself being backed into a corner but was determined to stand his ground.

Part of him still hoped Catherine might change her mind at the last minute and stay, even though that seemed unlikely, knowing how resolute she tended to be. Also, he could understand to a certain degree where she was coming from. It made sense in a weird kind of way when considered as part of the whole unusual situation.

The argument hinged on her death being more palatable for their child than the rejection of being abandoned. The former would be a tragedy, allowing the youngster to fondly imagine a loving mother killed in a cruel twist of fate. The latter would inevitably cast Catherine as a villain, raising all kinds of thorny questions and issues.

He had no desire for his son or daughter to grow up hating the mother they would never know. He was too fond of Catherine for that to happen.

On the other hand, lying about such an important matter, to a child no less, was morally wrong. Plus it would close the door on any chance of a future reunion.

He'd weighed up the pros and cons, giving the matter a great deal of thought, before coming here today to see his parents. Ultimately, he'd decided that going along with Catherine's request, as strange and unnatural as it might sound, was the best way forward. His visit wasn't to seek counsel, it was to get them on board, knowing he'd struggle to manage without their support. And so he presented himself as resolute, hiding all lingering doubts.

'It's not ideal, Mum, but it is what's going to happen. Our decision is made.'

'There's no need to rush into anything,' Stephen said. 'You could—'

'Look, both of you, Catherine and I are the baby's parents and this is what we've decided together. I'm here looking for your support, not a row. Yes, it's extremely unusual. I'm not denying that. But I've made my peace with it. Now I'm begging you to back your son and do the same.'

Taking a deep breath, he threw a stern look at his mum, summoning every bit of conviction he could manage, and added: 'If you don't agree to go along with this, I'm afraid I really don't see how I can involve you in the child's upbringing. You'll leave me with no choice but to go it alone. That's the last thing I want, believe me, but how else could it work? Do you want to be in your grandchild's life or not?'

He was fairly sure this was a bluff on his part, but he had to believe it at least a little in order to make it sound convincing.

So far, all of their discussions about going ahead without Catherine had focused on his wants and desires, as well as the needs of the baby. He'd never specifically asked his mum and dad if it was something they wanted. However, he'd noticed a spark in their eyes – particularly his mother's – as soon as he'd told them about the pregnancy. He wouldn't put it past Deborah to have already bought a gift for the baby: a cute little unisex outfit or a teddy bear, perhaps.

Anyway, the gamble paid off. By the time he left, they'd agreed. His mum had even offered to explain the situation to his sister, so she could prepare herself too.

'Sure, that would be great, if you don't mind,' he'd replied. 'It's only right that Bridget knows the truth. But don't tell anyone else what's going on, yeah? I don't want my child to grow up being the only one in the dark. We need to keep this strictly family only. Everyone else will have to be fed the fiction, once the time's right. For now, tell anyone who asks that we're pregnant and madly in love. I'll come up with a suitable twist in the tale.'

And he did, like the critically acclaimed novelist he was supposed to be, creating the narrative that Catherine died from a brain haemorrhage when Rose was only a few weeks old. He repeated the lie to his parents and sister until they all knew it inside out. And as soon as she'd gone, destined for Greece, he made sure they all stuck to it, including the falsehood that a small, private funeral had already taken place.

He and Catherine had pretty much lived in a bubble during their time together in Manchester. This made it a relatively easy lie to sell. So too did Catherine's lack of family and friends, plus the fact she'd barely stepped foot in the Ribble Valley or met any of the people he knew there.

Going through with it, though – actually telling the lie – was a terrible burden, not least having to accept all the heartfelt condolences: the cards, phone calls, flowers and even gifts for Rose. It felt so fraudulent, because that's exactly what it was. His parents struggled with it every

305

bit as much as he did, but they at least could say, honestly, that they'd barely had a chance to get to know Catherine.

As for him, he almost was in a state of mourning; he missed her terribly.

The whole process drained him of any remaining desire to write, seemingly sapping his talent for creating imaginary worlds once and for all.

Instead, he channelled his energies into the wonder that was Rose, his amazing baby girl. She was the prize that kept them going through that tough period, making it all worthwhile.

Right from the off – readying himself for the inevitable torment of having to lie to his own daughter – he started to consider all the questions Rose might one day ask and to prepare suitable answers.

'Where's Mummy buried?'

'She's not buried anywhere, darling. She was cremated and we scattered the ashes into Lake Windermere, in the Lake District, because she liked it there.'

'Can we go there?'

'Of course.'

And they did, on a few occasions, during which he pretended to recall a visit there with a heavily pregnant Catherine. Ironically, the two of them had actually discussed doing this, but for one reason or another, it had never happened.

'Didn't Mummy have any other family, like a mummy and daddy of her own?'

'I'm afraid not, Dimples. Her parents died when she was young. She was an orphan.'

'Am I a kind of orphan, because I don't have a mummy? Like a half-orphan.'

'No, love. You're not an orphan, because you have me, and I'm not going anywhere. Plus you have Nana and Grandad, as well as Aunt Bridget, Uncle Joseph and your little cousin Patrick. You have plenty of family and we all love you very much.'

Why Dave has never been able to show Rose any old pictures of her mother: that's always been a harder question to answer. Catherine's dislike of being photographed, presumably connected to her unpleasant early years, did mean there were precious few. And yet these photos could have been of some comfort to Rose as she grew up with only one parent.

However, unbeknown to anyone else, Dave deliberately burned them in a sleep-deprived fit of rage while Rose was still a baby.

He experienced a crisis of confidence – seriously doubting himself capable of the responsibility he'd taken on – so he lashed out at the only person, other than himself, who he could realistically blame.

'How could you leave us, Catherine?' he wailed, full of self-pity and hate, as the last images of her withered away into the flames. 'I can't do this. I can't manage alone.'

He quickly regretted his actions, but not soon enough to make a difference. And so, too mortified to admit the truth to anyone, least of all Rose, he slipped into telling yet another lie, claiming it was an accident.

*   *   *

Back in the present, Dave looks at the clock yet again: seven minutes now since he received Cassie's text. Right, he thinks, time to head inside.

He wants to be waiting outside the lounge when ten minutes pass, as they agreed. He has a sinking feeling he'll know when she makes the revelation. Rose is bound not to react well. That's why he's here: to try to soften the blow. To try to help explain. Not that it'll be easy. It was never going to be. But at least it'll be the truth at long last. Better late than never, right?

He gets out of the car, checking it's locked twice before heading into the hotel reception and through to where he knows the lounge to be. He's done his homework. He's been planning this for a while.

When he reaches the lounge, the door is open. He peers in as he walks past, but he can only see a small section of the room, which doesn't include where they must be sitting. Fortunately, the couch in the carpeted hallway outside is unoccupied. He takes a seat and pulls out his phone to make himself look busy. Nine minutes since he received the text. It won't be long now. Breathe, he thinks, inhaling and exhaling as slowly and regularly as possible in a bid to slow his racing heart.

He needs to keep his cool. He hopes to be the calming influence that sweeps in and maintains order. To what degree that will be possible depends on Rose and how she reacts to what Cassie tells her. It's quite possible she'll be too furious at everyone – him especially – to listen to anything he has to say. But he has to try.

CHAPTER 35

ROSE

'Rose, that was the name of my baby. It was you. I made your father agree to tell you I died.'

She hears the words, but they seem to emerge from Cassie's mouth in slow motion. Time pauses for a long, mind-bending moment as her world teeters on its axis.

Rose.

Cassie's baby, the one she gave up, was called Rose.

Her name.

Making Cassie . . .

Her mother?

Her dead mother.

Who's not actually dead?

Never has been. That's what she's saying.

Rose's entire life . . .

A lie?

No, that can't be right. Her dad isn't even called Max! Who the hell—

'Your father *is* your father, just to be clear,' Cassie adds, as if Rose's spiralling thoughts are emblazoned on her face. 'Max was, um, a nickname I used to call Dave when we were together.'

It's all too much for Rose. She blinks and is back in the past, where it's safe.

A scene from her childhood. Her tenth birthday.

Her father knocked on the ajar bedroom door as he walked in to see her.

'What's up, Dimples? Why are you hiding here when everyone's downstairs? They've all come to see you. You're the birthday girl.'

'I know,' she replied from where she was lying on her bed, staring out of the window. 'I'll come down in a minute, Daddy. I just needed . . . I don't know, really. I was opening my presents and got a bit sad.'

He walked over to her and, after ruffling her hair and kissing her forehead, took a seat next to her on top of her pink and white spotted quilt. 'How come?' he asked in a gentle voice. 'What made you sad, love? It's your birthday. You're supposed to be happy.'

She shrugged, not yet ready to tell him her reason for feeling blue. She picked up the soft toy next to her on the bed, a furry black and white cat she called Domino, and pulled it into her arms, giving it a tight squeeze.

'I know what will cheer you up,' her daddy said. 'What

about if I told you there was a very special present hidden nearby?'

'What?' She instantly perked up. 'Where? Here in my room?'

'Yep. Closer than you know.'

'What does that mean?'

'All I'm saying is that I'd have a look under my pillow, if I were you.'

'There's nothing under my pillow, Daddy. Don't be silly.'

'Are you certain?'

She did as he asked and, sure enough, she found a small box wrapped in shiny silver paper. 'What? When did this get here?'

He held up his hands, palms forward, like it was nothing to do with him, but his grin said otherwise. 'Daddy!' she said, frowning in mock anger. 'That's naughty.'

'I've no idea what you're talking about.'

'What is it?'

'You'll have to open it.'

She did, tearing off the wrapping with great excitement and finding a small velvety box, which contained a beautiful silver charm bracelet.

'Well?' he asked. 'Do you like it?'

She nodded her head enthusiastically. 'I love it. Can I wear it now?'

'Absolutely. And so you know, it's a very special charm bracelet, a family heirloom. It used to be—'

She gasped. 'Did it used to belong to my mummy? I was just talking to her, so it's an amazing—'

'Um, no love,' he said, clearing his throat and running a hand over his face. 'Sorry, I wish I could say it was. I'll tell you who it did originally belong to, though – my nana. She passed it on to Aunt Bridget, who in turn asked me to pass it on to you. She didn't think it would really be Patrick or Harry's scene, but she thought you might love it. You can add more charms to it, by the way. We could even look for one together with some of your birthday money, but only if that's what you want. No rush.'

She nodded and gave him her best smile but couldn't get any words out for a minute.

'Is that why you came up here: to chat to your mummy?' he asked.

He already knew this was something she did from time to time. They'd discussed it before and he'd been fine with it. He'd said it was 'very healthy'. Rose liked to pretend she was there with her in spirit and could hear what she said to her.

'Any particular reason you felt like doing this now?' he asked, tilting his head to one side. 'Weren't you enjoying your party?'

'Yes, I was. I am, honestly. I'll come down again in a minute.' She paused, weighing up whether or not to tell him why, and eventually deciding she would. 'I noticed most of the children at my party were dropped off by their mummies. It got me thinking and made me a bit upset.'

Her father pulled her into a warm, tight hug and held her like that for what felt like ages. When he pulled away, she could tell he'd been crying. They both had. But after

312

that they pulled themselves together, washed their faces in the bathroom and headed back down to the party, hand in hand.

She loved her father so much that afternoon, it felt like her heart wanted to burst out of her chest.

'Rose, are you all right? Can you hear me, Rose?'

She can see and hear Cassie, who's kneeling in front of her, looking troubled. However, Rose appears to have lost the ability to respond. Her whole body feels frozen solid.

Is this to allow her time to process what she's just heard? Maybe.

But what was that again?

It's floated to the edge of her mind, out of reach.

She probably could get to it with a little mental stretching, although she's not sure she wants to. It wasn't good: that's one thing she knows for certain.

Cassie is clicking her fingers in front of her face now. 'Rose,' she says. 'What's going on?' She holds up a glass of water. 'Come on now, Rose, why don't you drink some of this?'

Cassie presses the glass to her mouth, tipping it slightly so her lips feel wet. But Rose keeps them firmly shut and a dribble of water runs down her chin, quickly wiped away by Cassie with a serviette.

A blurry figure appears behind Cassie and taps her on the shoulder. She stands up and moves a short distance away, out of Rose's vision. The pair mutter a few words to each other before the new arrival returns, places his hands on his knees and leans forward, eyes squinting at

Rose. She recognises him as Greg, the nice bartender from this afternoon.

'Everything all right, Rose?' he asks.

She wants to respond, at least to say hello, but it's not happening. She's still frozen.

He stares at her, puzzled, shakes his head, then returns to a standing position.

'I'll go and find him,' Greg tells Cassie, who nods as she kneels before her again.

'I think you're in shock, Rose,' she says. 'That must be what this is and I get it, believe me. I know what I just told you must have come as a huge shock. I tried to build up to it as best I could, to soften the blow. But it was always going to be hard. For what it's worth, I'm sorry. For everything . . .'

She keeps talking, but Rose closes her eyes and tunes out.

She doesn't want to hear any more.

She's happy for now in this frozen state.

She remains like this until the speaking stops.

There's a shift, movement in front of her and a smell she instantly recognises: the fresh woody scent of her dad's favourite aftershave.

It couldn't be, could it?

She slides open her eyes and, incredibly, there he is, kneeling in front of her chair, having taken Cassie's place. Her body and mind thaw with a rush. She stretches her arms forward, craving his warmth and protection more than ever. 'Daddy,' she says, even though she rarely calls him that any more. 'It's you. You're here. Thank goodness.

314

This woman – Cassie she calls herself – has been making up all kinds of lies. She tried to convince me that—'

'Shh,' he whispers into her ear as they hold on tight to each other. 'It's all going to be okay, darling. Everything is going to be fine. I'm here now.'

She lets these words wash over her, soothe her, as she comes back to herself.

Then something clicks.

'Hang on,' she says, pulling away from his embrace and really looking at him for the first time, before turning to Cassie, who's back sitting in her armchair. 'What's going on? How come you're here now, Dad? Do you know this woman? What she told me can't be true.' She starts shaking her head and can't stop. 'Tell me it's not true. Tell me you had nothing to do with this. She's an impostor, right? I don't know what she's playing at. Dad, please say something.'

Inhaling deeply, he closes his eyes for a second. When he opens them again, still kneeling in front of Rose's chair, he speaks in a slow, steady voice, barely louder than a whisper.

'Rose, you know how much I love you. This is incredibly hard to say, and I can only imagine how difficult it must be for you to comprehend, but I'm afraid everything Cassie has told you *is* the truth. She *is* your mother.'

'No!' Rose replies. 'Why are you saying this? You've told me my whole life that my mother, Catherine, died when I was only a few weeks old. She had a brain haemorrhage. That has to be the truth. Why would you have said so otherwise?'

His face twitches on one side. 'I, um, don't know what

to say, Rose, other than what you've already heard. Telling you that story – that fiction – has never sat well with me. It's why I've always been uncomfortable talking to you about your mother. But as I hope Cassie – who used to go by her full name of Catherine when we were together – has explained, it was something I agreed to before you were born and had to stick to.

'Recently, now you're an adult building your own life, I've struggled even more with you not knowing the truth. After much soul-searching, I decided to try to contact your mother. She'd given me an email address before she left and had pledged to keep it active so I had a way to contact her in case of a dire emergency. I'd kept it safe but never used it. I had no idea whether or not it would still work after more than two decades. Honestly, I feared it wouldn't, but I tried anyway. I wanted to see whether, after all this time, she might have changed her mind and be open to getting to know you. I thought it unlikely, but I was pleasantly surprised.

'I hadn't expected her to be living as nearby as Ireland, nor to learn that she was settled down with a family of her own. I'd anticipated that the burden of telling you the truth would land on my shoulders. However, your mother was adamant that she should be the one to tell you.' He turns to Cassie, handing her the baton. 'That's right, isn't it?'

'Absolutely,' Cassie says, leaning forward in her chair. 'I was the one who left and who insisted on creating this, um, lie. I felt that it was my responsibility to try to explain it to you.'

'Just in time to ruin my wedding,' Rose snarls. 'How kind. Ever the caring, attentive parent.'

'That's fair,' Cassie replies. 'Whatever anger and hatred you have for me is totally understandable, Rose.'

'Don't you say my name!' The level of venom in Rose's slow, seething pronunciation of these words surprises even herself.

Cassie hesitates but continues: 'Think whatever you like about me. That's your right. I'll take it on the chin. But go easy on your dad. None of it was his idea and he's been there for you all the time that I haven't, dedicating his life to you. Yes, he didn't tell you the truth about me – but only because I put him in a terrible position and he's a man of his word.'

Rose wants to tell this woman to stop talking – to leave her the hell alone – but her body won't play along with her mind.

'As for you learning about all of this now,' Cassie continues, 'a week before your wedding, that's on me too. Your father first contacted me around six months ago, but I didn't reply immediately. I was too afraid. And when I did eventually get up the courage to speak to him, to hear what he had to say, I didn't say yes straight away. I had to think about it and consider all the possible repercussions.

'By the time I did agree, there were unforeseen things I had to deal with at home. Now's not the right moment to go into all that, but let's just say I was needed there for a while. I couldn't drop everything and jump on a plane, as I might have done in normal circumstances. I specified this weekend and insisted I should be the one to tell you. The cloak and dagger stuff, introducing myself as a stranger and so on, was also my idea. I desperately wanted the chance to give you an insight into my mind: why I did what I did. I wanted to be able to show you that all of this was about me – not you.

'Your father went along with it – gave me this chance – because that's the kind of selfless, considerate man he is. Whatever happens after this, please don't punish him for my mistakes. Remember that if it was down to me alone, you'd have been adopted and not been brought up by either of your birth parents. I'm the villain in this story. Your father is the hero.'

Rose's eyes linger on an uncomfortable-looking Dave, still kneeling on the floor in front of her chair. She can't bring herself to look at Cassie. Thinking how much time they've spent together today, while she was oblivious to the truth, makes her skin crawl.

It feels like a huge invasion of her privacy that she revealed so much of her own heart and mind to someone she was led to consider a friend. The fact her dad was in on it makes her even angrier. And who else knew about this in advance? Was Cara another conspirator? She desperately hopes not. But surely her departure was engineered, one way or another. Today's trickery wouldn't have worked with her maid of honour alongside her. If Rose hadn't been alone, she and Cassie would never have struck up such an intimate conversation.

The dawning realisation that she's been played, all of her life, is horrible. It makes her sick to her stomach, stifled and panicky. She can't make eye contact with either of them.

No one says anything for an eternity once Cassie falls

silent. It's only when Dave clears his throat, apparently about to speak, that Rose steps in and beats him to it. Digging deep and finding an inner strength, she jumps to her feet. 'I need some time alone.'

'Wait,' her father says. 'Please don't storm off. Surely it's better we talk this—'

'No, not now. Not today. Just leave me alone, okay? This is all too much.'

'But we need to speak to you about something else too,' he adds. 'It's important. It's to do with, er, Ryan.'

Rose can't deal with this any more. Without saying another word, she turns on her heel.

She runs out of the hotel lounge, gasping for fresh air, head spinning . . .

She's been blindsided – trapped in a living nightmare – and all she wants to do is escape.

CHAPTER 36

CASSIE

'That went well,' Dave says, taking a seat in the armchair vacated by Rose.

'At least she didn't start shouting and screaming, making a big fuss,' Cassie replies. 'That was kind of what I was expecting. It threw me when she fell silent like she did. If you hadn't turned up, I don't know what I'd have done to snap her out of it. I was already considering that I might have to throw a glass of water in her face.'

He frowns. 'Don't you think Rose has been through enough already today?'

'It would only have been a last resort. She looked almost catatonic.'

'It was a lot to take in. I only wish that was the end of it.'

'So what now?' she asks. 'Should we go after her together?'

He rubs his eyes, looking every bit as weary as Cassie feels.

'Leave it to me for now,' he says. 'But keep your phone on, yeah?'

'Of course.'

'I'd best go and see if I can find her.'

'Okay. I'll stay put, but do shout if you need me. I'll be there in a flash.'

He nods.

She doesn't envy him what he intends to tell Rose next. As he gets up to leave, she grabs hold of his arm and looks him in the eye. 'You're doing the right thing, even if it doesn't feel that way. She'll thank you for it in the long run.'

'I hope so.'

Once he's gone, Cassie exhales. Did that sound convincing? Fingers crossed it did. She was, after all, the one who argued the case for them making both of their big revelations on the same day.

'You think so?' he asked when they discussed it over the phone beforehand. 'Really? It's going to be one hell of a shitty day for her. What if she can't handle it? What if she does something stupid as a result? I'd never forgive myself. It's going to be very close to the wedding.'

'Rose is your daughter,' Cassie replied. 'I don't have any right to call her mine. You probably know her better than anyone: her mental state, what her reaction is likely to be, and how she'll deal with it. So it's your call. But my opinion, for what it's worth, is that it'll be easier to do in one go, like ripping a plaster off rather than peeling it away gradually.'

Now, after getting to know Rose a little and having witnessed her reaction to the first incendiary announcement at point-blank range, Cassie is less sure.

Part of her feels like she ought to have gone with him to find Rose, but she intends to respect his decision.

So she sits tight, as she said she would, and when a waiter passes by, she orders some tea. The perfect drink in any crisis, right? That's debatable – but going for more alcohol at this moment would feel inappropriate.

She texts Ed for the first time since late morning: *How are you, love? I hope you've got your feet up. You'd best not be overdoing things.*

He replies a couple of minutes later: *Don't you worry about me. I'm fine. The kids have me under lock and key. How are you, more's the point? Have you told her yet?*

Cassie: *Yep. She hasn't taken it well. No surprise.*
Ed: *Want to talk? I'm here if you do.*
Cassie: *Not tonight. Still might be needed. I'll call you in the morning. Love you. X*
Ed: *Love you too, honey. Thinking of you. Chin up. X*

This trip is the first time in months that she and Ed have been apart. The 'unforeseen things', which she told Rose had stopped her from coming earlier, were all to do with her husband. Soon after Dave's shock move to re-initiate contact with her, like a bolt from the blue, life threw them yet another curveball. There was an accident. Ed fell on to a concrete patio from the top of a stepladder while replacing an outside light in the garden at home.

He fractured a vertebra in the process, aka broke his back.

Following a scary evaluation period in A&E and several days on a hospital ward, he was sent home in a carbon fibre back brace meant to immobilise the injury, allowing it to heal. Thankfully, no surgery was required. The doctors said he'd been extremely lucky, escaping any damage to his spinal cord, which could have left him paralysed. All the same, he was in an awful lot of pain, and unable to do much other than rest and recuperate while pumped up on morphine. Initially, he had to wear his brace night and day, only briefly removing it to stand still in the shower while Cassie washed him.

Now, well on the road to recovery, he's allowed to remove the restrictive, uncomfortable brace in bed at night, finally enabling him to get some proper sleep. He's reasonably self-sufficient again, hence why Cassie's finally confident enough to leave him and come here to do this. Not that he's alone. Between the four children and several other close friends and family working on a rota Cassie created, there will be someone with him in the house the whole time she's away.

Still she worries. But actually, if anything, Ed's accident was one of the key things that spurred Cassie on to come here to meet Rose and tell her the truth. Experiencing that trauma – knowing how close Ed came to being paralysed – reminded her just how fragile life can be. And how important it is to live your life to the full, with no regrets, making time for what really matters, rather than sweating the small stuff.

The accident also brought her, Ed and the children closer, emphasising the importance of family.

So Cassie cast aside the doubts and fears she had about meeting her long-lost daughter and agreed to Dave's request to tell Rose the truth.

Now she's done that, faced her demons, it is undeniably like a weight has been lifted off her shoulders. And yet she's conflicted, considering how it's affected Rose. She must be so angry and confused, it's no wonder she ran off like she did. Cassie hopes Dave has found her already, made sure she's all right.

If only there wasn't more misery to come.

Her tea arrives and, as she pours it, her mind drifts, pondering on the past, when things still had the potential to end up so differently.

There was a pivotal moment when she almost turned back and didn't go to Greece.

Cassie's fairly certain Dave doesn't know about this. Otherwise, he surely would have mentioned it once they got back in touch. Deborah could still know, but Cassie suspects not. Her gut tells her that Dave's father took to his grave what happened between the two of them that evening when she arrived by train at Manchester Airport and experienced major last-minute jitters.

She'd only met Stephen in person on a handful of occasions, during which he'd always been civil but harder to like than his wife. Cassie had found him to be a cold fish: a man of few words, who shared only what he had to with the people around him. An astute businessman, by all accounts, she suspected he quickly wrote her off as a bad investment of his family's time and effort.

What neither he nor anyone else knew, however, was that she'd secretly had misgivings about relinquishing her baby ever since the birth.

Other than a passing mention of second thoughts, Cassie didn't go into this with Rose today. Why? Because she'd left, regardless. To say more would have sounded phoney and pathetic.

The truth was less clear cut.

She had managed to stay fairly detached during the pregnancy, trying not to humanise or overthink the contents of her bump. That all went out of the window when she held Rose in her arms, smelled her scent, felt her tiny hands and the tickle of her warm breath against her own skin.

Even as she whispered to her about leaving, when the two of them were alone for the first time in the hospital, a part of her wondered if she could truly go through with it.

Later, each time she saw baby Rose, having already passed her into her loving father's care, she felt a stab of guilt and longing.

And yet her hard-wired aversion to most things maternal remained, alongside frequent flashbacks to her own troubled childhood.

It felt as though for every moment of doubt she had about leaving, there was a memory to counter it: cowering on the threadbare carpet in her tiny bedroom, for instance, arms tightly wrapped around her knees, hearing her parents fighting; praying Mummy would be okay.

There were so many miserable memories to choose from, no wonder they haunted her, constant reminders of why she had to get away.

If she started to believe she could be a capable parent, she'd soon recall her mother's good intentions. How she'd initially been fun, kind and loving, only for all of that to be sucked away by heroin, the drug she chose over her own daughter.

There were lots more memories to support that: long nights spent alone in squalor, little or nothing to eat, afraid her mum might never return. Terrifying times she found her unconscious, covered in her own filth and impossible to rouse. Things no child should have to experience.

And then, after finally being taken into care, that awful sense of not belonging anywhere – not being loved or wanted – which slowly hardened her heart until any last dregs of hope were finally drained away by her mother's death.

Such painful memories were near constant companions back then. So she fought to bury her feelings for Rose, hiding them from the world, sticking to the plan.

Communicating her doubts to Dave would have been all too easy, but she couldn't do that to him. She was still too conflicted. She was terrified of leading him on, giving him hope, only to then let him down again.

Finally, alone at the airport, having declined his typically benevolent offer to wave her off, something happened. It was like her legs refused to take her to the check-in desk.

Next she was fumbling around for change to use a payphone and calling his parents' place, where he and

Rose were still staying until their own house was ready. She wasn't entirely sure what she was doing, but her heart was racing and it somehow felt right.

Once she heard his voice, she was sure she'd know what to say.

But it wasn't him who answered. It was Stephen.

'Oh, hello,' she said, thrown by this. 'It's Catherine. Please could I, er, speak to Dave? I don't mean to be rude, but I'm on a payphone and I'm not sure how long my money will last.'

'I thought you were leaving today?' Stephen replied, monotone.

'I, er . . . I'm at the airport now. That's why I'm calling. Is he there? It's important. I think I might have made a—'

'He's not here,' Stephen replied as she heard what sounded like a door shutting on the other end of the line. 'And even if he was, don't you think you've caused him enough trouble already?'

'Sorry? I—'

'David and Rose will be fine. Please don't mess them around any longer. Everything's under control here without you. You go off on your precious travels, okay? Have a nice life. Goodbye.'

He hung up, leaving her in no doubt that he did not want to hear from her again. If such a thing were to happen now, Cassie is confident she would challenge it, questioning his right to answer on behalf of his son. She'd ring back, find another way to contact him, refuse to take no for answer.

But at that time, she was a different person, too young

and taken aback to find the strength to stand up to Stephen. What he said was certainly a shock to the system. There were tears, but once they'd passed, she chose to take the phone call as a sign not to change course after all. She continued on her way to Greece, doing her utmost to leave her doubts behind.

Regrets? What would be the point? It may not have worked out well, anyway, had she stayed. Besides, if she hadn't left when she did, she wouldn't be the woman she is today. She wouldn't be Cassie. She'd almost certainly never have met and married Ed; been mother to Rory, Niall, Niamh and Shauna.

That said, did Stephen's intervention play a role in keeping her away, out of Dave and Rose's lives, for so long? His harsh words definitely came back to her at moments when she wondered how the two of them were getting on. When otherwise she might have been tempted to reach out. However, it would be dishonest to put all of that on him. It was more about the definitive nature of her exit. She was supposed to be dead, and that felt irreversible from her end, increasingly so as the years passed.

She did nearly send a letter once to test the waters. It was around the time when she formally adopted Ed's children as her own, which was no coincidence. She wrote it, put it in an envelope, addressed it and even added a stamp. But she just couldn't bring herself to send the damn thing. She ended up, somewhat dramatically, burning it in the fireplace instead.

The problem was, she knew that Dave could have contacted her at any point over the years, had he wanted or needed to. That was why she'd given him her email address and maintained it, as promised. But no email had ever arrived – and that spoke volumes. Until eventually one did, long after she'd written off the possibility, leading them to where they are today.

Cassie has no intention of ever mentioning her phone call with Stephen to Dave, Rose or Deborah. The man was long gone and, with hindsight – right or wrong – he was a parent acting in what he considered to be the best interests of his family. Also, what benefit would the knowledge be to anyone now, other than perhaps to make Cassie look a little better? With no proof, it could actually backfire, appearing to be a lie.

No, her lips will remain sealed.

CHAPTER 37

DAVE

It takes him a while to track her down, but after asking a few of the hotel staff if they've seen her, he eventually discovers Rose at a quiet spot in the grounds.

She's sitting on a long wooden bench next to a large fish pond, staring into the distance. If she's aware of him approaching, she doesn't let on, but she doesn't appear surprised when he sits down on the far end of the bench, not daring to place himself any closer. She doesn't look at him or say anything, so he takes the initiative.

'I'd ask you if you're okay,' he says, 'but it's a stupid question. Your head must be spinning. I wish I could have told you all of this myself much sooner. In fact, I wish there'd never been a need, because you'd known the truth from the start. That lie has eaten away at me for years. I almost came clean and told you more times than you can imagine, but . . . I was torn. There was the promise I made to your mother, for a start, which I never took lightly. Plus I couldn't see how it would be good for you to discover this without your, um, mother being around to explain. I was afraid it would scar you at a time when you were still forming your own sense of identity. Not that any of this justifies the lie. Of course it doesn't. I'm attempting to give you some context, that's all. I love you so very much, Rose. All I can do is apologise and hope that one day you might find it in your heart to forgive me.'

He stops talking, hoping Rose might respond.

She doesn't. She continues to look forward, eyes clouded over.

Dave desperately wants to take her hand or put his arm around her, but he knows his daughter well enough to sense that's not a good idea. He waits in silence.

Eventually, after a good few minutes of quiet, Rose says in a cold voice: 'Who else knew the truth before me?'

'Only me and Catherine – Cassie, I mean – plus your grandparents and Aunt Bridget. That's it, as far as I know.'

'Uncle Joseph?'

'Not that I'm aware of, although I suppose Bridget might have told him. They weren't together at the time. There's no way she's told your cousins, if you're worried about that. Absolutely not. It's not like any of us were talking about it behind your back either. There was an implicit agreement not to discuss it. After your mother left, it was barely ever mentioned again. Nana found it especially hard to accept. She only agreed because I insisted and gave her an ultimatum.'

'What about all of this, today? It must have taken some arranging. I had no idea you were such an accomplished liar.' She pauses then asks: 'Was Cara in on it? I just tried to call her, but her phone is turned off.'

'No, absolutely not. I wouldn't do that to you or her, Rose. I asked Cara's dad to help me out, that's all. And I didn't tell him why, other than saying it was a surprise I had planned for you ahead of the wedding.'

'A surprise?' She gives him a flinty stare.

'I had to say something, Rose.'

'It makes sense now why you never had any pictures of my supposedly dead mother to show me: a good way to keep the truth buried. So, tell me, was that a lie too, about her not liking to be photographed, and then the fire?'

Dave almost admits what he did so many years ago, deliberately burning those photos. But he can't bring himself to say the words. Not now, anyway. Not in the knowledge of the other news he's about to break to her.

'She genuinely didn't like having her photo taken, Rose,' he says instead, swerving an actual lie. 'Ask her yourself if you don't believe me.'

'Pah, like that would mean anything, with the two of you in cahoots. Have you been in touch with her the whole time – all my life?'

'No, absolutely not. It's like she said: I first contacted her around six months ago. There was no communication before that. Genuinely, I didn't even know where she was in the world. She could have settled in India or China, for all I knew.'

Dave had considered trying to contact her beforehand – many times over the years, despite the advice of his parents – his father in particular.

'She was trouble, that one,' Stephen told him repeatedly. 'You and Rose are better off without her, trust me. Don't look back. Don't give her a second thought.'

How could he not think of her, though? He regularly wondered where she was and what she was doing.

But she'd been the one to leave. And the extreme way she'd insisted on being written out of their lives was so permanent. He felt like there was no point in approaching her about coming clean to Rose, because if she'd had a change of heart, she'd have approached him already. Plus, he knew that learning the truth and uncovering all the lies in the process would be a huge mountain for his daughter to climb. It also had the potential to rock his own relationship with her to the core.

'So why the change of heart?' Rose asks. 'Why *did* you decide to contact her after so long?'

Dave presses his hands into the wood of the bench beneath him, smarting as he feels a splinter slide its way into one finger. Dammit. This is where things get tricky. Even trickier than they are already. Part of him is tempted not to give her the real reason now, after she's had to absorb so much already today, but the clock is against him. He needs to push forward with the plan, even though he knows it will lead to yet more hurt for his daughter. This is what everything's been leading to – today and all the preparation he put in beforehand to make it happen. It's the right thing to do in the long run, he's convinced of that. Being a parent sometimes means making tough decisions for the good of your child. They still hurt, though.

He feels every bit of pain that Rose experiences,

physical and mental, as if it's his own. It's always been that way, ever since she was tiny. Like the time she climbed on a chair when he was in the shower, fell and cut her chin open. He'll never forget the sheer panic and terror he felt. He can still hear her shriek of agony, picture all that blood. It was the first time that his precious Rose had been under real threat and vulnerable. He felt awful, berating himself for his poor parenting skills. It was a nightmare, but – somehow – he held himself together, did what had to be done and got them both safely through the episode in one piece.

Now he has to do the same again.

'You're an adult, Rose. You're about to embark on a life of your own, away from me and your childhood home. One of the key concerns your mother and I—'

'Do you have to keep calling her that?' Rose snaps. 'She might technically be my mother, assuming you're telling me the truth this time, but she lost the right to be called that when she ditched me as a baby.'

'Noted.' Dave clears his throat before continuing. 'We feared you could be damaged by having to grow up feeling abandoned by one of your birth parents. That it could get into your psyche while your personality and mindset were still forming. Now you're a strong, inde-pendent woman, more than capable of handling whatever life throws at you, I thought it was only right that you know.'

He stops to catch his breath. He can feel it running away from him and he forces himself to take a few seconds to steady the ship.

Rose continues to look straight ahead in stony silence, her face locked into a scowl.

'Now you're an adult,' he continues, 'I worry that growing up thinking your mother was dead might have affected you in ways we didn't foresee.'

She tuts. 'Like what?'

'I suspect, subconsciously, it made you crave the normality of a more traditional family – two parents, two or three kids – something along those lines. What I've never been able to give you. I wish I could have done. I wish I could have met someone I loved enough to want to invite them into our family, but you can't force these things. It wasn't only my desire to write fiction that left me when your . . . I mean, when Cassie left. My focus moved to more important things.'

'You mean me?'

'Yes.'

'And let me guess: you're about to tell me I shouldn't rush into getting married. That I'm too young and I still have my whole life ahead of me. Please, change the bloody record. I know you don't like Ryan, but I love him. I thought you'd accepted this now. Don't you think a week before our wedding is a bit late for such discussions?

'Meeting Cassie changes nothing, Dad. Do I want to settle down and have a family of my own? Too right I do. But why would knowing she's not dead change that? If anything, it makes me glad to be moving out and starting my own life, away from you and your lies. You say this whole charade today was about me. I think it was about you; you're afraid of being alone, so you're trying to stop me leaving. Are you hoping to get back together with Cassie too? Good luck with that. She moved on long ago, Dad, like you should have done.'

Dave takes a deep breath. He refuses to rise to or even consider the veracity of any of her jibes. She's lashing out, understandably, and he needs to get to the point.

'I have to tell you something about Ryan. You're not going to want to hear it, but you must.'

'Dad, you don't—'

'No, Rose, please don't interrupt me. This is too important. It can't wait any longer. Ryan's been cheating on you again. And not just once. It's happened a few times, including—'

'Stop, Dad. Just stop, for God's sake. We've been through this. Why won't you get the message? You're being pathetic, desperate. Don't you think I'd know if Ryan was cheating on me? As I've told you again and again, he made one huge mistake, ages ago, which he massively regrets. I forgave him. Why the hell can't you? I'd never have got back together with him if there was a chance he'd do it again. He wouldn't. He loves me too much. That's why I'm marrying him.'

Dave waits for her to stop, before continuing, as calmly as he can, like she hasn't interrupted him: '. . . including on his stag do in Brighton, when I understand a different woman stayed in his room with him on each of the two nights he was away.'

He gulps, hating the taste of those words in his mouth. But what choice does he have? He has to shock her out of her denial before it's too late.

336

She stares at the pond, stony-faced. 'I don't believe you. Haven't you lied enough to me already?'

Dave slides his phone out of his pocket, unlocks it and, with a heavy heart, selects the message he drafted earlier and presses send.

'I've sent you an email,' he says. 'There are photos attached, which you should look at. You might not believe this, feeling as you do about me now, but I truly wish I didn't have to tell you any of this. I'm not Ryan's biggest fan, but that doesn't mean I wanted to be proved right about him. Your happiness is far more important to me than my pride. But facts are facts. I've had my suspicions for a while, initially based on nothing more than fatherly intuition, which I put to one side for your sake. Then I started hearing occasional whispers, rumours about him.'

'What are you talking about?' Rose snipes. 'This is ridiculous.'

'I've lived around here a long time. I know a lot of people in the area and folk love to gossip.'

'Why are you doing this to me, Dad? It's cruel. Don't you think today's been hard enough already?'

She's still not looking at him, but he can see that her face is red; tears are streaming down her cheeks. He desperately wants to hold her, to console her, but that's not happening. For now at least, he's the enemy.

Stick with the plan, hold your nerve, he tells himself. You're doing what's best, as hard as it might be.

'Please look at the email, Rose. The photos speak for themselves, unfortunately.'

'What if I say no? What if I don't want to read your stupid email and I delete it without looking?'

'You need to look at it, Rose.' He stops talking and waits. His mind fills the gap by zipping him back to the memory of a meeting at the house, when Rose wasn't around, a couple of weeks earlier.

'Hello, come in,' he said after answering the doorbell to the man he'd only met in person once before. His name was Winston Jones, a tubby chap in his mid-forties, average height with short mousy brown hair.

Dressed in dark jeans, a grey polo shirt and a navy anorak, he was the kind of person you barely noticed. Even the way he spoke, with a neutral accent you'd struggle to place, was unremarkable, all of which presumably made him good at his job as a private investigator.

Dave had hired the former policeman as a last resort. He knew it wasn't exactly a normal thing to do, to pay someone to snoop on your daughter's fiancé. But he had to know once and for all whether his suspicions, fuelled by the rumours he'd heard from a couple of business contacts, were true.

'I'm told he's been playing around, getting over-friendly with some of his female clients,' he'd explained to Mr Jones during their first face-to-face meeting, at the investigator's office, above a takeaway in Whitefield, north of Manchester. 'It could be tittle-tattle – you know what gossips people can be – but he has cheated before. I want to find out for sure before he becomes an official part of my family.'

Mr Jones had returned with sufficient initial evidence to validate Dave's fears and to convince him of the need for the surveillance to continue, at considerable cost, when Ryan and his mates headed down to Brighton for the stag do.

'Can I get you a drink?' Dave asked his guest after showing him into the lounge.

'No, thank you.'

Mr Jones pulled a laptop out of his canvas bag and they got down to business: a final presentation of his findings, ahead of Dave settling the bill.

Dave's heart sank in empathy for Rose as he finally viewed the surveillance photos. He'd already been primed with details of their contents, but actually seeing them was far worse. There was no sense of 'I told you so'. He felt sick to his stomach, already worrying about how to break the news to his daughter.

'As you can see,' Mr Jones concluded. 'You were right to be concerned. Ryan Thorne is a love rat, plain and simple. I wouldn't want him within five miles of my daughter. He's bad news.' Handing Dave a USB stick containing all the evidence, he added: 'I hope that's sufficient for your requirements. You know where I am if you need anything else.'

Dave's heart is pounding when Rose finally takes her phone out to look at his email. He's only included three of the many photos he was supplied with, but they're arguably the most damning.

One picture shows Ryan entering his Brighton hotel

room at night with his hand groping the backside of a drunken young woman, who's hanging all over him in a skimpy black dress. Another depicts him brazenly kissing a different woman as he shows her out of the same bedroom in daylight, dressed only in his boxers. The third shows him in the front seat of his work van, parked in a quiet rural spot, while someone with black curly hair – most definitely not Rose – appears to be giving him oral sex.

Goodness knows how Mr Jones got in so close on these shots. Dave doesn't regret a single penny of what it cost to hire him. It's horrible evidence for Rose to have to see, but it's also exactly the kind of proof that's needed to change her mind about her fiancé at this very late stage in the run-up to their wedding.

Dave would have preferred to present it earlier. He tried to bring up the rumours with Rose on various occasions prior to gaining this hard evidence, but his appeals repeatedly fell on deaf ears. She always shut him down before he could get to the point, claiming he was unfairly biased against Ryan.

'Why do you keep scrabbling in the dirt for ways to try to break us up?' she said in one especially hard-to-stomach rant. 'I'm not interested. He's not the boy who once broke my heart. He's changed, whether you see that or not, and soon he'll be my husband. Don't make me choose between the two of you.'

So Dave did what he had to, pretending to drop the matter and biting his tongue, while secretly approaching Mr Jones.

However, by the time he finally had the necessary proof in his hands, the wedding was drawing close and the wheels were already in motion for today's meeting with Cassie: so far the only other person with whom he's discussed the investigation and its findings.

Hearing Rose's first gasp as she looks at her phone – the awful photos *he* sent her – Dave winces. It's a sound as uncomfortable to his ears as fingernails on a blackboard and she does so twice more, each new exclamation packed with more shock and disgust than the last. She slams her phone down next to her on the arm of the long wooden bench. She does nothing other than breathe heavily, until she turns to shoot daggers in his direction, eyes like slits.

'Where did you get these? How long have you had them for?'

'I, um, hired someone. A private investigator—'

'What? How could you? Who are you? So much deception. I barely recognise you any more.'

'I'm sorry. I know how it sounds, but I had to, Rose. I needed to get to the bottom of what was going on. I couldn't stand back and let him make a fool of you all over again.'

'Is that what you think I am, Dad: a fool?'

'Of course not. How could I think that of you? I love you more than anything, more than anyone. I'm trying to protect you. As you can see from the photos, my suspicions were not unfounded. Far from it. Ryan's been—'

'How do you even know these photos are real?' she snaps robotically, as Dave realises she still hasn't accepted the truth about her fiancé. 'They look fake to me.'

'Trust me, they're not,' he says.

'Trust you? Seriously? After everything I've just discovered? For all I know, you're the one who doctored the images.'

To Dave's surprise, she starts laughing. What begins as a giggle soon mutates into a head-thrown-back maniacal cackle, which he finds unnerving and alarming.

'Are you okay, Rose?' he asks, terrified that he's dealt with all of this totally wrong.

She turns to him with her eyes stretched wide and a wild grin carved across her face. 'Yes, I'm absolutely fine, Dad. Tickety-boo. Flipping fantastic. Oh, other than the tiny fact that my whole life has turned to bloody shit. But hey, you have to keep smiling, right? Hahaha! Hahaha!'

'Rose,' he says, struggling to stay calm. 'I think you need to—'

'No, I don't want to know what you think,' she says, springing to her feet and, before he can stop her, tossing her mobile into the middle of the pond.

'Rose!' he cries out. 'What the hell? Why did you do that?'

'Out of sight, out of mind.' She turns her back on him and walks towards the hotel. 'Don't you dare try and follow me,' she adds, her voice now stone-cold. 'And don't have me followed either by your creepy stalker. I want to be alone. Got it?'

'I'm here for you, Rose, whenever you want,' he says, grimacing.

He listens to the fading sound of her footsteps on the gravel path as she disappears into the distance.

CHAPTER 38

ROSE – ONE WEEK LATER

Rose wakes to the smell of coffee. She opens her eyes and blinks until her vision is clear, relishing the warm beams of sunshine that burst through every tiny gap they can find in the thin curtains.

'Morning, sleepyhead,' Cara's voice calls through the open door of their en suite bathroom. 'And what a lovely sunny Saturday morning it is. There's a fresh cup of coffee on your bedside table. I made it from one of those posh pad things.'

'So I see,' Rose says, her voice still husky from the night before. 'Thank you.'

'You're welcome.' Cara sounds chirpy, like she's already been awake for hours.

'How long have you been up?'

'Oh, not too long. Twenty minutes?'

Rose picks up her mobile: a replacement, courtesy of

Cara, for the one she threw into the pond last weekend, never to be seen again. It's 8.47 a.m. 'Checkout's at eleven, right?'

'Yep,' her friend replies. 'Plenty of time. How are you feeling? Big day today.'

As soon as Cara has said this, she sticks her head out of the bathroom door, toothbrush in one hand, toothpaste in the corner of her mouth, and pulls a face at Rose. 'Sorry! Bad choice of words. I didn't think, as usual.'

'Don't apologise. It's fine. Today was supposed to be my wedding day. There, I've said it. No need to avoid it now. And yeah, it's still a big day for me – just not the kind I was originally expecting. I'm feeling okay, I guess. Considering.'

Cara appears again. 'I've said it before, but I think you're amazing, Rose. It's incredible how well you're handling everything that's been thrown at you. I'd be a mess in your shoes. Crying and screaming. Probably smashing things up. I'd be all over the place. You seem so together.'

She should have seen me alone last Saturday night, Rose thinks. Her mind jumps back to that moment, in another hotel room, soon after she'd looked at those damn photos of Ryan, tossed her phone and told her dad to give her some space.

She just about held it together until Hornby Lodge room service had delivered the first bottle of white wine. However, by the time the second arrived, less than an hour later, she must have looked awful. The young chap at the door asked her if everything was all right.

'Not really,' she replied. 'There's been a death in the family.'

'Oh, I'm very sorry to hear that.' He shuffled awkwardly on the spot. 'If there's anything else we can get for you, please let us know.'

'I will.' She shut the door in his face.

Why had she told him that lie?

Why not? She'd been lied to plenty. She wanted to see what it felt like to tell a big fib of her own. Also, it got rid of him without any awkward questions. Death was rarely a topic people wanted to stay and discuss. Plus, who would begrudge a second bottle of wine to someone in the throes of grief, even if they looked like they'd already had enough?

She looked at her reflection in the bathroom mirror as she poured herself yet another large glass and immediately started to gulp it down.

No wonder he'd asked if she was okay. She looked awful: blotchy red skin, panda eyes and hair like a bird's nest, still wearing the outfit she'd gone to dinner in, but with her white bathrobe on top, because it felt soft and comforting.

Soon afterwards, the landline rang. Well, it felt soon, but she was rather drunk by that point, so impossible to know for sure.

It was her father. 'Sorry to bother you, Rose. I had to check on you. I'd have texted instead, but I know you don't have your mobile.'

'I'm fine. Leave me alone.' She hung up, then called down to reception and, doing her utmost to sound sober, asked them to hold any further calls.

She nearly phoned Ryan countless times. She knew his mobile number by heart and dialled it again and again, only to hang up at the last minute, before it connected. She couldn't bring herself to confront him yet. To make what she'd witnessed real.

She cried a lot that night. What felt like floods and floods of sorry-for-herself tears came out as she lay on the bed, wailing and moaning, thumping the pillows, wondering what on earth to do with her life in light of everything she'd learned. Eventually, she started feeling queasy. Soon she was running to the en suite and being sick in the bath, knocking her half-full wine bottle over in the process, thus curtailing her drinking for the night.

Her sobbing continued as she unsteadily undressed, having a shower to wash the foul-smelling mess away from herself and the bath.

Crying some more, she used two rolls of toilet paper to mop up the wine on the bedroom carpet.

And still she wept as she got into bed and drifted off into a fitful sleep full of nightmares almost as scary as the truth.

'Would you like me to come with you when you meet your, um, you know, parents?' Cara asks at breakfast. 'Sorry, is it okay for me to use that word?'

'It's fine – and kind of you to offer,' Rose replies. 'But no, thanks. I need to do it alone. Besides, you've done enough for me, bringing me here and listening to my incessant moans for the past few days. You have your own life to get back to.'

'Feel free to change your mind,' Cara says. 'I'd be happy to hold your hand. And I've loved being here with you, despite the difficult circumstances.'

Rose reaches across the table and squeezes her best friend's cool hand. 'What would I do without you?'

They smile at each other and Rose feels weepy for the umpteenth time these past few days. She gulps, takes a few slow, deep breaths and blinks back the tears. 'Thanks for everything,' she manages, a catch in her voice.

'Of course. That's exactly what friends are for, right?'

Rose nods and battles another wave of emotion.

They're downstairs in the small dining room of the isolated guest house. By chance, and somewhat ironically, it's a modernised former vicarage, just like the family home she's run away from. They've been here since Monday. It's in the Lake District, not far from Buttermere, pretty much in the middle of nowhere, surrounded by gorgeous green pasture land and dramatic Lakeland fells. Cara miraculously managed to find it, thanks to a late cancellation, and made a last-minute booking for the two of them to escape, as per Rose's request.

It's turned out to be a real delight, run by an attentive but easy-going husband and wife team called Bob and Suzie, who keep the place immaculate inside and out and serve the most wonderful breakfasts, from full Cumbrian to eggs Benedict, or scrambled eggs and smoked salmon. It's all free range, locally produced fare, alongside home-made preserves and honey from their own beehives. Rose has struggled with her appetite after everything she's been through, but Bob and Suzie have successfully managed to tempt her with something delicious most mornings. If either of them has noticed how up and down Rose has been emotionally during the visit, they've certainly not let on or asked anything intrusive, for which she's grateful.

She turned up on Cara's doorstep last Sunday afternoon, fresh from confronting Ryan, hungover and broken, and begged to stay with her and her parents for the night, not wanting to face her own father. Later, after bringing her friend up to date about what had happened, in between sobbing sessions, she said: 'I need to get out of here, as soon as possible. Will you come away with me for a few days, preferably somewhere quiet, where I can take shelter, lick my wounds and regroup?'

'Yes, it's the least I can do after leaving you like I did yesterday. Honestly, Rose, I had no idea what was coming. Obviously I knew something was going on after Dad told me there wasn't really a family emergency. He made me swear not to let on, so I didn't dare speak to you. Dave had told him he was arranging a surprise, which I was afraid of ruining. It sounded like something nice. How was I to know otherwise?'

'You weren't,' Rose said. 'Which is why I don't blame you at all, and why I'm hiding out here.'

Cara screwed up her face, adding: 'Cards on the table. I'm sure my parents will have tipped off your dad that you're here. But I've told them, in no uncertain terms, not to let him in to see you. Unless, of course, that's what you want.'

'No. I don't want to see anyone, apart from you.' She felt short of breath. 'And definitely not Ryan. If he shows up here, I don't know what I'll—'

Cara pulled her into a warm hug. 'He's not getting anywhere near you – not as long as I have anything to do with it.'

Back in the present, the full Cumbrian breakfast they've both opted for today arrives at the table courtesy of a smiling, moustachioed Bob. 'Here we are, my glorious guests,' he says with a theatrical flourish. 'Any extra condiments I can get for you on this final morning of yours?'

'Not for me, thanks,' Rose replies, while Cara requests some brown sauce, which he duly fetches.

'We'll be sorry to lose you,' Bob adds. 'It's been a particular pleasure to have you both stay with us. If you ever fancy a return to this green and pleasant land, you'll be most welcome.'

Cara beams at him. 'Thank you very much. We've had a lovely stay. We certainly fell on our feet finding you at the last minute. Thank goodness for whoever it was that cancelled.'

Bob chuckles. 'I was cursing them last Sunday morning, I must admit. But yes, all's well that ends well. I'll get out of your hair now before Suzie has my guts for garters. Enjoy your food.'

'So how are you feeling about everything today?' Cara asks Rose as they're both tucking into their sumptuous spread.

'A bit nervous, I guess, about seeing Dad and, um, Cassie later.' She hasn't seen or spoken to either since last Saturday night, communicating only with her father via an occasional text, which was how they arranged their meet-up, at a restaurant close to home at six o'clock this evening.

Nana will be there too, since she's flown back to the UK, regardless of the fact the wedding has been cancelled. Will that make the meeting easier or harder? Difficult to say, considering they haven't spoken about any of this yet. Rose has had several missed calls from her this week, but she's not been answering her phone to anyone, using the poor mobile reception up here as a convenient excuse.

Apparently, Nana didn't know that Dave was back in contact with Cassie or about Ryan's cheating. She was in on the whole dead mother deception from the start, of course, but only very reluctantly, it seems.

Rose isn't really angry with her. What would she gain from falling out with Nana now? Besides, Ryan's cheating has overshadowed everything else.

There have also been some missed calls from him, which isn't particularly surprising, considering they were supposed to get married today. She doesn't know what more there is for them to say to each other. It's done and dusted as far as she's concerned. And yes, she most definitely is angry at Ryan. How could she not be? Especially after she forgave him for cheating on her that first time, believing his promises, only for them to prove fake and meaningless. She really believed he'd changed; that he was a man worth dedicating the rest of her life to. He won't be getting any more opportunities to make a fool of her. What a prize idiot she must look to all those people who were supposed to be attending her wedding today. How will she ever face them? She knows she'll have to – it's one of the many things she and Cara have discussed on their short trip away – but that doesn't mean she's looking forward to it.

'Tell them the truth,' is Cara's advice. 'Say you discovered he was a lying cheat in the nick of time and pulled the plug.'

Thank goodness she's at least been spared the job of contacting everyone – guests, caterers, photographer, florists and the numerous other people involved – to inform them that the wedding is off.

Her dad texted: *Leave that all to me. Don't give it a second thought.* But of course she has. How could she not after living and breathing this wedding for so long?

She keeps panicking that he might have forgotten someone; wondering whether he's had any help, particularly with regards to contacting the invitees from Ryan's side. She hopes this job has fallen to her former fiancé himself, who she doubts very much Dave will have let off the hook. Cara has relayed a couple of questions along the way, but otherwise Rose has escaped all involvement. And when she has been tempted to query something, Cara has talked her down with an assurance that it's all under control.

'What did your dad say?'

'Not to give it a second thought.'

'There you go. Just forget about it.'

'It's hard, Cara. I keep thinking about all the financial implications. None of this will be covered by the wedding insurance.'

'Your dad and Ryan's parents were paying for most of it, right?'

'Yes, but still. I feel awful.'

'If anyone should be feeling bad, it's Ryan, not you. Let

go of it all, that's my advice. Worrying won't change a thing.'

In the car on the way back home, Cara drifts off to sleep in the passenger seat and Rose's mind drifts back to the moment she confronted Ryan.

CHAPTER 39

LAST SUNDAY

Rose pulled up outside Ryan's flat in Clitheroe at 1.32 p.m. She still felt rough from the night before, but her headache had at least been muffled by paracetamol and now the adrenaline running through her veins in anticipation of the confrontation to come.

She'd barely been able to think of anything else – not even the shock reappearance of her dead mother – since her dad had sent her those pictures last night. Those awful, heartbreaking, stomach-churning photos depicting a man she barely recognised as Ryan, trampling all over her hopes and dreams. And for what? Mindless sex.

The fact each photograph showed him with a different woman too! How could he do that to her, behind her back like a scumbag – a cowardly, horny little weasel? What did they give him that she couldn't? Was it the danger, the threat of getting caught, that got him off?

How was this even the same person who'd begged and pleaded with her for forgiveness, sworn never to stray again, and then gone to all that effort to propose to her in such a public, romantic, extravagant fashion?

It was definitely the same person who'd quietly slid a knife into her back while she was at uni. So why had he chased her, gone to all the effort of winning her back, only to cheat on her again, goodness knows how many times?

And that didn't even address the fact that he'd put her at risk of catching all kinds of horrible STIs. How could he do that to someone he genuinely loved and was about to marry?

She felt physically sick every time she recalled those images her father had sent her. She'd hoped to rid herself of them by ditching her phone, but it was too late: they'd already seared themselves into her memory.

When she'd seen the first picture – before that, even, if she was honest – she'd known in her heart it was true what her dad was telling her. The stuff she'd said to him about the photos looking fake was pure desperation, clutching at straws.

She'd had her suspicions before. Nothing serious. Only inklings, really, like Ryan being overly protective of his mobile, or not wanting to get close to her until he'd showered, saying he stank from sweating at work. She'd talked herself out of worrying about these things, writing them off as paranoia rather than intuition, which she now regretted. She should have listened to her father, who she'd rebuffed whenever he'd tried to warn her.

As she approached the entrance of Ryan's flat, it occurred to her that he might be in there with someone now – some floozy from the night before. He had said he was going out in town with some of his friends yesterday, and he wasn't expecting her, so it was definitely possible. Pulse racing at the thought of catching him in flagrante, she stood before his front door, steadying her nerves and building herself up to going inside.

Rose considered whether to ring the bell or to use her key. She opted for the latter – even though it scared her what she might see as a result.

As she gingerly slid the slice of metal into the lock, turned it and pushed, she closed her eyes for an instant, before snapping them open. She saw Ryan sprawled on the sofa in the lounge at the end of the short hallway, wearing boxers and a T-shirt.

'Oh, hello,' he said casually, unfazed. 'I wondered if you might call in this afternoon. How was yesterday? Nice and relaxing, I hope.'

'Hi,' she replied, raising her right hand in greeting, thrown by the prosaic scene before her.

What if none of it was true after all?

What if those photos really were fakes? Her dad didn't like Ryan – and he had already proved himself more than capable of lying to her.

The thoughts crossed her mind, to her shame, but her gut was having none of it. Not any more. Stop burying your head in the sand, it said to her. You know the truth. Now make him admit it.

'Yesterday was interesting,' she said, slowly walking

towards him. 'Not what I expected at all, but very illuminating.'

'Hang on,' Ryan said, looking away from her and towards the TV. 'Let me pause this.'

He was on his Xbox, playing some game involving zombies.

Rose stepped into the lounge, looking across to the open kitchen, still half-expecting to see a scantily clad stranger climbing out of the window. But unless he had someone hiding out in the bedroom or bathroom, which his relaxed demeanour suggested he did not, he was alone. Rather than joining him on the sofa, as she usually would, she sat down on the adjacent armchair, having first lifted an empty takeaway pizza box out of the way.

She met Ryan's gaze.

'No kiss?' he said, eyes narrowing as he finally appeared to sense that all was not well.

She shook her head. 'I need to talk to you about something, Ryan. Something serious.'

His Adam's apple jerked as he gulped, but still he kept his cool. Like a serial cheater, used to not getting caught, would do.

'I know what you've been up to,' she said in a low, steady voice, suddenly enveloped by a shield of calm detachment she'd not been expecting.

'Sorry, what do you mean?' Ryan replied.

'Either you tell me or I'll tell you.'

'W-what are you talking about, Rose? Is this some kind of wind-up? Because it's not funny. You're scaring me.'

'Poor little lamb,' she replied, an ice queen. 'Last chance. Confess. It's over anyway.'

'What's over? Rose, seriously, please stop this. It's creepy. I've got a hangover. I can't deal—'

'Fine, I'll tell you, then. You've been cheating on me, Ryan. Numerous times, with numerous women. On your stag do, in your work van . . . Do I need to continue?'

'What? Where's this coming from? I, um—'

'Don't try to deny it. I've seen hard proof. Turns out Dad was right about you all along. More fool me for falling for your bullshit again after you cheated the first time.'

Putting on a whiny, singsong voice to impersonate him, she continued: '"I'll never do it again, I promise." That's what you told me, right? "I love you so much, Rose. Please forgive me." What a load of old crap that was, Ryan. At least have the balls to admit it now you've been caught. Either way, the wedding is off. We're over once and for all. On my life, you'll never get another chance.'

Finally sensing he was beaten, out came the apologies and excuses.

'I'm so sorry. It was just sex – meaningless sex. Nothing like what we have. I don't know why I did it. I have these urges. I couldn't stop myself. I . . . I . . . please, Rose. I do love you. I was planning to stop once we were married. Honestly, I—'

'You just said you couldn't stop. And what on earth does honesty have to do with anything? You disgust me. You put *my* health at risk. You could have passed any number of nasty infections on to *me*. Maybe you have. Some STIs appear symptomless while having lifelong effects, like infertility. Didn't consider that, did you? And you know damn well how much I want to have children. I thought that was important to you too, but you're nowhere near ready to be a parent. You'd be an awful father. You're too much of a child yourself – and a bloody selfish one at that. I'll have to get myself checked out now, Ryan. Thanks so much. To think I nearly married you! You're repulsive.'

'No!' Ryan said, dazed, shrivelling back into the corner of the couch, a horrified look etched into his gurning features. 'I was careful. I, um . . . got myself checked out when I needed to. Several times.'

'Wow. What a gentleman. So you've got a season ticket at the GUM clinic, have you? Would you like a round of applause?'

'Seriously, Rose. I stayed away if I thought there was any, er, risk. I'd never do that to you. I care too much about you.'

'You what? Am I supposed to be thankful for that? Don't make me laugh and don't waste your breath, you deceitful prick.' Rose got to her feet, slid her engagement ring off her finger and hurled it at him with all of her might, hitting him on the forehead so he yelped in pain, hopefully causing a nasty bruise.

'Goodbye, Ryan,' she said, striding out of the room, heading for the front door. 'And good riddance.'

He called after her, spouting more meaningless words, but she'd already tuned out by that point. Thankfully, he was too busy nursing his head and looking for the ring to try to follow her.

She kept her composure all the way to the car, getting

in and driving it around the corner before pulling into a layby and finally letting herself go.

She sobbed her heart out once again, her whole body shaking uncontrollably.

It had been dreadful, having to face him like that, but at least she'd done it now and in a way that let her keep her dignity, not allowing him to see how much he'd truly hurt her. One thing she knew for sure: Ryan Thorne would never get the opportunity to shatter her heart again.

Eventually, she managed to pull herself back together enough to make her way to Cara's house.

CHAPTER 40

DAVE

His heart skips a beat when Rose finally walks into the restaurant at 6.15 p.m. It's been so incredibly hard not being able to see or talk to her this week. The fact she's here now is a huge relief.

He hasn't had any direct contact with her, other than the odd text, since she stormed off last Saturday night, leaving him alone by the pond. He did briefly consider trying to fish her mobile out for her, but it was quite a large pond and he'd have had to wade right into the water. The chances of him finding it would have been minuscule.

Luckily, Cara was able to furnish her with a spare. It was from this that she messaged Dave to say she'd called off the wedding, which was music to his ears. He offered to relieve Rose of the responsibility of cancelling everything. It was a big job, but he had plenty of assistance from Cassie, who was still in the area, as well as his mother, remotely while she was in Spain and in person once she flew in on Thursday.

Deborah was initially angry that he hadn't involved her in his decision to contact Cassie or the subsequent process of Rose learning the truth. Thankfully, she accepted his explanation that he'd deliberately kept her out of it to avoid harming her relationship with her granddaughter. She soon turned her fury on lying, cheating Ryan, relieved that Rose was no longer marrying him, while welcoming the fact that her granddaughter finally knew the truth about her mother. She was pretty cold with Cassie when they met but at least kept things civil.

As for cancelling the wedding arrangements, Dave made sure Ryan and his parents did their part too.

'Have you heard?' he asked Kelly after phoning her on Monday morning.

'Yes.' Her voice wavered with emotion. 'Oh, Dave, what a mess. Ryan's been here since last night. He's in bits, although from what he's told me, he only has himself to blame. He's my son – I'll love him whatever – but he makes it bloody difficult sometimes. I feel like I should apologise for him. I honestly didn't bring him up to behave that way. How's poor Rose?'

'Oh, you know,' Dave fudged, not having an accurate answer. 'As well as can be expected. I think she's hoping to get away for a few days to clear her head.'

'Tell her that Jeremy and I still love her to bits and we don't blame her whatsoever for calling it off. I'd have done exactly the same in her position. Ryan's an idiot – I've told him so myself. He doesn't deserve her.'

Dave obviously agreed, but he bit his tongue, seeing as how gracious Kelly was being. Instead, he moved the conversation on to the practicalities of what needed doing cancellation-wise.

In the present, at the restaurant, he gets to his feet and waves at Rose, who's talking to the man on reception.

She looks pale and drawn, he thinks, as she walks over. He's not sure how to play it in terms of greeting her, so he lets her take the lead. She gives him a brief peck on the cheek, which is better than he was expecting, although notably more formal than their usual tight squeeze. Next, she turns to her nana. Deborah jumps up out of her seat and takes the initiative, pulling her granddaughter into a bear hug and kissing her multiple times. 'How are you, my love? You poor, poor thing – everything you've had to go through. Not to worry. Nana's here now. We'll get past all this, I promise.'

All three of them have tears in their eyes when they sit down together at the table, Rose and Deborah on one side, with Dave opposite.

A puzzled look appears on Rose's gaunt face. 'Is, um, Cassie not here yet?'

Dave and his mother share a look before he answers. 'It's just going to be the three of us, I'm afraid. She really wanted to be here, having stayed in the area all week with the intention of seeing you again, but there was a family emergency in Ireland and she unexpectedly had to fly back this afternoon.'

'Really?' Rose sneers. 'A family emergency like the one Cara got called away for last Saturday?'

Dave tells her about the accident Cassie's husband had several months ago, explaining that was why she hadn't been able to come sooner. And then he adds: 'He was making a really good recovery, which was why she was able to come now, but apparently last night he had another fall. Lost his footing on the stairs. Now he's in hospital again.'

'That's awful,' a shocked Rose replies. 'Poor Ed. Is he going to be all right?'

'I really don't know, I'm afraid. Let's hope so. The thing is, she really did want to see you again, love, to answer any questions you might have, if nothing else. But she had to go back, of course. She's promised to contact you very soon. And she told me she'd love to hear from you, on your terms, if that's what you want.'

'I understand,' Rose says, blushing.

When Dave first reached out to Cassie, he was surprised to learn that she was married with four children. He hadn't expected that. Married, maybe. But a mother? No, that threw him, considering her former determination not to be a parent. He felt a brief burst of resentment, although he reminded himself that a lot could change in two decades and he had no right to judge her. Discovering her children were adopted was another shock. Initially this made her change of heart about being a mum easier to accept. However, on reflection, it felt worse, as he wondered how she could bring up another woman's children when she'd walked away from her own baby.

He didn't tell her any of these thoughts, though, even

when she asked for time to consider her position regarding her birth daughter. He kept his feelings to himself and, thankfully, after she agreed to get on board with his plan to tell Rose the truth, Dave was able to move past them. He accepted that the troubled soul he'd once known as Catherine had found happiness and peace of mind – and that was a good thing, not only for her, but also potentially for Rose. It opened up a door that had long been locked shut.

As for the strong romantic connection they'd once had, Dave respected the fact Cassie was married and clearly very much in love with Ed. Did he still find her attractive when they met again in person after so long? Yes, definitely, but he put that and their passionate past firmly to one side, for everyone's sake, focusing his attention on their daughter. Besides, their love story had ended long ago: they'd been more friends than anything else by the time Rose had been born.

They saw a lot of each other while Rose was up in the Lakes, and, honestly, it felt like catching up with an old pal.

In between worrying and cancelling wedding arrangements, Dave has found the odd moment in recent days to consider what Rose said to him last Saturday night. She accused him of wanting to get back together with Cassie and not having moved on, as he ought to have done.

Did her words, spoken in anger, contain any truth?

Absolutely not, he thought initially.

A week on, he's starting to wonder.

When he first contacted Cassie, he certainly wasn't

expecting a romantic reunion. It was never about that. It was all about Rose. And yet what if a subconscious part of him hasn't ever truly moved on from her? It could go some way towards explaining why he hasn't found, or even really looked for, someone new. Why he's been so picky. There's been the odd dalliance over the years, which he's kept well hidden from Rose, but nothing even approaching an actual relationship.

Maybe that should change. Perhaps it's finally time to put himself back out there.

First things first. Rose remains his immediate priority. She's going to need lots of support moving on with her life. To help provide that, he needs to heal the rift between them and, hopefully, win back her trust.

Rose visibly relaxes once she knows Cassie isn't joining them in the restaurant. On arrival, her body language – darting eyes, twitches, rigid posture – suggested she was incredibly tense. Now, in the familiar presence of only him and Deborah, she seems better able to unwind. Not totally, which is hardly surprising in the circumstances, but there's a significant shift in mood. It reminds Dave of when someone changes out of formal wear into joggers and a sweatshirt.

'I'm really glad to see you, Dimples,' he says, daring to use his pet name for her, testing the waters.

He's rewarded with a flash of a smile followed by a brief knotting of her brow that feels playful rather than a genuine frown. This signal that their relationship might weather the storm comes as such an immense relief to him that he feels himself starting to tear up. He has to divert his thoughts to more practical matters to avoid breaking down.

'What would you like to drink?' he asks his daughter. 'Nana and I are both on white wine, but you have whatever you want.'

Later, once they've ordered food, Dave decides to address the elephant in the room.

'Listen, Rose,' he says. 'To put it out there: your nana and I are happy to discuss anything you want to regarding Ryan, Cassie and so on. Whenever you want. But there's no pressure at all. We can take things at whatever pace you like.'

'Absolutely,' Deborah chimes in. 'We appreciate what an awful lot it is to take in and that you must have considerable anger and frustration to process, not least towards the pair of us. But we're so glad you're here now. Let's keep communicating so we can find a way to repair what's broken and move forward together. Your father and I are totally committed to that and to you. As long as it takes, love. We both adore you.'

Rose doesn't reply to either of them for what feels like forever. Instead, she stares blankly at the table before her, seemingly thinking. There's a long gap before she says: 'Can we not talk about any of it today? Can we just have a meal and chat about other stuff, as trivial as possible; pretend things are normal?'

'Of course,' a relieved Dave and Deborah reply in sync, looking at each other and smiling.

There are some things that will need discussing very

soon, however, Dave thinks, such as what they're going to do about the honeymoon. He and Deborah were chatting about it before Rose arrived. They think it might be possible to change Ryan's name on the tickets, for a fee. Maybe Rose could go with Cara instead, or someone else, if she prefers, assuming she still actually wants to go. He shelves the topic until tomorrow. There are still a few days to go.

'How was the weather up in the Lakes?' he asks instead, adhering to Rose's wishes.

'Not great. Typically British: drizzly and overcast. We had some lovely walks, though. Plus the guest house was brilliant. The breakfasts were to die for.'

Later, as they're all finishing the remnants of their main courses, Deborah winks at him before placing a hand on Rose's wrist and saying: 'You'll never guess what your father told me earlier.'

'What?' Rose asks, turning to him. 'Go on, tell me.'

He's a little embarrassed to say, partly wishing he'd not told his mother now, but he does so anyway. 'It's no big deal, but I got the urge to start writing again. I've barely made any headway yet and please don't ask me to tell you anything about it, because it's far too early in the process. But I have, er, started working on a new book.'

'Seriously?' she asks, a flash of her old self shining through as her tired eyes unexpectedly light up. 'Where on earth did that come from? After all these years.'

'Who knows? The desire, the inspiration if you like, it . . . just returned this week, out of nowhere. I got this idea in my head and, next thing I was rattling away on my computer into the early hours. It might yet fade away before I get anywhere with it. But yeah, for now at least, I'm writing again and it feels good.'

It's not until the meal is over and the three of them are walking to the car park that Dave dares to ask Rose where she's staying tonight.

'I'm going back to Cara's,' she says. 'For now.'

He does his utmost to hide his disappointment. 'Sure. No problem. I understand.'

Rose narrows her eyes. 'I could be persuaded to come over for brunch tomorrow if Nana happened to be making some of her special pancakes.'

'I think that could be arranged,' Deborah says, throwing a discreet wink in her son's direction.

A look of panic appears on Rose's face. 'There won't be anything at the house – in the garden or whatever – to remind me of, you know, the wedding, will there?'

'Absolutely not,' Dave replies. 'I promise.'

She breathes a sigh of relief. 'Okay. What time?'

'Half eleven?' Dave asks, eyes darting between Rose and Deborah, who both nod.

'Sounds good. I'll see you then,' Rose says.

He doesn't get a hug goodbye.

CHAPTER 41

ROSE

From: Cassie Doyle
To: Rose Hughes
Subject: So sorry

Hi Rose,

I hope you don't mind me emailing you. I had to let you know how unbelievably sorry I am for not being there with you this evening. I assume your dad has already explained what happened – Ed's original accident and now this second fall. He promised to tell you.

I really hope you understand. I'd never have left early under normal circumstances. I was desperate to see you again. That's the whole reason I stayed in Lancashire as long as I did, although I must admit, while you were in the Lakes, I used the opportunity to visit some old haunts and bury a few demons after all these years.

I'm writing this on the plane to Dublin. It should send as soon as we land and my phone gets a signal again, all being well. Before I forget, I'm so sorry that things haven't worked out between you and Ryan. I know how much you were looking forward to getting married. Your eyes sparkled when you talked about it, just as they did when you spoke about him. But I don't doubt for a second that you made the right decision to call it off. How could you not? He wasn't worthy of you, end of story. Better you found out now rather than later. And trust me when I say that you'll find someone else eventually – someone better – who'll give you all the happiness you deserve. You're still so young. You have your whole life ahead of you!

I'll be honest, I'm struggling to know what to say to you now, Rose. My brain's a bit mushed. I'm terribly anxious about Ed, although thankfully, from what I'm being told, it looks so far like there'll be a setback in his recovery but no scary new complications. Fingers crossed! He was at least wearing his back brace when he slipped, affording him some level of protection, and he was only a few stairs up from the bottom.

Anyway, I digress. I want to apologise to you, Rose, for so many things: particularly for not being there when you grew up and for making your father, grand-mother and so on lie to you and tell you I was dead. My actions have had a huge impact on your life, which I sincerely regret. At the time, I believed I was acting in everyone's best interests, but knowing what I do now, it was stupid. I was young and naive. I was miles and miles away from finding myself and becoming the person I am today.

I feel guilty for misleading you last Saturday – for not being upfront about who I was. Why did I do that? Selfishness, partly. I wanted you to get to know me as the woman I am today. I wanted the chance to tell you about the long, winding path I trod to get here. I hoped it might eventually stop you from hating me quite so much, which sounds awful now I put it down in words. But it wasn't only about that, Rose. I hoped that in knowing my story, you'd understand my leaving you as a baby had nothing whatsoever to do with you and everything to do with me. I can live with you hating me. It's what I deserve. But please don't allow any of this to knock your self-confidence, especially in light of Ryan's misdeeds. You're an incredible young woman and you deserve so much more.

Now we've met each other, I'd love to be a part of your life, however big or small – but only if that's what you want. Once things are, hopefully, on track again with Ed and his back, I'd be delighted to return to England to see you. You'd also be incredibly welcome to come and visit us here in Ireland. Rory, Niall, Niamh and Shauna would absolutely love to meet you, I'm sure, as would Ed. But no pressure, no rush. It's all entirely up to you, Rose. If you'd prefer never to see or hear from me again, that would be a shame, but I'd understand and respect that decision.

I must mention your father. Most guys in their early twenties would run a mile at the mere thought of bringing up a child alone. Not your dad. He's a special man, he really is; he's done such a wonderful job of raising you. Try to focus on that rather than the lie I made him tell, if you're struggling to forgive him. He loves you so much. You know he'd do anything for you.

I found you a real ray of sunshine to meet, Rose. I'll always treasure spending that day together in your warm company. You're such a kind, thoughtful, intelligent person – so much more than I ever was at your age. You have a bright future ahead, whatever you choose to do next. I know this for certain.

Here's hoping this is not the end for us.

All my very best,

Cassie X

*   *   *

Rose is startled by a light knocking on the window next to her. Still sitting behind the wheel of her car outside Cara's house, she looks up from her phone and the email she's been staring at for ages now. She sees Cara peering in through the grimy glass, which is badly in need of a wash since their trip to the Lakes. She winds down the window.

'There you are, my glorious guest,' Cara says, doing a decent impression of Bob from Buttermere, theatrical flourish and all. 'What are you doing sitting out here, alone in your car? It's a bit weird.' She narrows her eyes. 'Are you pretending to be a cop on a stakeout, or a stalker perhaps?'

'Very funny,' Rose replies, grinning and shaking her head.

'Hmm. Just to be clear, my parents have agreed to you staying over. There's really no need for you to live out of your car. Although, I mean, you can, if you really want to. At least I'll get to escape your snoring.'

'What? You're the one who snores, Cara, thank you very much.'

'Lies! Seriously, though, what are you up to out here? You've been parked for ages. Everything okay?'

'Oh, yeah. I was reading an email on my phone, that's all.'

Cara winks. 'On my phone, you mean?' Her face falls as she adds: 'Hang on, it's not from bloody Ryan, is it?'

'No, thankfully not.'

'Something interesting, though?'

Rose shrugs. 'Maybe.'

'Fine, don't tell me, Miss Mysterious. How was the meal?'

'Better than expected.'

'Good. And your mother? Sorry, Cassie, I mean.'

'She wasn't there. It was just Dad and Nana. Long story.'

'What? You're joking. What a—'

'No, it wasn't like that. She had to rush back home. Her husband had an accident. He's all right, kind of . . . I'll fill you in later.'

Cara nods. 'So are you coming in or what? You're still planning to stay here tonight, right?'

'Yes, if that's okay.'

'Obvs.'

As they walk inside, arm in arm, like they used to when they were girls, Rose asks: 'What's it like having a brother and sister?'

'Fine, I guess. Why do you ask?'

Rose scratches the side of her nose. 'Oh, no particular reason. I was wondering, that's all, me being an only child and everything.'

After pausing to think, Cara lowers her voice, adding: 'I didn't really appreciate them when I was younger, constantly living at home with them. They often annoyed the hell out of me, messing with my stuff and winding me up. But I don't mind them so much nowadays, particularly since I started at university. I even miss them at times when I'm in Edinburgh. Once we're all grown up, with our own lives, I reckon we'll get on quite well. I'll never be as close to them as I am to you – that's different – but yeah, I guess it's quite nice actually, having siblings.'

Rose nods and smiles at her friend. Good to know.

What would Cassie's four children be to her, she considers: step-siblings? No, more than that, since Cassie has adopted them. Half-brothers and sisters, then? That sounds about right.

Two sets of twins, quite close to her in age, twenty and seventeen.

Interesting. Maybe that big family she's always aspired to having is still within her grasp, despite the collapse of her marriage plans.

That would, however, mean letting Cassie into her life.

Is that something she'd be prepared to do after all that's happened?

It's too early to say. Her mind has been so busy processing her battered, reeling emotions regarding Ryan and their cancelled wedding that she hasn't properly considered the implications of Cassie's bombshell revelation yet. A person can only handle so much at once. Maybe that's why she's been walking around in a fog, the events of the past several days swirling around her head as if they happened in a dream.

Is this some kind of inbuilt emotional defence mechanism?

If so, it only works to a degree.

And yet, somehow, she knows in her heart that she's already partway towards forgiving her dad. How could she not, ultimately, considering everything else he's done to raise, protect and cherish her over the years? She's loved and adored him her entire life, knowing he feels every bit the same. She's her father's daughter. Always has been, always will be.

Trust is another matter. Another process. Rose doesn't even know where to begin with that, having seen hers demolished on so many fronts.

Will she ever truly trust anyone again?

As for Cassie, there's no shared history to fall back on, no love or family loyalty. Rose owes her nothing. And yet, as her email shows, Cassie knows that only too well. She's not asking Rose for anything. She's holding out an olive branch.

Would there really be any harm in accepting it, at least tentatively? What does Rose have to lose?

To gain, on the other hand . . . a mother?

No, it's way too soon to even think about that possibility. Far too painful.

Having brothers and sisters, though. How often did her childhood self use to fantasise about that very thing? Just one sibling would have been a dream come true. And now here she is, facing the possibility of meeting four of them.

That has to be worth considering.

EPILOGUE

TWO MONTHS LATER

Rose exits the busy double-decker train at Amsterdam Central Station, one hand clutching the shoulder strap of her weekend bag, the other clamped around her ticket.

It was only a short journey from Schiphol: a vast airport, but thankfully one in which English speakers are amply catered for. The way to the onsite railway station was well signposted; paying her fare and getting to the right platform was easy, thanks to a smiling, immaculately presented Dutchman.

'Do you speak English?' she asked him on approaching his ticket booth.

'Of course,' he replied, nodding gently. 'How can I help you today?'

Now she's impressed how the people waiting to board the train calmly make space to allow her and her fellow disembarkees to leave first. Very civilised, she thinks, especially in such a busy city.

But as she makes her way along the platform and down an escalator, soon entering the station's busy shopping area, she finds she can barely think at all. She's far too nervous.

After spotting the main entrance, outside of which is the meeting point she's heading towards, she moves to one side of the throng and takes a moment to compose herself.

'Come on, Rose,' she whispers, jaw clenched as she stares down at her suede ankle boots. 'You can do this. It won't be as awkward as you fear. It'll be fine.'

After taking several slow, deep breaths, she wipes her clammy palms on the back of her jeans and forces herself to continue, glad of the cool air as she steps outside.

'Rose!' she hears almost instantly 'Over here.'

She turns her head in the direction of the familiar voice – and sees Cassie wearing a broad smile and waving from a few metres away, already walking towards her.

What now? Her mind whizzes through various possibilities of how to greet the woman who gave birth to her. But before she can make a decision, Cassie does it for her, grabbing her gently but firmly by the shoulders, looking her in the eye, nodding, and then planting a quick kiss on Rose's right cheek.

'There you are!' Cassie says, her eyes twinkling with enthusiasm. 'Welcome to Amsterdam. It's so good to see you again at last, Rose. I was over the moon when you agreed to meet me here. I've barely thought of anything else for the past few days. How are you? You look wonderful. And wow, I love the new haircut. It's gorgeous.'

'I'm fine,' Rose replies, hoping she doesn't look as overwhelmed as she feels. 'I've actually had this hairstyle for a bit now. I got it not long after, um . . . you know.'

'Well, it really suits you. Good journey?'

'Yes, thanks. How, er, how are you?'

'Very well, thank you. All the better for seeing you again.'

'What about Ed?'

'He's not bad, thanks for asking. Definitely on the mend.' Cassie rolls her eyes. 'Getting under my feet and trying to do far too much, mind. You'd think he'd have learned his lesson by now, wouldn't you? Honestly, I despair sometimes.'

'What about Rory, Niall, Niamh and Shauna?'

A puzzled look flashes across Cassie's face in response to this question. Rose wonders if she expects her to feel hostile towards them, jealous perhaps? Quite the opposite is true. The prospect of eventually meeting the two sets of twins is one of the reasons she's here now. Maybe Cassie's just surprised that Rose remembers their names.

'They're all very well,' she replies after a short pause. 'They've been a big help with their father – and they're under strict orders to watch him like a hawk while I'm away this time. I know they'd love to meet you some day.'

I hope so, Rose thinks. She's planning to ask to see some photos later on. Cassie's bound to have plenty on her mobile.

It feels so weird seeing her again. They've exchanged

emails and had a couple of brief phone calls since Cassie returned to Ireland, but that's it. Rose spent much of her journey today wondering if the whole trip was a mistake. She almost didn't get out of the car when her dad dropped her off at Manchester Airport. He pretty much had to turf her out. But now she's here, she knows she has to at least give it a go.

Cassie suggested the idea on a call last month, picking Amsterdam because they'd spoken about it at length on that fateful spa day and she knew Rose had never visited the city before.

'I could come to you, otherwise,' Cassie said. 'Or, of course, you'd be very welcome to visit me here in Ireland. But I thought neutral ground might work best. And I'd love to have the chance to introduce you to such a special city.'

'Can I think about it?' Rose replied.

'Absolutely.'

She really wasn't sure, but after talking it through first with Cara, then with her dad and her nana, she decided to give it a go. Nothing ventured, and so on.

Cassie arrived yesterday, so she could visit her old friends Bianca and Jeroen. Tonight and tomorrow night, she and Rose are booked into a boutique hotel close to Rembrandtplein, near the bar where she once worked.

The idea of the trip? Rose isn't entirely sure.

To get to know each other better?

To try to cement an ongoing relationship?

To give her the chance to quiz Cassie further about everything she's done?

All possible. All potentially problematic.

'How's your dad?' Cassie asks, the two of them still standing at the front of the train station. 'I was so glad when I heard that you'd moved back home. Are the two of you—'

'We're fine.'

Not entirely true, but this is as much as she's prepared to divulge for now. All that's happened has, inevitably, put a degree of strain on Rose's relationship with her father. Returning home was initially a practical decision more than anything else. She could hardly crash at Cara's parents' house forever. And with no job yet in sight, it wasn't like she could afford a place of her own.

Since she's moved back, Dave's had to contend with quite a few tears and tantrums as she struggles to come to terms with the new normal. But to be fair to him, he's taken it all on the chin. And he's been there for her constantly, as he always was before: a sympathetic ear, a shoulder to cry on, a source of advice, a sounding board for ideas. Whatever she needs.

He's writing almost every day now. Annoyingly, he refuses to tell anyone what about, but he has at least promised that it's not based on anything to do with her.

Meanwhile, he's put no pressure on her about what to do next with her life, telling her to take as long as she requires to work things through. She definitely hasn't forgotten his role in keeping the truth from her for so long, yet she can't help but love him dearly.

The same is true of her grandmother, who, ultimately, was given very little choice but to go along with the big lie.

She was most understanding when Rose opted not to go on what should have been her honeymoon – and Nana's wedding gift – to St Lucia. There had been talk of possibly transferring Ryan's tickets to someone else, but Rose couldn't face it. There was no way she'd have been able to enjoy herself there, even with Cara. It was spoiled and would have been a constant reminder of her misery. She'd have probably ended up drinking like a fish in between crying and scowling at all the honeymooners. Definitely not a good idea.

In the present, nodding at Rose's brusque reply, Cassie gets the hint and moves on. 'What about you-know-who: the idiot who didn't deserve you? Have you heard anything more from him?'

'It's okay, you can mention his name without me bursting into tears.' Rose frowns. 'No, I've managed to avoid any direct contact with Ryan since I dumped him, thank goodness. And long may it remain that way. Don't worry, I won't make the mistake of forgiving him twice, and I think he knows that. Anyhow, should we make our way to the hotel so I can get rid of my bag and freshen up?'

'You took the words right out of my mouth,' Cassie says. 'But first I have a little surprise for you. Would you like to follow me?'

Rose agrees, despite feeling apprehensive, joining her as she turns around and, at a sprightly pace, walks away from the station entrance. Soon they arrive at what looks like a multistorey carpark – only it's not for cars, it's for bicycles.

'What on earth?'

'I told you they love their bikes here,' Cassie replies, beaming. 'Mine's up on the third floor. I hired it earlier. I'll cycle and you can sit on the rear bag rack. You know, just like I did with Bianca when I first arrived here all those years ago. You remember me telling you that, don't you?'

'Yes, of course.' Rose's stomach feels queasy at the mere thought of this. 'That, um. Yeah, okay, right. That sounds . . . interesting.'

'I mean, you can cycle if you prefer,' Cassie says, 'and I'll go on the back. But I'd have to shout directions to you. I'm fairly sure I remember the way. What do you think, Rose?'

She doesn't know how to answer. Neither option sounds remotely appealing, so she stands there, gawping, no words coming out.

A furrow appears in Cassie's brow as her face falls. She stares back, blinking several times, not saying anything either.

Oh no, this isn't going to end well, Rose thinks, fearing she's ruined the surprise. Not exactly a good start to the trip.

'Oh God, I've messed up, haven't I?' Cassie says eventually in a quiet, hurt voice. 'Sorry. I can't believe I thought this was a good idea. I was desperately trying to think of a fun way to make it up to you for, um, messing up the hotel booking. Clearly I've done the exact opposite.'

Her words take a second to sink in. 'What do you mean? What's messed up about the booking?'

Cassie pulls an awkward face. 'It's okay. I'm sure we'll

383

be able to work something out. There's always Bianca and Jeroen's place, although, saying that, they did mention something about having other guests tonight.'

'What's the problem with the hotel?' Rose asks again, feeling a sense of panic rise in her chest. 'Please just tell me.'

'They've put us together in one room.' Cassie utters this in little more than a whisper, pausing before adding, quieter still: 'A double.'

Rose looks away as she attempts to process this information on top of the ridiculous mode of transport. Her blood's boiling, but she tries desperately to hold in her rage. This isn't Cassie's fault, she thinks. Try to stay calm.

As composed as she can manage, Rose turns around . . . only to see Cassie crack a smile, which turns into a grin, soon accompanied by a chuckle.

'Your face!' she says, properly giggling now and placing a reassuring hand on Rose's arm. 'I'm sorry, I couldn't resist. Don't worry, it's not true. I have already been to the hotel and it's lovely. Everything's in order. We have separate rooms across from each other. And we're not going on a bicycle either. We'll take the tram, or a taxi if you prefer.'

Rose thinks about being angry for a split second, but it doesn't take. Cassie's well-meaning laughter is too infectious. Instead, she rolls her eyes and shakes her head. Smiling, she wags a finger in her mother's direction. 'I'll get you back for this. Just you wait.'

As they board the tram together a few minutes later, both still laughing about it, Rose realises that this could actually be an enjoyable trip, if she lets her hair down and rolls with it. Perhaps the two of them can find a way to make things work somehow, despite what's gone before. It won't be easy. There are still plenty of tough conversations to be had. But there's definitely a chink of light at the end of the tunnel.

It also dawns on Rose that, unconsciously and for the very first time, she just thought of Cassie as her mother.

ACKNOWLEDGEMENTS

Thank you to everyone who helped me to produce my sixth novel during such strange, distressing times.

Covid-19 has no role whatsoever to play in this story, partly because I planned and started writing it before the global pandemic took hold. But also, why would I do that to my fictional world? I was very happy to escape reality on this occasion.

Hats off to my wife – as always, my fantastic first reader – and my daughter. Somehow you both managed to put up with me through lockdown as I experienced the usual ups and downs of crafting a novel.

Thanks to my ever patient and supportive parents and sister for always being at the end of the phone when required. Mum, my chats with you about plot and characters really helped me to get unstuck on several occasions. Much appreciated!

And, of course, thank you to my wonderful literary agent Pat Lomax, my excellent editor Molly Walker-Sharp, eagle-eyed copy editor Laura McCallen, plus all the other brilliant staff at Avon, HarperCollins and Bell Lomax Moreton.

Lastly, here's to you, the reader, for picking up this book and joining me on my latest fictional journey. I really hope you've enjoyed it. If so, please help to spread the word by telling others. Personal recommendations are such a key way for people to hear about books. Leaving a quick review online, if you can spare a moment, is also incredibly helpful.

For all the latest information about me and my writing, including my social media details, please visit my website: www.sdrobertsonauthor.com

You can't have a rainbow
without a little rain . . .

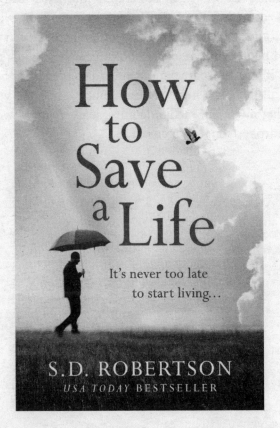

A life-affirming story about a man who is
given a second chance, perfect for fans of
Mike Gayle and Imogen Clark.

Hannah's life is pretty close to perfect.
But her sister, Diane, is carrying a
devastating secret that will turn
everything upside down.

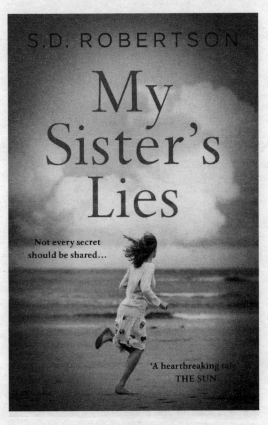

An emotional story that delves into the true
meaning of family, sisterhood and secrets.

Best friends since the day they met.

True friendship can last a lifetime . . .

'A heartbreaking tale' *Sun*

stand
by
me

S.D. Robertson

**They'll always have each other,
won't they?**

Is holding on harder than letting go?

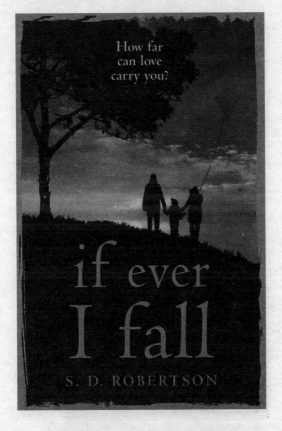

How far
can love
carry you?

if ever
I fall

S. D. ROBERTSON

**A beautiful story of love,
grief and redemption.**

How do you leave the person
you love the most?

Is there ever a right time to let go?

time
to say
goodbye

S. D. ROBERTSON

A heart-rending story about
a father's love for his daughter.